**Forge Books by
Larry Bond and Jim DeFelice**

Larry Bond's First Team
Larry Bond's First Team: Angels of Wrath
Larry Bond's First Team: Fires of War
Larry Bond's First Team: Soul of the Assassin
Larry Bond's Red Dragon Rising: Shadows of War
Larry Bond's Red Dragon Rising: Edge of War
Larry Bond's Red Dragon Rising: Shock of War
Larry Bond's Red Dragon Rising: Blood of War

LARRY BOND'S
Red Dragon Rising

EDGE
OF
WAR

LARRY BOND AND
JIM DeFELICE

FORGE®

A TOM DOHERTY ASSOCIATES BOOK • NEW YORK

LARRY BOND'S RED DRAGON RISING: EDGE OF WAR

Copyright © 2010 by Larry Bond and Jim DeFelice

A Forge Book
Published by Tom Doherty Associates, LLC
175 Fifth Avenue
New York, NY 10010

www.tor-forge.com

Forge® is a registered trademark of Tom Doherty Associates, LLC.

ISBN 978-0-7653-6099-1

Forge books may be purchased for educational, business, or promotional use. For information on bulk purchases, please contact Macmillan Corporate and Premium Sales Department at 1-800-221-7945 extension 5442 or write specialmarkets@macmillan.com.

First Edition: November 2010
First Mass Market Edition: November 2011

Printed in the United States of America

0 9 8 7 6 5 4 3 2

The term "global warming" is as misleading as it is inaccurate. True, the overall temperature of the earth as measured by annual average readings will rise. But averages tell us next to nothing. A shortening of a rainy season by two weeks in a given area might be reflected by an increase in the average annual temperature of only a third of a degree. But the impact on the water supply—and thus the growing season—would be considerably higher.

Paradoxically, rapid climate change may bring much lower temperatures in many places. It should also be noted that some changes may well benefit people in the affected areas, at least temporarily, by extending growing seasons, negating weather extremes, or having some other unpredictable effect.

Unfortunately, the sensationalistic term, combined with the slow evolution of the effects prior to the crisis point, will make it hard to convince the general population of the true danger. . . .

**—International Society of Environmental
Scientists report**

Major Characters

United States

Josh MacArthur, *scientist*

Mara Duncan, *CIA officer*

Peter Lucas, *CIA chief of station, Bangkok/Southeast Asia*

Major Zeus Murphy, *former Special Forces captain, adviser to Vietnam People's Army*

Lieutenant Ric Kerfer, *SEAL team platoon commander*

President George Chester Greene

CIA Director Peter Frost

National Security Adviser Walter Jackson

China

Lieutenant Jing Yo, *commander, First Commando Detachment*

Colonel Sun Li, *Commando regiment commander; executive officer, Task Force 1*

Premier Cho Lai

Vietnam

Premier Lein Thap

General Minh Trung, *head of the Vietnam People's Army*

Other

Jimmy Choi, *Korean mercenary*

February 2014

Commodity Prices—Chicago Board of Trade

COMMODITY	PRICE	1 YEAR AGO	5 YEARS AGO (2009)
Crude Oil	$735.87	$700.13	$74.86
Corn	$1,573	$1,234	$723
Wheat	$3,723	$1,534	$812
Rough Rice	$896	$310	$20.20

Average February Temperatures (Celsius)— Major World Cities

CITY	HIGH	LOW	2009 (average high)	2009 (average low)
Washington, D.C.	13.0	3.2	8.2	−1.2
Beijing	30.2	5.0	4.2	−7.0
Tokyo	12.3	3.0	9.2	0.1
Rome	16.5	5.2	13.5	4.7
Johannesburg	19.1	7.5	24.8	14.7

"Peace Is What We Want" Chinese Premier Declares

BEIJING, CHINA (World News Service)—Chinese Premier Cho Lai declared today that Chinese troops would leave Vietnam as soon as peace was assured there.

"The dastardly attack on our border, killing dozens of innocent civilians, must be avenged," declared Cho in an address to foreign ambassadors. "We will eliminate their capacity to conduct offensive war. When that is accomplished, Chinese troops will quickly withdraw to our borders."

The reception was generally favorable. Western analysts say . . .

Heating Oil Shortage Continues in Maine

BANGOR, MAINE (AP–Fox News)—Residents in the Bangor, Maine, area shivered through their third day of record cold temperatures as heating oil deliveries continued to be sparse.

The shutdown of two major refineries due to environmental concerns is blamed for the latest shortage.

Ironically, much of the rest of the Northeast is undergoing one of the warmest late winters on record. But that isn't helping Maine residents, who . . .

PERSONAL CHRONICLE: LOOKING BACK TO 2014 . . .

Markus:

When I wrote last I had taken the story up to late winter of 2014. Your uncle Josh had just found his way from behind the lines in Vietnam, returning to Hanoi with the help of the CIA and Navy SEALs. He thought he had escaped hell. The truth was, the worst part of his ordeal was just beginning.

I know it's hard for you to imagine what the world was like in 2014. It's probably impossible for you to think that the world believed China was innocent of aggression, or that its leader, Cho Lai, wasn't bent on taking over the world.

How could we have ignored such an obvious threat?

It's hard to explain, even looking back. People were under tremendous strains. Many of the world's economies had crashed. There was a great deal of turmoil. Right around the time this happened, there was an election in Italy that saw the Communist Party take control of the government! This was something that had not happened even right after World War II, when many of the partisans had been Communists. It was an incredible, stunning development. It just showed how crazed people were. The last thing they wanted was trouble with China, let alone a war.

Even America, which had been fortunate to escape the worst effects of the environmental changes, was struggling.

China had become an important country financially—the U.S. owed it trillions of dollars. Many politicians were honestly reluctant to anger Premier Cho Lai, worried that he would order Chinese banks to start selling U.S. treasury notes and bonds wholesale. That would have sent interest rates soaring and destroyed our economy.

But many politicians were simply blind. They refused to see the threat, even when it was staring them in the face. Only when their own lives were threatened did they wake up. By then it was too late. . . .

Run

跑

1

Hanoi, Vietnam

Josh slept through the bombing. He slept through the wail of the sirens. He slept through the rumble of the Plaza Hanoi across the street imploding. He slept through the strike at the new education ministry a half block away, and the collapse of the Vietnamese Private Commercial Enterprise Bank building a half mile away.

Josh MacArthur slept and slept, oblivious to the sounds of the war he had suddenly found himself in, a war that he was not only witness to, but a critical part of. He missed the grating *har-ush* of the Chinese jets as they roared overhead, the last-minute shriek of the air-to-ground missiles just before they struck, and the steady rattle of the antiaircraft guns, twin-barreled 23 mm and the larger 57s and 85s, their shrapnel exploding in an irregular pattern.

He missed the glass shattering everywhere, panes breaking like the thin ice over a pond on a late winter's day. He missed the rumble of the gas lines as they blew up, muffled by the ground. He missed the sharp cracks of old wood splintering beneath the weight of collapsing roofs and walls.

What woke him was the light touch of her footsteps in the hall, passing in front of his room on the way out.

They belonged to the woman who'd rescued him, Mara Duncan. Against all odds, the CIA officer had found Josh behind the lines of the Chinese advance and pulled him with her through the jungle, across the hills to a rendezvous with American SEALs, who had brought him to a truck commandeered by two U.S. Army officers. Together, they barely managed to make it past the advancing Chinese troops, but managed nonetheless.

The adventure would have been unimaginable for most people. But for Josh MacArthur, a weather scientist of all things, it seemed as unlikely as it could get. Josh had come to Vietnam to study the effects of the weather on the jungle. Instead, he had become a witness to man's more immediate impact on the environment—the cold-blooded massacre of a Vietnamese village in the hills by the Chinese.

The Chinese had also murdered his own colleagues. He'd missed that by chance, complete chance—his allergies had woken him and sent him away from the tents, out of concern for his colleagues and their sleep. His sneezing had saved him.

He'd run when the fighting began. Except that it wasn't fighting; it was a massacre. The scientists and their support staff had been killed in their sleep, without any possibility of resistance.

The killers had chased him as well. He'd run for his life, lost in the darkness in a country literally halfway around the world from his home.

He'd been defenseless and alone, and yet running seemed like an act of cowardice, of weakness, as if he might somehow have made a difference.

It was a foolish notion—the Chinese soldiers outnumbered him greatly, and in fact had barely missed him several times before his rescue. Josh had killed several himself, including one with his bare hands. There was no question, or should be no question, of his bravery.

And yet that idea, that feeling of failure, woke with him in the gray light of the Hanoi hotel room.

Josh sat upright in the bed. The hotel had never been one of the city's best, nor a favorite with the international tourist crowd. The furnishings had been old and battered well before the war. There was only a pair of bare sheets on the bed. They hadn't been changed in days, not since the war began. Josh had found them covered with dust and small bits of glass from the shattered windows, blown out from the attacks on the first night of the war. Too tired to talk to the staff—and guessing it would have been worthless to try—he'd pushed the small shards off on the floor and simply collapsed in bed a few hours before. Now he found grime stuck to him, held to his skin by his sweat.

He put his hands on his chest, gently brushing downward, more to reassure himself that he was still there than to clear the clinging grit.

As unglamorous as it was, the hotel was a solid, squat structure, dating from colonial times and overengineered by its French architect. Its sturdy walls had protected it from the shrapnel when the building across the street had collapsed, and while nothing was truly safe against a direct hit by one of the Chinese army's larger weapons, the hotel was one of the safest buildings in the city still open to foreigners. And of course it was obvious that Josh and his friends were foreigners.

He swung his legs out of bed. They were creaky and stiff. Josh had considered himself both athletic and in fairly good shape—he had taken letters in cross-country and baseball in high school, despite the asthma occasionally provoked by his allergies—but his ordeal in the jungle had tested his body. Both knees were sore, his right calf muscle had been pulled, and his neck felt as if it were a bolt twisted too tightly into its socket.

Glancing at the gray twilight outside the window, he

guessed it was roughly 5 a.m. His watch had been lost during the initial attack.

He walked slowly to the door, mindful of the glass. There were small piles of it along the front of the room, which faced a side street away from the hotel that had imploded. Someone had come in and swept the larger pieces into the piles, but neglected to come back and remove them.

Or maybe they had been killed before they got the chance. Several thousand civilians had died in Hanoi since the bombing began.

Josh undid the lock and pulled open the door. A large man stood in front of him, blocking the door. It was Jenkins, aka Squeaky, one of the SEALs who had rescued him.

"Hey, sir, where you going?" said Squeaky.

His nickname was Squeaky because his voice occasionally cracked, jumping a few octaves. He sounded like a teenage boy on bad mornings as his voice begins to deepen. There was no precise pattern to the squeaks; they seemed to occur a little less under pressure, the opposite of what Josh would have expected.

Squeaky was a big man, six ten and solidly built, stocky but not fat. He wore a pair of dungarees and a button-down shirt, in the Western style common in Vietnam's urban areas. The clothes were all black; they seemed to merge with his black skin, making him look like a dark spirit haunting the building, a hungry ghost looking for its ancestral offerings, as the local folklore would have it. He had an MP-5 submachine gun, and held it down next to his body discreetly, almost as if he were hiding it.

"I gotta use the john," said Josh.

"I'll walk you down."

Josh fell in behind him. Squeaky rocked a little as he walked, shoulders nearly scraping the walls.

"Hold on," the SEAL told him when they reached the doorway to the restroom.

He poked his head in, then reached back, took Josh's arm, and tugged him in. For a second, Josh thought he was going to stay—a problem, since Josh liked privacy—but Jenkins was just making doubly sure the place was empty.

"I'll be outside. Stay away from that window, you know?"

Josh nodded and stepped over to the commode. Fortunately, it was a Western-style toilet. But the water had been shut off sometime during the night, a fact Josh discovered when he tried to flush.

Squeaky was waiting outside.

"Water's off," Josh told him.

"Yeah."

"Hate to be the next guy that uses it."

"I'll remember that."

They started back for the room.

"What time is it?" Josh asked as they walked.

"Oh-four-ten," said Squeaky, his voice cracking. "Why?"

"Just curious."

Jenkins didn't say anything. Josh wondered if he was self-conscious about his voice.

"I heard someone walking in the hall before," said Josh when they reached his room. He suddenly didn't feel like going back inside. "Was it Mara?"

"You heard that?"

Josh shrugged. "What was up?"

"Ms. Duncan had to go out."

"At four?"

"I don't set her schedule, bro."

"What about Mạ?"

"The little girl?" Jenkins's face noticeably brightened. "Sleepin' like a peach. Cute little kid."

"Yeah," said Josh.

Josh had rescued the little girl after her parents and the rest of her village had been massacred by the invading Chinese. She was six or seven years old—Josh wasn't sure.

"We taking her with us?" Josh asked.

"Decision's above my pay grade." Jenkins grinned. "Why don't you go get yourself some sleep? Cap'll be looking for you in a few hours. We got a long way to go. Rumor is no flights out of the airport."

"We flying out of here?"

"We were supposed to."

"Oh."

"Don't know how the hell we're getting out of here," Squeaky added. He smiled. "Swimmin', maybe."

2

Northern Vietnam

Lieutenant Jing Yo knew better than to interrupt Colonel Sun Li when his commander was in the middle of a tirade. Neither patience nor understanding was among Sun's strong points under the best of circumstances, and at times when he was angry, like now, saying anything would only deepen his rage.

It was galling that Sun was bawling him out for failing to do the impossible. It was infuriating that the colonel's decision to ignore Jing Yo's advice had led to the very failure he was now complaining about. But making the slightest excuse would only lengthen the storm. The only solution was to weather it, as the young cherry tree weathers an unusually fierce winter, or the bamboo withstands the typhoon.

The metaphors were not strictly poetic. Jing Yo had seen both, time and again, during his time at the monastery where he had studied Shaolin. He had passed one particularly brutal winter night in bare feet, seated across from one of his mentors in a mountain pass they called Claw. Ostensibly they were there to help any lost travelers caught out in the storm. The unstated reason, Jing Yo was sure, was to test his dedication as a follower of the one true way, a walker along the path that has no name and no presence, and yet endlessly exists, without beginning or end.

That was what Shaolin was to him. The path of life. To others it was kung fu—the fighting way, the way of a monk warrior. Or an old, musty superstition.

"You are expressly ordered to kill him. Do you understand that?" thundered Sun. "Wherever you find him. Kill him. No matter the personal consequences to yourself."

Jing Yo tilted his head slightly. The colonel had jumped directly from his rant to the order. Jing Yo felt as if he had missed something.

"Colonel, if our spies say he has reached Hanoi," said Jing Yo softly, "how do you want me to proceed?"

"You call yourself a commando?" thundered Sun. "I have to outline everything for you?"

Jing Yo pressed his lips together. In truth, Sun was no more irrational than the monks had seemed when Jing Yo first came to the monastery. But in their case, the seeming illogic masked a much deeper sense and purpose. Sun's was chaos for chaos's sake—emotion, as those drunk on the surface of reality would perceive it.

"Our agents believe he is in the city already. You will be given instructions on how to contact them," said Sun. "And a briefing from intelligence. My advice to you is to leave as soon as you can. It will be more difficult to get into the city after dawn. Take whatever men you need. Here is a phone. Use it wisely."

Jing Yo took the satellite phone from Sun. It was a precious commodity. Even the army could not be trusted in the political upheaval roiling China.

"Do not fail," said Sun. He folded his arms. "You have tried my patience already."

3

The outskirts of Hanoi

Mara Duncan slumped in the backseat of the car, trying to make herself as inconspicuous as possible, even though it was the sedan, not her, that would attract attention. It was the only vehicle on the road that wasn't connected with the military.

Even before the war, Hanoi was generally deserted at four in the morning. Now it was like something out of a Dantean painting, the fires of hell burning around the city. The moonless night was tinged red by the flames, their glow occasionally clouded by black smoke furrowing from their center. The smoke threw vaporous shadows into the air, darkening the city beyond what seemed physically possible. It was as if Hanoi were at the epicenter of a black hole, its matter being pushed together into a mass that defied reason but was nonetheless mathematically correct. And Mara Duncan was a witness to it all.

"Train tracks, twenty meters," said Ric Kerfer. The SEAL lieutenant was sitting in the passenger seat, next to the driver, a Vietnamese man whom Mara had bribed to drive the vehicle. She figured that having a Vietnamese driver would help her cover story if they were stopped. She'd told him not to speak if that happened, and from the looks of his shaking hands, that wouldn't be a problem.

"*Đi thẳng,*" Mara told the driver. "Go straight over the tracks."

The driver slowed and inched over the crossing as if afraid a train might materialize out of the darkness.

"*Phải,*" said Mara. "Right. *Here.*"

He found the narrow trail parallel to the tracks and started down it. The car, a two-year-old Toyota, bounced violently.

"Stop here," Mara told him after they'd gone about thirty meters. She opened the door. Kerfer opened his.

"No, you stay," she told the SEAL lieutenant.

"What the fuck would I do that for?"

"How about so the car's here when I get back."

"Slant-eyes ain't gonna steal it."

"You're so damn charming," Mara said, closing her door. "Stay with the car."

She slipped her hand behind her back and pulled her Beretta pistol from her belt.

There was just enough glow to see the track to her right. After thirty meters, she spotted a signal box. She stopped and looked around carefully. Then she resumed walking, glancing left and right and continuing to watch everything around her. After she'd gone another thirty meters, she stopped and dropped to her haunches, listening.

Every so often in the distance she could hear automatic weapons being fired, undoubtedly by nervous soldiers on guard duty. The real war was still some miles to the west. Hanoi was safe enough for now, except for the missiles and bombs.

And spies, which she expected China would have here by the dozens.

Satisfied that no one was nearby, Mara crossed the tracks and walked back in the direction she had come. She stopped when she was roughly parallel to the signal box, then walked into the weeds.

There was supposed to be a footlocker with supplies here. She didn't see it.

Mara moved forward slowly. There were many possibilities about why it might not be here, and she tried not to think of them. She also fought off her inclination to start composing a Plan B. There was no sense devoting her energy to it yet; better to make sure first that it was needed.

Besides, she was already on Plan Z, not B. She'd have to start the alphabet over.

Her foot kicked something. She stopped, bent to it slowly.

It was a bottle.

Mara straightened, walked again. There was no box here, nothing but weeds and a few stones.

Mara retraced her steps to the bottle and knelt down, patting with her hands in the weeds until she found it. It was a Coke bottle, an old-fashioned, hourglass-shaped Coke bottle.

And there were no other bottles in the area, or along the tracks now that she thought about it. Trash like that wouldn't be unusual in America, where railroad tracks were often used as open-air trash bins, but in Southeast Asia, northern Vietnam especially, trash was a valuable commodity. An intact bottle had dozens of potential uses.

Including, perhaps, a signal that the box was buried below.

She poked the dirt with her fingers. The ground in front of her was hard, but the weeds to her right came up easily.

They'd been removed, then replaced.

Her fingers scraped the top of the footlocker within a few seconds, but it took her nearly ten minutes to clear enough of the dirt away so she could lift the box from the ground. She stopped several times, listening, still afraid that this might be a trap.

As she reached for the latch, she hesitated again, worried that it might be booby-trapped. It had been left by a contact sent by the CIA station at the American embassy—a station she knew had been penetrated by Vietnamese spies. It was because of that breach that she had been sent to Vietnam in the first place; then the war had begun, and her mission morphed from routine to *interesting.*

Interesting.

Would someone who wanted to kill her go to the trouble of burying the box? He'd have just left it out where it would easily be found.

But burying it would make her drop her guard. Burying it might lull her into complacency. Burying it would be exactly the sort of precision, the exact attention to detail, to expect from a smart enemy.

There was no way really to know. Mara took her folding knife from her pocket and opened it, teasing the latch. She started to run the point around the edge—but what was the point?

Because she mustn't drop her guard, ever. She'd learned that lesson many times, long before Vietnam.

Mara worked the knife around the box, opposite the latch. When she reached the first hinge, she pushed it in, levering it up.

The hinge snapped. She froze for a moment, then lowered her ear to listen.

"Shit, you gonna kiss it next?"

Mara dove over the box, pistol raised. She just barely kept herself from firing at the voice behind her.

She would have hit the driver, not Kerfer, who was standing behind him, MP-5 in the poor man's ribs.

"Calm the fuck down," said Kerfer.

"You're lucky you aren't dead," said Mara, getting up for her knife.

"Jesus H. Christ—you really think one of your own people booby-trapped it?" said the SEAL.

Mara ignored him. She snapped off the second hinge.

"Stand back," she said, first in English, then in Vietnamese. "Just in case."

Kerfer snickered, but he pulled the driver back a few steps with him. Mara slid the top to the left, then to the right, then finally pushed it open.

There were old clothes on top. She took her small LED penlight and shone it around the interior of the box. Two AK-47s, ammunition, a satellite radio, two cell phones, which most likely would be worthless, and maps. A backpack.

That was it.

Son of a bitch.

Mara unfolded the backpack, made sure it was empty. She looked at the clothes—peasant wear, useful in the countryside but out of sync here, and in any event similar to what she already had—a black pair of baggy pants, Vietnamese style, with a longish black shirt.

She took the weapons, made sure the box was empty. Then, following an impulse, she dropped down and examined the hole again, digging deeper and on the sides. But the ground was hard. She worked her light around, making sure there was nothing else.

"We set?" asked Kerfer, standing over her.

Mara didn't answer. She rose, and tossed him one of the rifles.

"Come on," she said, heading for the car.

"You expecting something else?" Kerfer asked.

"Money," she said. "A lot of money. The fucks."

In the air, approaching Hanoi

Jing Yo steadied himself in the door frame of the Harbin A180, watching the gray and black tops of the trees pass by. The Harbin—a Chinese "interpretation" of a Cessna 180—was flying barely twenty meters off the ground, skimming low to avoid any possibility of being picked up on Vietnamese air defense radar. Every so often the pilot had to pull up to avoid colliding with something in his path. Several times branches of trees had brushed against the belly of the plane, tiger claws scratching the metal, hoping to rip it open and expose the meat inside.

The near misses suited Jing Yo fine. They meant the pilot was doing his job. Stealth was all-important.

"Hanoi is ahead," said the man.

He was a member of the air commando brigade. Jing Yo knew him slightly; his unit had worked on some exercises with the brigade the year before.

"Third time I've been here," said the pilot when Jing Yo didn't reply. "Twice last night. Fires get brighter."

He seemed to mean that as a joke.

"Won't be much left to burn soon," added the pilot. "Uh-oh, watch out!"

The plane tilted abruptly to the right. A yellow cone of light rose just behind them: a searchlight, activated by someone who had either seen a shadow or somehow heard the heavily muffled engine.

The plane began to rock. A stream of red and yellow fire arced into the air above, first behind them, then all around them.

"Hang on," said the pilot. The bonhomie was gone from his voice; he spoke like a machine, cold and impersonal.

Jing Yo welcomed the change.

The intelligence service had identified his subject: an American scientist named Joshua MacArthur. He was in Hanoi, but not at the embassy—the service had excellent contacts there, and the briefer assured Jing Yo that they would know if he was there. A spy had been designated as a local contact, and important information would be delivered by sat phone if necessary, but for the most part, Jing Yo was on his own.

The plane zigged to the left, then to the right, then turned hard in a bank. It seemed to Jing Yo that they were turning around. He waited by the door, silent, watching the fires in the distance. On an ordinary night before the war, there would have been at least a few lights on below, and many more in the distance, in Hanoi itself. But now it was a black hole in the landscape, marked only by fires and a few searchlights.

More lights flashed on. They worked across the sky, pens crossing out sections they had examined. The pilot ducked around them, trying to fly into the areas where they weren't.

Fountains of red appeared, fresh gushes in the night. Their glow came from tracer rounds, showing the gunners where their bullets were going. The tracers were loaded every five or six bullets—Jing Yo wasn't sure; perhaps it was even less. So for every streak he saw, there were several more bullets he couldn't see. The slugs were large, thick pieces of metal the size of a clenched fist. They would tear through the light aircraft like a knife poking through paper. One hit and the tiny airplane would go down.

"Three minutes," said the pilot calmly.

"Are we going east?" asked Jing Yo.

"South. Don't worry. You'll go out where planned."

Jing Yo waited. The flak from below had not abated. He took a slow breath, counseling the muscles in his body to relax. They had been battered severely over the past several days; they would be battered again in the next few.

Jing Yo had chosen to carry out the mission by himself. This was partly a practical matter. It seemed to him that it would be easier to slip into the city under the cover of darkness, and with dawn rapidly approaching—it was already almost six—even the few minutes it would have taken to return to his unit's temporary barracks at the captured Vietnamese base and have one of his men gather his things could not be spared.

Even with more time, Jing Yo would most likely have chosen to come alone. He trusted most of the men in his squad, and could have found one or two on short notice worthy of such a difficult mission. But he had been trained to act alone, and preferred doing so.

Alone, there was less chance of a random error preventing him from accomplishing his mission. Alone, he could focus on the task at hand, and not worry about an underling's welfare. For even on a mission such as this, a commander had responsibilities to his people.

The nose of the plane tilted upward. They were getting close.

"The flak trucks are very close to the first position," said the pilot. "There will be ground patrols there, guarding them, and perhaps they will see you. Would you prefer one of the fallback zones?"

"Which?"

"I can drop you exactly two kilometers south of Bay Mau Lake," said the pilot. "Will that do?"

"It is fine."

"The Vietnamese have moved all of their army headquarters south of the city," said the pilot. He was back to being friendly. "They have bunkers. They're out there, three kilometers south. They think we don't know."

Jing Yo stared into the darkness. If there were bunkers, they were well beyond the flak, where he couldn't see them.

"Hold on now, we're turning," said the pilot. "We'll either go into a calm spot in the sky, or we'll be shot down."

He laughed.

Jing Yo gripped the handle at the side of the door. The plane jerked hard, making the turn. Its nose came up abruptly. Jing Yo felt his stomach fall toward the bottom of his chest.

They flew like that for five seconds, then ten more. The sky cleared.

"Three hundred meters," said the pilot. "I'm climbing to five."

Suddenly the sky filled with searchlights. The pilot cursed. Tracers appeared near the door.

"I'm going," said Jing Yo, leaning toward the door.

"I can't let you out here. You'll be killed!"

"You have no choice," said Jing Yo, stepping into the night.

Central Hanoi

As a newly minted second lieutenant, Zeus Murphy had served in Iraq at the height of the second Gulf War. Much of his time had been spent in Baghdad and the surrounding areas, when suicide bombings and random mortar and rocket attacks were still common. The days had been hell, but he'd always managed to sleep easily at night, even when he was staying outside of what later became the protected Green Zone. In fact, he'd slept through at least two mortar attacks on his building, including one that damaged the room next to his.

It was the same way now, in Hanoi. Perhaps it was the exhilaration of having cobbled together a mission to help the SEALs and CIA officer Mara Duncan retrieve the American scientist. Zeus hadn't had a "real" mission since making major and being promoted out of Special Forces nearly a year before. Or maybe it was just jet lag. In any event, Zeus had fallen asleep as soon as he hit his mattress. None of the Chinese bombs and missiles, let alone the antiaircraft guns stationed across the street, put the slightest dent in his slumber.

The hotel called itself, without ironic intent, Hanoi's Finest Hotel. The title was impressive in Vietnamese, where the characters were drawn and arranged in a way that could be interpreted as having several lucky meanings. The hotel building itself was somewhat less so. It consisted of three different sections, all built by the French during their occupation. The oldest, taken up by the reception hall and offices, had some slight pretensions toward Architecture, with a capital A. There were columns and plasterwork so elaborate that decades' worth of white paint couldn't entirely obliterate them. The draperies and rugs were threadbare but their patterns hinted, if not at opulence, at least at some appreciation of design and color.

But the two additions, which folded out from each other in a train behind the oldest, were utilitarian block houses, with low ceilings and narrow hallways. The rooms were small even by Vietnamese standards: the door hit Zeus's single bed when it was opened more than halfway.

The hotel had somehow managed to escape damage during the war with America. The Vietnamese considered this a sign of its superiority, making prominent mention of the fact in not one but two placards in the lobby. In fact, most buildings south of the central business areas had not been damaged. As inaccurate as American bombing sometimes was, even the massive B-52 raids that dropped bushels of unguided iron bombs had always been aimed away from obvious civilian areas.

Neither Zeus nor General Harland Perry, his boss, thought the Chinese would take such pains in this war.

Perry had been put up in a guesthouse a mile away. His driver and his security people were staying with him. The rest of his small staff—Zeus, Major Win Christian, and two sergeants with expertise in intelligence and communications—had been put up in the hotel after a brief stay at the U.S. embassy.

Officially, they weren't in Vietnam. They wore civilian clothes, and in the unlikely case that someone asked what they were doing, had been instructed to give vague replies about being attached to the embassy.

Unofficially, they were there as observers to see what the hell the Chinese were up to, and possibly learn if the Chinese claims that Vietnam had started the war were true.

Secretly, and in reality, they were there under the direct orders of the president of the United States, to do whatever they could to keep the Chinese from rolling through Vietnam.

"Major?"

Zeus rolled over in the bed.

Jenna was with him—in his dream. He pushed himself against her side, then wrapped his arm around her, his left hand searching for her breast.

"Major Murphy?"

Gradually, Zeus realized there was someone else in the room. A woman.

But not Jenna. And not in his bed.

Damn.

"Zeus?"

"Mmmmmm," he mumbled.

"Zeus? Are you awake?"

A hand touched him. Big, warm, somewhat soft.

"Zeus?"

"Mmmm."

"Zeus, I need to talk to you."

Zeus rolled back over and opened his eyes. Mara Duncan stood next to the bed. The door to his room was open to the hall.

"Mara," he mumbled.

"Zeus. Come on, wake up."

"How'd you get in?"

"I picked the lock. Come on. We need to talk."

"Uh, what about?" he asked.

"Not here. Get dressed. I'll wait for you in the lobby."

Just as demanding as Jenna, thought Zeus, though not in a good way.

Mara waited for Zeus on one of the massive French couches in the lobby, sipping coffee and eating one of the croissants the hotel employees had brought. A Western-style continental breakfast was an old tradition at the hotel, and the manager insisted on keeping it up, even though his staff was greatly reduced.

The pastries were at least a day old, if not two or three. The croissants, however, were fresh, still warm from the oven, Mara thought. She'd been in Paris several times, and appreciated a good croissant—flaky and airy, the inside porous enough to soak up jelly.

Little luxuries were like pearls when you were on an assignment, her boss, Peter Lucas, always said. Grab them when you can.

Mara took another croissant, and split it in half with her fingers, dabbing both sides with jelly. The jelly was grape, relatively rare and probably not much in demand before the war, she thought.

It came in a small plastic tub, sealed against germs and bugs, and dust. But ultimately not against war.

Zeus came out from the back, passing the reception desk. He had an easy, confident gait. Though sleepy-eyed, he walked with purpose, the sort of man who swept into a room and took control of it. He was handsome, but without the rugged edge Kerfer displayed. Zeus was clearly headed for the upper ranks.

"You played football in high school," Mara said as he sat down.

"Are you asking?"

"No." She sipped her coffee.

"You read some sort of dossier?"

"No. I can just tell."

"Yeah, I did."

"Quarterback?"

"School record for passing. Broken the next year by a guy who went to Michigan State." Zeus smiled. The waiter began pouring him a cup of coffee.

"Yeah," said Mara. "Try the croissants."

"What's going on?"

She shook her head slightly. She assumed the hotel was bugged.

"Oh," said Zeus, catching on. He took a big swallow of coffee.

"I expected more chaos," said Mara. "And destruction."

"There's plenty of both," said Zeus.

"But there's also this." She held the croissant up.

"That good, huh?"

"Try one. Then let's go for a walk."

The coffee was stronger than Zeus was used to, and he had a slight caffeine buzz as they walked outside. A Vietnamese army unit had been assigned to protect the Americans in the hotel. Two trucks sat across the street. A half dozen soldiers milled around nearby. To a man, each had a cigarette in his mouth.

They stared at Zeus and Mara as they came out of the building. They are as curious about the westerners, Zeus thought, as they would be about circus performers come to town.

"You think the hotel is bugged?" Zeus asked as they turned down a side street.

"Hmm," she said.

It was the barest of syllables, just a sharp hum really, but the tone told him to be quiet. He walked along at her side, chastened, crossing at the corner onto a broader avenue. The sun had not yet risen

"I've never been to Hanoi," said Zeus. "Not in real life. But I've played all sorts of war games here. In our simulations—they look a hell of a lot like the real thing."

"You couldn't die in one of the simulations if the bricks of the buildings fell apart," said Mara.

"Or if a bomb hit," said Zeus.

He meant it as a joke—a quip, something to break the tension. But it fell flat. Mara seemed cross, angry about something. The night before, driving in from Hanoi, she had been much less cynical and snappy.

Well, they were in a war. People were trying to kill them. That didn't make most people happy.

Mara wasn't pretty in a conventional way. Not that she was ugly, or even unattractive. She was tall, almost six feet, and maybe a little too much like a tomboy for his taste. Her Vietnamese-style clothes—baggy, draping, in black—didn't do much for her either.

"Don't trust the American embassy," she said, abruptly starting across the street.

"Huh?"

She moved so fast Zeus had trouble keeping up.

"Don't trust them," said Mara.

"The ambassador seems nice."

"Nice is meaningless. And she's not the problem."

Mara turned to the right. She seemed to know exactly where she was going. The buildings around them were two- and three-story masonry structures, storefronts and apartment houses, with the occasional office building thrown in. The signs were a colorful mishmash of Vietnamese characters, occasionally punctuated by English and familiar trademarks. There was a Canon sign; across the street on a bank was a logo for HSBC. The words "Out of Order" were written on a piece of cardboard over it, in English and Vietnamese.

"I need to get down to Saigon," Mara told him. "The airport here is too dangerous to use. It could be overrun at any minute."

"That's not true," said Zeus. "It's not in any immediate danger."

"I don't have time to argue with Langley," Mara told him, referring to the CIA brass by naming the agency's headquarters. "And if they're not going to believe what I tell them, they're not going to buy anyone else's arguments. There's a plane for me in Saigon. I need to get there."

"I don't understand," said Zeus. "Last night, you and the SEALs were going to be evaced from the airport by plane this morning."

"Yeah. Things change. Especially in Vietnam."

Mara walked on, wending her way through central Hanoi's business district. The soldiers from the hotel were probably following, but she wasn't able to see them.

Which was good enough. As long as they weren't in direct sight, they wouldn't be able to use a shotgun-type mike to pick up the conversation. Not that she'd seen one.

Maybe she was being too paranoid. Unless one of them was bugged . . .

Shit.

"Stop!" Mara said, turning to him. "Take off your shoes."

"My shoes?"

"Where'd you get them?"

"I brought them with me."

He stood on one foot in the middle of the sidewalk and removed his right shoe. Mara took it, examining the sole, and then the interior.

"You looking for a bomb?" he asked.

"Other shoe," she insisted, holding out her hand.

He gave it to her. Then she demanded his shirt.

"You gonna ask for my pants, too?"

"You can check that yourself," said Mara, running her fingers across the seams. The CIA had bugs that were so small they could be sewn into the facing of a shirt, or placed along the side of a buttonhole. But the Vietnamese didn't possess such technology, or at least no one in the agency thought they did.

Which, Mara knew, wasn't the same thing as their not having it.

It wasn't just paranoia she was feeling. She was angry, mad at the agency, furious with Langley and the idiots there who ran things. She wasn't even too happy with Peter Lucas. She needed to talk to him, but despite trying, she couldn't get through. She'd been with the Company long enough to guess the reason: Lucas, temporarily heading the agency's Southeast Asia operation, had been called back to the States to give a command performance for the White House.

Idiots.

And then there was the problem of the ten thousand

dollars missing from the drop. Which, at best, indicated that the station was employing thieves.

"So do I get to check your clothes now?" Zeus asked.

"Very funny," said Mara, handing him back the shirt. "Did the Vietnamese give you anything?"

"Indigestion."

"In case you haven't guessed, I'm not in a very good mood, Major."

"Really? You were just about bowling me over with your jokes."

"Walk," she said, starting again.

"So your plans were changed," said Zeus, falling into stride. "Which is what has you in such a good mood."

"The airport was closed. As if nobody could fucking foresee that."

"Go out by ship."

"Apparently the Chinese have set up a blockade and we're not going near enough to the coast to test it," said Mara.

The SEALs had come from a submarine farther offshore, which had rendezvoused with a helicopter. The submarine had gone northward near the Chinese coast immediately after the SEALs left and was not available to even try for a pickup.

"You sound a little bitter," said Zeus.

"I am."

Mara realized she was almost running. She slowed her pace, trying to calm herself. There was no sense being angry; plans changed all the time.

"Too much coffee," she told Zeus.

"Didn't get much sleep, huh?"

A jet rocketed overhead. Zeus stopped and spun in the direction of the sound, braced for a bomb. Mara felt comforted somehow, his tension proof that her jangling nerves were normal, were deserved.

"Probably a reconnaissance flight," said Zeus.

"In any event, the upshot is, I need to get south," said Mara.

"I can talk to General Trung," said Zeus. "I'm sure we can get an escort."

"I don't want an escort. I don't want anything that will draw attention to us. More than the obvious," said Mara. As foreigners, they would stand out no matter what.

"You don't trust the Vietnamese?"

"No," said Mara.

"Not even Trung?"

Mara had been told by Langley to treat the Vietnamese army as if the general staff had been penetrated by the Chinese—which to Mara meant that it had been. She wasn't supposed to tell Zeus that, since it could possibly jeopardize whatever means the agency was using to gather its own intelligence from the Chinese. But she wanted him to put two and two together, for his own safety.

"I wouldn't trust anyone," said Mara. "The Chinese have a huge spy network here. A very efficient one."

"Okay."

"Anyway, I'm supposed to get south quietly," added Mara. "The Vietnamese don't know about Josh. They know very little about the UN mission that he was on."

A mission that had been penetrated by the CIA, a fact that also had to stay secret, though it did not involve Josh. The spy had been killed in the Chinese massacre.

"I need to know what roads south are open," said Mara. "That's number one."

"They're all open," said Zeus. "South of the reservoir."

"Will they be open twelve hours from now?"

"Hard to say. It depends on what the Chinese do next. If I were them, I would be swinging eastward to hit Hanoi," said Zeus. "And I'd be coming in from the sea. But if I were them, I would have had a different strategy to begin with."

"I may need to find out what's going on," said Mara. "I need to be able to talk to you."

"Call me."

"Good idea."

"You're being sarcastic?"

Mara turned at the corner and picked up her pace again, walking to a building in the middle of the block whose door was painted bright green. She stopped, looked around, then walked to a set of steps leading downward just beyond the main door. Zeus followed.

She knocked. The door was opened by a short, gray-haired Vietnamese woman, who looked at her expectantly.

"Four," said Mara in Vietnamese.

The woman told her that the price was one hundred dollars apiece.

"One million dong for all," said Mara.

"Dollars."

"I've always paid in dong."

Mara had never bought a phone here, or anywhere else in Vietnam for that matter. But it was a plausible lie. Mara knew she wasn't going to pay in dong, but she had to try and get the price down as far as possible to preserve her small supply of American money.

"Phone always in dollar," said the woman, switching to English.

"You won't be able to change them," said Mara, sticking to Vietnamese.

"Changing them is my problem," said the woman, back in Vietnamese. She offered Mara ninety a phone.

Mara told her that was unacceptable, waited for a moment, then turned to go.

"I know that trick," said the woman.

Mara ignored her. She had reached the sidewalk when the woman offered the phones for fifty apiece.

"Too much," said Mara.

"Mister, buy for your wife," said the woman, appealing to Zeus in English.

"She's not my wife," said Zeus.

The words confused the woman.

"One hundred for all the phones," said Mara in Vietnamese.

The woman made a face. "Your Vietnamese is very good," she told Mara. "So you must know how poor our country is."

What Mara knew was that the phones had surely been stolen. Pointing that out would not be helpful at this stage in the negotiations, however.

"One hundred for all of the phones," Mara repeated.

The woman closed her eyes.

"I will give you three phones for that," she said finally.

Mara took the deal.

The phones had numbers taped to the back. But those weren't the numbers they were going to use. Two blocks away, Mara found a wooden crate to sit on. She carefully opened the phones and inserted new SIM cards, in effect changing the brains of the phones. She gave Zeus one and kept the other two.

"I should only have to call you once," said Mara. "But don't get rid of the phone until I call and tell you to do so. You realize the Vietnamese listen to all cell phone conversations, right?"

"Uh—"

"So we have to assume that they're going to be listening in. Maybe even the Chinese will by then. I'll give you a number. That will be the highway number. Then I'll give you a place. I'll be asking you if the road is clear south of that place. You tell me yes or no. That's it. Nothing more. Assume they're listening."

"What if you have a more complicated question?"

"Then I'll have to play it by ear," said Mara.

"This is all the help you want?"

Mara contemplated giving him a copy of the video and stills Josh had shot of the massacre. Washington had ordered her not to transmit the files, since she couldn't safely encrypt them. It was likely the Chinese would intercept the transmission, and they could break any commercial encryption, just as the CIA could. Once they had the images, they would find a way to alter them, releasing versions before the U.S. did.

But what if she didn't make it? Murphy could be a backup.

No. Her orders were specific: trust absolutely no one with the files, even Americans. Even Zeus, though he hadn't been named.

"It's all the help you can give me," she said. "Can you find your way back to your hotel?"

He looked around. "I'm honestly not sure."

"Take a right there, go two blocks, then take a left," said Mara, pointing. "You'll be back on the avenue. Keep going and you'll reach your hotel. If you get stuck, you can always ask the soldiers who are trailing you. They're a block and a half behind."

6

Over Hanoi

Stepping into the air was a relief.

Jing Yo pinned his elbows close to his ribs, his legs tucked up. He wanted to wait until the last possible moment to deploy his chute.

The city grew before his eyes, the yellow speckles resolving into spotlights and guns. He'd parachuted so often that he didn't even need to glance at the altimeter on his wrist to know when to pull the cord; he could just wait for the twinkles to stop.

He thought of what would happen if he didn't pull, if he just continued to fall.

Oblivion was everyone's eventual reward. But it was hubris to try to steal it from fate, to seek it before one's assigned time. The way was unending; attempt to cheat it on one turn of the wheel and the next would make you pay.

Jing Yo pulled the cord. The chute exploded into the air behind him. He felt the strong tug on his shoulders and at his thighs. He took hold of the toggles and began to steer.

He wanted a black spot to land on. He fought off the blur, steadied his eyes. The guns were still firing, but they had moved northwest, following the small aircraft that had flown him here.

Jing Yo aimed for what he thought was a field, then realized almost too late that it was the flat roof of a large single-story building at the end of a road. He pitched himself right, and managed to swing the parachute into the small yard behind the building. His rucksack hit the ground a moment before he did, giving him just enough warning.

The next few minutes rushed by. He gathered the parachute. He found a large garbage bin behind the building and placed it inside. He put the jump helmet and goggles there as well. He unpacked the rucksack, unfolding the bicycle he would use to get into the city. He took his pistol and positioned it beneath his belt. He made sure his knife was ready. He considered changing his boots—he'd worn heavy combat wear for the jump—but thought better of it.

Finally, he started to ride.

Only when his foot touched the pedal did he hear the dogs barking. Even then, he thought they were just random sounds, the sort of alarm a nosy pet might make when catching an unfamiliar scent in the field.

Then he heard shouts, and he realized someone was hunting for him.

Jing Yo began pedaling in earnest. The street before him lit up—headlights, coming from behind him. The beams caught the rusted crisscross of a chain-link fence on the right side of the road, then swung back, reflecting off the houses that lined the left.

He glanced over his shoulder. A pickup was following him.

Though a strong cycler, Jing Yo was no match for the truck. It accelerated toward him, pulling alongside.

Two dogs, along with two men, were in the truck bed. The driver rolled down his window.

"You," shouted the driver. "What are you doing?"

"I have to report for work," replied Jing Yo, still pumping his legs. There were houses on both sides of the road; if necessary, he could run behind them.

How could he lose the dogs?

"Where do you work?" asked the driver.

Before Jing Yo could answer, one of the men in the rear of truck yelled at him, asking if he had seen a paratrooper.

Jing Yo's Vietnamese was very good; he had trained for the mission inside the country, working with a tutor for months. But his vocabulary wasn't encyclopedic, and he didn't recognize the Vietnamese word for paratrooper.

"What?" he asked.

"Soldiers. Did you see them?"

"I don't know," said Jing Yo.

"From the sky," said the man.

"An airplane?" Jing Yo asked.

"Dumb peasant."

The driver pushed harder on the gas, starting to pull away. Jing Yo put his head down, pedaling. He heard the men in the back shout something over the barking dogs.

The truck stopped abruptly.

His path to the left was blocked by a cluster of houses, tightly packed together. Jumping the fence into the open field was a better bet, though it would leave him vulnerable as he climbed. And either way, he would lose his bike.

"What kind of shoes are those?" yelled one of the men in the rear of the truck as he approached.

Jing Yo stopped. "My shoes?"

"Are you a deserter?"

"Maybe you're pilot of the fighter that was shot down," said the other man in the back. They were holding their dogs tightly on a leash. The animals were large, foreign dogs, the type trained as watchdogs. He guessed that the men were part of some sort of militia, or perhaps policemen out of uniform.

"Do I look like a pilot?" Jing Yo asked.

Jing Yo put his foot on the pedal, and started to pass them. He looked straight ahead.

The dogs' barking intensified, then suddenly stopped. They had been released.

There is a point of balance, in every man, in every situation. Stasis, a calm balance free from turmoil, internal and external. Jing Yo reached for that point, and found it in his mind.

Then he attacked.

The bike flew out from under him as the first dog grabbed at his pant leg. Jing Yo stomped the dog's skull, crushing it. His maneuver left him vulnerable to the second dog, which jumped at him. Jing Yo raised his arms, barely catching the animal as it lunged. He rolled to his left, using the animal's weight and momentum against it as he pinned it to the ground. His knee broke its rib cage.

The animal yelped, snapping its teeth. Then it dropped its snout, helpless, dying, wheezing in pain.

Jing Yo jumped to his feet. The two men in the back of the pickup truck were gaping at him, stunned. Jing Yo launched himself, flying into the two men, fists raised. He caught the first man in the throat but missed the second. Jing Yo turned, found the man, and kicked him in the chest, sending him against the window of the truck. He kicked him again in the face, then chopped his neck with the side of his hand.

The man's neck snapped.

The other man had fallen to the ground under the force of Jing Yo's initial blow. Jing Yo jumped on top of him, landing on his back. He kicked him over, then with his heel crushed the man's esophagus, in effect strangling him.

The truck lurched forward. Jing Yo threw himself into the bed. Scrambling to his knees, he grabbed one of the AK-47s as the driver screeched around the corner. Jing Yo put the gun to the rear window and pulled the trigger.

The truck began to veer as the driver fell forward against the steering wheel, killed by Jing Yo's shot. With the dead man's foot still hard against the gas pedal, the truck veered sideways, then rushed off the pavement into the front yard of a small house.

Jing Yo put his left hand on the cab roof and pushed off, managing to jump off the opposite side as the truck flipped and crashed into the house. He rolled on the ground, his senses momentarily gone.

There was silence.

A woman screamed. A child began to cry.

Jing Yo jumped to his feet and began to run.

B y the time Jing Yo got to central Hanoi, it was nearly eight o'clock, and the city was wide awake. He'd had to duck only a single checkpoint, but his experience with the dogs and the pickup truck made him wary. He'd gotten rid of his boots, and while tempted to keep the AK-47 for protection, he'd ditched it as well. He looked like a Vietnamese student, in Western blue jeans, with cheap athletic shoes and a bulky sweatshirt to hide his pistol. His backpack bore the insignia of a Vietnamese company.

It had been more than a year since Jing Yo had been in Hanoi. That visit had in no way prepared him for the city he saw now. Black smoke hung over the northern half, thickest above the airport and the area where the government and army had their official buildings. Jing Yo made his way to the banks of the Red River, walking in the direction of Phu Tan Port. Both the Chuong Dong Bridge and the Long Bien Bridge farther north had been destroyed. Burned-out shells of cars littered the roads near the water. Several small freighters had either been bombed or run aground, perhaps out of panic. The stern of the nearest vessel, a gasoline tanker blackened by the smoke of a fire, stood high above the water, its screw and rudder exposed like the genitals of an old, naked man.

Jing Yo walked northward, his stoic expression mirrored in the faces of the people he passed. They, too, were on a mission. A woman was taking dried sweet potatoes home from the market, dinner for a week. A man in a clean suit strode through the dusty street toward work, his manner daring the grit to settle on him.

Soldiers were posted at several of the intersections, but they took little notice of the clusters of people walking past. Jing Yo turned onto Hang Gai, one of the main roads north of the Tháp Rùa or Turtle Tower, the famous temple in the middle of Sword Lake in the center part of the city. There was a gaping hole in the row of buildings on the first street he turned down. He knew the area from his last stay, but couldn't place the building that had been there.

He walked slowly, trying to prod his memory. Whatever had been there was now a hole filled with debris. The house behind it leaned over, as if peeking downward. Stray rocks and bricks were strewn at the sides. A small pile lined the gutter on the far side.

The theater. It had been a theater.

The memory came full force. He saw himself sitting in the audience, enchanted by the show, completely taken by the strange dance onstage.

Jing Yo pushed the memory away. It was an indulgence he couldn't afford.

He continued down the block, then turned into a street of old and cramped buildings.

A strong odor hung in the air. Burnt metal and rotting flesh.

Jing Yo found the building and knocked on the door. There was no answer. He knocked again. This time there was a rustle. Someone came to the door.

"Who?" asked a voice, so softly he could barely hear.

"Jing Yo."

The door opened. A woman about Jing Yo's age, wearing a Western-style dress, her hair undone down her back, stood gaping.

"Jing Yo?"

"It has been a long time," he told her as she collapsed into his arms.

Hanoi

Josh studied his face in the mirror. The razor the SEAL had given him had removed about three-fourths of his week-old beard, leaving an uneven stubble covering his face.

There wasn't enough shaving cream for a second try. He lathered up the soap as best he could, and began scraping gently. Bits of hair poked up from the corners of his mouth like pimples erupting on a teenager's face.

His forehead was red, his nose blistered. His right eye drooped down, ringed by a deep, puffy bruise. He didn't remember how he'd gotten it; it was simply one of the assorted minor injuries he'd suffered.

Better this than dead, he thought. Much better.

"Hey, kid, how's it coming?" said Little Joe from the hallway. Little Joe—his full name was Ensign Riccardo Joseph Crabtree—had replaced Squeaky on guard duty while Josh slept.

"I'm getting there," said Josh.

"You shaving?"

"Yeah."

"Mind if I use the facilities? My stomach's gonna explode."

"Yeah, yeah, come on in," said Josh.

There was only one commode in the washroom, open to the rest of the room. Josh threw water on his face and started to clear out to give the SEAL some privacy.

"Where you goin'?" said Little Joe.

"I'm not watching."

Little Joe had a chortling laugh, the sort of sound a pig might make while grinding food.

"I don't blame you. Take this." He handed Josh his MP-5. "Don't shoot yourself. I'll be out in a second."

Josh took the submachine gun and went out into the hall.

Josh had learned to hunt and handle guns as a young boy, but the submachine was a different sort of weapon. A rifle, a shotgun, even a pistol—all were tools for a certain kind of work, taking food. They were little different from the tractor his uncle used to plow the fields on their farm. You respected your rifle because it was a powerful tool, one that could easily get you into trouble if used improperly.

The submachine gun was a tool, too, but its purpose had nothing to do with food. You killed with it. Not food, but other people.

Kill or be killed. It wasn't a theoretical or philosophical construct, not a scientific theory or hypothesis.

Josh understood it completely, in his gut as well as his head—he'd just lived it. He'd witnessed the results of what happened when you didn't or couldn't defend yourself. And he'd managed to survive *only* at the expense of others.

And yet, after all that, there was something about the *idea* of killing another human being that weighed greatly on him.

As a scientist, he believed his mission was to help people. He studied the weather and its effect on biomes because he wanted to help humans deal with it. What other reason was there? Idle curiosity?

"You need purpose in your work," a professor had told him in college. It was back in his junior year, his Philosophy of Science class. Professor Van Garten. Considering that it was a science class, and that Van Garten was a biologist, the lectures veered very close to religion. "If science's discoveries are not in service of mankind, what good are they?" Van Garten had said on the very first day.

Van Garten was a realist; he'd spoken of the dark side of science—the atom bomb, mutations gone awry. But in the end, again and again, he maintained that science's aim must overall be toward the good. He invoked Teilhard de Chardin—Catholic priest and philosopher—to imply that man's innate nature was good, and that science, if true to that nature, would be good as well.

But having seen what he'd seen in the jungle, Josh had to question whether that was really true.

The old men and women massacred by the Chinese in the village: what did they know of man's innate nature? What about the infants?

Man's nature was brutal, and ugly, and beyond redemption. What science could possibly redeem the acts of the killers?

Kill or be killed? That wasn't even in the equation. Kill for the sake of killing.

But that wasn't what he was about. Was it?

"Smart thing, getting out of there," said Little Joe, pulling open the door. "Whew."

The SEAL waved his hand in front of his face, smiling. His nickname was apt. Little Joe stood only about five four. He wasn't particularly broad-shouldered, and while all SEALs exuded a certain toughness, he didn't seem particularly threatening. Even when they'd been escaping under fire from the Chinese, he'd had the demeanor of a guy grabbing a beer at a keg party, the sort of guy who'd smile at you when you walked up, give you his plastic cup, and get himself another one.

He'd also fed grenades into his grenade launcher like they were M&M's. He'd hung off the back of the van firing while a half dozen Chinese soldiers tried to perforate him, firing well over a hundred rounds into everything but his flesh.

The easygoing smile and shrugs made the more lasting impression.

"Jeez, you hold that like you know what you're doing," said Little Joe, pointing at the submachine gun. "Ya gonna give it back, or ya gonna make me wrestle ya for it?"

Josh handed the weapon over.

"You all packed? Ready to go?" asked Little Joe.

"I don't have much," said Josh.

"Travel light, right?" Little Joe gave one of his chortles. "Let's go then. We gotta meet the spook lady."

Josh followed the SEAL through the hall toward the back of the building. They came out in a narrow alley. Another SEAL, Eric Wright, was there with a pickup truck they'd commandeered.

Mạ was sitting next to him, sucking her thumb. She

opened her mouth wide as Josh slid in, then threw herself on him.

"Hey, I'm happy to see you, too," he told her. "How are ya?"

Mạ didn't understand what he said; she spoke only Vietnamese.

"She's a doll," said Eric. "Cute kid."

"Been through hell," said Little Joe, squeezing in on the other side of Josh. Mạ sat on Josh's lap, giving them all room.

"Where'd you get the truck?" Josh asked. It was a two-door Toyota, maybe a year old.

"Nice wheels, huh?" said Little Joe. "Not even a dent."

"Where'd you get it?" asked Josh, trying to make conversation.

"Rental lot," said Eric.

"How much is a rental here?"

"Cheap," Little Joe chortled. "We paid with SEAL."

"Call it an exchange," said Eric. "We took the truck, and, in exchange, we didn't blow nothin' up."

As they drove out of the alley onto the main street, both men became silent, watching their surroundings. Little Joe was still smiling, but his eyes were darting.

"Patrol up there," he said. "Two guys on the deuce."

"Yeah," grunted Eric.

Technically, the truck they'd spotted wasn't a deuce-and-a-half, military slang for a two-and-a-half-ton transport used by the army to haul men and supplies. But the description was close enough: the vehicle was a troop truck with a canvas back, similar in purpose if not exact detail. Ironically, the vehicle was made by China, which before the war had done a fair amount of trade with Vietnam.

"Sniper up on that building," said Eric.

Little Joe leaned forward to look as they passed.

"Just guarding something," he said. "Just watching. Not a sniper."

"You know what the hell I mean, man."

"Well then say it."

"Hey, fuck you. He's a sniper, all right?"

"Watch the language. We got a kid."

"Sorry."

"What's he going to snipe at?"

"The rabble."

Little Joe laughed. "They have these guys in the city to show the people they're safe," he told Josh. "It's psychological. They don't want panic."

"That's bull," said Eric. "They're looking for SEALs. And spies. And Santa Claus, 'cause they know he comes by rooftop."

"Don't listen to him," said Little Joe. "He's nuts. He flunked colors in kindergarten."

"Look who's talking," said Eric. "Don't listen to him, kid. He can't find his dick in a bathroom. Stick with me. I'll give you the straight story."

"Hey—watch it for the kid."

"Sorry."

The two SEALs traded put-downs—without any more four-letter words—as they wended their way through the capital. The streets were far less crowded than they had been two weeks before, when Josh was here with the expedition team, gathering supplies and preparing to go into the jungle.

And yet, the destruction he saw was less than he would have expected.

"I'm amazed there's so many buildings still standing," he said.

"Don't let that fool you," said Little Joe. "Airport's pretty much leveled, and a lot of the important government buildings are wiped out."

"Takes a lot to steamroll a city," added Eric. "But they're working on it."

"Come back next week," said Little Joe. "City'll be one big pile of rubble."

"Nah, they won't waste the ammo," said Eric. "Waste of time to blow everything up."

"Chinese invented gunpowder. They like blowing sh—stuff up," he added, amending his language midstream because of Mạ.

"So do I, but I wouldn't waste it on Hanoi."

"That's it," said Little Joe, pointing to a brown brick building. "Shop's around the back."

Eric pulled over. Little Joe hopped out, pushing the door closed behind him. He eyed the street left and right, then motioned Josh out. He took Mạ by the hand and walked with her through the alley side by side to a blue door. It was a small restaurant. Mara was sitting at a table in the corner, speaking to a hollow-cheeked Vietnamese man. The man fidgeted almost violently, turning his head left and right and flailing his elbows almost as if they were wings and he was trying to take off. Mara looked up as they came in and glared at them.

"Here," said Josh, realizing that she didn't want them to interrupt. "Let's take this table."

Little Joe pulled out a chair and sat down, positioning himself so he could see the entire room. His back was to Mara and the man.

A woman came over. Josh had only enough Vietnamese to realize she was asking what they wanted.

"*Cà phê sữa,*" he said, asking for white coffee.

"Me, too," said Little Joe, in English.

The woman glanced nervously at his submachine gun, which he'd put on his lap. Josh signaled with his fingers that they wanted two of the coffees.

"Milk for Mạ?" he said.

The woman said something in Vietnamese that he didn't understand. Mạ answered.

"Okay, Joe?" asked the woman.

"Yup," said Josh, who didn't understand what she had ordered, but figured it would be okay.

"She tell us it was on the house?" asked Little Joe.

"I have no idea," said Josh.

"You don't know Vietnamese?"

"Not really. They taught some phrases and things, and we practiced a little, but when people talk real fast, I can't get it," Josh said. "The tones are tough—the same sound can mean a bunch of things, depending on how they inflect it."

"Well that's a bitch. We'll have to take pot luck, huh?"

"I ordered white coffee. It's coffee with milk."

"What if I wanted tea?"

"Oh. Um—"

"Just busting you, kid. Coffee's good."

Though Little Joe called him "kid," the SEAL seemed to be about his age. Maybe being in combat made him feel older than other people.

"So you're a scientist, right?" said Little Joe. "What do you do? You know, science-wise?"

"I'm a weather scientist. Actually, what I study is the relationship between weather and biomes. We were looking at the plant life, how it's changed in the last two years."

"Global warming, right?" Little Joe smirked.

"I really hate that term. It doesn't describe what's going on. Vietnam's average temperature is actually lower than it was a decade ago. People think everything's getting hotter but it really isn't."

Josh began explaining that the effects of rapid weather change were extremely complicated. In Vietnam's case, the changes had actually increased the arable land and lengthened the growing season.

Little Joe chortled. "What's 'arable'?" he said.

"Just farmland," said Josh. "They grow a lot of rice, and what they've been able to do with increased crops—as much from genetic engineering on the rice as from the weather, but the weather did really help. Anyway, what they have now are two and even three crops per year, with yields that five years ago would have been unimaginable. They even do better than we do back home. That's given them an incredible boost. That's why China's invading. They want the food."

"Nah, it's their oil," said Little Joe. "They got tons of it offshore. That's what this is about."

"Oil's important," said Josh, who knew that the oil fields off Vietnam's eastern shores were reputed to hold over twelve billion barrels, nearly double the estimate of a few years before. China was a voracious consumer. "But food is the reason people go to war. Vietnam has food and China doesn't. Or not enough, anyway."

"Nah. Always about oil, kid. It's always oil."

Mara tried to stay focused on what Phai was telling her about his cousin, but it was difficult. The SEAL and his submachine gun had drawn the attention of everyone in the room. It would be clear that they were together.

"The difficult problem in his village is thinking the Americans are friends," Phai said. "No one accepts that. Always be on guard."

"I understand."

"Then good luck." He started to rise.

"Wait," said Mara, grabbing his hand.

It was a breach of etiquette, a mildly serious one, since they were different genders, and Phai immediately tensed. Mara let go.

She apologized. He nodded stiffly and asked what she needed.

"I have some things to sell. Satellite phones. I need to find a place—".

"I can take them."

"No. They may be bugged. I don't want you connected to them."

He named a gold shop on Ha Trung, and gave her directions. Then he rose and walked out quickly, arms tight to his body as if he were trying to shrivel into the air.

Mara fished out money for the bill, adding extra dong to cover Mạ, Josh, and Little Joe. She got up and walked to their table.

"Leave. Now," she said, and without waiting dropped the cash on the table and walked out.

The SEAL with the truck was waiting at the head of the alley. Nothing like being conspicuous. Mara gritted her back teeth.

"Hey, spook," said Little Joe, practically swinging as he came out the door. "Where to now?"

"You jackass. What the hell did you go in there with your gun for?"

"Bunches of people have their guns with them," said Little Joe.

"Bunches of people aren't Americans. They're the militia."

"Nobody complained."

"Get in the fucking truck," said Mara. She turned to Josh. "You have to have more sense."

"I uh—"

"Get Mạ in the truck," said Mara.

"Listen—"

"You thought he knew what he was doing, is that what you were going to say?"

"No. I mean—"

"He's got a brain the size of a pea. They all do."

The three walked back to the pickup. Josh started to get into the open bed.

"Joe goes back there," said Mara. "You stay in the front with me."

Inside the truck, she told Eric to take them to Hotel Nikko.

"I don't know where that is," said Eric.

"It's on Tran Nhan Tong Street. In Dong Da."

"If it ain't in Michigan, I don't have a clue."

"It's south," said Mara. "Go up a block and take a left. Go down Ba Trieu. There aren't too many troops."

"Direct me."

The hotel was one of the city's best. A large Western-style building near Hoan Kiem Lake, it was located in a neighborhood that included several embassies, and so far had escaped damage.

"Stay with the girl and the truck," Mara told the SEALs as they pulled up to the thick overhang that marked the entrance. There were soldiers around the corner, but none in the plaza at the front of the hotel.

"No, we're with Josh until the place is secure," said Little Joe. "Orders."

"Screw your orders," she told him. "The more attention we attract, the less secure we all are."

"Hey, I'll go inside and scout," said Eric, jumping out of the driver's seat. "If I spin around, something's up. You stay with Ma."

"Fine with me," said Little Joe.

Eric pulled his shirt out, making sure the front concealed his holster. Mara frowned. She waited a few seconds, then led Josh inside. The lobby was crowded with foreigners sitting on the couches or milling around, making nervous conversation.

Kerfer was sitting near the bar, nursing a beer. "Took your time," he said.

"I'm not on your schedule," said Mara.

"Longer we wait to leave, the more chance the Chinks have to overrun the place."

"I wish you'd watch your language."

"That's rich. You think any of these people would object? Fucking Chinks are breathing down their necks." Kerfer took a swig of his beer. It was a Sapporo. "You know the restaurant's supposed to be pretty good. I ate here a couple of years ago. How are ya today, Doc? You eat yet?"

"I'm not that hungry," said Josh.

"Don't blame you. Heard you didn't sleep well."

Josh shrugged. "I slept okay."

Kerfer pushed the beer toward the bartender. "Couple more," he said in English.

"We have to talk, Lieutenant," said Mara. "Over there. In private."

Kerfer got up and followed her toward the side of the room. "You sure this place ain't bugged?" he asked.

"We're not talking inside."

She went down the hall through a staff-only door and out into the back lot.

"You know your way around pretty well," said Kerfer.

"Listen, your men have to keep their weapons out of sight."

"Eric's is under his shirt."

"Little Joe was swinging his around like he was exposing himself in a girl's boarding school."

Kerfer laughed. "Well, you got him pegged." He took out a cigar. "Copped this from the bartender. Cost me ten U.S. You figure that's a good deal?"

"Conserve your money," she told him. "I need to run a few more errands. We'll meet at the train station at noon."

"Train station?"

Mara stared at him.

"You're out of your fucking mind, lady." Kerfer clipped the end of the cigar with a cutter, then poked it in his mouth. "We're going to take a train?"

"Why not?"

"Chinese'll bomb it as soon as they can spare the iron."

"We'll be in Saigon by then."

"I wouldn't bet on it."

"I know my way around. I don't need you to hold my hand."

"I'm supposed to get you back in one piece. You and Junior in there."

"You were assigned to get me out from behind the lines. You did a fine job. I can take it from here."

Kerfer laughed. He puffed up his cigar, pushing the flame with a series of sharp breaths.

"You're just good enough to be dangerous," he told her.

"Just get Josh to the station in one piece, okay? If you don't want to come with us, then you don't have to. We're probably safer traveling on our own."

"You believe that?"

"Yes."

He laughed again, then blew a ring of smoke from his mouth. "I'll have him there," said Kerfer. "You trust me to do that?"

"Not really."

8

Hanoi

Jing Yo had first met Hyuen Bo three years before, when he was assigned to visit Vietnam as part of a training regime for the commando regiment. He'd already been in combat for nearly a year, assisting guerrillas in Malaysia; the assignment was intended mostly as a rest period, but also helped familiarize him with the country of a traditional enemy. It would turn out to be the first of several trips, though at the time neither he nor his superiors knew that.

Hanoi had been his base of operations. As cover, he had enrolled in the college of science as a biology student. It was there that he met Hyuen Bo.

She was working as a clerk for the registrar, and helped him with his paperwork. He stared at her long black hair as she showed him the forms, entranced by her face and the scent of jasmine surrounding her.

He found an excuse to come back the next day, telling her that he was confused about whether he was assigned to the right class. There was no mistake, of course, and she looked at him oddly.

Raised in the cloistered monastery, Jing Yo had always been shy with women. With Hyuen Bo he was beyond awkward. But his attraction was so strong that he delayed his plans to travel to Saigon. He went to class a third day, and afterward went to the registrar, determined to see her again, though even as he came through the door he didn't know what excuse he would invent.

Another woman was in her place.

All the blood seemed to drain from his head. He had faced gunfire more times than he could count, but the fear he felt at the possibility of never seeing the girl again was more palpable than anything he had felt during war.

The woman at the desk explained that Hyuen Bo had been given a new job. She was due to start in the central ministry as an aide and translator within a few days. The office had given her the rest of the week off as a reward for her good service.

Jing Yo managed to get her address. He went directly to the house. Hyuen Bo wasn't there. He waited, sitting on the pavement in front of the door as the afternoon grew into evening. When darkness fell, he began to feel sick to his stomach—the only reason she could be staying out this late, he reasoned, was that she must be seeing a boyfriend.

Hyuen Bo's neighbors watched from a distance. He could see them stealing glances, but none approached. He would have ignored them if they had.

Jing Yo sat cross-legged near the door to the house, sitting and staring into the growing blackness. He emptied his mind. He had done the same thing at the monastery for years and years, and so it did not feel overly difficult or boring. But his stomach continued in turmoil.

And then finally a cab pulled up, and Hyuen Bo stepped out.

Jing Yo felt his heart stop.

She started to walk right by him. He couldn't say a word.

"You want something?" she said, turning her head.

"It's me, the student, Jing Yo. I heard you are gone from the college."

"I . . . What are you doing here?"

He rose. His tongue felt frozen but he forced it to work.

"I wanted to ask you to go out with me," he said.

"A date?"

"Yes."

She stared at him. "When?"

"Now. Or another time. Now would be better," he added, feeling his heart would never work again if she didn't say yes.

"We could take a walk," she said finally.

And so they did.

"**W**hy are you here?" Hyuen Bo whispered as he pushed her gently away from him.

"I have to find an American," he told her.

"What?"

"Is there anyone in your apartment?"

"No. Come on in, yes. You don't want anyone to see you."

The small apartment was exactly as he remembered it. Two thinly upholstered chairs dominated the front room. A table sat to one side. A stereo rested on the top, an MP3 player connected by a snaking wire to its USB port.

"Do you want some tea?" she asked.

"Yes."

Jing Yo sat in the chair closest to the door. It was one he'd always sat in. If he closed his eyes, he might wake up and find out that everything that had happened since he had been here eighteen months before was a dream.

Hyuen Bo came back with a cup of tea.

"China has invaded Vietnam," she said accusingly as she gave him the cup. "Why?"

Jing Yo shook his head.

"They are claiming Vietnam started the war," added Hyuen Bo.

Jing Yo said nothing. There was no way to justify the actions of the government, and even if there were, he would not have expected Hyuen Bo to understand or accept the logic.

She knelt down at his feet, putting her head on his right knee. "Why have you returned now?"

"I have a mission," he said softly. He leaned down, covering his face with his hands. They were barely inches away, their breaths intertwined. Yet he suddenly felt the separation of time and distance as an immense, uncrossable border. "There is an American agent."

"Where?"

"He has come to Hanoi. I'm not yet sure where."

"And you want my help?"

"Yes," answered Jing Yo, though at that moment his mission was the furthest thing from his mind.

It was a moment of temptation—weakness. But what he wanted was not duty, not even adherence to the Way. He wanted her.

"My superiors would want to know why I was asking questions," said Hyuen Bo.

Jing Yo steeled himself.

"A friend might be looking for him," he said. "It's not a lie."

A tear slid from the corner of Hyuen Bo's eye. A second and then a third followed.

"Why are you crying?" Jing Yo asked.

"Chinese bombs killed my mother at the theater the other night," she told him, raising her face to gaze into his eyes.

Jing Yo didn't know what to say. The woman had

always been kind to him. She lived around the corner, with Hyuen Bo's sister and brother-in-law and their children.

"I'll help," said Hyuen Bo. She collapsed onto his lap, shaking.

Jing Yo put his hand on her back.

"Tell me what to do," she said between her sobs.

Washington, D.C.

President Greene hated videoconferences, especially when he took them downstairs in the National Security Council facilities. The larger-than-life screens made them feel like television talk shows, and there was always a certain amount of preening for the camera. Even one-on-one they seemed fake, promising intimacy and subtlety but ultimately failing to deliver.

But he couldn't very well fly to Vietnam to hear what General Harland Perry had to say. Nor did he want Perry to leave Hanoi just then. So this would have to do.

"The attack on the reservoir stalled them, temporarily at least," said Perry, speaking from the secure communications room of the U.S. embassy. "They didn't anticipate it. They've sent some units on probing attacks to the east. So far, the Vietnamese have turned everything back."

Greene leaned his chin on his hand, his elbow resting on the large table that dominated the conference room. Besides the president and the communications specialist handling the gear, the only other person in the room was the national security adviser, Walter Jackson. Washington and Vietnam were twelve hours apart—when it was 11 a.m. in Vietnam, as it was now, it was eleven at night in Washington.

"How long do you think they can continue to hold the Chinese back?" asked the president.

"Yes, sir, good question."

Which was Perry's way of saying he had no way of knowing.

"The Vietnamese are shelling them from across the reservoir," continued the general. "The Chinese haven't dug in. That means they're going to move again. If I had to guess, I'd say there'll be a new push in a few days."

"Which way?"

"If they're planning an invasion from the coast, they'll try to come east," said Perry. "They've got to. Going into Laos now will slow them down. That's what Major Murphy thinks."

"His track record is pretty good," said the president. He remembered Zeus—the major had correctly predicted the route of China's surprise charge into Vietnam. "So how do we stop them from going east?"

"Short of deploying the Twenty-fifth Infantry in the highlands north of Da Bac, I don't know that we can."

The Twenty-fifth was an American light infantry unit stationed in Japan. There was no chance it was going to be thrown into the battle, even if it were able to get there.

"What's your wonder boy say?" Greene asked.

"Zeus is looking to punt." Perry grinned. "I think he'd like to see the Twenty-fifth Infantry here, too."

"Not going to happen, General. The Vietnamese are going to have to hold them themselves."

"We're working on it, Mr. President. We are. But if there's an invasion along the coast, the Vietnamese are going to have to withdraw some of the forces in front of the Chinese to deal with it. Once that happens, their line will be so thin a breakthrough will be inevitable. Frankly, sir, I don't know how long they can hold out."

"Understood. Keep doing your best. My best wishes to all your men."

"Thank you, Mr. President."

The screen went blank. Greene turned to Jackson.

"What do you think, Walt?"

"The Chinese have a lot of troops there. If they land near Hue they'll cut the country in half. They can skip Hanoi if they want. They'll go down the coast, take the oil fields, then get the rice. Hanoi will have to surrender. Then, as soon as they've got Vietnam under control, they go into Thailand. After that, maybe they show their teeth in Malaysia."

"I would look at Japan," said Greene.

"No food in Japan," said Jackson. "Besides, Russia will have something to say about that."

"Russia will say go ahead."

Greene walked back and forth in the room, his energy getting the better of him. He was overdue for his evening workout, but it was too late for it now. He still had to call the education secretary to discuss strategy on the new education bill.

"Russia and China will clash eventually," said Jackson. "They're natural enemies. Maybe we can encourage that. Maybe the Russians will go along with us in the UN."

"The first thing we have to do is stop the landing," said Greene. "We need ships there."

Jackson's silence spoke volumes. The national security

adviser was hardly a dove, but clearly he thought the situation was hopeless. There were only two American ships in the general vicinity. Both were too far south to confront the Chinese aircraft carrier and destroyers that had steamed into the Gulf of Bac Bo and the waters off northern Vietnam. USS *Kitty Hawk* and her battle group were nearly two thousand miles away. And the Joint Chiefs of Staff were arguing vociferously that the carrier be kept there.

"I know, I don't ask for small miracles," said the president finally. He turned to the communications specialist. "See if you can get General Perry back on the line."

"What are you thinking?" asked Jackson.

"If I'm going to ask for a miracle, I ought to talk to the miracle man, right?"

10

Hanoi

Half a world away from Washington, Zeus Murphy was waiting for General Perry to finish briefing the U.S. ambassador on the latest developments before going with him to the Vietnamese army headquarters. While he faced a long afternoon working the Vietnamese through the latest U.S. intelligence, Zeus wasn't thinking about the language problems or the difficult tactical situation the Vietnamese found themselves in. He was worried about his Corvette back home in the States, debating whether to have his brother put it in storage in his garage. Which would necessitate allowing his brother to drive it—never a good idea, given his driving record.

One of the embassy employees, a Vietnamese woman in her early twenties, came down the stairs. She was thin, dressed in a skirt whose looseness somehow managed to emphasize the narrow contours of her body. Very pretty, yet brittle-looking at the same time.

"Major Murphy?" she asked.

"Call me Zeus."

She smiled. Zeus wondered if there was some sort of rule against fraternizing with embassy employees, and if there was, whether she'd be worth breaking it.

Almost certainly.

"The general would like to see you upstairs."

"Great. After you," said Zeus.

She blushed, actually blushed—Zeus knew opportunity when he saw it. But before he could take advantage, before he could even admire the rise of her hips up the steps, he was rudely interrupted by Major Win Christian, who shouted from the front hall behind him.

"Yo, Zeus—we leaving today or what?"

"Ask your boss," said Zeus.

"My boss. Yeah." Christian walked to the foot of the steps, lowering his voice. "You're his golden-haired boy."

Christian was Perry's chief of staff, and resented Zeus's inclusion as Perry's special adviser in Hanoi. Zeus had never been too crazy about Christian, though his opinion had warmed ever so slightly during their mission together to help the SEALs and Josh MacArthur. They'd taken a van and driven past an enemy ambush to grab them.

"The general just asked me to come and talk to him," said Zeus. "He's on with the president."

Zeus didn't actually think the president wanted to talk to him; it was just a way of tweaking Christian.

He jogged up the steps, looking for the staffer with the magic hips. Instead he found one of the American employees, a middle-aged male CIA officer who naturally claimed not to be a CIA officer. The man led him to the secure room.

Zeus was surprised to find that General Perry was still on the line with the president, and even more surprised when Perry put him on the line.

"Mr. President," said Zeus.

"You need to push to talk, Zeus," said Perry. "And tone down the exuberance a bit. It's not quite professional."

"Yes, sir." Zeus found the button. "Mr. President?"

"Major Murphy, good to talk to you again," said Greene. "Nice work with our scientist friend. Excellent."

"I just drove the van, sir."

"Here's why the general and I wanted to talk to you. Everyone agrees that the Chinese are going to launch a sea assault on Vietnam's eastern coast."

"Yes, sir. They have all those landing ships on Hainan, the island to the east. And meanwhile, their carriers—"

"Your job," said President Greene, not allowing himself to be interrupted, "is to stop the invasion."

"Um, stop it?"

"Yes. Come up with a plan to stop it. Then get the Vietnamese to implement it."

"I'm not sure it can be done, sir. The Vietnamese—their navy is, uh, tiny to nonexistent."

"Then use something different." The president sounded like a high school football coach, telling him to find a way around the blitz. "Think outside of the box. That's your job. You're good at it."

"Yes, sir."

"You figured out how to stop the ground advance," added Greene.

"Well, temporarily."

"Come up with something for the ships."

"I'll do my best, sir."

"That's all we ask. General?"

"I'm done on my end," said Perry.

"Very well. Keep up the good work, Zeus," added President Greene. "We're counting on you."

The screen went blank. Zeus looked at Perry.

"It's kind of impossible," said Zeus.

"I thought it'd be better if you heard it directly from him," said the general.

Hanoi

A certain amount of paranoia was absolutely essential to succeed as a covert agent. The problem was figuring out exactly how much was the right amount.

Mara had arrived in Vietnam knowing the CIA station in Hanoi had been compromised, so the theft of the money shouldn't have come as much of a surprise. And the fact that the box was actually where it was supposed to be could be interpreted as a good sign. Since her goal was simply to get out of Vietnam, whatever else was going on didn't really matter. She'd learned long ago to focus on the goal rather than the messy stuff it took to get there.

Still, despite the fact that the U.S. was now covertly

supplying advice and aid to Vietnam, she'd been told explicitly not to rely on the Vietnamese for help, not even transportation. The implication wasn't simply that they had a different agenda than the U.S. did: the Chinese were legendary in their ability to penetrate Asian governments and their militaries, as Mara had learned to her detriment time and again in Malaysia. Asking the Vietnamese for help might very well be the same as asking the Chinese for help.

Her suspicions and doubts wrapped themselves tighter and tighter as she drove her scooter over to the shop Phai had mentioned to sell the sat phones. Mara didn't particularly trust Phai, either, even though she knew him from Thailand. She rode around the block twice, making sure she wasn't followed, then parked in an alley about a block away. Even so, she circled around on foot to make sure there wasn't an ambush waiting.

Under other circumstances, Mara might have simply left the sat phones in the city somewhere. But she needed money as well as misdirection.

The fantasies she'd had as a child about being a spy—she'd grown up on *Where in the World Is Carmen Sandiego?*, then graduated to old James Bond movies—didn't involve credit cards or ATM machines. But they turned out to be an agent's best friend in the real world. When they weren't working, life was a hell of a lot harder.

Gold shops were common in the city, combination pawnbrokers and banks as well as jewelers. Like others, the owner of Ha Trung Finest conducted several other businesses on the side concurrently—tourist knick-knacks and bottled water were featured in the window, along with hand-woven place mats and a rug.

He offered her fifty thousand dong apiece for the two phones—a total of roughly six dollars.

"Be serious," scolded Mara. She was in no mood to bargain.

The proprietor pretended to look at the phones again, then upped his offer to two hundred thousand dong.

"No," said Mara loudly, this time using English. She turned to leave the store.

"Wait, wait, lady," said a woman, rushing from the back room. She spoke in English. "Don't worry about husband. Eels for brains."

Mara showed her the phones impatiently. The woman turned them over, looking at them as if they were pieces of jewelry. She flicked one on.

"These active," said the woman.

"I figured you'd take care of getting new accounts," said Mara.

"Without accounts they're worthless," said the man in Vietnamese.

"You just have to reprogram them," snapped Mara in English. "I know that happens all the time."

What actually happened all the time—and what Mara was counting on—was that the phones would be used on the existing accounts until the phone company finally got around to shutting them off. That could be days if not weeks. Of course, stating that explicitly meant acknowledging that the phones were stolen.

The store owners didn't just suspect the phones were stolen; they were counting on it. But if Mara said that, they wouldn't take them.

The wife looked at her. "Five hundred thousand dong."

"One million dong each."

Mara pushed the phones into the woman's hands. The woman tried to give them back. The man behind the counter harangued her for interfering.

"Eight hundred thousand," said Mara, speaking Vietnamese. "The account is good."

They settled on seven hundred and fifty, with the woman throwing in a sling bag Mara decided she could use for her gun. Once the money changed hands, the man became gracious, insisting on giving Mara a bottle of water. He would have tried selling her the rug if she hadn't left abruptly.

Mara had expected the trains south to be packed, but the station was almost empty when she arrived. Kerfer, Josh, and the others were huddled at the far end of the large room, camped out around a dozen of the light blue chairs. They'd bought some civilian luggage, and used them to stow their weapons and other gear. The SEALs had even found some new clothes and a doll for Mạ. She held the doll in her arms, rocking it gently and humming to it as she leaned against Josh.

"I'm assuming you have some sort of plan," said Kerfer when she arrived. All six of his men—Eric, Little Joe, Stevens, Jenkins, Mancho, and Silvestri—were sprawled nearby.

"Are the trains still running?" Mara asked.

"You sent us here without knowing?"

"They were running this morning," she said defensively.

Kerfer made a face. Mara went over to the ticket stand, a small podium-style desk near the door. The clerk assured her that the full schedule of trains was operating. She asked for tickets for Hai Phong—the cheapest trip available—and tried to pay with her credit card. The clerk told her that they were accepting only cash. She tried to use dongs but he would only take dollars, greatly depleting her supply.

Josh sat on the chair, his head hanging down about midway over his knees. His face looked even whiter than normal, and his eyes were gazing into space. Mạ leaned against him, but he didn't seem to be paying much attention to her.

"You with us, Josh?" Mara asked.

"I'm here."

"He's got some sort of bug," volunteered Little Joe. "He ain't pissing too well."

Great, thought Mara. She had the images Josh had made of massacre, but Washington wanted Josh and the girl as well. There was no substitute for a first-hand story.

She put her hand against his forehead. He seemed a little warm. "You take aspirin?" she asked.

"Eric gave me some. I think it's something I ate," he added.

Hopefully. Otherwise they'd all have it soon.

"Hang in there," Mara told him. Shouldering her backpack and sling bag—her folding-stock AK-47 was in the pack, her pistol in the bag—she pointed to the door out to the tracks. "Our train leaves in ten minutes. Let's go."

Mara walked across to the southbound train. It wasn't the one she had tickets to, but it was the one she wanted. This train traveled along the coast, with stops at Dong Hoi, Hue, and Da Nang, among others, before heading inland to Saigon. It was a sleeper, and ordinarily would have been at least half full with tourists and business-people. But it was empty.

"Hey, they even got TV," said Little Joe, pointing.

They spread out in the cars.

"You gonna give us all tickets?" Kerfer asked.

"They're not for this train," said Mara, handing them out.

"What?"

"They aren't going to collect them," said Mara. "We're not going to be on long anyway."

"What do you mean?"

She shook her head.

"Listen, I gotta know what's going on here," said Kerfer. "I don't like being on a train to begin with."

"Neither do I," said Mara. "I didn't have enough cash for the right train. Besides, we're going to jump out down the line. A friend has arranged to leave some vehicles for us."

"You should have said that before."

"What difference does it make?"

"It makes a difference."

"Well, that's what we're doing. It was a backup plan," she added. "And now we're using it. Because I don't like the fact that the train is so empty. The ones this morning weren't."

Kerfer frowned, then went and gave his men the tickets.

Two minutes later, the train started out of the station. They still hadn't seen a conductor.

J osh slumped against the window. His pelvis felt as if it were burning up. He breathed slowly, trying to dissipate the pain.

He imagined it was something he ate, but had no way of knowing for sure. Maybe it was a urinary infection, but he hadn't had sex in weeks.

Three months now, actually. When he and his girlfriend broke up. So that couldn't be the cause. It must just be something he ate or drank.

"They have bathrooms on these?" he said, feeling the urge to pee.

"Up there," said Mara, pointing.

The small closet reeked of human waste and ammonia. Josh felt his stomach churning and leaned over to retch. But nothing came out.

"Let it all out, man," said Squeaky, who was standing outside. "Just let it go. You'll feel tons better."

"Trying," muttered Josh, steadying himself against the side of the coach as the train began to pick up speed.

The train ran along a highway through the city and immediately south. It chugged along slowly, barely approaching thirty miles an hour. Mara nervously watched the countryside pass by. Knots of Vietnamese troops were parked every quarter mile or so along the road. This was the safest way past the military bunkers where most of the government and army officials had taken shelter to the south, but it took them perversely close to them, as well as to several military installations along the sidings.

Mara left Josh and Mạ in the seat near the back of the car and went up the aisle to the first row, not expecting a conductor but prepared to deal with one if he showed up. A small bribe would be sufficient to take care of any problem about their destination, especially since they weren't going to be on the train for very long.

"So when exactly is it we're getting off?" said Kerfer, settling down beside her. He leaned forward and rested his arm on the seat back of the row in front of him, leaning toward her.

"Soon," she said.

"That ain't good enough, kid."

"You're calling me kid now?"

"I call everybody kid. I figure that's better than lady, right?"

"Mara works."

Kerfer frowned. She could only guess at his age—late twenties, maybe thirties. He had a rough face that seemed made of unpolished stone. His green civilian shirt and blue jeans made him look more military, not less, even though he was unshaven and his hair edged over his ears.

"All right. So Mara—what are we doing?"

"We need to get south of Phú Xuyên," she told him.

"Where's that?"

"Twenty-one miles south of Hanoi. Things are less tense there. We shouldn't have to worry about being stopped."

"I thought Major Murphy said these guys are on our side now."

"I wouldn't trust them for the time of day."

Kerfer frowned again—it seemed to be his basic facial expression—then slowly nodded.

"What about the little girl?" he asked.

"Washington says she can come back with us," said Mara. "That's what you want, right?"

"Hey, I don't care. Better than an orphanage, right?"

Mạ had a hell of a story to tell, which was the real reason Washington wanted her back. Still, she could live a far better life in the States than she could here. Regardless of the war.

"When are we getting out?" Kerfer asked.

"I'll tell you in plenty of time."

Kerfer pushed himself back in the seat, extending his legs to relax. "Girl jumping, too?"

"She can come with me. We'll go out uphill. It's like stepping off an escalator."

"I've done it before." He smelled of sweat. "Country's falling apart?"

"Not really," said Mara. "If that was happening, the train would be packed."

"People are afraid to take the train because they know the Chinese will bomb it soon," said Kerfer. "It's an easy target."

"They haven't bombed it yet," said Mara.

"That's because they figured they would waltz right through. They wanted the train. Now that they're starting to slow down, they'll bomb everything in sight. They won't care about how many they kill. They'll just lay it all to waste." He turned to her. "That bother you?"

"It's not my job to be bothered by that."

Kerfer laughed. "You do a good imitation of being a hard-ass," he told her. "I'll give you that."

The train started braking. Mara looked out the window. She wasn't sure where they were, but she knew they couldn't be much more than halfway there; they hadn't even passed Phú yet. She got up and walked to the vestibule of the car.

"Problem?" asked Kerfer, following.

"We shouldn't be stopping," she said, taking a train key from her pocket and opening the door.

"Nice," said Kerfer.

Mara leaned out of the car and saw a contingent of soldiers near the side of the track ahead. They must be the reason the train was stopping.

It was too late to run for it.

"Back in the car. Group together," she told Kerfer. "I do the talking."

"They going to ask us for passports?" said Kerfer.

"Hopefully not."

"We got 'em." The SEALs had prepared civilian covers for this very contingency. They were a soccer team, in the country for an international goodwill tour.

"Hold on to them," said Mara. "The girl is my daughter. I talk. No one else."

Squeaky banged on the door of the restroom. "Come on, come on," he said in his high-pitched whisper.

Josh straightened and took a slow breath. The putrid air of the closet-sized bathroom only made him feel worse. What he needed was fresh air.

"Josh? Stay in there," said Mara outside. "You're all right?"

"Yeah."

"There are soldiers coming onto the car. Stay in the bathroom. Don't come out unless I tell you."

Josh heard her tell Squeaky to stay there as well. He pressed the tap to get some water and wash his hands, but nothing flowed. And then there were Vietnamese voices in the car.

Mara watched the soldiers as they came into the train. They were teenagers, joking about something one of them had done while waiting for the train. The sight of the foreigners silenced them momentarily. They moved into the middle of the car and sat in a clump together, a half dozen of them, all lugging AK-47s and light packs.

Mara had gone back to sit with Mạ. The little girl was tense, sitting stiffly upright. They were two seats from the end of the rear door, just up from the restroom.

She wouldn't have minded the soldiers at all, except for the fact that she had to jump from the train. She wasn't sure how they were going to react if half a dozen foreigners went off the side.

The train began moving. Mara pretended to be interested in the scenery.

Josh was still in the restroom as the train started to move again. Now that the soldiers were in their seats, Mara decided it was time to get him back out. So she went over and put her head to the door. Squeaky blinked at her, trying to puzzle out what she had in mind.

"Honey, are you okay?" asked Mara. She made her voice just loud enough for the soldiers to hear, guessing that they would know at least a little English.

"I'm okay," said Josh.

"Come out and sit with me," said Mara, her voice softer.

Josh immediately opened the door. Squeaky hesitated for a second, then slipped inside as if he'd been waiting.

"What are we doing?" asked Josh.

"You can have the window," said Mara, gently pushing his side.

He slipped Mạ between them and sat down. A few seconds later, the door at the front of the car opened. Another pair of Vietnamese soldiers entered—a lieutenant and a corporal.

The lieutenant immediately frowned at the foreigners. "Why are you on this train?" he said to Kerfer, who was sitting alone in the seat closest to the door.

"Going to Ho Chi Minh City," said Kerfer. He held his ticket, folded down, in his hand.

The lieutenant shook his head. "You're Americans?" His English was good, his accent by now familiar.

Mara got out of her seat. "We were all here on a visit to Hanoi University," she told the soldier, walking forward. She switched to Vietnamese. "The government advised us to join the rest of our group in Saigon."

"Who?" said the lieutenant, still in English.

Mara used the first name that came into her head—Phú, claiming he was from the education ministry, which had sponsored their soccer visit. The soldier would have no way of checking, and she calculated that if she seemed sure and exact, he would eventually drop the matter.

But she calculated wrongly.

"We will search your bags," said the lieutenant.

"Why?" said Mara, switching to English as well so Kerfer would know what was going on. "Why are you going to search our bags? Do you think we are thieves?"

"Let me see your passport and visa," demanded the lieutenant.

"Okay. Let me get it."

Mara turned and walked to the back, even though her passport was in her pocket. Only one of the soldiers was watching; the others were either listening to MP3 players or reading.

Mara opened her sling bag, poked around quickly—making sure not to expose her pistol—then began patting the pockets of her clothes. She reached inside and pulled out the passport. There was a twenty-dollar bill in it.

The lieutenant opened the passport, keeping the bill in place.

"Is there a problem?" Mara asked him.

"All transportation must be organized by the army," said the lieutenant. "The minister of education is nothing."

Mara saw Kerfer coming down the aisle behind the Vietnamese officer.

Go back to your seat, she thought. We're almost through with this.

"Where in Ho Chi Minh City are you going?" asked

the Vietnamese lieutenant, still looking at her passport.

"We're supposed to call when we get to the station," she said. "I would imagine they will send a car. I hope they will send a car, or we will have to walk. We'll do whatever they tell us, of course."

"Whose child?"

"Mine."

"She's not on your passport?"

"That's not necessary in America," she lied.

The lieutenant closed the passport, tapping it against his hand. He seemed to be deciding whether to take the money or not.

Finally he slipped the bill out and handed her the passport back.

"Now let me see your bags," he said.

Kerfer raised his arm, revealing a pistol. Before Mara could say anything, he'd pulled the trigger, putting a bullet through the side of the officer's head.

12

Hanoi

Jing Yo put it simply to Hyuen Bo—he was looking for an American scientist who had come to the country a few days before the war started. Hyuen Bo's job in the central ministry gave her the perfect pretext for checking with the Hanoi police to see if the scientist had registered at the local hotels, as required.

Jing Yo did not try to soften the fact that she was, in

effect, betraying her country. He walked her halfway to work, promising to meet her at lunch. Then he walked southward, cautious but more confident than he had been before.

Hanoi was on high alert, with soldiers scattered through the streets. But mostly they ignored him. He was dressed like many Vietnamese his age, those with good jobs at least: fresh black slacks and a light blue shirt, pulled from his rucksack and nicely pressed by Hyuen Bo. He was tall for a Vietnamese man, and might look somewhat more Chinese than many others, but he had identification, a license, and other miscellaneous papers if he needed to establish his bona fides.

There were soldiers stationed along some of the streets, and on several of the corners sandbags had been piled to make crude strongpoints. Rolls of barbed wire were coiled by the side. The Vietnamese seemed to be planning to fight street by street, if it came to that.

That was unlikely, Jing Yo guessed. From what he knew, China planned to let Hanoi wither on the vine, cutting it off from the rest of the country. The Vietnamese would eventually be allowed to sue for peace—assuming, of course, that the rest of the world did not intervene.

Which was why he was here.

Jing Yo caught the eye of a soldier across the street, staring at him. He frowned but put his head down, walking as he imagined a compliant Vietnamese citizen would walk, anxious not to cause any trouble. He crossed the street and turned the corner onto a block lined with stores. Ordinarily, the street would be choked with traffic, but there was little today. Even the usual clusters of scooters and bicycles were much thinner than Jing Yo remembered from his previous stays in the city.

His destination sat squarely in the middle of the block, a small clothing and dry cleaning store where one could get handmade clothes. The trade for tailored goods had declined sharply over the past decade, as fashions became more and more westernized—and imported. The shop was now regarded as somewhat dusty and old, a place that mostly served an older generation.

Jing Yo went in cautiously. The proprietor was seated at a chair, speaking with another man. They looked up as he came in.

"I'd like to be measured for a suit," Jing Yo said.

The tailor rose without comment. He reached into his pocket for a measuring tape, and slowly unfurled it.

"You are an awful optimist," said the other customer.

Jing Yo didn't reply. He was afraid that if he spoke too much, his accent would betray him.

The tailor began taking his measurements. He moved slowly, feet shuffling. His whole manner was glacial, except for the way he moved his hands—they pulled the tape out as if snapping a line over a piece of wood at a construction site. His fingers furled the tape back between them with the quick efficiency of a fisherman reeling in an errant cast. He smelled of perfumed tea.

"Have they gotten far with the defenses?" asked the other customer.

Jing Yo shrugged.

"Have they barricaded the street?"

"No," answered Jing Yo.

"I don't think they will be barricading the street," said the tailor, his voice a bare whisper. But the customer heard it, and replied.

"They will. You'll see."

"They made no such preparations during the American war," said the tailor.

"The Chinese are not the Americans. The Chinese are murderers. They will carry off the women, if they ever enter Hanoi."

"They will not enter Hanoi," said the tailor. He pushed Jing Yo's right leg slightly to the side, so he could measure his inseam.

"The Chinese are devils," said the customer.

"Yes," said Jing Yo.

"You disagree?"

"They are devils."

"I think they will retreat," said the tailor, continuing with his measurements. "This will be the way it was with the border war. They will see that we cannot be defeated. They will run away."

"The Americans are egging them on," said the customer. "They are probably the ones who planned this. They want revenge."

"Ah, revenge," said the tailor. "They have been gone forty years. They care as much for us as you do for the dust under your stove."

The tailor shambled over to a small table at the side of the room. He took a pencil from a cup, wet the tip, and began writing numbers on a pad. Then he turned to Jing Yo.

"What style do you want?" he asked.

Jing Yo hesitated. He didn't know what the options were.

"Let me show you my most popular suit. They wear this in Hong Kong."

"Hong Kong is China," said the other customer. "Show him something else."

"It's up to him to decide." The tailor stepped toward a rack at the side of the shop.

"Why do you want a suit anyway?" asked the other customer. "To be buried in?"

"For work," muttered Jing Yo.

"Work? You don't need a suit for work."

"This is something popular in Paris," said the tailor. "Many young men such as yourself choose a suit like this to make an impression."

"Hmmm," said Jing Yo.

"Well, I must get to the market," said the other customer, rising. "I will see you later, Mr. Loa."

"Later, Dr. Hung."

The tailor pulled out another suit to show Jing Yo. "This is also French," he said as the door closed.

"I am interested in a hat," said Jing Yo.

The tailor pushed the suit back into the rack and fished for another.

Jing Yo wondered if he had made a mistake and come to the wrong place.

"This is a lighter fabric," said the tailor.

"I've changed my mind," said Jing Yo abruptly. "Your friend was right. This is a bad time for a suit."

The tailor clutched his arm as he turned to go. Despite the old man's fragile appearance, his clasp was strong.

"People are watching everywhere," whispered the tailor in Chinese. "You must be extremely careful."

"Yes," said Jing Yo.

"The Paris suit would be the best." The tailor once more was speaking in Vietnamese. "In black, I think."

"I am in your hands."

Jing Yo explained that he had a mission, and was looking for an American scientist. He showed the picture that had been obtained from the UN Web site by Chinese intelligence. The tailor did not recognize the man, and made no promises, except to pass on the message.

The old man was a low-level operative, more of a cutout than a spy, a person used to insulate the upper ranks from the people in the field who were constantly in danger of being caught. There might be several cutouts in any given chain of information.

Then again, there might not. For all Jing Yo knew, this old man might actually be China's Hanoi spymaster.

After warning Jing Yo that he must be careful, the tailor said that the airport had been bombed sufficiently that it was now closed. The word from Da Nang was that the airport was no longer open. The only flights out of the country were leaving through Saigon. Most likely, said the tailor, the American would head there.

"I need better information than guesses," said Jing Yo.

"Many foreigners were taken south the first day of the war," said the tailor. "Beyond that, I cannot say."

The old man seemed more interested in getting rid of him than in doing his job. Jing Yo decided he would not mention the two hotels he'd been told to check.

"What kind of transportation can I find to get south?" he asked.

"Hmmm," said the tailor. He went into the back. Jing Yo waited. He returned with a small satellite phone.

"You will receive a phone call after six p.m. There will be instructions," said the tailor. "Do you have money?"

"Yes."

"The suit will be ready when you return," said the tailor loudly, as if someone were listening to their conversation.

"Thank you very much," said Jing Yo.

13

South of Hanoi

Mara reacted automatically, pushing Mạ down as she grabbed for the pistol in her sling bag. By the time she had the Beretta in her fist, the car had erupted with automatic-rifle fire: the five SEALs had slaughtered the Vietnamese soldiers.

"Out the back," said Mara, grabbing Mạ into her arms. "Come on, let's go!"

When she reached the vestibule at the back of the car, Mara took the train key and jabbed it into the lock that opened the door. The door flew open.

The train was going just over ten miles an hour. There was no time to do anything but jump.

"Try to roll when you hit the ground," Mara told Josh, and then she leapt out with Mạ, pushing off hard to make sure they cleared the track. She rolled, taking the force of the fall on her back, protecting the child.

Mara got up and looked at Mạ. She expected the girl to be crying. Instead, she had a determined look on her face, eyes slit.

"They were bad men," said Mạ in Vietnamese.

"Yes, but we're all right," Mara told her.

The adrenaline that had spiked with the gunfire vanished as soon as Josh hit the ground. His body exploded with pain. He couldn't breathe.

"Come on, come on," said Mara, pulling him to his feet.

"I need—I can't breathe. . . ."

"Come on, come on," she insisted, pulling him along.
Mạ grabbed his leg, urging him to run.

The SEALs were jumping from the train behind him.
Josh pushed himself forward. He was dizzy and nauseous, and his head pounded.

A road ran parallel to the tracks. As Josh struggled
to breathe, Mara ran into the path of traffic, her pistol
out. She signaled wildly as a car approached. The frightened driver hit the brakes.

Mara yanked at the door and yelled at the woman
driver in Vietnamese. The woman got out, running
across the road.

"In," Mara told Josh.

Josh pulled tentatively at the passenger-side door.
Little Joe grabbed him from behind, took the door
handle, and opened the car. As soon as they were in,
Mara hit the gas, spinning the car into a three-point
turn. Another car narrowly missed her.

"We need Lieutenant Kerfer," said Little Joe. "Unlock the door."

Josh had slipped into a confused haze. Mạ was
next to him, climbing into his lap. Little Joe reached
across him and unlocked the door. Another SEAL,
Squeaky, threw himself in, pushing Josh into the
other sailor.

"The lieutenant has the other car," said Squeaky.
"Go! Go!"

Mara stepped on the gas pedal. Tires squealing, they
drove up the wrong side of the highway for about five
hundred yards before coming to an intersection. Mara
turned, bumping over the railroad tracks, and speeding
onto the road heading eastward, finally on the right side.

"I think I have to throw up," said Josh.

"Go for it," said Mara. "We're not stopping."

Mara didn't stop until she'd gone nearly five miles. Fortunately, the roads were clear of almost all traffic, the only exceptions being a few old farm trucks.

Even better, Josh managed to keep his stomach under control.

They stayed on back roads, moving through the outskirts of towns clustered along the highways. The terrain was mostly partitioned into paddies and fields, completely given over to agriculture.

Kerfer was behind her. He'd grabbed a pickup; two of his men were in the back, no doubt looking for someone else to shoot.

Mara was furious with him, so angry that she was having a hard time keeping the car on the road.

"You okay back there?" she asked Josh.

He moaned an answer.

"Better stop soon," suggested Squeaky.

Mara spotted a small dirt road on the left that led to an abandoned, ramshackle building. She braked and cranked the wheel hard to make the turn, skidding in the dirt. She pulled up in front of the building and hopped out, her gun in her hand.

Kerfer pulled in behind her.

"Why the hell did you do that?" she screamed at him.

"What do you think he was going to do when he found your gun in the handbag?" Kerfer said.

"I was bribing him," said Mara. "That was his way of asking for more money. If it came to that, I would have told him we were armed because of the war. He wouldn't have said anything. Except to ask for more money."

"Right. You think twenty bucks gets you a get-out-of-jail-free card? You can't corrupt everyone. You probably pissed him off by offering him the bribe."

"His unit is probably following us."

"It'll take them a while to catch up," said Kerfer. "They probably don't even know what happened yet. The train sound covered the shots."

"You're a jackass, Lieutenant. You just killed seven of our allies."

"If they're allies, why the hell do we have to sneak out of their country?"

Mara stomped back to the car. Josh was bent over near the building. Squeaky and Little Joe were standing between him and the car, looking at her. She got behind the wheel. Squeaky got in the front, immediately pushing back the seat to try and get more legroom.

"Where we going?" he asked.

"South," said Mara.

Josh, pale, got in the car. Little Joe pushed in beside him.

"It was a do-or-die thing," said Squeaky. "Just a reaction. It's how we're trained."

"I'm sure you're very good at what you do," said Mara. "But sometimes you have to take a risk."

"The lieutenant lost some people in an extraction out of Afghanistan a year ago," said the SEAL. "We were trying to get them out as civilians. Those were the orders. Taliban came up, disguised as policemen . . ."

Squeaky's voice trailed off.

"This isn't Afghanistan," said Mara.

They drove with the windows down. Gradually, the fresh air helped clear Josh's head.

At first, what had happened in the train car seemed far away, further than anything that had happened while he was near China, behind the advancing line of the Chinese. But gradually it came into sharper focus.

"How ya feeling?" asked Little Joe.

"A little better."

"You looked like you were sleeping for a while."

"Yeah, I guess I was."

"You puked?"

"Only slime came out." Josh wiped his mouth on his sleeve, the taste lingering in his mouth. "Why did the Vietnamese shoot at us?" he asked.

"They didn't. We didn't give them a chance."

"Don't they understand we're on their side?" Josh asked.

"We're not on anybody's side but our own," Little Joe told him.

"No, that's not true. We have to—the whole world has to deal with this."

"Dream on."

Phai had arranged for Mara to get two vehicles in a small town southeast of Phú Xuyên. Besides the vehicles, Phai had arranged for some other supplies, including gas cans and water.

Mara debated whether it was worth the risk to cut back east. They needed cars or trucks, and holding on to these seemed far too risky. But going back in the direction of the army would be an even bigger risk.

Saigon—or Ho Chi Minh City, as it was officially but only occasionally called—lay over seven hundred miles away as the crow flew, and they weren't crows. The twisted route and the Vietnamese highway system made the trip from Hanoi a twenty-hour marathon—if everything was with you. She'd calculated that it would take them close to two full days of driving.

Mara kept driving due south, following a checkerboard pattern of secondary roads through the farmland, staying as far away from settled areas as possible. After they'd gone about a half hour, she noticed Kerfer flashing his lights.

She pulled over to the side of the road.

"Gas is getting toward empty," said the SEAL lieutenant.

As she started back for the car, she heard a pair of aircraft approaching. They were jets, low, very low.

Kerfer leapt out of the truck. "Out, get out!" he yelled. "Off the road."

Josh and the others were already getting out, taking cover in the ditch at the side of the shoulder. The jets were over and gone before Mara reached them.

"J-12s," said Stevens. "Brand-new. Chinese stealth jets."

"That was a big bomb they were carrying," said Josh.

"That's a fuel tank under the belly," said Stevens. "Gives them more distance. Except that it's a bad sign—means they're not scared of Vietnamese radar anymore. Probably blew it all up in the first hour of the war."

"Hey, pilot wannabe," said Kerfer, "you figure they're doing recce?"

"Probably testing defenses," said Stevens. "Or just trying to see what the Vietnamese got left. They'll be using UAVs for reconnaissance."

"Kerfer, you take the car," said Mara. "And the girl. Josh and I will get the gas. Just us two."

"No way. You need protection," said Kerfer.

"Protection?"

"Don't be foolish."

"One person with us in the cab," she said, realizing he was right. "It looks too suspicious in the back."

"The hell with suspicious. These people are at war, spook girl. You think they're really putting a lot of thought into anything but saving their own asses?"

Mara was insistent. She told Kerfer to follow her; when they came to a gas station, she would go in; he should drive on and wait a short distance away.

"You ain't gonna run out on me, right?" said Kerfer, finally agreeing.

"I'm tempted," she said.

The pumps at the gas station looked like the ones back home, more or less, with bright fluorescents and an illuminated sign announcing PETRO. A silver-haired man dressed in a white shirt and black pants came out of the cement-block building beyond the pumps. He walked with a limp that tilted him almost sideways, dragging his right foot across the crumbling macadam.

Mara and Squeaky both got out, leaving Josh alone in the truck.

The contrast between the calm if rundown station and what had happened in the railroad car—not to mention the past few days—was stark. The station belonged to a world that had never known war, and didn't have much use for the rest of the world, either. A cluster of buildings sat just beyond it, spilling off the roadside into the farmland beyond. They were small, mostly made of block like the gas station, with shed roofs of metal in various stages of rust and disintegration. The ones closer to the road were stores as well as houses, and Josh could see people sitting or squatting on the stoops in front of them. A boy of about eight stared at the truck intently, perhaps thinking of what he would do if he had such a thing.

Mara spoke to the gas station owner as he filled the truck's tank. She seemed to be doing most of the talking, though every so often the man would turn and say a few words, gesturing with great intensity. Their conversation continued for several minutes after the truck was full. Then the man and Mara walked into the building. They emerged a few minutes later with a pair of five-gallon gas cans. These, too, were filled, and placed in the back of the truck.

"I'm going to have Kerfer come back and fill up," Mara said when she got back in the truck. "The old man says he's the only place around that has gas."

"Maybe he's just saying that to drum up business," said Squeaky.

"No, I don't think so. He hasn't gotten any deliveries for the past week, and I doubt anyone else has, either. Once the war started, the gas the Chinese didn't blow up was probably confiscated by the army."

Kerfer and the others were waiting about a half mile down the road. Mara insisted that she would be the one to go back, since Kerfer didn't know much Vietnamese. They left Josh and the SEALs and went back. Josh sat in the front seat, staring through the windshield, his mind jumbled. The lower part of his stomach and groin felt as if they were on fire. Heat poured from his forehead. But whatever disease or sickness he'd picked up was only part of what was bothering him. His brain felt scrambled, unable and unwilling to process what was going on around him. There were too many jumbled contrasts, too much death and contradiction.

Mạ, drowsy, leaned against him, once more sucking her thumb.

She was sleeping. Gazing at her, Josh realized she

didn't have her doll. She'd lost it somewhere in the train car.

Damn.

Outside the truck, the SEALs plopped down in the shade, watching the road and waiting. One of the men—Silvestri, an Italian-American who claimed to be the only "wop" who lived in Texas—realized that he had bits of blood on his shirt from the railcar, and pulled it off, stripping to his undershirt. The others began joking, making cracks about his physique, then about the blood, then about the ghosts that would be clinging to Silvestri's shirt.

The jokes were mild by SEAL standards, but Josh was appalled.

"How can you guys joke?" he said. He repeated the question several times, talking more to himself, though his voice was just loud enough for Squeaky to hear.

"What's up, Josh?" Squeaky asked, coming over to the truck.

"You guys are joking."

"Just blowing off some steam."

"The officer's head burst open like it was a tomato," said Josh.

"Yeah." Squeaky smiled awkwardly. "That's what happens."

"It sucks."

"Would you rather it'd been you?" asked Mancho. His voice was sharp and defensive.

"No," said Josh.

"I know what he means," said Little Joe. "You're that close to something like that—it gets to you."

"Everything gets to you," said Mancho. "Because you're a wimp."

"I'm worse than a wimp," said Little Joe. "I'm a little girly wimp." He laughed.

"You okay?" Squeaky asked Josh.

Josh nodded.

Squeaky reached in. "Man, you're burnin' up. You got a fever. You know that?"

"I guess."

"You want some aspirin?"

"I took some."

"Baby sleepin'?"

"Yeah."

"If you're sick, you think you oughta be that close?"

"I carried her through the jungle a couple of days," said Josh. "If she's going to catch it, she'd have it by now."

"True."

Squeaky went back to the others, joking by the side of the truck again.

Josh went back to staring out the windshield.

Mara and Kerfer returned a few minutes later. Mara and Squeaky got in the truck, leaving Josh between them.

"We should be able to get pretty close to Saigon with the gas we have," she told him as they turned onto the road. "I don't know what the conditions are going to be. We haven't seen any panic yet, but it may be different in the south."

"Yeah."

"The Chinese army is moving down the western valleys," Mara continued. "They were stopped at the Hoa Binh Lake area, but once they get past that, they have a clear shot at Ninh Binh. That's the next concentration of troops we have to get around. We should start seeing them in about an hour. The people here haven't seen much of the war yet."

Mara stopped talking and turned to Josh. Her face was close, only inches away. "Are you all right?" she asked him.

"I'm here," he answered.

"Your stomach?"

"It hurts when I pee."

"And you have a fever."

"Yeah."

"We'll have help for you soon," she said, a worried look on her face. "Hang in there."

"I'm here."

14

Hanoi

After leaving the tailor shop, Jing Yo went back toward the Hai Ba Trung district in the city's business area, aiming to check the two hotels the intelligence reports had recommended.

Jing Yo had left his weapons at Hyuen Bo's house. He was worried that explaining even a pistol might be difficult, and until he located his target and had a plan, the risk did not make sense. Besides, if circumstances were right, Jing Yo could easily kill him with his hands and feet.

Lenin Park had been turned into an antiaircraft site. Tanks and a throng of soldiers blocked off access. Beyond them, Jing Yo could see trucks with antiaircraft cannon mounted on their backs.

He walked in the direction of the river for a few blocks, then headed north. His first stop was the Hilton Hanoi

Opera, an overwhelming building of grand design, mirroring the city's opera house next door.

The men at the door were wearing pistols conspicuously strapped to their hips. One stopped Jing Yo as he started inside.

"Are you a guest?" the man asked.

"I'm to meet someone here," he said.

"Who?"

Jing Yo considered his answer.

"An American," he said finally.

"Who?" demanded the guard.

"Joshua MacArthur," said Jing Yo, deciding there was no sense in not naming his subject. "He works for the UN."

"Wait here," said the guard.

Jing Yo folded his arms and took a step back from the door. The two other doormen were frowning at him. Neither could have stopped him from going in if he'd wanted, but it seemed pointless.

The doorman returned quickly.

"There is no MacArthur here," he said.

"I am not sure whether he is a guest," said Jing Yo. "He told me to meet him in the lobby."

"You can't come in unless you are a guest," replied the doorman.

"You could call him," said one of the other men. "Call him on your cell phone."

"Are the phones working now?" Jing Yo asked. He looked at the man.

"Sometimes."

Jing Yo could see that the man was lying. He had made the suggestion in an effort to seem helpful—to seem like a nice person. The man wanted people to like him. He had acted on that emotion, without thinking of the implications. Now he was trapped in the lie.

A weak emotion—the need to be liked.

To be loved. Was that why he had gone to Hyuen Bo?

He had succumbed to his own weakness, Jing Yo thought.

"I will have to think of another way to contact him," Jing Yo told them. "Thank you."

The Sofitel Metropole was another executive-class hotel, featuring the best French restaurant in the city. No guards barred the way here; the doormen, if armed, were as discreet as the others had been obvious. The lobby was packed with foreigners. Jing Yo moved through them, picking up pieces of conversations.

It seemed all the people were Europeans. A lot were French.

One of them mistook him for a waiter, and asked that he fetch him a brandy. He realized his mistake as Jing Yo stared at him.

"*Excusez moi,*" said the man in French.

"*Ca ne fait rein,*" answered Jing Yo, somewhat haltingly trying to say it didn't matter. His French was not particularly good.

"*Ca va,*" answered the man. "Do you speak English? I don't speak Vietnamese."

"Some English," said Jing Yo. It was of course a lie; like most Chinese students, he had studied English from the time he was a small boy; and then he'd continued his education in the army.

"This war—a—" The Frenchman struggled for the right word. "A disaster."

"Yes."

"Are you a guest?"

"I am looking for a friend," said Jing Yo. "I am worried for him. He's an American."

The Frenchman offered to buy him a drink. Jing Yo went with him to the bar, though when the man offered, all he would take was water.

There were not many Americans in Hanoi, according to the Frenchman. The best place to look, he added as he sipped his brandy, was the Hilton.

"Yes," said Jing Yo. "But he is not there."

The Frenchman rattled off a list of other hotels. He seemed to need to talk. His fluency in English grew as he drank a second brandy, though his accent thickened. Jing Yo had to listen hard to understand the words.

"There are a lot of people at Hotel Nikko," said the man. "Mostly Asian, though. The airport is closed. There's a train south to the coast, but everyone says it is foolish to take it—it's sure to be bombed."

"So are you going to stay here then?" Jing Yo asked.

"I'm getting out as soon as I can."

"I see."

"I'm a businessman, not a warrior. I sell toiletries." The Frenchman smiled awkwardly. "Another drink?"

Hyuen Bo was waiting for Jing Yo at the small café where they said they'd meet, sitting at a table on the sidewalk, protected from the street by an iron rail. She lowered her gaze as he approached. He sat without greeting her. He was angry with himself for involving her, even though she had the potential to help.

"The agency has given up keeping track of the foreigners," said Hyuen Bo.

"I understand."

The waiter came. Jing Yo ordered *cha ca,* a casserole made from fried fish.

Hyuen Bo ordered nothing.

"I have to get back to work," she told him. "I'm sorry."

"Go," said Jing Yo softly.

She looked at him, then rose.

"Tonight?" she asked, touching him.

Jing Yo didn't reply. He didn't want to see her. And yet of course he did, more than anything in the world.

She bent quickly and kissed him.

A knife, plunging past his mouth.

Jing Yo lost his breath, and sat in shock—not at the kiss, though that had been unexpected, but at the flush of heat it left.

After lunch, Jing Yo remembered the list of the hotels the Frenchman had given him and began systematically checking them, going to each in turn. By the third hotel his pattern was perfected. There was no great trick to it. Jing Yo went in the front door—only the Hilton, it turned out, was carefully guarded—and looked for groups of foreigners, first in the lobby, then in the bar. Because he looked Vietnamese, they took him as a potential source of information and tried to befriend him. They asked about possible evacuation routes, about how close the Chinese were, whether the army was collapsing. Jing Yo answered as optimistically as he could. This cheered them up and made his own questions easier.

He was looking for an American who worked for

the UN, he would say, and from there add whatever details seemed helpful.

There were some recommendations, some hints, but it was clear enough that no one he spoke to had seen Joshua MacArthur. An announcement had been made that power would be turned off at 6 p.m., and this spurred considerable concern, distracting most of the people he spoke to. Few thought it would be turned back on again.

One man offered him ten thousand American dollars to get him safely out of the country.

"I heard the trains are still running," said Jing Yo coldly.

By four thirty, Jing Yo realized that if he was in Hanoi at all, the scientist had decided to avoid the most obvious hotels. A hotel that completely catered to Vietnamese would not be a good choice, as he and whatever security was with him would stick out. But hotels on the edges of the tourist area, or ones whose primary guests were foreigners but not Americans—those were the places Jing Yo should look at.

I have underestimated him, Jing Yo told himself. That was a serious mistake.

The scientist would choose a hotel that could be guarded. Or, lacking that, one where lookouts could be posted and an easy escape planned.

There were many hotels in that category. Jing Yo remembered the Hotel Nikko and went there. But it was difficult to strike up a conversation. A man mentioned that there had been several Americans there earlier. He described a woman—tall, blond—and a man who might be the American Jing Yo wanted, or might not. He hadn't spoken to either.

No one at the desk knew him.

Jing Yo left the hotel and began walking toward

Hyuen Bo's apartment. He had resolved not to return, but he was doing it anyway.

He remembered the kiss, still felt her lips and the warmth.

S he met him at the door. She wore a long silk chemise, a Western-style gown so thin her body seemed to flow through it. His resistance, bare as it was, melted completely. Hyuen Bo pulled him inside and pushed her mouth to his. As their lips touched, Jing Yo gave up everything—not merely his honor or his commitment to duty, but his will and his life.

They made love on her cot on the floor. The war did not exist. He pushed gently into her, and then he did not exist.

J ing Yo was starting to doze when the sat phone rang. He'd left it in the pocket of his pants, a world away.

Hyuen Bo grabbed at his chest as he started to get up. He pushed her away gently.

"Yes," he said.

"Hanoi's Finest Hotel." The voice spoke calmly but mechanically. "Soldiers are escorting them. But we believe they may have left to go south. The airport is open at Saigon. We have people looking there."

"Are you sure they have gone there?" asked Jing Yo.

"We have nothing else. We will call at six tomorrow."

The phone circuit died.

Jing Yo sat at the edge of the bed. He was at the precipice, teetering between everything he believed in, everything he was, and Hyuen Bo.

Several of his mentors among the monks used to say that voices came to them at times of stress, apparitions that seemed to float from the mountain where they lived and trained. They guided them back to the path, clearing their minds the way a rising sun burns off mist.

No such voice came to Jing Yo now, though he longed for it. Never had he felt so alienated from himself. The decision to leave the monastery and accept his commission in the army was, by contrast, the decision between different flavors of ice cream.

"Jing Yo?"

Hyuen Bo put her hand on his back.

"I have to go," he said, standing.

"Where?"

She reached for him as he stood, her hand slipping down his naked back.

"I need to go to Ho Chi Minh City. Tonight," he added. "Are the trains running?"

"The army commandeers them. Spies are suspected of using them." She stopped, suddenly aware of what she had said—aware of which side she was on, he thought. "There was—an accident on one today."

"What kind of accident?"

"Some soldiers were killed. They think it was a deserter."

In that moment, Jing Yo knew. He knew both that his quarry had been on that train, and that he would follow him. There was no logic to his knowledge—and yet he knew it.

"Where was the train going?"

"Ho Chi Minh City."

Jing Yo turned and looked at her. He wanted a last glimpse before he left. For he had to leave.

"I'm going with you," she told him.

"Your mother's memorial is the day after next."

"I'm going with you," she said.

"Take me to the train station."

"I'm going with you."

15

Northern Vietnam

Mara reached over and hit the radio's Scan button as the station faded, hoping to find something else. Several Vietnamese stations were still broadcasting; she didn't know whether it was because the Vietnamese were resourceful in keeping them on the air, or if the Chinese were allowing them to continue for some reason that suited their purposes, such as sending messages along their spy network.

She got a pop music station; the radio stayed there for a moment, then scanned again, then found the same station. She punched the button to keep the music there, then put her full attention back on the road. It was dark, and to help avoid detection they were driving without lights. She needed to stay as focused as possible.

Josh was sleeping, slumped over toward Squeaky. She could feel the heat coming off his body. He was burning up.

His getting sick was one thing she hadn't counted on. The Chinese blockade—and Washington politics— were two others.

But they'd be out of here soon. Get to the airport, get the plane—she'd be due for a *long* vacation.

"How we doing for time?" asked Squeaky. He was drifting in and out of sleep.

"We're getting there," said Mara.

"Lucky we haven't hit any checkpoints."

"That's not a good sign."

"Why not?"

"There should be troops all over the place, rushing to defend the country," said Mara. "The Chinese are going to roll all over them."

"As long as we're out of here first, who cares?"

"They won't stop with Vietnam," said Mara.

Squeaky didn't answer. Mara didn't feel like talking geopolitics with him anyway. She fiddled with the radio again as the pop station faded. It scanned and scanned. Finally she turned it off.

"I'd kind of like to take a leak soon," said Squeaky. "You think it's okay to pull over?"

"I'll find a place," Mara told him.

She tapped her brake gently, signaling to Kerfer, then eased off onto the shoulder. There wasn't quite enough to hold the entire truck off the pavement, but it had been a while since they'd seen another vehicle, and straddling the line didn't look like it would be a major problem. Mara turned off the ignition to save gas, then got out, stretching her arms and back in the damp night air.

"What's going on?" asked Kerfer, who'd stopped behind her. They'd switched off the team radios to preserve the batteries, planning to use them only when they were closer to Saigon, or in an emergency.

"Potty time," said Mara sarcastically. "And I gotta call home. How's Ma?"

"Sleepin' like a SEAL. She lost her doll," added Kerfer. "We're gonna have to get her a new one."

"I'll put you in charge of that."

Beyond the shoulder of the road the ground sloped downward to a field. Mara picked her way down, but in the dark sidestepped into a ditch filled with water. She climbed out on the other side, muddy to her calves.

Wheat stalks brushed at her legs, about a month from harvest. Even five years ago, the field would have been fallow, the crop not even a figment of the local farmers' imaginations.

Mara pulled her sat phone from the sling bag, took a breath, then turned it on.

Jesse DeBiase, the deputy station chief in Bangkok, answered the duty line. "Well, hello there, sweet thing," he drawled. "I was starting to worry about you."

"Hi, Jess."

"Using proper names. Aren't we formal?"

Mara, like everyone else who worked with him, usually called DeBiase by his nickname, Million Dollar Man. But she was in no mood for the usual kidding and bantering, good-natured as it was.

"I'm wondering what the road situation is," she told him.

"I'm looking at an image right now. You're five miles north of the Vietnamese Second Regiment. They have two checkpoints along the highway. If you detour east at your next macadam road, you'll miss them completely."

"Thanks."

"They're sending random patrols farther south. I'd like to call you to warn you if I see something."

"I don't trust leaving the phone on," said Mara.

"Well now, darlin', you're going to have to trust something."

"Where are the Chinese?"

"They don't know you exist."

"Says you."

"True. The nearest Chinese units are stalled at the reservoir west of Hanoi. They look as if they're going to try making an end run through Laos and Cambodia. Or maybe wait for a beach invasion to the east. In any event, you have nothing to worry about from them."

"I'm glad you're so confident."

"The Vietnamese can't track your phone, Mara. You can leave it on. The Chinese know we have people in country, and they're not going to come for you. You don't have to worry."

"You're not paranoid enough, Jesse."

He didn't answer for a moment. Mara knew that he was simply trying to be as encouraging as possible, even if that meant overselling how safe they were.

"What's going on at Langley?" asked Mara.

"I would use very strong words if I were not on the phone with a woman."

Mara laughed. She could see DeBiase smiling as well. He loved playing the old-school southern gentleman, the pontificator and professor. He also loved to complain about a dozen different things, starting with a hernia he always claimed he was going to get fixed. But he also had a great deal of experience, and she knew he could be counted on in a crisis.

"You'll be better off with the phone on," said DeBiase. "I can't help you if I can't talk to you."

"All right," she told him. "I'll leave it on."

"Thank you."

"We're going to need a doctor in Saigon," Mara added. "Josh is sick."

"What's he got?"

"A fever. Stomach trouble. It hurts when he pees."

"I hope it's not catching," said DeBiase.

"I think it's something he ate. Uncle Ho's revenge."

DeBiase wasn't put off so lightly. "When did he get sick?"

"This morning it started coming on."

"Did you tell Peter?"

"I didn't talk to Peter. I talked to a communications specialist and I wasn't about to unload."

"Communications specialist. Hmmm."

"Hmmm, what?"

"Just hmmm."

"There're no curse words with that?"

"Too many to report." DeBiase laughed. Mara sensed that the fact she'd spoken to a low-level operator rather than a supervisor troubled him, even though it was far from unusual. But all he did was change the subject. "Are those SEALs treating you right?"

Mara knew she had to tell someone about what had happened on the train. But this wasn't the time or the place. And besides, she already knew what DeBiase would say . . . something along the lines of, for every omelet, a few eggs get broken.

Which, ultimately, was probably the right response. But she had to think about it first.

"They're good."

"Shoot 'em if they get fresh. Remember what I said about keeping the phone on."

Hanoi

The Chinese had sent their two aircraft carriers into the Gulf of Bac Bo, ostensibly to blockade the northern ports of Vietnam; additional ships, mostly destroyers and a single cruiser, were working their way south to complete the blockade. As Zeus saw it, though, the primary purpose of the fleet was to secure a path for an invasion force, which U.S. satellites showed had been gathered on the large island of Hainan, which on the map looked like a fist about to punch northern Vietnam. The bulk of the force was located at Sanya, a civilian port and tourist city at the southern end of the island. The military facilities to the east of the city center— ordinarily used only by ballistic-missile submarines— were so crowded that ships were docked temporarily outside them.

They would be an easy target from the air, but Vietnam's air force, ragged to begin with, was now essentially wiped out. And a sea attack seemed suicidal. The Chinese had plenty of air bases on the island, so that even without the aircraft carriers and their escorts nearby, the attackers would be in mortal danger. The shallow waters around the island made a mass submarine attack less than attractive as well—and since Vietnam didn't have any submarines, it wasn't even a possibility.

Actually, Vietnam did have two submarines—ancient North Korean death traps masquerading as midget submarines, so decrepit that they would surely sink if their lines were cut from the Hai Phong dock where they were berthed.

Which gave Zeus an idea. An incredibly risky, unorthodox, outrageous, and even ridiculous idea—but one he thought might work.

Albeit, with a great deal of luck.

"See, the thing is, the Chinese don't think the Vietnamese pose any threat to the invasion force. Zero threat. Nada. Look at how these ships are aligned." Zeus went over to the wall of the command bunker, where the images from his laptop were being projected onto the whitewashed cement. There were a dozen Vietnamese generals gathered around the conference table, but he was really talking to only one man: General Minh Trung, the head of the army.

Trung was the oldest person in the room. Zeus wasn't sure exactly how old he was, but he would not have been surprised to learn that Trung had fought against the Japanese during World War II.

"The Chinese plan rests entirely on the belief that they cannot be harmed," continued Zeus. "It's more than a feeling of superiority. It's like the belief in gravity. Everything is based on the invincibility of the force at Hainan. So if we do something to disrupt that belief, they'll have to change their plans. Or at least postpone them," added Zeus. "And every day we can get them to delay is another day we have to prepare."

For the inevitable defeat, probably, but Zeus didn't say that.

"So how do we fool them?" continued Zeus, now in full lecture mode. "We attack them at their base, and in the process, make them think Vietnam has a large force they don't know about. It's a classic commando raid. Except we make it look like something else."

The first step was to make sure the Chinese saw the midget submarines—and a lot of them. Then they'd have to disappear. Then there would be a SpecOp attack on the ports that would look as if it had been launched by the submarines.

"The Chinese will put two and two together and come up with four," said Zeus. "Or better yet, four hundred."

He looked at the translator, who stared blankly at him.

"It's a joke," Zeus told him.

The translator explained. The Vietnamese generals didn't seem to know what to make of it. They looked at one another, but said nothing. Finally, Trung got to his feet. He walked to the projection of the island on the wall, studying the satellite image.

"These ships are fuel tenders," said the Vietnamese supreme war commander. He did not use a translator when he spoke to Zeus. "They would carry the fuel for the aircraft carriers."

"That's true," said Zeus. He knew he shouldn't be surprised at Trung's mastery of details, and yet he was.

The general walked back to his seat and sat down. His aides began talking among themselves in Vietnamese. Zeus looked at Perry, who didn't offer much encouragement. Zeus sensed that Perry thought it was a bad idea.

But there were no good ideas: with no air force, a navy that was a joke, a thin army—what could they really expect?

"This is not a bad idea," said Trung in his characteristically soft voice. "But there are a number of things to be added."

Trung paused, silent for a full minute, considering.

"If the tenders were blown up, the carriers would

have to retreat," he said. "Their aircraft would lack fuel."

"That's true," said Zeus.

"So that would be a prime target."

"Okay."

"The main problem is how to get the force there," said Trung.

"I've thought of that, too." Zeus pointed at the image. "We have a diversion here, just close enough to the carriers' attention. A force of commandos comes out from here and cuts across the gulf north of Buch Long Vi Island. Small, fast boats, stay away from the Chinese patrols farther north. You could make it."

"That is over two hundred kilometers," said one of Trung's assistants in Vietnamese. Zeus waited for it to be translated.

"It is far," admitted Zeus. "But from there it gets easier. Once you're on the island, they're not expecting you. You arrange in the harbor to make it seem as if there's a massive attack. And we take the tankers out somehow, as General Trung suggested. The attack doesn't have to be huge. It just has to look like a submarine attack. The Chinese will have to bring in more ASW assets. It'll be days, if not weeks, before that happens."

ASW stood for antisubmarine warfare. The force left behind on Hainan had mostly second- and third-tier defenses.

Zeus glanced around the room. There wasn't a single enthusiastic face.

And why should there be? Even if the mission succeeded, it would buy the Vietnamese only a few days—three or four weeks, maybe, with Trung's adjustment. At the same time, it would be incredibly difficult, a suicide mission in all but name.

"I believe it is worth a try," said Trung finally. "We will go ahead."

Zeus was surprised. But before he could say anything, Trung raised his hand and continued to speak.

"What the plan most requires is a dedicated commander, one who can not only plan it but lead it. The only person I can think of who would qualify, Major Murphy, is you."

"I don't even want to raise the point with the president, Zeus," said General Perry as he, Christian, and Zeus drove back to the city. "Even if he would reverse his stand against using our troops here, I wouldn't let you go. You're too damn valuable."

"Thank you, sir," said Zeus. "I mean, thank you for saying I'm valuable. But . . ."

"What's the but?"

Zeus wasn't sure. Now that he had come up with the plan, a long shot if ever there was one, he felt obliged to defend it. And defending it meant being willing to go on the mission.

The more he thought about it, in fact, the more he thought he could make it work. Once on Hainan, he could pose as a Western businessman. Businessmen were plentiful in the autonomous economic development zone, especially in the cities. Give him one Chinese speaker and some well-trained men, and they could make the attack look realistic enough. It didn't even have to succeed—as long as the Chinese thought there were more submarines than they'd known, and that the vessels had the capability to get past the screen, they'd be forced to regroup and rethink.

Zeus was starting to understand the Chinese military mind much better than he had before coming here. The

Chinese were brilliant planners and could easily move large numbers of men. But when their initial plans broke down, the army stalled. The attack on the dam, flooding their assault path, was a prime example. An American army faced with a problem like that would have adopted a solution within hours. It might be the *wrong* solution—Zeus knew from his war games that most American officers would head into Laos, where mountains and high jungle would greatly complicate their advance—but they would do something. The Chinese were just sitting and waiting.

"I don't know, General," said Christian. "If Zeus wants to put his neck on the line, I say let him."

"Careful, Win. Or you'll be going with him."

"I—have no problem with that," stuttered Christian.

Zeus barely stifled a laugh. The asshole.

The driver brought them back to the embassy, where General Perry had to use the secure communications center to talk to Washington.

"You boys can go back to the hotel," Perry said as he got out of the car. "Zeus?"

"Yes, General?"

"You think this idea has *any* chance of succeeding?"

"Sir, if it were up to me I'd lead it myself," said Zeus. "That's how much I believe in it."

Perry grimaced, then closed the door.

"Man, who's the brownnoser now?" said Christian as the car pulled away from the embassy gate.

"I wasn't bullshitting. I would."

"Yeah, right."

"You forget, *Win*, I was in Special Forces."

"Big fucking deal. You got your ticket punched there because you figured it was a quick path to a star on your shoulder."

"Right."

"Hey, you don't have to snow me. I know the score. I know how the politics work, believe me. I pull the strings myself when I can."

"Duh."

"Yeah, duh."

"You don't know crap. You were an engineering major. What are you going to do, build roads?"

"I could build a fuckin' road if I had to," said Christian. "And for your information, my engineering degree is in mechanical—"

"I'm shocked. You actually used an expletive."

"Fuck you."

"Fuck you back."

Zeus looked toward the front of the car. The driver was Vietnamese, and didn't know much English.

A good thing, thought Zeus. He'd be looking at them like they were kindergartners.

17

Washington, D.C.

President Greene rose from his desk in the Oval Office, took a last swig of coffee, then hurried out to the hall, Secret Service detail and aides in tow. It was nearly one. He was due in the secure communications area for another phone call from General Perry in Hanoi.

Then the real fun would begin. Lunch with Senator Grasso et al.

Dickson Theodore, his chief of staff, met him on the steps.

"What crisis do you have now, Dix?" asked the president.

"Which one do you want?"

"Which one should I worry about?"

"Teamsters are threatening a three-day walkout beginning of next week over the price of diesel."

"Good. That will send it down."

"George—"

"I have no influence with them. And I'm not joking—if the trucks don't drive for three days, demand will be less and the price will go down."

"I was thinking you could have Senator Leiber try and talk to them. You're going to see him at breakfast."

"The only friendly face I'll see all day. Not counting yours."

"Mine's not friendly. The Fed is going to raise interest rates—"

"Again? My God, is the recession not deep enough for them? Unemployment is over sixteen percent!"

"What we need to do is get some bankers unemployed," said Theodore. "Then it will come down."

"Give that to Jablonski. Tell him I want to use it. In New York, at the Al Smith Dinner."

"You're not invited."

"I will be. Next problem."

"I wouldn't be so sure." The dinner, the major political event of the year in New York City, was only a few days away.

"I'll bet you on it if you want," said Greene. "What's the next problem? More talk of impeachment if we help Vietnam?"

"I thought you didn't want to hear reports on that anymore."

"I don't want reports. I want names."

"Half of Congress will impeach you if you ask for aid to Vietnam. The other half is ready to impeach you no matter what."

"Good to have a mandate."

They continued their half banter, half briefing all the way down to the Secure Communications Room. National Security Adviser Walter Jackson and Peter Frost, the CIA chief, were waiting.

"So who made the coffee?" President Greene asked as he walked into the room.

"It was here already," said Jackson.

"Always dangerous," said Greene, helping himself.

"There's sandwiches," said Frost.

"Can't eat. Gotta break bread in the lion's den after this."

"Grasso?" said Frost.

"Who else?"

"You have assassins on your payroll, don't you, Peter?" asked Jackson.

"Don't even tempt me," said Greene.

"Mr. President, Hanoi is ready," said the communications specialist.

"Let 'er rip."

Greene pulled his seat out just in time to see General Perry's face come on the screen. The transmission quality was a little off; the general's face was blotched with patches of magenta.

"Have you had a good day, General?" asked Greene.

"So far, it's been acceptable. Vietnam is still here."

"That's a plus."

"If they don't get some sort of relief very soon, Mr. President—"

"I'm working on it, Harland. Trust me, I'm working on it."

"Major Murphy did come up with an idea, as you

requested," said Perry, who didn't look at all relieved by the president's assurances. "He believes a diversionary raid against the Chinese assault force before they have a chance to actually launch their invasion will delay it at least a week. I have to say, Mr. President, I think it's a bit far-fetched."

"Just a week?" Greene rubbed his forehead. It was one of several tics he had when he was trying to figure a way out of a bad situation—a habit he'd picked up while in a prisoner of war camp in Vietnam, ironically enough.

"Maybe more," conceded General Perry. "It's designed to get the Chinese thinking they left a major hole in their intelligence. The Chinese seem to react to every new situation with caution. They still haven't broken out of the reservoir perimeter."

"So let's hear it," said Greene.

Perry briefly described it. Greene liked it—but then he liked most special operations. He turned to Frost.

"You think it will work, Pete?" he asked.

"Well . . . If it goes off exactly as planned, if they buy it, it will confuse them. But . . . I will say that if those tenders were destroyed . . ."

Frost was hesitating, calculating in his head. Greene had known him for so long that he could read the hesitation: the plan was close, but not quite there yet.

"If the tenders are destroyed, then you've got real possibilities," said the CIA chief. His words started coming faster. "Because that's going to be where the fuel for their aircraft is. They won't launch an invasion if they don't have air cover. A lot of it, and not just from Hainan. They're very cautious."

"How many commandos does Major Murphy say the Vietnamese need?" asked Jackson, his voice clearly skeptical. "And when are they thinking of launching this mission?"

"Those are good questions, sir," said Perry. "Major Murphy recommends a relatively small but highly trained force. The Vietnamese really don't have a dedicated special ops force. They could put together some spies and marines, but it would be very ad hoc."

"They'll never take out the tenders," said Jackson. "There's no time. You know how long SEALs would practice to do something like this? And they train all the time."

"The right people could do it," said Frost. "SEALs could do it."

"How hard would it be to hit those tankers with Tomahawk missiles?" Greene asked.

"Child's play," said Jackson drily. "And then the Chinese will declare war on us. And you'll be impeached."

"Not if they don't know they were Tomahawks," said the president.

"Easily identified," said Jackson.

"I'm afraid he's right, George," said Frost.

"We used them against the dams," said Perry. "The Chinese haven't identified them yet."

"The missiles struck the bottom of the dams," said Jackson. "The evidence is buried under a lake. We won't get away with that here. Or at least we can't count on it."

"What kind of missiles do the Vietnamese have?" Greene asked General Perry.

"Very few."

"They have about a half dozen Kingbolts in their inventory," said Frost. "Probably rusting at a base near Ho Chi Minh City."

"Kingbolt. What is that? Chinese?"

The name sounded familiar to Greene, a former Navy aviator, but his memory was faulty: it was an air-launched Russian weapon, sold to some foreign governments—including Dubai's. Jackson, who loved to show off his knowledge of military minutiae, lovingly detailed the missile's origin and capabilities.

Greene cut him off before he got down to mentioning the type of explosive the warheads held.

"We can get some of those from Dubai easily enough," said Greene. "And quietly. Can we launch them?"

"Have to talk to the Navy about that," said Jackson. "I don't know if they'd go for it."

"We'll see about that," said Greene.

"We might use some of the assets we used in Malaysia," suggested Frost. He was referring to mercenaries loosely connected with the government air force—and not so loosely on the CIA payroll.

"Good," said Greene. "So if we made this look like a Vietnamese attack—add an air element in there—"

"Easier said than done," said Jackson. "The only air bases operating are in the south."

"Launch it from a helicopter," said Frost.

"I doubt that would work."

"It doesn't have to work," said Greene. "It just has to look as if it could."

"I don't know, George. You're awful close to the line," said Jackson.

"The hell with the line."

"What are the senators you're having lunch with going to say if you tell them we're helping Vietnam on the sly?"

"I'm not going to tell them. Besides, this isn't much more than I've already done."

"I don't want to contradict you," said Jackson.

"Then don't."

"Even sending General Perry was over the line."

"I'll worry about the line," said Greene. "It's only politics anyway."

"Mr. President, there is one other factor that you

should know about," interrupted General Perry. "The Vietnamese—in order to go along with this, sir, they want Major Murphy to lead the operation."

"I couldn't pick a better man myself," said the president.

Hanoi

Soldiers were guarding the Hanoi train station. Jing Yo drove past slowly, then stopped the scooter down the street.

Hyuen Bo tightened her grip around his midsection. "I'm coming with you," she whispered.

"It's too dangerous." He pried her hand away and got off.

"I'll turn you in."

"You could never do that." He touched her gently, then walked down the street toward the station, steeling himself not to look back.

He'd felt the same way when the time had come to leave the monastery. It was a difficult walk.

Jing Yo kept his head down as he passed the soldiers. One or two glanced in his direction, then ignored him. He wasn't important.

Like the rest of the city, the main lights inside the station had been blacked out; a pair of small kerosene lanterns had been set up near the center of the waiting area. While in theory the blackout was a precaution against bombers, in truth the lights made no difference to the weapons the Chinese used, as the glow of fresh fires from the north and east proved. But turning off the lights was a tangible, if feeble, action the city could take in its own defense, important for morale if nothing else.

A man three times Jing Yo's age stood at the desk in the far corner of the station's waiting room, standing stiffly, as if at attention. The only other occupants of the waiting room were two men stretched out along the chairs, snoring. The plastic seats were improbable beds, but with their heads covered they were oblivious of the world.

"I wanted to book a sleeper on the midnight train to Ho Chi Minh City," Jing Yo told the ticket clerk.

"The trains have been shut down as of five o'clock. The military has commandeered them. I'm sorry."

Jing Yo nodded. He turned to leave, and was surprised to see Hyuen Bo there.

She brushed past him.

"Isn't there a way?" Hyuen Bo asked the man. "My mother is there alone. We are afraid for her."

"There's nothing I can do. I'm sorry."

"Nothing?"

Her voice was so plaintive and convincing that Jing Yo almost couldn't tell that she was acting.

"Perhaps one of the buses," said the man. "They're still running."

"When do they leave?"

"At five."

Jing Yo left Hyuen Bo in the station, walking quickly out and back up along the road. He had to get away from her. After that, it would be a simple matter to steal a car.

"Halt," said one of the soldiers, barring his way.

Puzzled, Jing Yo stopped.

"Why are you out on the street?" demanded the soldier.

"I was trying to get a train."

"Papers," demanded the soldier.

Jing Yo reached into his pocket. He was unsure whether the soldier was just being officious, or had some reason to be suspicious.

He could take the gun from the private's hand easily enough. But there were a dozen other men here. Could he kill enough of them to get away?

And what of Hyuen Bo?

The soldier grabbed the documents. "What unit are you in?"

"I am not in the army. I have a disability."

"You're not blind."

"My heart is weak."

The soldier scowled.

"What is the matter?" asked Hyuen Bo, running up to him. "I found out where the buses are."

"Who are you?" asked the soldier.

"His wife. We were hoping to go to Saigon—"

"The place has been called Ho Chi Minh City since before you were born," snapped the soldier.

"My mother is there."

"Use some sense then. Use the proper name."

"Do you know when the trains will run again?" asked Hyuen Bo. "We have to get to her."

"Everyone is to remain where they are. You're not afraid of the Chinese, are you?"

"Of course not."

"Your boy is." He threw the papers at Jing Yo, dismissing him.

"You shouldn't have done that," said Jing Yo when they reached the scooter. He spoke softly, sensing the soldiers were still watching them.

"You need me," said Hyuen Bo.

———

Hyuen Bo had a small scooter. It held about three gallons of gas, and though it could get nearly a hundred miles per gallon, its capacity was far too small to get them to Ho Chi Minh City.

But it was the best option. Jing Yo had some plastic tubing to use as a siphon; he would steal gas along the way if he couldn't find a gas station. He found a pair of water jugs on the street a short distance from the station and took them to use for extra fuel.

He thought of leaving Hyuen Bo, of just pushing her off and driving on, but he couldn't do it. There were practical reasons—she'd already demonstrated how useful she could be dealing with the soldiers and officials—but the real reason was his love for her. He did not want to leave her, or lose her.

And yet, he would have to, at some point. Taking her with him surely exposed her to more danger, far more danger. If she was caught with him, she would surely be hanged as a spy.

"It's a long ride," he told her as they approached the highway. "Many hours. And it will be very hard."

"We will be together," she told him, wrapping her arms firmly around his chest.

The night air gradually turned damp, the moisture and darkness interconnected. Stars faded behind thickening clouds.

They had been traveling for almost an hour when they came to the first military checkpoint. Jing Yo didn't see the trucks across the road in time to turn off without arousing suspicion. The trucks were Chinese-made troop transports, and at first their boxy silhouettes confused him. He thought for a moment that he had stumbled onto a Chinese army unit, and while under orders to conduct his mission with complete secrecy, he decided he would have the soldiers take him immediately to their superior. He'd ask his help getting farther south. But Jing Yo's first glimpse of the soldiers warned him that he had been wrong; these were Vietnamese units, ordered to hold the road to Cam Thuy against a possible advance.

Jing Yo throttled down, keeping the scooter in a low idle as he stopped before the soldiers. He could tell they were nervous. There were three men in the road, with others off the road nearby. Jing Yo knew from his own experience in the army that bored, nervous soldiers suddenly presented with excitement were apt to do many things, including killing innocent civilians.

"Why are you on this road?" demanded the first soldier.

"We are going to help my mother," said Hyuen Bo behind him. "She is an old woman and needs our help."

"I'm not talking to you," said the soldier.

"It's true," said Jing Yo. He began to cough, a ruse in case his accent seemed unnatural.

"Where is your mother?"

"Saigon," said Hyuen Bo.

"Saigon?"

"Where in Saigon?" asked another soldier. "You answer, not her."

Jing Yo named a district at the southern end of the city where he had stayed during his last visit. The soldier asked if he knew of a restaurant at a certain address. Jing Yo said that he didn't, but that the address itself seemed to be wrong. Perhaps it was in another city district—a common problem in Saigon, where the border of each small district meant the street numbering system was restarted.

The answer seemed to mollify the soldier. "You

should look it up when you get there," he said. "I recommend it."

"I will."

"Has the enemy broken through?" asked Hyuen Bo. "Will we be able to get there?"

"Since you ask, I would not advise driving any farther," said the first soldier. "Where have you come from?"

"Hanoi," said Hyuen Bo.

"You shouldn't drive at night," said the soldier who had asked about the restaurant. "The Chinese send their airplanes out to strike anything on the road. They don't care if you are civilians or the army."

"You're in danger yourself," said Hyuen Bo.

"It's our job to be in danger," said the first soldier. "And we're not afraid of any Chinese bastards."

"I hope I see one. I'd shoot the bastard in the face," said the third soldier, speaking for the first time.

"Are they that close?" asked Hyuen Bo.

"Only their planes," answered the first soldier. "Their army has been stopped at the reservoir. They'll be kicked back to China soon. They are dogs. We have always beaten them, from ancient times."

"What's the safest way south?" asked Jing Yo. "If we have to go."

"The Ho Chi Minh Highway," said the third soldier. "It's the only way."

"That is for military use only," said the first soldier. "It's closed to civilians. And I would stay away from it—the Chinese will bomb it."

"Could we drive it?" Hyuen Bo asked, addressing the soldier who had mentioned the Saigon restaurant. "Would it be fastest?"

"Why are you talking to him? I told you already it's closed." The first soldier practically shouted. Jing Yo was familiar with the type—a small-minded man, suddenly handed a little authority, who became completely unnerved at the slightest perceived threat to his position.

"We must stay away from the highway," said Jing Yo before descending into a coughing fit.

"Go," said the soldier, waving his hand. "Don't say we didn't warn you."

They avoided the cities. Jing Yo worried that there would be additional patrols on the outskirts. Much of the land had only recently been claimed from the jungle, and the roads were rough and twisting, old trails that connected new farm fields and skirted bogs and sudden sharp rises in the terrain.

It took them nearly a half hour to go only ten miles south. The twists and turns jumbled Jing Yo's sense of direction, and he was able to navigate only by catching occasional glimpses of dim lights and the sound of trucks close to the city, which lay to his west.

Finally, Jing Yo realized he had no choice but to go through the heavier populated areas that lay near Cam Thuy. And if he was going to do that, then he might as well take the Ho Chi Minh Highway, military restriction or no. They drove into the city and, noticing that the gas tank was only about half full, found a block where several cars were parked and stole more fuel.

Hyuen Bo continued to be more helpful than he could have wished; she held the tube down into the other car's tank, and when they heard someone coming, she managed to free the tube and hop on the scooter so calmly he would have sworn she was a guerrilla herself.

The city was under blackout restrictions, and in theory under a curfew. But people were gathered on the main streets in the business district, crowded together on the sidewalk, talking—or so Jing Yo imagined—about the war and their prospects for remaining safe. There were several tanks parked near the bridge over the Ma River, but no soldiers made an effort to stop them as they crossed, even though they were technically on the Ho Chi Minh Highway. A pair of motorcycles and a small car passed them going the other way.

There were more vehicles moving in the southern suburbs. A Mercedes sped past them, so close that the wind almost threw them into a ditch.

A short while later, a pair of military jeeps, old Russian models, rushed past in the opposite direction. Jing Yo took this as a sign that others would follow. He found a side street that paralleled the main highway, and got off, swinging away from main road. But within a quarter mile the road came back to the highway, and Jing Yo had no choice but to follow.

Two more small trucks passed. These slowed as he approached. One flipped on a small searchlight mounted near the driver's side. Jing Yo pushed his head down and revved the throttle, willing the small scooter forward. As they whizzed past, he tensed, expecting gunfire, but no one fired and the trucks didn't stop.

The road began climbing a hill, negotiating a gentle curve. As they rounded it, Jing Yo caught sight of a line of shadows moving ahead.

A large gravel pit had been built into the side of the highway during its construction. Jing Yo drove into it, angling toward the steep slope where he could hide in the darkest of the shadows. But just as he reached it, the scooter hit a rock hidden in the weeds, and he and Hyuen Bo went flying off.

Jing Yo's reaction was automatic. He entered a realm where thought and action, body and mind, are joined completely to each other. He felt himself flying, and without thought or other preparation, moved his elbows and tucked his shoulder to roll on the ground. The uneven gravel bit at his body, but Jing Yo had taken many such falls. His momentum brought him to his feet. He ran to the scooter and turned off the engine, then looked for Hyuen Bo.

She lay heaped on the ground. He scooped her up and ran with her into the shadows, collapsing into the brush as trucks approached. He sat with his lover in his arms, her head and upper body cradled in his lap. Never had a grown person seemed so small, or so fragile.

"Hyuen Bo?" he said softly. "Hyuen Bo?"

She didn't respond. Jing Yo took a breath, steeling himself against her death.

No matter what one believed about the universe, whether it was a place filled with heavens and hells, or simply an empty consortium of atoms, there was no easy acceptance of death. Brave words about passing to a better place would be meaningless to Jing Yo, and all his training no consolation for Hyuen Bo's loss.

He prepared himself.

But then she stirred, alive.

Jing Yo let go of the iron armor he'd bound himself in. "Ssssh," he whispered. "You'll be all right."

She turned her head toward him in the darkness and opened her eyes. "I know I will."

"What hurts?"

"My head."

"Can you move your arms? Careful," he added quickly. "The army trucks are coming up the highway."

As soon as Hyuen Bo demonstrated she had not broken any bones, Jing Yo gently removed her from his lap, laying her softly on the ground. He told her not to move.

"I want to see the trucks, what they are," he whispered. Then he crawled away, moving carefully to a point a dozen meters away where he could see the road.

There were tanks as well as trucks. They made an easily discernible sound, their treads grinding against the smooth pavement of the highway. They were T-55s, and even if Jing Yo hadn't been familiar with the whine of their engines from his time in Malaysia, he would have easily recognized them by their silhouettes and long gun barrels.

The crews were driving with their hatches open, anxious to escape the stifling interior. Jing Yo counted twenty-two before the line was broken by a pair of low-slung command vehicles. The sharp angles at the front indicated they were probably BTR-40s, very old trucks that were still used for various purposes by the Vietnamese.

A second group of tanks followed, this one bigger than the first, with the tanks taking two files rather than one. Most of these were T-55s as well, but there were bigger tanks mixed in, T-59 main battle tanks. Jing Yo counted thirty-two.

Supply vehicles followed, then towed artillery. Jing Yo concluded that he was looking at elements from three or four different units, perhaps tank battalions stripped from their normal infantry division and rushed north to reinforce whatever was trying to bog down the advance at the reservoir the soldiers had mentioned earlier. He thought of using his phone to warn of the advance, but realized that would be foolish. For one thing, the

Chinese air force would undoubtedly be watching, either by satellite or by UAV. For another, his mission required complete secrecy, and every use of the phone threatened that.

Jing Yo crawled back to Hyuen Bo. She had pulled herself upright, and sat with her knees curled against her chest.

"Is the scooter okay?" she asked.

"We'll check it in a minute. There may be other trucks coming," said Jing Yo. "There are always stragglers."

"In every army?"

"It's universal."

He knelt next to her, wanting to inspect her head for cuts. She misinterpreted his intentions and turned to kiss him. He tried to pull back but her lips pressed into his, and he yielded to her insistence. She unfolded her arms and they moved into an embrace. Worried that they might be seen above the weeds, Jing Yo leaned to his right, bringing her down gently to the ground with him.

They stayed like that for nearly a half hour. There were several stragglers, all troop trucks.

Finally, Jing Yo renewed his resolve and pushed himself back up to his knees. Hyuen Bo clung to him.

"We have to check the scooter," he told her. "We can't stay here."

The bike started right up. He didn't realize the front wheel was badly bent until he tried to drive it out of the quarry. The scooter bucked violently, its wheel wobbling.

They worked together to fix it. Hyuen Bo found a pair of large rocks, and helped anchor the bike in place while Jing Yo used his feet as levers, returning the hub to round.

Or almost round. The scooter pulled to the right once they were on the highway. But it was far better than walking, and even at forty miles an hour, Jing Yo found he could hold it steady with relatively little pressure.

They drove for roughly another hour, still on the Ho Chi Minh Highway. Nearing Thai Hoa, Jing Yo got off to use local roads. He ran into a pair of roadblocks almost immediately. At the first, a bored Vietnamese sergeant barely looked at their papers before waving them away. The soldiers manning the second, however, told them that the curfew was being strictly enforced. They threatened to put them in jail until Hyuen Bo began to sob. They relented, but insisted the pair find a place to stay until dawn, warning that other patrols would be stricter, and that sooner or later they would be arrested.

Jing Yo was wondering whether to take this advice to heart when he heard a high-pitched whistle in the distance.

He reached his hand to his chest where Hyuen Bo's were, grasping them and squeezing. In the next moment, there was a low crash, the sound thunder makes when lightning splits trees ten or twelve miles away.

White light flashed in the distance ahead. The flashes looked like signals sent from a ship in the distance, whiteness streaming through shutters opening and closing.

The sound of the explosions followed.

And then, finally, air-raid sirens began to sound. Antiaircraft weapons began spewing streams of tracers into the air. The ground shook with a dozen different vibrations, and the air popped with rounds as they were expelled. Searchlights began to sweep the clouds. Jing Yo heard jets in the distance.

He angled back toward the highway. It took several minutes to find it. Just before he did, he heard the whistle of bombs falling toward him.

Or thought he did. Jing Yo reasoned later that if he had truly heard the bombs, he would have been blown up by their explosions. And he was not blown up, merely covered with dust and severely rattled. The ground heaved violently and he nearly went over, but with all of the other sounds and chaos, it was impossible to say if the concussions were nearby or not.

Hyuen Bo tightened her hold on his chest.

"Hang on," he said, squeezing the throttle. "We must get as far south as we can while the attack continues."

19

Near Thai Hoa, Vietnam

Mara had just crossed out of the city's precincts when DeBiase called and warned her that an attack was on the way. She drove to a high spot south of the city, then pulled over and got the others out of the vehicles, fearing that the approaching Chinese aircraft would mistake them for soldiers.

The air strikes began with a fury of explosions, half a dozen cruise missiles striking ahead of the airplanes. At first, the Chinese seemed to be aiming at a Vietnamese division headquarters, which was located along the Ho Chi Minh Highway south of the city. But within minutes, unguided bombs were falling in a broad semicircle that took in the residential areas of the city. Some missiles in a third wave even fell on nonmilitary targets, striking the buildings on the eastern side of the highway and flattening the business area beneath a tremendous red and black mushroom cloud.

"Caught a gasoline tank," said Kerfer. "The Chinese aren't pulling many punches."

"I wouldn't expect them to," said Mara.

"You know them well?"

"I fought against their commandos in Malaysia. They're bastards."

Kerfer remained silent. Maybe, she thought, that was his way of apologizing for having underestimated her.

Probably not. He wasn't the sort that apologized for anything, not even subtly.

"Now's the best time to drive," said Kerfer as the planes flew off. "Everybody'll be hunkered down."

"They'll be nervous, too."

"They're always nervous."

Mara watched for a few more seconds. Fires burned in the distance, the fingers of a man buried alive groping from the grave.

"I wish to hell you hadn't shot up that train car," Mara told Kerfer.

"If I hadn't we'd be dead by now," he told her, walking back to the car.

Mara let Squeaky drive as they pressed south. The patrols seemed almost nonexistent. DeBiase was cagey in his updates, not giving her exact information about what was going on. That made sense, of course: if she was captured, anything he told her would have to be considered forfeit to the Chinese. Knowing what the Americans knew and when they knew it would tell them quite a bit about the intelligence-gathering methods.

Josh was still sleeping in the middle seat of the truck next to her. He began mumbling to himself incoherently, humming almost, his teeth held close together.

Bad dream, probably. Maybe based on what he had seen behind the lines.

He'd told her very little of it. An entire village buried in a field. An arm poking up from the ground after the rain. His fellow scientists, murdered in their sleep. The body of child who'd crawled under a bed to hide after being wounded, then left there to die, its toy doll in its arms.

The sat phone rang. DeBiase with another update.

"Hey, darling, how are you?"

"I'm doing good, Million Dollar Man," Mara answered. "How's your hernia?"

"Ailing me greatly. You're not making very good time."

"We're driving through a country that has a war on," said Mara. "I didn't know you had your stopwatch out."

"Listen, the Chinese navy is gathering off the coast, south of Hainan Island. There's big trouble brewing."

"You told me that already."

"This is big trouble. It looks like they have an invasion force getting ready."

"When?"

"Can't tell. But we want you home. Come on now," he said, switching to his cheerleader voice. "Pick up your pace. Once you get below Hue, you'll have free sailing. I have a plane lined up for you in Saigon."

"There has to be an airstrip closer that we can get to," Mara told him. "Come on."

"Darlin', I've been trying. But the best alternative I can do to Ho Chi Minh is a puddle jumper that can

meet you near Cambodia. That'll be twice as dangerous. The Chinese have complete air superiority, as you
just saw."

"And the pilot's a drunk, right?"

"Could well be."

It was an inside joke between them, a reference to a
story DeBiase liked to tell of one of his own hairy es-
capes by plane, when the pilot had been so smashed
that DeBiase had taken over the controls midflight.
DeBiase, of course, had no clue what he was doing and
just barely succeeded in keeping the plane moving in
the right direction. Miraculously, the real pilot revived
about ten minutes from the airfield where they were
supposed to touch down, and landed the plane without a hitch. The story was probably largely apocryphal,
like many a DeBiase tale, but it was told with such gusto
that it deserved to be entirely true.

"If you start to get into trouble south of Hue," added
DeBiase, "we'll consider asking the Vietnamese for help.
The closer we are to Saigon, the harder it should be for
the Chinese to interfere."

"I don't think asking the Vietnamese for help at this
point is a good idea," said Mara.

"Why not?"

"There have to be more spies in Saigon than in Hanoi,"
she said.

"I'm sure there are. What else is up?" asked DeBiase.
His voice had a subtle edge to it.

"We had some trouble on the train," said Mara, deciding to come clean. "With the Vietnamese."

"What kind of trouble?"

"The kind that got them killed."

"That sounds like bad trouble," said DeBiase.

"I don't know that I've ever seen good trouble."

"Well." He paused. She knew he was considering whether to ask what had happened. "To make an omelet, eggs are often broken."

"They are."

"We won't talk to the Vietnamese at all," he said.

"Good."

"But you get going. Things are falling apart there damn fast."

20

Washington, D.C.

The thing that really frosted Greene was the fact that *all* of the senators he'd invited to lunch in the White House dining room were members of his own party. All had stood onstage with him this past November and proclaimed their undying support. They'd been the first on their feet in January to applaud at the inauguration.

And the first with their hands out the next day.

He didn't have one vote among them to give aid to Vietnam. Maybe he had Leiber. Maybe. But even the Connecticut senator looked like he was a little beaten down. He sat at the far end of the table near the windows and the painting of Geronimo that Greene liked, hunched over a bowl of soup. He'd said less than two words the entire time.

"So obviously we're here for a reason, Mr. President," said Phillip Grasso, whom Greene had seated at his right hand. "You're going to push us on China."

"Damn right I'm going to push you on China," said Greene.

"They're taking over the world again, right?" Grasso turned and winked at the other senators.

"I wouldn't underestimate their threat," said Greene.

"I take China very seriously," said Grasso. "I just don't think we should go to war with them."

"If we don't stand up to them now, we will be at war with them eventually," Greene told him. "That's why I want to help Vietnam."

"We can't send arms," said Senator Roosevelt, who despite his last name was not related to either president, either through blood or character. "People will view it as a hostile act."

"And invading Vietnam was not?" said Greene in disbelief.

Everyone looked at their plates. Greene took a breath and tried to recalibrate.

"I think a good step here," said Leiber, "would be to go to the UN and get sanctions. We can build a coalition. Like George Bush did during the first Gulf War. The first George Bush," he added.

"No one takes the UN seriously," said Grasso. "Besides, you don't have the votes there. Frankly, I think I'd oppose sanctions myself. China is our biggest trading partner."

Grasso headed the Armed Services Committee. If he wasn't taking a hard stand against China, no one on his committee would. Not a single one.

Grasso was a guy who could tell which way popular opinion was running. He'd started out as a machinist in a small family-owned business, a "real blue-collar guy," as the talking heads put it. He'd wandered into politics because the state wanted to take his backyard to expand a highway. He ended up on the town board, became a county party chairman, then a congressman and a real power in New York. He had numerous connections on both sides of the political aisle. And a long, long list of contributors.

Many of whom undoubtedly had Chinese connections.

Greene needed to persuade him.

"I am for sanctions," said the president. "I'm going to push them personally in front of the UN. We're raising a stink."

"Why raise a stink when the Vietnamese started it?" asked Senator Jennifer Kraft. Kraft was the junior senator from Wisconsin, and until now, a vote Greene could generally count on.

"Maybe they didn't start the war," said Greene. "What would your reaction be then?"

"I'd need some very good proof that they didn't."

"We've seen footage from the Chinese," said Grasso. "We've seen their satellite photos. Is there proof they're lying?"

"If I have proof, that would change your mind?" asked Greene.

"I would consider it," fudged Grasso. "Do you have proof?"

Greene did have proof—Josh MacArthur, and the little orphan girl he'd found. But he wasn't ready to share that proof with anyone outside the administration. Even there, most didn't know about it. The problem was that once he said something, especially here, it would get out, and the Chinese would find a way to rebut it.

"We're examining the situation," Greene said.

"What's 'examining' mean?" asked Kraft.

"Reviewing the intelligence. Let's say we have proof—what then?"

"Convince the UN. Start with sanctions," suggested Kraft. "Then you might be able to get some votes."

You might get some votes—not *we*. Greene boiled inside. He had very little use for the UN. No use, in fact.

Yet he couldn't go to war without the support of the American people. And their elected representatives.

"I am going to the UN," he said. "You can count on that." He looked around the table. "Could someone pass me the pepper? My chicken is a little bland."

Vinh Province, Vietnam

Jing Yo stopped again to siphon gas, this time from a small farm not far from the road. Hyuen Bo had fallen asleep against his back, and nearly fell off when he stopped. Jing Yo left her with the scooter near the road and went alone to scout the yard.

A few years before, this would have been a rich farm for Vietnam, with several acres and several buildings. Now it was commonplace. He guessed that it would have a tractor and at least one car or motorbike, but he couldn't find them. There were two sheds near the road. Neither had a vehicle. In one, he found a small fuel can, but it smelled of diesel or kerosene, and its fuel was too thick to be gasoline.

Jing Yo found a path that led back to the two small houses. It started to rain as he approached the nearer house. The small droplets felt good at first, but soon they started to fall faster and thicker, and it became harder to see.

A tractor was parked in a hollow next to the house. A motorcycle leaned against it. Jing Yo unscrewed the top to the motorcycle's gas tank. There was gas almost to the brim. He pushed his hose in to fill his makeshift gas tank, then got another idea. He picked up the bike and backed it away from the house, walking with it to the spot where he'd left Hyuen Bo.

He didn't see her or the scooter. A hole opened in his chest as he stood still, turning around slowly as he looked for her.

Perhaps it is good that she has left, he thought.

"I'm here," she whispered. And his heart jumped.

"Across the road," Hyuen Bo added. "I was afraid we could be seen."

She pushed the bike out from around the brush where she'd been hiding.

"You found another bike?"

"Just for the gas," said Jing Yo, changing his mind about taking it.

He didn't want to be separated from her.

Not yet.

They rigged the hose, taking advantage of the different heights between the machines. The slope and the full tank of gas in the bike made it easy.

"Are you hungry?" Jing Yo asked when they finished.

"Why? Is there food?"

"There are houses. There's bound to be something."

"You shouldn't take the food from the people," said Hyuen Bo. "They probably have very little."

"It's a rich farm," said Jing Yo. "A person with a farm this size would be very well off in China. If not for the drought."

"Is that how you justify stealing?"

Jing Yo didn't answer. He took the bike and pushed it back to its resting spot. He leaned it against the tractor just as the sat phone rang.

"We have found a transmission on the frequencies used by the CIA," said a man whose voice he did not recognize. "There have been three transmissions in the past several hours, moving in a general direction south. The last was fifteen minutes ago, in southern Vinh Province. There have been no other transmissions from the American spies in the past two days."

"Give me directions," said Jing Yo.

The last signal had come from a position barely thirty kilometers, or twenty miles, away. Jing Yo drove with new focus. It might be nothing—there was no way of knowing from the signal itself, and his informer had made no promises—but he was convinced that he was now on his quarry's trail. And close to him.

Rain continued to fall steadily. The scooter's small wheels slipped on the pavement, and he had to keep his speed down to roughly forty kilometers an hour. It was an exercise in patience.

He had learned to be patient in the monastery by spending whole days sitting outside the prayer hall, waiting for the monk he was assigned to accompany. During this phase of his training, the monks were completely unpredictable. They would arrive before morning prayer; they would not come until nightfall. This was all absolutely intentional—they had perceived in Jing Yo a weakness for action. They interpreted this as impetuousness, a vice. Not trained, the tendency could overcome careful thought. And so they had taught him to harness it, first by teaching patience, and then by instructing him in the physical skills of kung fu.

The rain made it harder to see in the distance, and Jing Yo nearly missed the intersection where he needed to turn. He braked a little too hard and the bike began to slide to its left. He let off on the brake, shifted his weight. It was all automatic; he had his balance before he could even open his mouth to warn Hyuen Bo. But the incident warned him against his wandering thoughts. He needed to concentrate and focus on what he was doing.

A truck blocked the highway about two miles later. Jing Yo slowed gently, easing the brake against the wheel. The truck was a civilian vehicle, and it was parked on a diagonal, nose facing south. As he came close, Jing saw that he could slip around on the left shoulder. As he did, two men came out from behind the truck. They had guns. He pushed down toward the handlebars and accelerated, trying to speed past.

One of the men lurched at them. He hit Hyuen Bo and spun the scooter into a skid.

Jing Yo fell away from the vehicle, tumbling across the pavement into the ditch beyond the shoulder. In the dark night with the rain he was momentarily blind, his bearings scrambled.

Caught by surprise, Hyuen Bo fell with the scooter, landing at the edge of the road.

"We will take your bike!" yelled one of the men. "We will take your money as well."

"This one's a girl," said the man who had lurched at the scooter. "We'll have her."

"They're both girls, I'll bet," said the other. "Put her in the truck while I get the other."

Jing Yo scrambled to his feet.

"Come on and don't make this hard," said the other man, unsure in the darkness where Jing Yo was. "You'll escape with your life, and be glad for it!"

Jing Yo's eyes focused on the shadow, barely ten feet away on his right, up on the road. The man had a rifle in his hand.

"Come on," said the man, who still hadn't seen him. "Don't make me shoot you!"

The man squared as if to fire, though it was clear from his aim that he didn't know where Jing Yo was.

"You'd best shoot then," said Jing Yo, taking a step and throwing himself feetfirst at the man.

The gun went off as they went down, a loud, violent rattle in the rain. Jing Yo landed square on the man's chest, knocking him down. He sprang up, then went down into the man's side, knee-first.

The man bashed his rifle against Jing Yo's head, hitting him just above his eye. As he reared back to strike again, Jing Yo grabbed the gun and rolled forward with him, both men holding the rifle as they went down the embankment.

His enemy's face pressed against his as Jing Yo fell beneath him. The man's breath smelled of rotten fish. Jing Yo started to push to the left, trying to slip out from under him. The man raised his skull, then smashed it into Jing Yo's forehead. Jing Yo hit him on the temple with his left fist. Still the man fought back, hitting him with another head butt.

Both were still holding the rifle between them. As long as they did that, neither would have an advantage. But to let go of the gun was to risk giving the other an insurmountable edge.

When his punches failed to move the man off him, Jing Yo grabbed the man's hair and tried to pull him down. But his enemy's bulk protected him, and he was able to push back and attack with another head smash.

I must take the risk, Jing Yo thought.

He pushed the rifle against his enemy's chest. The sudden change in direction caught him off guard. As the man fell back, Jing Yo pitched his elbow and forearm up, smacking the rifle into the man's face and striking his eye. The man winced, instinctively ducking back and loosening his grip on the gun.

That was all the advantage that Jing Yo needed. He tossed the rifle aside, and with his upper body free, his hands flew to the man's head, his knee up into his groin. With one hard twist, the man's neck was broken.

Jing Yo threw him to the side and scrambled for the gun.

The man's accomplice was by the truck, shouting. Jing Yo grabbed the rifle, then threw himself flat, unsure where the other man was.

"Pean!" the man yelled to his companion. "*Pean!* What are you doing? Where are you?"

Jing Yo crawled up the side of the ditch, willing his eyes to focus. He saw two shadows near the cab of the truck. The man had Hyuen Bo.

"Pean!" he called again. "Where are you? Should I kill the girl?"

Jing Yo raised the rifle. He wasn't sure which of the shadows was the man, which was Hyuen Bo.

She was behind the man, very close, held around the neck.

Ten yards. An easy shot.

Jing Yo pressed the trigger. The AK-47 clicked. It had run out of bullets.

"*Pean!*"

"Drop the girl and I'll let you live," said Jing Yo.

"Who are you?" yelled the man.

"Let go of the girl."

Jing Yo heard her struggle. The man twisted around, pulling her in front of him.

"You think I'm a fool?" said the other man. "Where is Pean?"

"You'll meet him soon enough if you don't let her go."

"Perhaps I'll shoot her."

"Then I'll eat your heart while you're still alive," replied Jing Yo.

The man began edging toward the scooter. Jing Yo rose.

"I see you!" shouted the man. "Any closer and she dies."

"Let the girl go, or you will die."

"Not today."

As the man reached the scooter, Hyuen Bo started to pull away. The man let go of her and fumbled for the ignition. Jing Yo launched himself, flying to his back as the motor caught. They both went over the handlebars, the scooter's engine catching.

Three hard punches to the back of the man's head rendered him unconscious.

Jing Yo struggled to control his anger. He rose, wanting nothing else but to tear the man's head off his body. He picked up the man's rifle, placed it next to his skull, and fired once, killing him.

It was an act of mercy, compared to what he wanted to do.

In the meantime, Hyuen Bo ran to the scooter and righted it.

"We should go," she said as Jing Yo stood over the body.

"They're soldiers," said Jing Yo, pointing at the

men's uniforms. They'd pulled their patches from their shoulders. They were deserters. "They may have something we can use."

"Come on, Yo."

Jing Yo stared at her. In his heart he wanted her to go, to just leave, to save herself from the future she would be trapped in.

"They may have something useful," he said, pulling the man he had just killed off the road and starting to search their pockets.

The rain eased as Jing Yo searched the dead men's truck, which was more than likely stolen. There were a few extra rounds for the rifles, but nothing else of value, not even a few crumpled banknotes.

This was the army they were fighting against? An army of cowards without even enough sense to steal a vehicle that had gas? Without even a thousand dong in their pockets?

His true enemy was somewhere on the road south, getting farther away with each moment he dawdled.

"Are you sure you are okay?" Jing Yo asked Hyuen Bo when he returned to the scooter.

"I've had much worse."

"There will be much worse to come."

Hyuen Bo said nothing, tightening her grip around his waist as he took the scooter once more back on the road.

22

Hue, Vietnam

It was nearly dawn when Mara and the others reached the outskirts of Hue. The Vietnamese army had two camps along the Hue City Bypass immediately to the west of the city, and DeBiase told Mara the easiest and fastest way would be to take Route 1, which cut down the side of the Citadel, the core of the old French city. A thick mist hid the landmarks, even the flag gate.

Squished between Mara and Squeaky, Josh felt as if he were wrapped in a sweaty blanket. Mara was driving; Squeaky had dozed off next to him.

The headlights were on. The light filtered through the droplets of water, reflecting off the sides of the buildings that lined the road. There was traffic, cars and trucks coming with supplies and workers for the day. There weren't a lot of vehicles, but there were certainly more than he'd seen before falling asleep.

"How far are we from Ho Chi Minh City?" he asked.

"We should be there by nightfall," said Mara. "We still have a ways to go. How are you feeling?"

"My insides kind of hurt. I must have eaten something bad."

"You have a fever."

"Yeah."

Mara put her hand up to his forehead. Her hand felt cool and soft, the touch gentle.

"We'll see a doctor as soon as we get to Saigon," she told him. "I don't want to stop."

"I'm okay," said Josh. "Maybe . . ." His voice trailed off.

"Maybe what?" Mara asked.

"Maybe we could stop and I could . . ." He couldn't find a delicate way to say it.

"Take a whiz?" asked Mara.

"Yeah."

"Once we're across the Perfume River, we'll stop," said Mara. "We'll get some breakfast."

"Is it far?"

"It's just ahead."

"How's Mạ?"

"She's with the SEALs. They have a little more room. Don't worry; they seem to be taking good care of her."

"I know. They bought her a doll. We lost it . . ."

Josh's voice trailed off. All he could think about was the blood in the train car.

There was a train bridge. The road turned sharply to the east, following the river. Finally the bridge loomed from the fog. Mara crossed over, checking her rearview mirror to make sure that Kerfer and the car were still behind her.

"You really know your way around," said Josh.

"Not really," said Mara.

"You've been here before?" he asked.

"Couple of times. To get an idea of what was where. I like to travel," she added. "It's interesting."

"Yeah."

"We don't have time for sightseeing, or we could have gone into the Citadel," said Mara. "The Forbidden City has some restored ruins. It's very pretty."

"Forbidden City?"

"It's like the city within the city."

"Why is it forbidden?"

"It was the emperor's home. It's like in Beijing. It's actually not that old—1805 or something like that. Hue was a provincial capital, and the French helped the emperor or encouraged him to build the Citadel as a fort. The Forbidden City is within the Citadel, which itself is a city within a city. A lot of it was destroyed during the war," she added. "There was a huge battle here during the Tet Offensive. The Communists took over the city. When the Marines finally drove them out, they discovered mass graves. The Communists had massacred, like, six thousand people. Some they just buried alive."

"And now we're trying to save them from the Chinese," said Josh.

"Something like that," said Mara.

They ate at a noodle shop. Josh didn't have anything, his bowels and bladder still on fire. While he suffered from a variety of allergies, he'd been lucky with his health otherwise, and this was one of the worst sicknesses he'd ever had, or at least that he could remember. He joked with the SEALs that it was like having a hangover without the good part, but it wasn't much like that at all.

"There's no gas in the city," Mara told the others after talking to the shop owner and some of the other locals. "Everyone claims there are stations with gas on the roads farther south. The south hasn't been attacked."

"That won't last for long," said Kerfer. "Assuming it's true."

Squeaky claimed he was rested from his nap and told Mara that he would drive for a while. She agreed. When Josh got up to leave, Mạ clung to him, so he carried her with him, even though his arms felt like lead weights.

She slipped in between Josh and Mara, draping her arms across Josh. She was asleep before they started.

"Just stay on Route One to Da Nang," Mara told Squeaky. "We'll take that as far south as we can."

"No more roadblocks?" asked Squeaky.

"I wouldn't count on there being no more road-blocks," she said. "But things should be easier. We only have to get to Saigon. We should be there by dark."

A half hour later, they were at Da Nang, climbing past the crowded city. There were no troops on the roads, no fortified strongpoints, not even a stray tank at the turnoffs. It seemed like another country.

The airport came into view as they climbed and turned toward the coast. It was a long, wide expanse of black just to the west of the city's most populated areas.

"Why don't we just take a plane from here?" asked Squeaky.

"Good question," said Mara. "They don't think it's safe."

"And driving all the way down the country is?" said Squeaky.

"The Chinese control the air," said Mara. "Suppos-edly they cratered the runway the other day."

"Send a helo."

"I ain't arguing," said Mara, though she suspected that the limited range of helicopters would have made that difficult.

They had gone no more than a quarter mile when the ground on their left exploded, a volcano appearing before their eyes. The ground shuddered and the car lurched to the right.

"Stay on the road," said Mara, reaching across Josh for the wheel.

"I got it, I got it," said Squeaky. "Relax."

Another bomb landed ahead, a few hundred yards to the left—not quite close enough to do any damage, but it certainly got their attention.

"Keep going," Mara ordered.

"I ain't stoppin'," said Squeaky.

Josh saw something fly across the sky in front of them. At first he thought it was a large bird, a vulture swooping toward the road to pounce on a carcass before the cars mangled it further. Then he saw a splatter of white and black and red, splinters flying—a second shell struck a row of houses.

"Bombs," he said.

"They're shells," said Squeaky. "There must be ships offshore. All right, so now I see why we can't take a helo."

"We have to cross the bridge before they hit it," said Mara.

"How do you know they're aiming at the bridge?" asked Squeaky.

"Go faster!" Mara shouted.

Mạ jerked up in Josh's lap. He put his hand over her eyes as a shell flew down to the right, east of the bridge as they started across. Water exploded in a geyser. The right half of the bridge, which was used by trains, was covered in steam.

A train had just started across from the other side. As it pushed forward, a spray of water came up and splashed the lead engine. As it emerged from the geyser, the train seemed to duck, as if afraid of another shell. One of the shells had twisted away the support for the track, which collapsed under the weight of the engines.

It was too late for the train to stop. Josh watched the cars tumble forward, driving mostly straight ahead, doomed by their connection to each other. They kept coming, and falling, one after another.

Then a geyser exploded ahead to the left.

Mạ screamed.

"It's okay," said Josh, holding her tighter. "It's all right."

"Faster!" yelled Mara. "Go! Go! Go!"

The riverbank in front of them turned black. Their pickup truck jerked upward. Josh's head flew backward, then whipped forward, his chin clunking onto Mạ's head. The truck veered right, moved sideways, then straightened.

They were in a cloud of smoke, dust, and water. Mara yelled at Squeaky, urging him to go faster. Squeaky said nothing, struggling to keep the truck headed straight as the bridge began vibrating crazily.

"Just stay on the road!" said Mara as they reached the other side.

"Skipper," said Squeaky, his voice cracking.

"Just keep going. They're behind us," said Mara. "Keep going."

The smoke cleared suddenly. There were trees near them, and a row of buildings. It was as if the attack had never happened.

It hadn't—here. Behind them, the bridge had just collapsed. The buildings along the river were now being targeted.

"Stop up there," said Mara, pointing to an open lot at the left ahead. There was a large barnlike building at the back of the lot. A pair of gas tanks sat just in front of it.

Mara jumped from the truck and ran to the pumps. Kerfer and the car pulled in behind them.

"What are you doing?" yelled the SEAL commander.

"There's gas here. Come on!" yelled Mara from the tanks.

"You're nuts, lady," said Kerfer.

Squeaky put the truck in gear and steered over to the pumps. Mara already had the handle out. As she pushed it into the opening, a fresh salvo of shells, these much closer, rocked the ground nearby.

A small, thin man came running from the building and began yelling at them.

Mara reached into her pocket and held up some bills, but they didn't seem to calm him. He stood a few feet from her, arms pumping up and down.

Squeaky leaned out the window of the truck. "Should I pop him?"

"No. Go. You're full." Mara pulled the pump out of the truck. "Get out of the way."

The truck lurched forward. Josh twisted around to see what was going on behind them and saw the old man grab the pump handle as Kerfer drove up.

A shell whizzed overheard, crashing across the road close enough to throw some bits of dirt on the truck. Mara tried pushing the old man away, until finally she'd had enough—she slugged him in the side of the head, sending him into the dirt.

"Whoa, she's got some fight, spook lady does," Squeaky told Josh.

Two more shells landed nearby, this time on the left. The old man got to his feet and started yelling again, even as he backed away from Mara. She topped off the car, then put the hose and nozzle back. She held out money, but he refused to take it. Finally she threw it in his direction and ran to the truck as more shells hit the ground.

"Go, let's get out of here," she said.

The wheels kicked dirt and dust everywhere as they sped back onto the highway.

"Didn't want to take your money, huh?" said Squeaky.

"The gas was for his family," said Mara.

"That's too bad," said Squeaky. "You shoulda kept the money, maybe. 'Cause we're so low."

Mara didn't answer.

"What was firing at us?" Josh asked.

"Probably some sort of Chinese destroyer," said Squeaky. "More than one. We're not too far from the water."

"Were they close?" asked Josh.

"In the bay, at least. Maybe up the river. Vietnam doesn't have much of a navy," Squeaky added. "Probably right offshore. Take care of whatever defenses they might have—probably pathetic to begin with. They probably sailed right up, bombing whatever they wanted. Nothing the Viets can do to them."

Josh slumped back in the seat. Mạ's face was buried in his shoulder. She sobbed silently.

"So it gets easier from here, right?" Squeaky asked Mara.

"'Easy' is a relative term," she said, turning her face to her window.

23

Da Nang, Vietnam

Jing Yo sensed he was getting close to his prey when the shelling started. He was only two miles or so from the river, but the bombardment quickly grew more intense. Finally, he saw a row of cars and flashing lights ahead and realized that the bridge must have been destroyed.

He took a U-turn and got off National Road 1A, treading back toward Cam Le Bridge. But the attacking Chinese ships had already put it out of commission. His only alternative would be to go farther inland, through the Tuy Loan suburb, before heading southward.

He found a row of cars stretching before him on the highway when he reached Route 14B. Several were abandoned, and the way was clogged with traffic. Even with the scooter, it was difficult to get around the jam. He treaded back and forth, hunting for open spaces, stopping and starting, several times going backward to try a different path.

The side roads were just as bad.

It took nearly two hours to travel three miles. By then the Chinese vessels had withdrawn. Smoke wafted on the breeze, clinging to the highway and the area around the rivers.

The bridge that took 14B over the river had been damaged by the assault. A barricade had been placed on the eastern bank; opposite him, a lone policeman stood in front of a small sawhorse, warning away cars and the curious.

Jing Yo stopped near the barricade, examining the roadway. It sagged about halfway across but otherwise looked intact. The bridge itself was only fifty meters long.

Jing Yo decided he would brave it.

"Are we going across?" asked Hyuen Bo.

"If we don't go here, it will take us another hour to find a crossing," he said. "And we'll be even farther from our direction. Do you think we can make it?"

"If you do."

"Hold me tightly," he said, pulling her arms around him.

He revved the scooter and shot forward. He'd gone no farther than ten meters when the road started to give way below. It dipped, then sprang back, as if it were a diving board. Jing Yo tacked left, easing off his accelerator. The road swayed left, and there was a loud noise, the crack a tree limb makes as it collapses in a heavy storm.

Jing Yo knew the road would not come back up this time. He accelerated, charging forward as the steel supports under the bridge swayed and snapped, one after another.

The policeman turned around and began waving his arms at him.

Ten meters from the end of the bridge, the right side of the road folded and fell below. Jing Yo hunkered against the handlebars, willing the scooter to the extreme left, clearing the remaining pavement as the deck collapsed.

He nearly ran into the policeman, who was too stunned to react as they sped past.

They drove on the highway for a few more minutes, until they were almost in Dai Hiep. Jing Yo slowed as they neared a cluster of stores and shops.

"Are you hungry?" he asked Hyuen Bo.

"If you are."

"We'll get something to eat," he said. "They have too much of a head start now for us to catch up."

Rat

Bystander Killed in Hotel Melee

BOSTON (AP–Fox News)—A mother of two was killed by a stray bullet today as armed hotel guards broke up a robbery attempt outside the Boston Crown Hotel.

The guards, all off-duty policemen, are a common sight at business-class hotels in Boston and most major cities, as crime against businessmen has spiked. The robberies are seen as part of the general spike of crime and violence against the wealthy as the country's economic downturn continues. . . .

Germans May Disband Health Care

BERLIN, GERMANY (World News Service)—The latest victim in the continuing worldwide depression may be one of the lynchpins of Germany's welfare state, universal health care.

The continuing fiscal crisis, which has hit Europe particularly hard, is causing governments across the region to cut services. Nowhere are the fiscal problems more severe than in Germany, where the government has traditionally eschewed deficits and other so-called tricks of the trade. . . .

Ho Chi Minh City (Saigon), Vietnam

A state of emergency had been declared in Ho Chi Minh City. The army as well as the police patrolled the streets, and a strict curfew had been imposed. Army units were gathered at different points along the highways; tanks were being dug in and other defenses prepared. Militia—in most cases little more than vigilantes with rifles older than they were—mustered at various municipal buildings and trolled the residential areas in pickups and the occasional van.

But the city itself seemed to be taking little notice of the crisis. Motorbikes, buses, cars, and trucks filled the highways in both directions; there was no mass panic or exodus.

Concerned that the regularly scheduled planes would be booked or even diverted, DeBiase had arranged for a plane to meet Mara and the others. The charter would then take them to Tokyo. Leased from a small Japanese airline named Goodwill Japan, the aircraft was one of several used on an occasional basis by the CIA.

The arrangement was straightforward. Mara would bring everyone to the airport, get through security, then go to the main terminal. She would page a ticket agent working for a regular airline but on the CIA payroll as a "friend." The employee would help them through passport control and out to the flight, which was due to arrive no later than 5 p.m.

Two hours from now.

Josh was sleeping again. He'd have to wait until they landed in Tokyo to see a doctor. But it seemed like the best way to do things.

They bogged down in traffic about four miles from the airport, and Mara had Squeaky change places with her so she was behind the wheel. Kerfer beeped the horn at her as she ran around the truck. He tapped his ear, indicating that he wanted her to turn on her radio. She got the truck going again, then did so.

"What's the game plan?" he asked.

"Straight to the airport, like I said."

"No shit."

"Just follow me."

"Leave the radios on."

"The batteries going to last?"

"We're taking off in two hours, right? We got plenty of juice for that. Little Joe's coming up to ride shotgun in the back."

"Why?"

"'Cause I'm fucking nervous, that's why."

Mara shook her head, but at this point there was nothing she could do about it. The SEAL hopped over the tailgate.

"Little Joe, you got your radio on?" she asked over the circuit.

"Big-time."

"Keep your gun in the bag. We don't want to be stopped."

"We saw a lot of people with weapons."

"They're militia. And they're not white."

Mara saw a 757 lifting off in the distance as the traffic snaked forward. They'd be doing the same soon.

As they edged toward the exit for Ha Huy Giap to get down to the airport, Squeaky saw that the ramp was closed, blocked off by a pair of military vehicles. Mara decided to try and talk her way through. She pulled off in front of the trucks, angled so she might squeeze past if one pulled back. The soldiers went over to the passenger-side window, eying Little Joe in the back suspiciously.

Mara had to lean across the others to talk. She spoke in the quickest Vietnamese she could muster.

"We have to get to the airport," she said. "I need to get on the highway."

"The highway is closed," said the sergeant in charge of the detail.

"But I need to get to the airport."

"Not by this road. It's closed."

She pleaded some more, but the soldier and the two privates with him simply walked away. Mara had to edge back into traffic.

"Why didn't you try bribing him?" asked Squeaky.

"I'm just about out of money," she said. "We could maybe buy a few loaves of bread; that's it."

"Can't grease a palm with spit," said Squeaky philosophically.

The ramp to Highway 22 was closed as well. Mara continued in traffic for another mile and a half, well past the airport, until she saw an open emergency ramp that led down to a city street. She followed several cars off, then began wending through the crowded, narrow city streets back in the direction of the airport.

The traffic thickened steadily, gradually choking off to an unsteady crawl. When finally she came in sight of Tuong Son, the main road to the terminal, she saw why—the airport entrance was closed. Cars were being sent down the road to make U-turns before fighting their way back into traffic.

"Stay with the truck while I find out what's going on," said Mara, hopping out.

Kerfer got out as well, trotting up behind as she walked down the line of cars. A pair of armored personnel carriers sat in the middle of the airport entrance. Two military policemen were directing traffic—or rather, trying to wave it onward.

"How do you get into the airport?" Mara shouted.

One of the men held his hand up to his ear. Mara squeezed around the tangle of cars and ran over to him.

"I have a flight," said Mara. "How do I get in?"

"No more flights today," said the policeman.

"I just saw a plane take off."

"No more flights."

"I need to talk to someone in charge."

The man ignored her.

"Hey!" she yelled.

He didn't answer, turning instead to a nearby car whose driver was crying that she was lost.

"We can just walk in," said Kerfer. He pointed to the lot across from them.

"What about the soldiers?" she asked.

"We duck around the side, back on the block where we turned. Near the end of that taxiway. There's no one there."

"You don't think there are soldiers inside?"

"We worry about them when we find them."

"It's too risky. If we get arrested, we may never get out," Mara told him. "Go back with Josh and the others. I'll find the officer in charge here and find out what's going on."

"Not by yourself," insisted Kerfer.

"You're a pain in the ass," she told him, starting toward the parking lot.

"And you're a bitch," said Kerfer, walking with her. "I'd say we're made for each other."

"Touch me and I'll deck you."

"I'd love to get physical."

"I doubt I'm your type."

"I'll just throw a paper bag over your head."

Mara would have decked him if they weren't being watched.

Kerfer started to giggle like a thirteen-year-old.

Jerk.

The soldiers wouldn't even listen to her questions. Mara walked parallel to the building, looking for an officer. She found a lieutenant having a cigarette on the sidewalk. He told her the airport was completely closed.

"I have a plane that's meeting me," Mara told him. "It's a charter. I have a little girl and—"

The officer cut her off, saying that she would need to take up her problems with the travel ministry. When she asked where the office was in the terminal, he replied that it was downtown, not here.

"Who can I talk to here?" she asked.

"No one," he insisted. Mara pressed him for his commander's name; the lieutenant finally gave her the name of a captain, who, he said, was back by the trucks where the traffic was being diverted.

"We can walk down that alley there, hop the fence, and get in," said Kerfer as the lieutenant went back to his men. "Easier than this bullshit."

"Yeah."

"What time's our flight?"

"It should be here in an hour," said Mara. "But they'll wait."

The area around the perimeter of the airport was packed tightly with buildings. They were halfway through them, heading toward the fence at the end of the runway, when DeBiase called her on the sat phone.

"Bad news, angel. Your airport's closed."

"No shit," said Mara. "Tell the pilot we're going to hop the fence. Ask him where to meet."

"You're not following me. They can't land. The Vietnamese closed the airport to civilian traffic. They mean business. There are armored cars on the runway. Word is they're using it for fighter operations tonight."

"You're joking, right?" she said.

"I wish. Apparently they have a dozen MiGs left and they want to make it easy for the Chinese to blow them all up," said DeBiase, as sarcastic as ever. "We'll get you out, don't worry. Why don't you go get something to eat? Get some rooms and relax for a while."

"You make it sound like we're on vacation."

"You're not?"

Washington, D.C.

This was not the way they taught it in civics class.

Then again, they didn't teach civics anymore. They didn't teach history, either. It was social studies, which was about as far from an accurate description as possible.

President Greene leaned forward against the long table in the White House Cabinet Room, trying to contain his anger as Admiral Matthews lectured him on the dangers presented to aircraft carriers by aircraft. This was just the latest round of whining, protest, and foot-dragging from the service Chiefs, who were determined to resist Greene's efforts to help the Vietnamese. Most of their resistance was passive-aggressive—find *that* in the social studies textbooks under separation of powers—but it was no less effective because of that. As far as Greene was concerned, it was a small step away from mutiny.

A very small step.

But the lecture was especially galling coming at five o'clock in the morning, an ungodly hour undoubtedly selected by the service Chiefs to keep him off guard. The bastards always fought at night.

The president decided that it was time to put the admiral and his fellow members of the Joint Chiefs of Staff in their place.

"Apparently, Admiral, you've forgotten that I was not only in the Navy for over twenty years, but that I was an aviator and flew off of aircraft carriers. And protected them, I might add."

The admiral shut up. The generals around him looked—"chastised" wasn't the word.

"Peeved" was.

Pampered jackasses.

"Now listen to me," said Greene. "You work for me. I understand the military damn well. I know pushback when I see it. I'm not going to stand for it."

Tommy Stills, the commander of the Air Force and a personal friend, started to protest. Greene put up his hand to indicate he shouldn't interrupt.

"I want U.S. ships close to the Vietnamese coast," continued Greene. "I don't give a crap about how the North Koreans are acting up, or how Russia's alleged battle fleet needs to be looked after. Taiwan can rot in hell for the moment. I want ships close to the oil fields. Period. Now."

"Do you want us to run the blockade?" asked Admiral Matthews. "That's the bottom line."

"I want us to *ignore* the blockade," said Greene. "We had a submarine off Hai Phong. It was supporting a mission—why the *hell* was it ordered to leave?"

"It had another mission."

"And that mission was more important?"

The admiral took a second before answering. Undoubtedly he was thinking of Greene's rank at retirement—captain—and found it galling to be questioned by him.

When he finally did speak, Greene cut him off.

"I thought it prudent to—"

"You thought it prudent?" Greene was having difficulty controlling himself. Showing his temper was counterproductive to the Chiefs. Outbursts only built resentment, which encouraged more backstabbing, greater foot-dragging, and even less candor later on. Any display of temper would surely be reported to Greene's enemies in Congress—now the Chiefs' best allies—within minutes of the session's end.

But damn it, he was commander in chief.

"Look, I'm not asking for a shooting war here," said Greene, trying to dial back his emotions and change tactics. "I want us to act like a superpower. That's what we are. We're the only ones who can stand up to this bully. Admiral, I know you feel the same way. This is pure Navy doctrine."

Matthews nodded. Greene wasn't really sure he did feel the same way. Matthews's predecessor had been lambasted for acting too aggressively at several points during the Malaysian conflict. As the previous administration's term wound down, he'd been dragged before not one but three different congressional committees and interrogated for his sins. The Army chief of staff, Renata Gold, had gone through the same process—one reason, Greene thought, that she hadn't said a word the entire meeting.

It was often said that generals always refought their last war. In this case, the war they were fighting was the one their predecessors had lost in Congress.

But to be fair, Malaysia had been a real fiasco, with Greene's predecessor caving disastrously toward the end of his term. The service Chiefs had no reason to see this any differently—there was no sense risking the lives of their people, or their careers, for a lost cause.

"You realize that this is 1939 all over again," said Greene. "Or maybe 1937. Same thing. Vietnam is Czechoslovakia."

"I don't think anyone is suggesting we partition Vietnam," said General Gold.

"Good." Greene didn't know what else to say. He turned back toward Admiral Matthews. "Tell the *Kitty Hawk* to turn up the steam. And let's have that destroyer—which one was it?"

"USS *McCampbell*, sir. DDG-85."

"Get it near the oil fields below Saigon," said Greene. "Posthaste."

"Aye, aye."

"Aye, aye, yourself," said Greene, trying, though failing, to inject a lighter mood. "More coffee, anyone?"

Ho Chi Minh City

Jing Yo's decision to stop chasing his quarry for the time being was not a surrender, but a recognition of the simple fact that he had to bow to fate. He must accept things as they were, bend like the tree in winter under the weight of the snow.

Nature made its own gesture, removing the rain that had made it difficult to drive and see. Jing Yo and Hyuen Bo stopped for a brief lunch, then set out again, moving at a good but not desperate pace. Considering the shelling an omen, he turned westward, reaching Route 14 in an hour. They passed several military convoys, but the soldiers took no notice of them, rushing north to meet the advancing Chinese army.

Jing Yo was able to buy gas in Buon Ho; they bought some vegetables as well as a snack. They stopped once more in Dong Nar, a small town north of Cat Tien National Park. With their gauge near empty and their reserves gone, they found the town's only gas station closed.

Jing Yo drove down the quietest side street he could find. He found a row of cars parked behind some houses. He drove next to them, and within moments fuel was flowing down his tube to the scooter. But as he checked to see how close to full he was, a man came out from one of the houses and began shouting. Jing Yo yanked the tube out and whipped away, losing the scooter's gas cap in the process.

It was nearly six before they came within sight of

Ho Chi Minh City. Jing Yo made his way to the Go Vap district on the northern side of the city.

The area combined dense residential neighborhoods with farm fields close to the river. Jing Yo navigated toward a set of large fuel-storage tanks not far from the city university, crisscrossing through the traffic as he zigzagged toward them. Finally he turned down a dirt road that dead-ended at a field near the tanks. He turned down the lone intersection and drove to a large house that sat incongruously between small sweatshops and broken-down warehouses.

A wide five-bay garage sat at the side of a large gravel parking area before the house. A gray panel van with a single round window sat in front of the last bay. Jing Yo parked his bike next to the van. He knew he was being watched, though there was no sign of a watchman.

"You have to wait for me," he told Hyuen Bo. "Just stay."

The house was nearly two hundred years old, built in a European style with a two-story portico in front. Two men stood behind the pillars at the front. They held guns—not the AK-47s common in the Vietnamese army and militia, but newer and deadlier German submachine guns.

As Jing Yo came up the steps, a thin man in his forties opened the door and stood on the threshold. He wore a black pin-striped business suit, and looked more like a banker than a butler or doorman.

He was neither. His name was Tong, and he was one of a rotating group of assistants used by the woman Jing Yo had come to see.

"Can I help you?" asked Mr. Tong, using English.

"My name is Jing Yo. I have come to speak to Ms. Hu."

Mr. Tong stepped back, letting Jing Yo in. Jing Yo had been here several times before, but if the man recognized him, he gave no hint of it.

"Sit here, please."

Jing Yo remained standing. The building smelled of exotic spices, jasmine and vanilla mixing with star anise and an earthy pepper. The wooden inlay of a dragon peeked out from beneath two heavy rugs. The chairs Jing Yo had been bidden to use were more than a hundred years old, made in and imported from France, and covered with Chinese silk that looked brand new, though it was as old as the wood.

Mr. Tong returned. "This way."

Jing Yo followed him through the central hall of the house, out onto a glass-enclosed patio, and from there into a garden at the back of the house. An older woman, known to Jing Yo only as Ms. Hu, sat at a small table near the center of the garden, sipping tea. Behind her, water bubbled in a large fountain. Statues lined the pebbled paths and grottoes in front of the trees, shrubs, and flowers that were arranged in the various beds: Here a Buddha sat under the tree after his rapture. There a Foo lion guarded the symbol of life.

"We have been expecting you, Jing Yo," said Ms. Hu.

Jing Yo bowed his head. Ms. Hu was small, not quite five feet. She was thin, though not quite so thin as to seem fragile. Her skin was extremely white, almost bleached, and far smoother than normal for her age, which Jing Yo had been told was near sixty. She wore a long dress. While of modern design, it was cut in a way that suggested tradition.

Hu in Chinese meant "fox," and Ms. Hu had all of the mythological characteristics associated with one. Jing was not in a position to know her exact responsibilities and duties, but he gathered that the petite

woman ran a sizable portion of the Chinese spy network in Ho Chi Minh City, and perhaps all of Vietnam.

"They doubted you would make it by nightfall,"
said Ms. Hu. "Did you have a difficult time?"

"It was easier than you would imagine."

"Good."

"You have information for me?"

"I have much information. Have some tea."

A butler stepped forward from the nearby shrubs, a
cup in his hand. Jing Yo waited while he poured. The
light scent of jasmine tickled his nose.

"Thank you," said Jing Yo before taking his cup.

"The man you are after is on his way to Ho Chi Minh
City. We believe he was trying to get to the airport, but
the authorities closed it a few hours ago. Where he will
go from there we don't know. Not yet."

"I see."

"Most likely he will go to District One and stay in
one of the hotels," continued Ms. Hu. "I have several
men in the area, searching. We have people throughout
the city."

"Is he using his satellite phone?"

"He has. But it is not as easy to track in the city. The
Americans have not been so kind as to share all of their
technology with us."

Ms. Hu took another sip of her tea. Her style was
reminiscent of a cloistered medieval Chinese empress,
concocting political plots behind the emperor's back
with understated finesse.

"I'm grateful for your help," said Jing Yo.

"Do not take this as an insult, Jing Yo," said Ms. Hu.
"I admire your persistence. But it seems that you have
not been your usual effective self. Not everyone is pleased
with you."

Jing Yo lowered his head. It was a warning more than an admonition.

"If our men are in position to kill him, they will do so," continued Ms. Hu. "I mean no insult, but this is a matter of some importance. I have heard from the premier's office directly."

"I appreciate your assistance," said Jing Yo again.

Ms. Hu nodded. "Why did they give you this mission?" she asked.

"I did not ask the question."

"Sending you behind the lines on your own—does your commander not wish to see you return?"

"I could have selected men to accompany me."

Ms. Hu took another sip of her tea. "You have someone with you," she said. "A girl?"

"She helped me get out of Hanoi. She has been very useful."

"She may prove to be a chain around your neck. You brought her here. That is not a good thing. Not for her."

"I vouch for her."

"I'm sure. Mr. Tong will give you an address where you can stay. Take the girl to the house and have her stay there. Mr. Tong has a phone for you as well. When we have information, you will be called."

"I intend to continue searching for him," said Jing Yo.

"Do as you wish. Just remember all that I have said."

"Thank you, Ms. Hu," said Jing Yo, rising. "I will."

4

Ho Chi Minh City

Most of the large foreign hotels were located in or near District 1, the heart of the city adjacent to the Saigon River. DeBiase arranged for rooms at the Renoir Riverside Hotel, a well-appointed skyscraper on the riverfront. Mara spent the last of her money buying some luggage and a few shirts at a secondhand store, hoping to make the SEALs look less like soldiers and more like tourists when they checked in.

"We don't want to all check in together," she told Kerfer as they cleaned up a bit in the back of a small restaurant. "Why don't you go in first, get a room, and make sure things look good."

"No shit."

"Don't get pissy with me. I'm not the one who closed the airport."

"They should have evaced us out of Hanoi," said Kerfer. "Nobody's got any balls."

"Hey, the submarine belongs to the Navy, not us," retorted Mara. "Where the hell was it?"

"I would have swum for it, if was up to me," said Kerfer.

Back in the vehicles, they started hunting for a place to park. Mara wanted the truck and car near enough to the hotel so that they could retrieve them if they needed to, yet far enough away to avoid suspicion if the vehicles were discovered. By now, even Squeaky was getting cranky. As they circled through the crowded downtown area, he groused that the police had far better things to do than check for stolen registrations.

"The plates show where the cars come from," Mara said. "Let's not screw this up by getting lazy."

"I'm not saying to get lazy."

Mara finally found a place to park in a lot at the back of a row of small stores. She pushed the truck against a chain-link fence, and had everyone get out on the other side. Kerfer did the same thing behind her.

"We stay together until we get two blocks from the hotel," said Kerfer. "Then Little Joe and I go ahead. We get our room, Joey comes down and gives the high sign. You, Josh, and the tyke go in, register. Then everyone else. Ones and twos. Sound good, lady?"

"It'll do."

"You with us, mad scientist?" Kerfer asked Josh.

"Hanging in there."

A t first, being out of the truck invigorated Josh. It felt good to move his legs. There was a gentle breeze, and the air, though damper than it had been up north, had a cool feel to it. But after a block, Josh felt his energy running down. His stomach and lower abdomen felt as if they were on fire. He struggled to keep up even with Mạ, who tugged at his hand as she walked.

"It's not too far," said Mara, slowing her pace.

"I'm okay," he insisted.

"We can sit up ahead and rest. There's a bench there."

"Let's just go to the hotel."

"We're going to make sure it's safe first." She put her hand to his forehead. "You're not as hot as you were."

"Good. Your hand feels nice."

"Are you hungry?"

"No. It hurts."

"Where?"

"Here. When I eat. And everything."

"Here, let's sit on this bench."

She took his elbow and guided him to the bench. Josh folded his arms in front of his chest, wishing away whatever it was that had gotten into his system. He closed his eyes.

He thought of the train, then the hand poking from the ground. . . .

A siren wailing nearby jarred him. He jerked up, alert, worried. A police van rushed by, then another—they were at the head of a group of black Mercedes sedans. A pair of motorcycles escorted them. A troop truck took up the rear.

"What was that?" Josh asked.

"Just a diplomat," said Mara. "Can you walk?"

Josh got up, legs stiff. Mạ looked at him doubtfully.

"Just two blocks," said Mara. She hooked her arm in his. Mạ took his other hand.

Mara was nearly as tall as he was, far taller than any woman he'd ever dated.

"The hotel's up there," said Mara. "I'll talk."

Was he attracted to her? Or just feeling lonely?

He wasn't lonely. Sick, yes. Tired. Not lonely.

The grip of her arm was reassuring.

"Okay?" she asked. "I'll get the room."

"Of course."

D eBiase had arranged to forward money through the hotel's international parent, but the hotel would disperse only a few hundred dollars cash. The clerk told Mara that the banks were still operating, and he gave her a list of nearby ATMs. She sensed that he was just trying to get rid of her.

She took Josh and Mạ up to the suite room. Mạ threw herself on the couch and immediately dozed off. Josh insisted he was fine, but Mara told him to go to bed. DeBiase had arranged for a doctor; as soon as she was sure all of the SEALs were squared away—they were all in rooms on the same floor, Kerfer right next door— she called his office.

He was there a half hour later. He introduced himself as Dr. Jacques. His accent seemed more Russian than French, but Mara wasn't about to question him. He took Josh's temperature, then sent him to the bathroom with a cup for what he delicately called "le sample."

"You've had sex?" the doctor asked.

"No," said Josh. "Not recently."

The doctor looked at Mara.

"I don't know if he had sex," said Mara. "And it wasn't with me."

"You have a urinary infection," the doctor told Josh.

"What about my stomach?"

"There, too."

Jacques opened the battered North Face backpack he used as a medicine bag. He took a prescription pad out. "This is an antibiotic," he said. "The hotel can help you get it filled."

He wrote out the prescription and handed it to Josh. Then he wrote another one and gave it to Mara.

"What's this?" Mara asked. "A backup?"

"Both people need them."

"We didn't have sex."

The doctor zipped up his bag without saying anything else.

Kerfer stayed with Josh while Mara went down to the desk to see about getting the prescription filled. After giving it to the concierge, she took a walk around the hotel, getting a feel for what was going on. The atrium lounge, normally fairly busy at this time of day, was almost empty; the only guests were a nervous-looking European woman and two small children, who were fidgeting on a couch packed with suitcases.

The hotel's Kabin Chinese Restaurant was considered one of the best in Southeast Asia; Peter Lucas raved about its fish and dim sum. It was about a quarter full. Upstairs at the Club Lounge on the penthouse level, all of the tables overlooking the river were empty; the few patrons in the place were huddled near the bar.

The sun had just set. Ordinarily, the view of the river and nearby city would have been spectacular, lights beginning to glow everywhere, ships passing below. But now the view was one of a darkened city. Boats passed as shadows below in the waning light. The far bank looked like a cluster of cards set down on an uneven table, waiting for players to arrive.

A waiter approached as Mara scanned the horizon. "The lights will be turned off very soon," he warned in English, "because of the war restrictions. Would you like a drink?"

"No, I'm good," she said, though she instantly craved one. "I was just leaving."

Josh and Kerfer were watching television when she got back to the room. The newscaster was telling a story about how the "glorious forces" had won a "courageous victory" against the "dastardly invaders." The newscast was in Vietnamese, but an English translation, more or less accurate, rolled across the bottom of the screen.

"Things must be worse off than we thought," said Kerfer, "if they're already declaring victory."

He drained the beer he had in his hand and went to the minifridge to fetch another.

"Better go easy on that," said Mara.

"I'm not driving."

The can opened with a loud pop. Kerfer took a swig, then went over to the desk and took a pad of paper from the top drawer.

Place bugged? he wrote.

"Maybe," answered Mara.

"When do we get out of here?"

Good question, she thought. She bent over and wrote, *I have to call home in a few minutes. I'll find out.*

"Good," said Kerfer.

It will take a few minutes. I have to find a good place to call where I won't be overhead.

Kerfer put his hand on her back. She almost jumped.

"Sooner we're out of here, the better," he whispered.

Mara straightened. "Yes."

Kerfer pulled over the pad. *You want me to go with you?*

"I can manage," she said.

"**S**he ain't that bad-looking," Kerfer told Josh after Mara left.

"I didn't say she was."

"But that's what you were thinking. You go for the brainy type, I'll bet."

"I don't have a type."

"Sure you do. Everybody's got a type."

"What's your type?"

"Naked and drunk. In that order." Kerfer laughed and sat down in his chair. "I think she likes me. What do you think?"

Josh shrugged.

"You want her for yourself, huh?" Kerfer laughed again. "Don't worry, Josh. If it turns out we're going to be here for a while, we'll find somebody for you. Plenty of girls in this town."

"Uh-huh."

"That how you got sick?"

"No."

"You sure?"

"Yeah."

"Probably from something you drank," said Kerfer. "Shame, though. You gotta pay the price, you oughta at least enjoy the meal."

Mara crossed the street in front of the hotel and began walking north along the edge of the park bordering the river. A naval patrol craft was tied up at the landing nearby. She walked past it, catching glimpses of the ship through the trees.

Mara spotted a bench as she neared the entrance to the ferry slip across the Saigon River. There was no one else nearby, so she sat down and took out the phone.

DeBiase answered as soon as she called. "I hope they fluffed the pillows for you," he told her.

"First-class service," she said. "What's the deal on our flight?"

"We're still working on it. We're trying to stay under the radar."

"Damn it, Jess, this is bullshit. Just get us the hell out of here."

DeBiase took a long, slow breath, the sort he always took before putting on his sturdy professional voice. Sure enough, his next words were almost surreally calm.

"We'll get you out. There's a lot of politics involved, Mara. Not just there, but at home."

"Crap on the politics."

"I know you're tired. Keep it together."

"I'm not tired," she said. "Josh is sick. He's got some sort of urinary tract infection. The doctor said it might be in his kidneys. We have to get him out."

"Did you get him medicine?"

"I'm working on it. That's not the point."

"Tomorrow the airport will reopen. The airplane will come in. You'll go out. Why don't you get a good night's sleep? That's what you need."

Politics. Mara wondered if maybe some people in the agency didn't want them to get out. Maybe they wanted to see Vietnam crushed. Or maybe a few dead Americans would help whatever cause they were pushing.

Maybe somebody's father or uncle or brother had been killed during the Vietnam War. Ancient history to most people—but not if the war took someone close to you. Personal grudges had a lot more to do with what happened in the geopolitical world than people thought.

"You're still with me, Mara?"

"I'm here."

"Listen, I'm getting pinged," he said, using one of his slang expressions for receiving a message over the secure text message system. "Lucas wants to talk to you. He needs to talk to Josh, too. He's in D.C."

"Josh isn't with me."

"That's okay. Can you get him?"

"I don't know. He may be sleeping. I told you, he's sick."

"I know. . . . Why don't you see if you can get him, though? We'll call you in a half hour."

"When you call, tell me when the airplane is going to pick us up," she said.

"I'm doing my best."

Ho Chi Minh City

Ms. Hu's assistant Mr. Tong gave Jing Yo the key to an apartment in District 5, better known as Cholon, or Chinatown. The area would not have been Jing Yo's first choice. But he was not in a position to argue.

A notice was posted in the entrance hallway to the building declaring that the city was under complete blackout rules as of 8 p.m. All patriotic citizens were expected to comply. A similar handbill had been pushed under the door of the apartment.

The unit was spacious, with two bedrooms besides a large living room and kitchen. There were a few pieces of furniture, low couches and tables in the Vietnamese style, as well as two Western-style easy chairs.

"Some tea?" Jing Yo asked.

Hyuen Bo went to the kitchen to make it. Jing Yo followed.

"I don't want this tea," said Jing Yo loudly, inspecting the cupboard. "I've had this tea—it is always disagreeable."

Hyuen Bo looked at him, confused.

"Let's see if there's a shop on the street," he told her. "It should take only a minute. Come."

She followed him out silently. He explained on the street.

"It is likely our conversations will be overheard by spies," Jing Yo told her. "I should have realized this before. You must be very careful. Talk very little."

"How long are we staying?"

"I'm not sure," said Jing Yo truthfully.

His phone rang. It was Mr. Tong.

"Your subject is in District One. Near the river. We will give you more details shortly."

The line went dead.

"I have to go see someone," Jing Yo told Hyuen Bo. "I'll be back."

"When?"

"Soon. I'm not sure. In the meantime, trust no one."

"I trust you."

Jing Yo felt a pang. He was the last person she should trust, though he didn't have the heart to tell her.

Ho Chi Minh City

Kerfer insisted that Josh eat something and had a burger and fries sent up from room service. As a precaution he had it delivered to Little Joe's room, but it still got to Josh steaming hot.

The grilled meat tasted far better than Josh had thought it would, and he quickly finished it, surprised at how hungry he was.

"One thing you have to learn, kid, is keep your strength up." Kerfer nursed his beer. "Your body's a furnace. Keep it hot."

"Isn't that how I got sick? Eating stuff?"

"You just ate the wrong stuff. Besides, who cares how you got sick? You work on getting better. War is an endurance race," added Kerfer. "It's a marathon. You're a scientist. You ought to know this shit."

"I have allergies. I can't eat certain things."

"Like burgers?"

"Burgers I can eat."

"Then you're good. What kind of allergies?" Kerfer asked. "Like hay fever?"

"Yeah. It has to do with the enzymes. They're the same as in the pollen. I can't eat apples. Nuts."

"Beer?"

"Beer I'm okay with."

Kerfer went over to the minifridge.

"You have your choice of a Foster's that looks like it's been in the fridge since Saigon belonged to the French, or a Tsing Tao. Chinese beer. Foster's is a can," added Kerfer, "Tsing Tao is a bottle."

"Bottle."

"Reasonable choice." Kerfer took it out.

"Doesn't seem to twist off," said Josh, after nearly tearing his hand on it.

"Gimme."

Josh handed it over. He wouldn't have been surprised if the SEAL had used his teeth to rip the top off. But his solution was much more elegant, not to mention dentally hygienic—he placed the cap against his belt buckle and popped it off.

"You'll feel better in a few," said Kerfer, handing it over.

Josh took a small sip. The cold liquid was bitter in his mouth.

Mạ was sleeping on the couch. Kerfer had put a blanket over her.

"Wish I could sleep like that," said Josh.

"You do. You just don't realize it," said Kerfer. He pulled over the chair and leaned back. "You like being a scientist?"

"Scientist? Yeah."

"Why?"

"Always find something new."

"About the weather?"

"About how plants interact with it. And how we interact with plants."

"We eat them."

"If there are any."

"Plenty of plants, kid."

"Not really. That's what this war is about."

"It's about oil, kid. You notice how cheap gas is here compared to anywhere else? Hell, you can fill up a car with less than a hundred bucks."

"The government subsidizes it."

"Sure, because they're Commies. But the reason they can do that is they have the oil fields offshore. You know what gas goes for back in the States. You think we could subsidize it?"

"No. But we're not Communists."

"Not yet," said Kerfer.

"Really, it is about food," said Josh. "China's in a drought. Their crop production has been cut in half each year over the past three. That's a huge amount of rice."

"And?"

"Vietnam is getting two and three crops a year."

"That's because of the weather?"

"Partly. And changes in the seeds and the way they grow. That's what the war's about. Food."

There was a knock on the door. Kerfer went over, pistol out. "Yeah?"

"It's Mara. Let me in."

He cracked the door open, peeking into the hallway before letting her in.

"What are you doing with a beer?" demanded Mara as soon as she saw Josh. "You're supposed to be sick."

"Don't go schoolmarm on the poor kid, for Christ's sake," said Kerfer. "He's trying to get better."

"What is that, SEAL medicine?"

Kerfer smiled. But Mara remained cross.

"They told me downstairs the prescription came," said Mara.

"Little Joe brought it up," said Josh.

"Let me see the pills."

"Man, you are a schoolmarm," said Kerfer.

Josh handed over the bottle.

"They're some sort of penicillin thing," said Kerfer. "I checked them. You think I'm going to let him take poison?"

"You have him drinking beer."

"It's good for him."

Mara rolled her eyes. "Put the beer down. We have to go for a walk," she told Josh. "Do you feel up to it?"

"I can walk."

"What's up?" asked Kerfer.

Mara pointed to her mouth. Josh guessed that she was reminding them that the room might be bugged. Then she pulled the headset out of her collar, indicating she'd have the radio on. Meanwhile, Josh pulled on his shoes.

Stevens and Little Joe were sitting in the lobby when Josh and Mara came down. The SEALs shadowed them out of the hotel, staying a few yards back as they crossed the street.

Night had fallen, and most if not all of the buildings in the city were observing the blackout rules. But with a clear sky, there was enough light to see through the trees to the river. A few people walked along the sidewalks, passing them quickly, heads down. But as they walked northward, Josh spotted groups of people gathered near the riverbank, talking among themselves, or occasionally staring at the water. A few young couples held hands.

"Let's go back the other way," said Mara. "There are more people than before."

They turned around and went back, walking past a naval ship tied up at the dock. Mara took his hand, wrapping her fingers in his. Then she leaned toward him.

"Are you okay?" she whispered.

"Yeah."

"You're slowing down."

"I'm okay."

"I want a spot where it's not easy to hear us," she said. "All right?"

"Okay."

"You have to talk to my boss. Peter. Is that all right?"

"Sure."

Mara guided him through the trees to a cluster of rocks on the shoreline. As soon as they sat down, she took out her phone. Josh leaned back, elbows against a rock, trying to look at ease.

He definitely felt a little better than he had earlier. Maybe Kerfer was right about the beer.

A small fishing boat moved across the river in their direction. As it drew near, a woman pushed out from under the canvas tent at the middle of the boat and went to the prow. She had something in her hand, and Josh felt a moment of anxiety, worried that she might have a gun. But it was just a line; she was getting ready to tie up at the dock about thirty yards to his right.

"Peter wants to talk to you," said Mara, handing Josh the satellite phone.

"Yes?"

"Josh, how are you?" said Peter Lucas.

"I'm okay," Josh told him. "A little tired."

"I've heard what's on the video, the files you gave Mara. It's incredible," said the CIA officer. "Everything."

"I hope it can help."

"It *will* help," said Lucas. "I have someone here who'd like to speak to you. All right?"

"Sure, I guess."

The phone clicked. A new voice came on, a little louder and clearer.

"Josh MacArthur?"

"I'm here."

"This is George Greene. Are our people taking care of you?"

"Mr. President? President Greene?"

"I'm here. Are you getting good care?"

"Yes. She's, they're—I'm doing fine."

"Good. I heard what happened. It's a terrible tragedy. Horrible."

"Yes, sir."

"You have pictures and video?"

"Yes, sir."

"Can you tell me where you got them?"

"Um, well, I had this little Flip 5 video camera. It's not very good quality, but it's good for snapshots and little videos."

"Where were you when you took the video, Josh?" asked the president.

"I don't—see, that's our base camp. But the others . . . I had to go through this village. I don't know how far away I went."

"But it was definitely in Vietnam?"

"Yes, sir. We were pretty far from the border. I mean, a couple of miles. You know—I don't know. Five?" Josh felt he was making a fool of himself by being so tongue-tied. He closed his eyes, trying to concentrate. "It was definitely inside Vietnam. I went—that night, I think it was, I found the border to the north. I was always in

Vietnam. There was a big fence. And guards. And then these trucks came down. They looked like Vietnamese trucks but—"

"Was there resistance at the science camp?" asked the president.

"No, sir. Well—I started to sneeze and I woke, and I had, uh, I had to uh, uh—"

"Nature called," said the president drily.

"Yes, sir. Anyway, I walked away from the camp, and then I was sneezing and I wanted not to wake anyone. So I went a little deeper into the jungle. The next thing I knew there was gunfire."

"The scientists didn't have guns, did they?"

"No, sir. Not that I know of. We had a couple of Vietnamese soldiers with us, but they'd gone to bed."

There was a pause. For a second, Josh thought the line had gone dead.

"Josh, we're looking forward to talking to you when you get back," said Peter Lucas, coming back on the line. "All right?"

"Yeah, of course."

"You're going to be home real soon. Please give me Mara."

"Okay. Uh, thanks."

"No, thank you."

7

Aboard USS *McCampbell*, South China Sea

Dauntless in Battle.

A nice phrase, surely; the perfect motto for a warship. But they were just words until put to the test.

Commander Dirk "Hurricane" Silas thought about his ship's motto as he strode across the bridge, casting a wary eye on the helmsman and the long row of controls and instruments necessary for her to do her job. Like all members of his family—including and especially the nine-thousand-ton guided-missile destroyer that held them—the petty officer was dedicated and squared away. Her eyes were focused, her hair very neatly trimmed.

Silas stopped and peered forward through the destroyer's bridge windows, into the dark, vast emptiness before him. To all appearances, the *McCampbell* was alone on the ocean, alone in the universe, a solitary ship making close to thirty knots, a hair off its listed top speed.

But appearances were deceiving. A Chinese cruiser and frigate were just beyond the horizon to his right, shadowing his course. The cruiser was one of the most accomplished vessels in the Chinese fleet, aside from the country's two recently completed aircraft carriers. Commissioned as the *Wen Jiabao* and named after a recently deceased premier, it was an extensively refitted Ukrainian ship, the *Moskva*, sold to China ostensibly as scrap two years before. At 186 meters long and nearly 21 meters at beam, it was a good bit bigger than the *McCampbell*. The *Wen* carried at least sixteen long-range P-500 Bazalts, known to NATO as SS-N-12s, antiship cruise missiles with a range of roughly 550 kilometers or about 340 miles.

The weapons posed a formidable challenge, easily capable of sinking most ships. But the *McCampbell*'s Aegis system had been specifically designed to handle this sort of threat. Like her sister *Arleigh Burkes*, she could put three or four SM2 Block IV missiles into the air against each P-500 in less than a minute. It would be a serious workout, but one the DDG could probably handle.

Silas would love to see it try.

He stepped out of the enclosed bridge onto the deck. There was something about standing here, high above the waves, that still seemed magical some twenty years after his first "real" ocean voyage. It was more than the physical sensation of the wind and the light, salt-mixed spray in the air. Silas felt a link to the men he'd grown up reading about, the old captains and seadogs who put themselves on the line, warriors whose every breath seemed to inspire heroic deeds.

Looking back on the stories from the perspective of an adult, he knew that they had glossed over many things—hardships for one, failures for another. No man facing the sea was *always* courageous, and no one facing an enemy's gun could claim that his stomach didn't occasionally hint of mutiny. But the omissions were unimportant; on the whole, those stories told a greater truth about human nature than a meticulously accurate log ever could.

Or at least what Silas thought human nature should be.

Unfortunately, the days of heroes were gone. The Navy wasn't anything like it had been during the cold war, let alone back in the days when the crisp crack of a sail filling with wind told a sailor all he needed to know about the weather. The idea that a single captain and crew could take destiny into their own hands was a quaint, even forlorn notion. The *McCampbell* was connected to the rest of the world by a suite of communications systems and sensors. Silas's commander could look at a screen and know instantly where the destroyer was.

So could half the Pentagon.

The day was not far off, the captain believed, when the Tomahawks and enhanced Standard missiles in his vertical launching tubes would be fired by some desk admiral in the basement of the Pentagon.

"Captain, you have a minute?"

Silas turned and saw his executive officer, Lieutenant Commander Dorothy Li.

"Sneaking up on me, Exec?"

"No, sir."

Silas sensed trouble in Li's voice. She wasn't usually half this formal with him.

"Shoot," he told her.

"Captain, as I understand our orders, we're to proceed toward Cam Ranh Bay, staying in international waters. Correct?"

"You know the orders as well as I do."

"Permission to speak freely."

"Hell, Dorie, you don't have to be so formal. What's up?"

"Back channel on this is not that good." She shook her head. The stiff tone remained in her voice, and it was obvious she was choosing her words very carefully. "Desron's passing along orders, but flashing stop signs everywhere. Dirk, I think we're being set up for something political."

Desron referred to the destroyer squadron the *Mc-Campbell* was assigned to. Li had spent considerable time working under the squadron's commander before joining the *McCampbell* as its new executive officer four months ago. Silas had no doubt that she was able to hear things that he wasn't—that was pretty much her job description as the ship's second in command.

"All right. So tell me. What exactly is the back channel?" Silas asked.

"Well." Li paused and looked behind her, making sure there were no other sailors within earshot. "A lot of people think the president is itching for a war. The Chinese have announced a blockade of Vietnam. Our orders are basically to test it."

"That's not in the orders."

"No, not in so many words. But the words that are there add up to that."

Silas turned to starboard. "You see that over there, Dorie?"

"I don't see anything."

"There are two Chinese ships over there, shadowing us."

"I realize that."

"A few hundred miles farther north, they have a carrier task force."

"Uh-huh."

"The captains on those ships know that we know they're there. But they haven't attacked us. You know why?"

"Because we're not at war."

"Because they know if they try to attack us, we'll sink them both. It's about force, Dor. They know we're stronger than they are. That's why they don't attack. That's the reason we sail to Cam Ranh. And beyond if we have to."

"I'm missing you, Cap. I don't get the logic."

"We have to show them we're not afraid. Or a year from now, maybe six months, they won't hesitate to attack us. And then there'll be real problems."

8

Ho Chi Minh City

Jing Yo was not surprised that the American would go to the Dong Khoi district, the downtown area that contained not only most of the large foreign hotels, but also the most familiar tourist landmarks. It was an area that would have the most foreigners, and make it harder to spot him.

The traffic was extremely light, and until Jing Yo left Cholon he saw few police officers or soldiers on the streets. Near the river the number of policemen multiplied exponentially. Several streets were blocked off. When Jing Yo reached Nguyen Thi Minh Khai—one of the main thoroughfares through the district—he was stopped by a roadblock.

"Why are you out driving?" demanded the policeman who stopped his scooter. "You should be home."

"I'm going to work," said Jing Yo. "My wife said the same thing."

"Where do you work?"

"Bun Cha Hanoi," he said, naming a famous restaurant in the area.

"I am sure the restaurant is closed," said the policeman, but he waved Jing Yo through without even bothering to look at his papers.

The area Mr. Tong had directed him to was over a mile long, and without more information it would be extremely difficult to locate the scientist. Jing Yo decided he would cruise along the waterfront, not so much in hopes of finding him but so that he was likely to be nearby when Tong called with more information.

He got less than halfway before meeting another roadblock. A pair of army trucks had been parked across Ben Chuong Duong, the main road running near the water. Here there was no possibility of being let through, so Jing Yo turned back westward, found a place to park, then set out on foot.

He'd gone a block when his phone rang.

"He is near Bach Dang Jetty," said Mr. Tong. "They are still talking."

Jing Yo resisted the urge to run. He was already walking in the right direction, just three blocks from the jetty itself.

Jing Yo walked across Ben Chuong Duong, normally choked with traffic at this hour. Small groups of Vietnamese were standing on the opposite side, clustered around the park that ran along the riverfront. There were more in the park itself, close to the water, almost as if they were gathering for a performance or some entertainment—fireworks, perhaps. Jing Yo caught bits of their conversation as he passed. They gossiped not about the war or the danger they were in, but about trivial matters—work, an in-law's boorish manners.

Jing Yo had seen the photographs of the scientist from the UN Web sites, but he wasn't sure whom Josh MacArthur was with. Soldiers had helped rescue him from behind the lines, but how many was impossible to say.

A half dozen, he thought, had been involved in the firefight when the scientist managed to escape. Jing Yo assumed they would be with him now.

The bodyguards would not stop him from achieving his mission. On the contrary, if they were with him they would make the scientist easier to spot—most foreigners stood several inches taller than Vietnamese, and a cluster of them would stand out from the others.

Jing Yo walked all the way north to the ferry station without spotting anyone who might be his subject. He turned back, wending his way closer to the clusters of people this time.

If MacArthur was calling from this area, it was likely that he was staying in one of the nearby hotels. A number lined the block, and there were more scattered behind them. Jing Yo decided he would check out each of them after one more pass between the jetty and the ferry terminal.

The difficulty of his mission gnawed at him. He tried to clear his mind, to focus on the task at hand.

Instead, he thought of Hyuen Bo.

It had been a mistake to bring her with him to see Ms. Hu.

She might be in danger—she *was* in danger. Ms. Hu had made that clear enough.

This might be a ruse to get him away from the apartment. It had to be.

Just as the idea occurred to him, he saw a pair of figures climbing off the nearby rocks. They were tall, foreign. One was putting away a phone.

He was too far away to see, but immediately he assumed it was Josh MacArthur.

"**W**hat do we do now?" Josh asked Mara as they started up from the riverbank.

"We get some sleep," she said. "Our flight should be here first thing in the morning. How are you feeling?"

"Well, I kinda gotta pee."

"Kinda gotta?" She laughed.

"Yeah. I'm just—my stomach and my sides are sore, but I feel better than I was."

Mara threw her hand up, catching Josh in the chest. "Hold on," she told him.

J ing Yo realized one of the people was a woman. That couldn't be right.

He was three or four meters away. The shadows made it hard to see faces.

The pistol was in his belt, beneath his shirt.

Two people? Just two? A man and a woman?

His instinct was clearly wrong.

And yet, it felt right.

Desire, tricking him.

Jing Yo saw them stop. He stopped himself, then decided he would walk as close to them as possible. But as he took his first step, someone bumped into him from the back, shoving him to the ground.

"Hey!" shouted the man in English, very loudly. "Watch where you're going! What are you doing?"

Jing Yo rolled over. The man was an American, smelly and obnoxious.

"My wallet!" yelled the man. "Help! My wallet!"

His instinct must have been right—this could only be a member of the scientist's security team, posing as a tourist.

Jing Yo looked to the right—the man and the woman had fled.

"Sorry, sorry," said Jing Yo, holding up his hands as he got up. He spoke in English as well. "Sorry, mister. Sorry, sorry."

He backed away as the man continued to shout.

———

M ara steered Josh out of the park as Little Joe continued to shout behind them.

"What's going on?" asked Josh.

"Keep moving."

Squeaky was near the street. "We're clear," he said over the team radio. "Spook?"

"Yeah, we're good," answered Mara. "You see us?"

"Yeah, yeah, yeah. Stevens is on your left."

"All right, I see him. I'm hiding the radio," she added, sticking it down under her collar. "We're going to the hotel. You see anyone else?"

"Negative. Get inside. We're watching."

They went in a back entrance to the hotel, trotting up fifteen flights of stairs because Mara didn't want to risk the elevator. By the time they reached their floor, Josh looked pale.

Kerfer met them at the room. "What happened?"

"I don't know," said Mara.

Kerfer got the pad and gave it to her.

Little Joe thought the guy was following us, she wrote.

One guy? wrote Kerfer.

Maybe there were more.

You see him?

No, but Little Joe bumped into him. He'll have a description.

We shouldn't stay here, wrote Kerfer.

I agree.

Wow, no argument?

"Give me a break, Navy," said Mara.

She went to the bathroom and ran some water on her face. Mara doubted the man was anything but a random stranger who'd had the misfortune of walking a little too close to them, but there was no point in dropping their guard now. He could easily be a spy. Saigon was full of them.

Back in the suite room, Mara took one of her paper maps of Vietnam and sat in a chair. They could retrieve the cars and drive to the Cambodian border. Embassy staff in Cambodia could help them get to Phnom Penh; from there they could fly to Thailand and then back home.

"Whatcha doing with the map?" asked Kerfer.

Mara shook her head. She didn't want to say anything, in case the room was bugged.

"There's a club on the roof." Kerfer motioned that they could talk up there. "Want some air?"

"Sure." Mara looked at Josh, who was lying on the bed. "You want to come?" she asked.

"I don't want to leave Ma."

"We'll take her," said Kerfer. He went over and picked the little girl up in his arms.

Josh got off the bed slowly. They went up in two elevators.

"Easier to protect you if we're all together," Kerfer explained as they reached the club.

Technically, the club was closed. But about a dozen guests were there, milling around tables that were lit by small candles in dark-colored vases. Mara led the way to a glass door she'd seen earlier. The door opened onto a narrow terrace overlooking the riverfront.

"Nice night," said Kerfer.

"It's a beaut." Mara walked toward the edge of the large patio. A pair of lovers stared into the southern distance on the opposite end of the roof terrace. Otherwise, the Americans and Ma were the only ones here.

"So what are you thinking?" Kerfer asked.

"Maybe we should just get the hell out of here," she

told him. "Drive over the border. We can probably get there in a couple of hours."

"You don't think there's going to be all sorts of refugees lining up?" asked Kerfer. "It'll be nuts. Especially now that they closed the airport."

"I don't think so. It doesn't look like they're taking the war too seriously here. They're ignoring it."

"Can you get gas?"

"I don't know. Maybe Bangkok can find some."

Little Joe, Squeaky, and Stevens came up to the terrace with an armful of food and beer. They'd walked around half the town to make sure they weren't followed, buying supplies before returning.

"Don't go too crazy with the beer," said Kerfer, grabbing a pair out of the bag. "We may be moving out tonight."

"Who was the guy in the park?" Mara asked.

"Just some slant-eye local," said Little Joe. "But he was kind of close. I didn't like it."

"You just wanted to hit somebody," said Squeaky.

"Maybe."

"Don't call him a slant-eye," said Mara.

Kerfer smirked.

"So we leaving, skip, or what?" Stevens asked.

"Me and the spook are working that out," said Kerfer. "Why don't you guys go get a little rest? Be ready to leave in an hour."

"Fuck, an hour," said Stevens. "Ain't worth taking a nap."

"Go get some rest. We'll wake you up if we have to. Take Josh and Junior down, too." Kerfer turned to Josh. "Okay? You get some sleep. We'll wake you up if we're moving."

"All right," said Josh.

"What was so funny?" Mara asked when they had left.

"Which?"

"Slant-eye."

"Ah, give it a rest, spook."

Mara saw a dark line growing at the edge of the sky behind him. She stared at it for a moment, not comprehending what she was seeing. It was as if the sky had a fold in it, and the fold was moving, arcing. It dropped sharply below the building.

Kerfer turned around to see what she was staring at.

The city flashed white where the black line had fallen. The sound of the blast came a moment later. The hotel shook with the force.

"Shit," he said. "More of them, there."

The missiles were all aimed at the airport. Three more exploded in rapid succession. A massive orange and red flame erupted in the distance.

Mara heard the sound of jets in the distance. They were following up the missile raid with bombs. Antiaircraft batteries began to fire. There were large flares in the distance—missile launches, Mara guessed. Sirens began to wail.

"Gonna be a lot harder for these people to ignore the war now," said Kerfer.

CIA Headquarters, Virginia

Peter Lucas hated being at Loony Corners, his nickname for CIA headquarters. It was his impression that no matter what else was going on in the world, the top priority for everyone in the building was internal politics.

With the exception of the people on the top floor, who were concerned with administration politics as well.

But having been summoned from the field, Lucas did his best to play his role as grizzled field agent, recalled to reinforce whatever opinions were current for the day.

Lucas walked down the glass-lined hallway toward the Starbucks on the first floor. There was free coffee upstairs where he was working, but he preferred the harsher brew Starbucks served.

That and he wanted the walk from the stifling surroundings.

"How's it going?" Ken Combs asked as he got on line.

"Not bad," Lucas told Combs, surprised to see him at headquarters. "How about yourself?"

"I could tell stories. But they won't get me anywhere."

Lucas knew a few of the stories Combs could tell. They had both been in Baghdad when a conflict with the FBI cost two Americans their lives. Combs had blamed himself for following procedure and notifying the FBI of the situation. Of course, if he hadn't done that, he would have been fired—and the Americans would probably still have been killed.

"Back for a while?" Lucas asked.

"Back for a bit. Yourself?"

"Not sure."

"Maybe we should have a beer sometime."

"Sounds good."

Lucas bought his coffee, then went back to his desk to prepare a briefing paper for the agency chief, Peter Frost. Lucas liked Frost, largely because he was an unlikely choice for the job: Frost had been a field officer, then rose through the ranks to become the deputy director of operations—the head of covert activity—before retiring. A personal friend of the president, he had been appointed DCI—director, central intelligence—as soon as Greene came into office. While it was certainly a political appointment, Frost was the first director in quite a while to have such an extensive operational pedigree.

On the other hand, Frost had served in Asia two decades before, covering a lot of the ground Lucas did now. Frost's experiences colored his perceptions, and he tended to micromanage based on things that were dead and buried years ago.

Lucas was worried about Mara. Getting her out of Ho Chi Minh City had looked like a no-brainer just twelve hours before. Now the reports said the country's situation was deteriorating rapidly. The airport had just been bombed, and the border up near Cambodia was a mess. Vietnamese troops had reportedly been shooting at people trying to flee over the border. Cambodian border guards had done the same.

Lucas returned to the small cubicle he'd been given to prepare his report. With his coffee cooling, he reviewed the military updates from the past hour. When he did, he realized that the destroyer *McCampbell* was steaming on a direct line for Ho Chi Minh City. It was still far off—but almost close enough, he thought, to send a helicopter to pick Mara and company up.

With a little work, some prompting and arm-twisting.

Lucas jumped up and started for the Secure Communications Room. The phone on his desk rang as he turned back for his coffee.

It was undoubtedly one of Frost's assistants, asking when the briefing was going to be ready.

"Soon," said Lucas, grabbing the coffee and rushing to the hall.

10

Ho Chi Minh City

Jing Yo sipped his cup of tea pensively, staring across the plain of darkness before him. The flashes of bombs and secondary explosions turned the night into a cityscape of white staccato. The light seemed to be attacking from below, cracking through the surface. The gunboat on the river behind him began firing its weapons. The bullets were undoubtedly useless, but Jing Yo understood the impulse, the need to respond in some way, to show that you were not merely a victim.

It was another manifestation of ego, an empty gesture born from the temporary world, not the permanent Way. And yet, at this moment he felt closer to the men firing those guns than to the commander who had sent him here.

The monks would nod sagaciously at that.

Jing Yo thought of Hyuen Bo. The apartment he had left her in was southwest of where he was sitting, to his left. The attacks were to the north, concentrating on the airport and military facilities nearby.

The ground rumbled with a trio of salvos. A great red glow erupted in the distance. Jing Yo turned his gaze toward it, losing himself in meditation as if staring at the flame of a candle. Conscious thought floated away. His mind became a cloud, easing toward a hilltop, filtering into the trees, assimilating everything.

He would have his target. He was somewhere nearby.

The satellite phone rang. Jing Yo reached for it mechanically.

"Yes," he said.

"Did you find him?" asked Mr. Tong, speaking Chinese.

"He was in the park at the river, with a woman and at least two other Americans," said Jing Yo. "I lost him. But he remains nearby. I can sense it."

"Where are you?" asked Mr. Tong.

"I am across from the Renoir Hotel."

"You should be in a shelter."

Jing Yo didn't answer.

"Go to the basement of a building, and stay there until the attack ends," said Mr. Tong.

Again, Jing Yo didn't answer.

"Our people will help you find him," said Mr. Tong, whose voice rose with his anxiety. "It is dangerous at the moment. Not just because of the attack. If the soldiers see you outside, they'll think you're crazy. They could lock you up as an insane person. You should not be outside."

"As you wish," said Jing Yo, ending the call.

Hyuen Bo was still sitting on the floor of the apartment when he returned. She'd left the door unlocked.

Jing Yo sat next to her. By now the bombing had stopped. The stars and moon gave enough light for him to see the smooth curve of her cheek as it glided toward her mouth. Her skin was that of a doll, unblemished, its pale hue glowing.

"I saw my mother," she said. "She came to me with her hand outstretched. She needed food."

"What did you do?"

"I had nothing for her."

"You're with me now."

He put his arm around her. Hyuen Bo's body folded

into his, becoming another arm and leg. Their lungs filled in a tight rhythm, his breathing hers.

The ground shook. More missiles were striking the city. This time the explosions were closer. Jing Yo guessed that the government buildings were being attacked. They were barely a mile away. The walls seemed to heave with the loud claps of the explosives as they ignited. A baby cried somewhere nearby.

Hyuen Bo's body trembled against his. Gently, he pushed her to the floor and they began to make love.

11

Aboard USS _McCampbell_

"Message for you, sir."

Commander Silas grunted into the phone, then hung it up. Some things about being in the Navy never changed—no matter when it was you went to bed, someone was bound to wake you up.

In this case, it was Washington.

Or actually, suburban Maryland. When Silas keyed up the secure e-mail system, he found a message requesting that he contact the CIA officer supervising Southeast Asia on a secure line as soon as possible.

Which got his attention. A few minutes later, he found himself talking to Peter Lucas.

"We have people in Ho Chi Minh we need to get out," said Lucas. "They were coming out by plane but it looks like the airport may be closed down permanently. Could you pick them up?"

"I'll have to check the Saigon port facilities," said Silas. "But it shouldn't be a problem."

"How long will it take?" Lucas asked finally.

Silas did a mental calculation. "Less than twenty-four hours, more than eighteen," he said finally. "We may be able to shave—"

"That may be too long. I want to get them out of there by daybreak."

"Daybreak?"

"Saigon's been bombed. The Chinese navy is moving down the coast. The sooner we can get them out of there, the better."

"We have a pair of Seahawks," said Silas. "I may be able to get close enough to the coast to have them there early in the morning. Not quite dawn. But by noon."

"That'll have to do. I'll find a landing strip and call you back."

12

Ho Chi Minh City

Things had gone to hell in less than an hour. The attack on the airport had been bad enough, but the strike on the downtown government buildings had provoked a panic. Mara, looking out the window facing north, counted eight different fires and knew there would be many more to the west. Army, militia, and police vehicles raced up and down, without a discernible pattern. Sporadic gunfire rang through the streets. The city had gone mad.

The hotel staff began going door to door, telling the

guests that they must meet for "special instructions" on the emergency, and escorting them down to the hotel's grand ballroom. Kerfer suggested they bug out of the hotel immediately, but Mara decided it would be wiser to see exactly what the authorities were up to. The street didn't seem to be a particularly safe place at the moment.

The ballroom wasn't as crowded as she'd thought it would be. Fewer than two hundred guests were still at the Renoir, somewhere between half and a third of its normal complement. Management had rolled out a table with pastries and cookies, along with an array of non-alcoholic beverages. Mạ, clinging to Josh, grabbed a fistful of cookies and stuffed them in her mouth.

Senior staff walked through the room, trying to make light chatter. The only thing guests wanted to talk about was the possibility of leaving the city, but this was the one thing the staffers couldn't address. The stillborn conversations simply increased the anxiety. Mara stayed next to Josh and Mạ. Little Joe and Stevens huddled next to them, taking turns making faces at the little girl. Kerfer and the rest of the SEALs filtered out through the room, always circling nearby to keep an eye on them.

A young Australian couple introduced themselves to Mara and Josh, the woman swearing she had seen them at breakfast.

"Oh, uh-huh," said Mara. She was certain that the pair must be intelligence agents of some sort, most likely curious about whether they were as well. "How long have you been in Saigon?"

"Just a few days," said the Australian wife. "We got here before the war started. I didn't think it was real until this evening. And how long have you been here?"

"Two weeks," said Mara. "My husband is a scientist."

"What do you do?" asked the woman.

"He's a biologist," said Mara, purposely misunderstanding. "He's not feeling very well tonight. Something he ate."

"Is this your daughter?" she asked.

Mạ hid her face.

"She's adopted," said Mara.

"She's very cute."

"Thank you."

"She was an orphan," said Josh protectively.

Mara sharpened her gaze, trying to remind him to keep the details fuzzy.

"Ladies and gentlemens, please," said the manager, speaking at a small mobile podium at the front of the ballroom. "If I could have everyone's attention."

Mara pushed Josh gently to the side, edging away from the Australians. She reached for Mạ, who reluctantly climbed over to her.

"You're getting heavy," Mara whispered in Vietnamese.

"Can we have more cookies?" replied Mạ.

"Sshhh. I'll get some."

"You are all aware that there has been an attack—two attacks—on the city," said the manager. His English was heavily accented, and Mara had to concentrate to understand what he was saying. "I apologize for the inconvenience this has caused. Please under-sand that this attack is a terrible breach of international law and we are doing everything we can to avenge it. Our forces are pushing the Chinese back this very moment. . . ."

The manager kept glancing toward two men in business suits near the doors. It wasn't too hard to guess that these were party or government officials, and the real audience of the manager's speech.

"Tan Son Nhat International Airport will reopen in

the morning," continued the manager. "At that time, we will be providing free buses to the airport. The buses will be accompanied by some of our finest troops and police officers. There will be not reason for concern or alarm. Your safety is our utmost. Thank you. Thank you for staying with us. Please enjoy our snacks and beverages."

Guests began shouting questions. The manager started away from the podium. Glancing at the men in the back, he changed his mind and returned to answer the questions. But most were about things he had no answer for—when the phones would be working, where the Chinese troops were, how planes would be available at the airport.

Mara felt her satellite phone beginning to vibrate.

"Come on," she told Josh, signaling with her eyes.

One of the men in the suits called to them as they reached the hall. His English was crisp and, while accented, clear.

"Where are you going?" he said.

"We have to go to the women's room," said Mara. She held Mạ up slightly, as if she were the reason. Mạ kept her face buried in Mara's shoulder.

"And you?"

"Me, too. To the men's," said Josh.

The man frowned but said nothing else. Mara heard his footsteps behind them as she walked across the reception area toward the hall where the restrooms were. She didn't want to split up, but she had no choice; the man in the suit would most likely follow Josh into the restroom.

"Go to the last stall," she told him. "I'll tell Kerfer you're there."

"I do have to pee," said Josh.

"Good," said Mara. "Just go. Act normal."

"Is she okay?"

"Just go."

Mara gave him a peck on the cheek in case their follower had reached the corner. Then she pushed into the ladies' room, took the first stall, and put Mạ down.

"Kerfer—if you can hear me—Josh is in the men's. Send someone."

She pulled the earset up just in time to hear him growl that they were already on it.

Mara pulled out her phone and dialed Bangkok. DeBiase came on the line immediately.

"Bad timing?" he asked.

"Hotel management is explaining how Vietnam is winning the war," she said.

"How long will it take you to get down to Vung Tau?" he asked.

"Where?"

"The peninsula. Down where you picked up Starry when we were trying to get those RPGS over to—"

"Okay, okay, yeah. I can get there. The airport?"

"Yeah."

"It's open? It's got a really short runway."

"That's not a problem."

"I don't know when we can leave," Mara told him. "They're enforcing the curfew. We've heard gunfire outside on the streets. One of the SEALs heard rumors that the Chinese were sending paratroopers."

"That's nonsense."

"I realize that." Mara looked down at Mạ. The tired girl clutched Mara's pants leg, her fingers squeezing the cloth so tightly her knuckles were white. "I'm not sure if we'll be able to get gas. Or that our cars are still going to be there."

"I have fresh cars for you."

"How?"

"They're clean, don't worry."

"Jess, I don't know. That guy in the park—"

"Mara, I'm every bit as paranoid as you are," said DeBiase. "Waiting around in Saigon isn't a great idea."

No shit, Mara wanted to scream.

"We'll have a big party when you get back," added DeBiase. "Maybe I'll even get my hernia done."

"Tell me where the cars are," she said finally. "I'm not sure when I'm leaving. I have to think about it. We'll get there eventually."

"I'm sure you will, darling." DeBiase's voice flickered with concern. Then he added lightly, "You gotta make the call. Go when you're comfortable."

J osh's cheek stung where Mara had kissed him, as if her lips had somehow short-circuited his nerves there. He sat on the commode, waiting while the Vietnamese official pretended to wash his hands. Or maybe he really did wash his hands—the dryer whooshed on three times before the man left the restroom. A moment later, Kerfer came in, humming a tune.

"Going to the chapel, gonna get ma-a-ar-ried."

It was such an incongruous song for the grizzled lieutenant that Josh started to laugh.

"Gonna get mah-ah-ahrried," repeated Kerfer, going over to the urinals.

"Hey," said Josh.

"Don't forget to flush."

Josh came out and washed his hands.

"Where're the girls?" asked Kerfer.

"Went next door."

"If you guys want to have a quickie, remember to hand the kid off to Squeaky first."

Josh felt his face flush. He waved his hands under the dryer.

"Still hurt when you pee?" said Kerfer.

"Yeah."

"Go ahead out," said Kerfer, going to the dryer. "Squeaky's out in the hall."

"You think you have to stick this close?"

"Gives the guys something to do," said Kerfer. "Otherwise they'll end up with the same thing you got."

"I say we get the hell out of here," said Kerfer. "Sooner the better."

Mara reached down to the banquet table at the back of the ballroom. The manager had been replaced by a small string ensemble playing something by Mozart. Fifty or sixty guests remained, including the Australian couple, who were busy chatting up a tall Frenchman on the other side of the room.

"We're going to have to wait until morning to leave," said Mara. "They're enforcing the curfew on the streets."

Kerfer made a face.

"I know you don't think much of the Vietnamese," Mara said. "But their guns have real bullets."

"Once we're outside of the city limits, it'll be easy," said the SEAL. "And my guess is that they're only patrolling here, calming the tourists. Or cowing them."

"What's the gunfire about then?"

"Idiots panicking," said Kerfer. "Where are these cars?"

"Across the river. I'm sure the bridges will be blocked."

"We go by water then."

"The ferry isn't running. You want to swim?"

"I've swum a lot farther," he said. "We'll put you, Junior, and the kid in a life raft and tow you across."

"You probably would."

They stayed in the ballroom for another half hour. Stevens reported that guests were being barred from the lobby area, and that guards had been posted at all of the doorways. He'd tried to get upstairs to the lounge, but the doors were all locked.

"And they cut the electricity above this floor," said Stevens. "We gotta walk up to our rooms."

"Probably a miracle that there's electricity anyway," said Kerfer. "I'd like to get up to the roof and see what's going on."

"Club's locked, Cap."

"Spook can get us in," said Kerfer. "Right, beautiful?"

"Maybe if you stop calling me beautiful."

"Okay, ugly puss."

"You don't give up, do you?"

"Not in my vocabulary."

The video surveillance cameras worked off the electricity, and with no electricity they weren't operating. Mara had to get through two locks to get them into the club and out to the terrace. Neither was very difficult. Little Joe and Stevens stayed below as lookouts; everyone else came up. Squeaky carried Mạ, who'd fallen asleep. She looked almost like a doll in the big man's arms.

A huge fire was burning only a few blocks from the hotel. Its glow was so intense that the nearby streets seemed to have turned orange, as if the sun had set between the buildings.

"Balmy night," said Kerfer.

"Picture perfect," replied Mara.

"What's on fire?" Josh asked.

"That's the airport in the distance," said Mara. "They probably set the fuel stores on fire. Closer in, I'm guessing government buildings. Those over there are natural-gas fires. That's just a big building."

"You an expert on fires?" said Kerfer.

"I've seen more than a few."

Mara walked over to the edge, scanning the river. The gunboat that had been tied up nearby had moved northward to the middle of the channel. A smattering of small boats were docked on the far shore, but otherwise the river was empty. The street in front of the hotel was empty. A troop truck sat in the nearby intersection, but Mara couldn't see any soldiers.

"I'm gettin' kinda tired," said Josh. "Are we goin' back to our rooms or what?"

"Maybe we'd better," said Mara. "We'll leave in the morning."

She started for the doorway to get back into the enclosed area.

"Hold on," said Kerfer, his hand over his radio earphone. "Someone's coming up the steps."

13

Ho Chi Minh City

Jing Yo had dozed off on the mat where they'd made love, falling into a dreamless sleep. He missed the final round of attacks, which struck fuel supplies north of the city as well as a military base to the west, and slept through the roar of the fire engines and military vehicles racing to deal with the destruction. He woke more than an hour later, in the quietest part of the night, with no reason to wake but the internal mechanisms of his mind. When he woke, he was refreshed, as calm and alert as on any of several thousand mornings as a young man in the mountains, studying to become an adept. He woke with his mind decided on what to do:

After he completed his mission, he would take Hyuen Bo and escape to Myanmar. There were countless places to escape there, and as long as his mission was completed the government wouldn't press too hard to find him.

Colonel Sun might. But that was a separate problem.

Hyuen Bo was sleeping next to him. He put his hand down on her back, pressing it gently. He realized now that their fates were intertwined. He was not seeking to escape his karma, but fulfilling it.

The phone Mr. Tong had given him began to ring. Jing Yo rose, and took it with him to the kitchen.

"This is Jing Yo," he said.

"We have located your subject."

"Where?"

"Meet us behind the Rex Hotel as quickly as you can."

"I'm on my way," he said, though the connection had already been broken.

When Jing Yo looked up from the phone, he saw Hyuen Bo standing at the door to the kitchen.

"Where are you going?" she asked.

"I'll be back."

"I want to go with you."

"No."

He started past her. She clutched at his chest. "Please."

"It won't be safe. I'll be back in an hour."

"You're lying," she said. "You told me you never lie."

"I'm not sure when I'll be back." Jing Yo felt ashamed for lying, but he simply couldn't allow her to come. "I will be back. Be ready to leave."

"Will they let us?"

"Don't worry," he said, putting his finger to his lips.

The location sounded wrong to Jing Yo—it was in the center of the city, far from where he had seen the Americans earlier. And to get there, he would have to pass through part of the city that had been bombed earlier.

The more he considered it, the more he told himself that he must take Hyuen Bo with him.

Not that there was any question of her staying in any event.

He thought of running then, of leaving the country and going to Myanmar. But he had no proof of their treachery, and in the end, Jing Yo decided he must at least try to do his duty.

The Rex Hotel was to the northwest, more than two miles away. Hand in hand, they left the building where they were staying and went down the street. Within a block, Jing Yo began to trot. Hyuen Bo kept pace.

His plan was simple. He would hide her near the building when they arrived, then come for her when he was done. They would leave immediately, never to return.

They'd gone only a few blocks when Jing Yo heard the sound of trucks approaching. He pulled Hyuen Bo back into an alley they'd just passed, and pushed her behind some garbage cans to hide. Then he ducked next to her, craning his neck to see.

Two pickup trucks drove by, the beds crammed with militiamen in street clothes, red rags and bandannas on their arms and heads to identify themselves, at least to one another.

As soon as the trucks passed, Jing Yo ran up to the corner. He watched as the trucks pulled into the middle of the intersection ahead. The men at the rear jumped out.

One of them yelled angrily. Several lifted their rifles and began to fire, spraying the nearby buildings with slugs. Men spread out in each direction, shouting and walking, firing indiscriminately at the buildings.

"They're saying the Chinese citizens are traitors," whispered Hyuen Bo. She'd come up so quietly that he hadn't heard her. "They're taking revenge for the attacks. This is Chinatown."

"I heard them," said Jing Yo. "Why aren't you hiding?"

"I need to be with you."

"The people who live here are Vietnamese."

"Not in their eyes."

Two of the men approached down the block. Jing Yo eased Hyuen Bo back against the wall, tucking her into the shadows, then edged to the corner.

Even if they both hid behind the garbage cans, the militiamen would have no trouble seeing them if they walked down the alley. Escape would be impossible.

Jing Yo would have the advantage if he struck them as they walked past, but doing that might bring the attention of the others.

Let them walk past? What if they turned at the last second and saw him?

Too much of a risk, Jing Yo decided as the first man drew parallel to the alley. The second followed a half moment later.

"Traitors!" yelled the first man, lifting his gun to the sky.

Jing Yo's foot caught him in the throat as he leapt into him. Rolling off the kick, Jing Yo caught the second man with hard punch to his startled face. A second chop rendered him unconscious, collapsing his windpipe and making it impossible to breathe.

Jing Yo grabbed the man's rifle as it clattered to the ground. Then he ran to the first man and with a fast kick to his forehead sent him to eternity.

"Stay!" Jing Yo hissed to Hyuen Bo, tossing her the gun. "Wait for me!"

He grabbed one of the bandannas, then ran down the block, in the direction of the trucks.

The other militiamen were too busy shooting their weapons to pay much attention to what was happening to their comrades down the street. The two men detailed to guard the trucks had their own pressing project—breaking into a small liquor store near the corner. They left the trucks to the drivers and began looting it.

The drivers had parked the trucks so they could talk to each other. They leaned out their windows, chatting, as Jing Yo ran toward them.

"What are you doing?" snapped one.

Jing Yo shot from the hip as he ran. His first bullets sailed right, but he pulled the gun back smoothly, and with three bursts killed both men.

The guards came out of the liquor store just as he reached the back of the nearest truck. Their arms were filled with bottles. Jing Yo stopped, turned, and fired, cutting both of them down with the last bullets in the magazine.

Jing Yo ran to the bodies, searching for more bullets and grabbing a bandanna for Hyuen Bo. As he did, he heard her shriek a warning from down the block.

He threw himself down, tumbling as the slugs from a militiaman's rifle shot overhead. The man let go of the trigger and took a step forward, lowering his rifle.

A single shot rang out. Hyuen Bo had killed the man.

14

Ho Chi Minh City

Josh knelt by the side of the table, waiting with Mạ behind the others for whoever was coming up the stairs. He was tired—beyond tired. His eyelids felt as if they were on fire.

And he was angry. He wanted to just get the hell out of there, to go home.

And he was frustrated. He wanted to help—he was still awed by the president's words, by the fact that the president himself had spoken to him. But sitting here, on the roof of a hotel, hiding—it was a waste of time.

"Here we go," whispered Kerfer.

Josh wrapped Mạ in his arms. "Gonna be okay," he whispered.

The door opened. A man with a pair of night goggles appeared in the doorway.

A light shone in his face—a flashlight blinding him. Before he could react, Kerfer had leapt from the side and run his knife across the man's throat. He dragged him out of the doorway, blood gurgling from the slit in his throat.

Josh kept Mạ's face buried in his chest.

Mara took the man's gun. It was a Chang Feng—a small 9mm Chinese submachine gun.

"Those goggles may be handy, too," said Kerfer. "Still think this place is safe?"

"I didn't say it was safe," snapped Mara.

Mara put her hand to her ear, listening to something over the radio.

"Two more on the stairs," she said. "Josh, let's go. You okay with her?"

"I'm okay."

Mara said something to the girl in Vietnamese. Mạ didn't react.

Kerfer went to the door. Mara knelt on the other side, waiting.

Josh knelt next to Mara. He felt his mind empty, as if it were a dump truck and the back had just tilted up to let go of its load. He waited, sure that he would kill someone if it came to that, but not in the least having an idea how that would be done. His first job was to protect the girl.

The door opened slowly. It seemed to take an hour for it to move the first inch, then another hour for the second. Suddenly it was flung open.

Nothing happened. A minute passed. To Josh it felt like an entire day passing.

Then there was a yell, and one of the men leaped inside.

Kerfer took him out with a single shot to the head. Mara rolled on her shoulder, firing the small gun she had taken from the other man into the stairwell.

There was a quick burst in the stairwell below.

"Clear!" yelled Stevens.

"Let's get the hell out of here," said Kerfer, grabbing the night glasses from the dead man and starting down the stairs.

Josh scooped up the fallen man's submachine gun, then followed Mara down the steps.

15

Ho Chi Minh City

Jing Yo took the truck, speeding down the street before the rest of the militiamen realized what was going on.

"Put the bandanna on," he told Hyuen Bo.

As he passed the alley, he saw the bodies of the men he had killed and got another idea. He stopped, grabbed the smaller of the two men, and threw him into the back of the truck. A few blocks later, he stopped again.

"Put his shirt and cap on," he told Hyuen Bo. "Tuck your hair up. You'll look more like one of them."

She did so. It worked—to a point.

The soldiers manning the first blockade they came to accepted them as militiamen, but would not let them through.

"Our orders are no one, not even government officials," said the sergeant who stopped them.

Jing Yo backed the truck away without arguing. He went down the block and took a turn toward the river. There were soldiers on the corners, but no roadblocks until Dien Bien Phu. Here a policeman waved him to the right without bothering to question them, recognizing the vehicle as one of the militia trucks.

A crowd of soldiers massed at Ho Ky Hoa Park, and the overflow extended down toward the main roads, with military jeeps and trucks blocking sidewalks. Jing Yo drove around the back of a row of stores and found a place to park in a small yard next to a garage.

"Stay close to me," he told Hyuen Bo, leading her across the back alley to the row of small buildings on the opposite side. He helped her onto the roof of a small shed at the back of one of the buildings, then brought over a garbage can for a boost and climbed up. From there they made their way to a fire escape that went up four stories to the back of the tallest building on the block.

Jing Yo surveyed the downtown area from the roof. There were several fires to the west and the north, in the general vicinity of the government buildings. By contrast, the area near the river, where he had seen the scientist earlier, was dark.

Had he been sent in the wrong direction? Were the spies so confident of their position that they would purposely risk his capture?

Or was the scientist actually where they said?

He didn't have the luxury of puzzling it out. He had to act. Jing Yo decided to look by the river, where he had seen him earlier.

If he didn't find him, he would cross the water and take Hyuen Bo to a new hiding place. The old one was in too dangerous an area, even if he had not been betrayed.

Ho Chi Minh City

Mara edged down the stairway, right hand on the wall. The night glasses were not quite as good as American models, with a very fuzzy grain. But in the pitch-black darkness, they were a godsend.

Stevens was waiting at the first landing below the club level. The man he had killed was crumpled against the wall. He was wearing dark clothes, and had no identification on him. Like the others, he was armed with a Chang Feng.

Stevens had already taken the goggles and was two floors below. Kerfer sent Squeaky and Little Joe to round up the others and meet them in the basement.

"We'll take the stairs down," Kerfer told Mara. "I say we hurry."

"I want to see if he has a wallet," said Mara, rifling the dead man's pockets.

"What are you going to do, steal his credit cards?"

"I want to see who it is who's out to kill us," said Mara.

"Gotta be Chink spies," said Kerfer. "Don'tcha think?"

Mara ignored him. The man's pockets were empty. It was possible he was just a thief, but Kerfer's theory—minus the ethnic slurs—made the most sense to Mara.

"Josh, you okay?" she asked.

"I'm good. Feeling better."

"How's Mạ?"

"Okay." He had his hand covering the back of her head, pressing gently so her face stayed toward his shoulder. Given everything she'd seen earlier, though, it was doubtful he was protecting her from very much.

"Do you have your medicine?" Mara asked.

"I, uh—"

"You left it in the room," said Mara.

"Yeah."

"We ain't goin' back to get it," said Kerfer.

"I'll get it," said Mara.

Kerfer grabbed her arm as she started down the steps. "I don't think it's a good idea. You think they sent only three people into the hotel?"

"I don't know how many they sent," said Mara. "But we're only one floor away. He needs the damn medicine."

"We'll get more once we're out of here."

"Who knows when that will be?"

Mara knew she was being stubborn, but she pushed on anyway, going down to the next level and cautiously opening the door. The battery-fed emergency lights had come on, bathing the hallway in a pale yellow. She pulled the goggles down around her neck and eased out into the hall.

"Clear," she whispered.

"We're staying here," said Kerfer.

"That's fine."

Mara slipped into the hallway. She started to tiptoe, then realized that made no sense. She walked slowly, sliding against the wall as she came to the elevators. One of them had stopped on the floor, door open; it was empty.

She eased past and walked to the room, taking the key card out of her pocket.

The nearby emergency light would frame her as she entered. She backed over to it, then reached up with the butt of the gun and broke both bulbs.

Most likely, there was no one in the room, she told herself.

Most likely.

Mara got down on one knee, her body against the wall, and reached over to put the card in the lock. She plunged it down.

The lock's LED didn't light. Apparently emergency power wasn't routed to the locks.

Mara put her hand on the door handle and pressed down. It didn't budge. Even without power, it remained locked.

Mara pulled out her wallet and retrieved a thin piece of metal from behind the credit cards. She slid it into the lock space, positioned the hard surface of her fist against it, and gave it a sharp rap, opening the lock.

Then she threw herself down as bullets exploded through the wood.

A second later, something protruded from the door.

A head.

A gunshot rang out from down the hall. The man went down. A second man, behind him, fired a burst, then retreated.

"You shoulda opened it from the side," grunted Kerfer, running up next to her. His gun stank of cordite.

The man he'd shot had fallen against the door, propping it open. Mara, submachine gun ready, slid down on her belly and eased toward the room, angling slightly toward the opposite wall.

Whoever was inside had retreated into the bedroom at the right or into the bath area on the left. It was impossible to tell which one.

There was no way to get inside without exposing herself.

It wasn't worth it.

"What are we doing?" Kerfer asked.

Mara was just about to start backing out when she heard something on her left.

The bathroom.

She threw herself forward, firing two bursts at the door.

There was no answering fire. She got up.

"Mara!" hissed Kerfer.

"Stay," she commanded. She kicked at the door just below the handle, fired a burst into the empty room.

The bullets shattered the commode and part of the sink, but they were unnecessary. The Chinese agent was lying in a pool of his own blood on the floor, already dead.

"What the fuck, '*stay*'?" said Kerfer behind her. "You think I'm a dog?"

"Ask Josh where his medicine is," she told him.

He growled into the radio. Mara spotted the bottle on the ledge above the sink before anyone responded. She grabbed it.

"Bathroom above the sink," said Kerfer. " Come on, let's go. We got people coming up from the stairs. Shit."

Mara heard the sound of gunfire below.

"They're coming up the stairs, six of them," said Kerfer as they reached the hall. "We'll have to go back to the roof."

Mara passed the elevator, then went back to it and looked in the car. There was a trapdoor in the ceiling, an escape hatch.

"We can take the elevator shaft," she yelled. "One of the cars is here."

"There's no electricity."

"I know. We'll climb down."

"Now you're using your head."

Mara waited by the elevator as Josh and Stevens came out from the stairwell.

"The medicine wasn't worth this," said Kerfer.

"If it weren't for the medicine, we would have run right into them," said Mara. "Where's the rest of the team?"

"They're on floor five."

"Tell them to meet us outside."

"We may need them," said Kerfer.

"Give me a boost," she said, standing under the trap-door.

Kerfer stepped over, cradling his hands together. Mara climbed up.

"You're heavy," said the SEAL.

"Are you going to criticize *everything* about me?"

She pushed the door open and pulled herself up into the space, then pulled the goggles up to her eyes.

Josh came up behind her, then reached down for Mạ. Mara handed him the pills.

"I'm sorry I forgot them," he said.

"Don't worry about it. Can you see anything?"

"No."

"Just stay here. You're two feet from the edge."

"Okay."

Mara leaned over. "It's going to be okay," she told Mạ in Vietnamese.

"Yes," said the girl in a voice so soft Mara could barely hear it.

The two elevator shafts were separated by a set of girders that were easy to pass through. The next car was several stories below, though Mara couldn't tell exactly how far. Maintenance ladders were mounted in race-ways on the far side of the opposite shaft, as well as the near side here. The easiest thing to do was to climb down the ladder in this shaft and look for a mainte-nance door, hopefully in the basement. From there, they could get out.

But first they needed to collect the rest of the SEALs, who now found themselves trapped on floor 5 between the Chinese and three Vietnamese policemen who'd responded to the call of gunfire. Kerfer told them to go to the elevator and try to open it. But with nothing to use as a lever, even Squeaky couldn't pry the doors apart. Worse, more black-clad gunmen appeared as he tried. The SEALs managed to get to the stairway, but they were taking gunfire from both above and below.

"The best we can do is come up behind them," said Mara. "We climb down, get over to the other elevator car, get out there, and then ambush them in the stairs. How many are there below them?"

Kerfer asked his men. They weren't sure. Two or three.

"Are they sure they're Vietnamese?" Mara asked.

"They didn't ask for IDs."

Kerfer went to the side ladder and began climbing down.

The rungs of the ladder were covered with a greasy grime, and there was considerable dust in the air. Mạ, her arms around Josh's neck, clung to him as he descended. The submachine gun hung off his back, occasionally swinging out with his momentum and then smacking him in the kidneys as he climbed back.

Josh felt a sneeze coming on. He tried holding his breath to snuff it out, but finally it exploded. His whole body shook.

"God bless you," said Stevens above him.

Josh sneezed again. He moved his foot down to the next rung, but started to slip. He caught his balance and buried his face in his shoulder as he sneezed again.

"Hope that ain't catchin'," said Stevens.

"Allergies. Dust."

"You okay, Josh?" asked Mara below him. "Let me take her."

"No, I'm okay," he said, sneezing again.

The space from the side of the elevator shaft to the cables at the center was too wide to get across easily, so Kerfer kept going all the way to the basement. He waited until Mara reached him before trying the small hatchway door.

It was locked.

"Little Joe, how are you guys doing?" Kerfer asked over the radio.

"We have them pinned down near the stairs."

"Make some noise when I count three, all right?"

"Bullets?"

"Unless you got a foghorn." Kerfer looked at Mara. "On three, we kick this thing out."

"All right," she told him, moving over.

"They may be waiting," he said. "You have right, I have left. Be ready."

Mara positioned the submachine gun. She had about half the magazine left.

Josh was still sneezing above them. Mara heard Mạ starting to whimper.

"One," said Kerfer, counting over the radio.

As soon as he hit three, the SEALs on floor 5 began shooting. Mara kicked at the door with her heel. It gave way easily, flying open. She uncurled herself and dove into the basement, rolling in a thicket of spiderwebs.

Kerfer jumped in after her. Her side of the basement was clear; the only things on the wide floor were support pillars.

"Stevens will stay with you," said Kerfer. "Get across the river as quickly as you can."

"We can back you up."

"No, get the hell out of here. We'll keep them busy."

"Listen—"

"Do your job, spook. You got a baby and the mad scientist to worry about."

Mara frowned at him. But he was right. Her job was to take Josh out alive.

And Mạ. Though now she regretted not finding her an orphanage.

"You stop sneezing?" she asked.

"For now," said Josh, sniffling into his arm.

"You're allergic to dust?"

"And about a million other things."

"Come with me," she said, taking hold of his arm. "How are you doing?"

"My bladder feels like it's on fire," confessed Josh.

"Stay close to me."

"There's no light."

"Hold my shirt."

She tugged him along as she explored the basement, looking for a way out. A large freight elevator sat at the north side of the complex, apparently connecting to the backstage area of the ballroom above. There was a large steel door on the wall diagonally across from it, but it was chained shut.

"We can shoot off the lock," said Stevens, raising his gun.

"They may hear it upstairs and realize someone's down here," said Mara. "They'll catch your captain from the back."

"You're right. Okay."

Mara inspected the freight elevator. It was large and

simple, open on both sides and the top. A set of rungs extended up the right side. The first opening was two floors up and protected by a metal cage that looked as if it would swing out when the elevator arrived.

Or maybe it was locked. There was some sort of mechanism near the shaft.

There was only one way to find out. Mara began climbing.

She could hear Kerfer's heavy breathing on the radio.

"You out yet?" he whispered.

"We're working on it," said Mara.

"Well get it going."

The cage was made of mesh. Mara could barely get her fingertips in. There was a small lip on the floor where it met the shaft, but this was only three inches wide. She eased out toward a cross-member, pushing gently, then a little harder. It didn't budge.

The screen extended only halfway up the opening, and Mara thought she could squeeze over it and get down on the other side. The problem was, she didn't think Josh could. And Stevens would never fit.

"The gate is a mesh fence," she told Stevens. "It's locked. I'm going to try climbing over it and then find the lock. Hold on. It's very hard to climb."

"I can do it," said the SEAL.

"Your fingers are fatter than mine," she told him. "Just relax."

Mara managed to get a few feet up, then quickly slid down. Her fingers were just too big for the holes.

She looked at the locking mechanism. It was a simple lever, but there didn't seem to be a way to reach it from this side.

"What about the kid?" asked Stevens.

"You mean have her climb over?" asked Josh.

Mara looked at Mạ. Was she strong enough to climb over?

The girl was tired, and just a few minutes ago had been crying.

"I don't think so," said Mara.

J osh looked at Mạ. The girl sensed that they were talking about her, though since she didn't speak English, she had no idea what they were saying.

Could she climb up over the fence?

He'd seen her dash through the jungle, swinging like Tarzan on some of the vines. But this was different.

They could catch her if she fell on this side, but on the other side, she'd be hurt.

No worse than if the Chinese caught them. If the Chinese caught them, she'd be dead.

"We gotta do something," said Stevens.

"Josh—do you think she could?" asked Mara.

"I don't know."

"You said she was tough in the jungle."

"Ask her," he said, dropping to his knee and putting her feet on the ground. "Ask her."

M ara repeated her question twice. Mạ didn't answer.

"Like this," said Mara, putting her fingers against the grid.

Mạ leaned away from Josh, her left hand still on his shoulder. It was almost as if she were protecting him, not the other way around.

She put her right hand on the fence. Then her left. Josh gave her a boost.

In seconds, she was at the top.

Mara held her breath as the child flipped over. Her feet couldn't find a grip.

"Against the fence," Mara told her in Vietnamese. "Like you went up."

Mạ finally started down. It was harder—tears came to her eyes from the pain, but the little girl made it.

"Push the latch," said Mara, motioning.

The door unlatched. Mara slid it to the side and pushed the gate upward. They were in.

Josh scooped Mạ into his arms. They all hugged the girl. Mara kissed her.

"Way to go, little SEAL!" Stevens told her.

"Now all we have to do is figure out where the hell we are," said Mara. "Stay here."

Rows of boxes sat on steel shelves directly in front of them. About fifty feet long, the room was some sort of storage area. Mara walked to her right slowly, her eyes still adjusting to the goggles. The shelves ended in an aisle that led to more shelves. The boxes gave way to a large row of white plates; the storeroom, she concluded, was for the restaurant. Sure enough, she found a pair of swinging doors leading into the kitchen, visible through windows in the top panels. The doors were key-locked from both sides, but Mara had little difficulty picking the lock. She eased the doors open into the dark room, then crawled in, moving past a large walk-in freezer and a row of smaller refrigerators and dishwashers.

Mara heard a low murmur of voices in the distance. She crawled steadily through the kitchen, down a row of stoves and prep tables. As she turned the corner, she saw two red marbles staring at her from the corner.

A rat.

Mara shuddered. She continued to one of the doors,

still on her hands and knees. There was no window on the door, and while Mara suspected it led directly to the dining room, she couldn't tell. She rose to a sitting position and listened. The voices were indistinct, and it was impossible to tell if they were in the next room, and if they were, where in the room they might be.

Mara crawled to the next door, hoping that this one would have a window, but it did not.

She got up and put her hand on the door, easing it open ever so gently and slowly. A faint glow came through the crack—candlelight, she thought.

Mara eased the door open a tiny bit more. Her view was blocked by a screen separating the kitchen from the actual dining area. She pushed the door open a little farther, and saw that the screen covered a long wait station, where extra silverware, trays, and plates were kept.

Mara moved back from the door.

"There may be someone in the dining room," she told Stevens. "Can you move up here?"

"Be right there," said Stevens.

"Get by the stoves. You'll be able to ambush anyone if it comes to that."

Stevens, Josh, and Mạ moved up silently, crouching about ten feet away.

Mara took the night glasses off and eased back into the dining room, listening from behind the screen. Two men were talking, but it wasn't clear what they were saying. She heard the word "militia" and something about "control," but the men were at the far end of the room and she couldn't make out every word.

She spread out on her belly and began crawling. As she reached the edge of the screen, gunfire erupted above.

One of the men shouted. Mara leaned out in time to see their feet disappearing.

"Let's go!" she hissed. "It's clear."

Josh banged against the door in the dark. He pushed into the dimly lit dining room and saw Mara standing a few feet away, gun ready, waving at them to hurry.

"The atrium is that way," she said, pointing in the direction of the doors. Beyond them was a balcony that overlooked the lobby and registration area. "There are people down there. I think we'll have an easier time going through the patio this way. We're on the third level, but there should be some way to get down."

"What about the others?" asked Josh. Mạ clung to his side.

"They're creating a diversion."

"Are they going to be okay?"

Mara frowned.

"We can't just leave them," said Josh.

"Don't worry about the skipper," said Stevens. "He can take care of himself."

That wasn't the point, thought Josh as Mara led them to a glass door.

The outside air, warm and damp, invigorated Josh. He took a deep breath, as if he'd been breathing stale air for days.

"Two soldiers, near the intersection," said Stevens, checking over the wall. "Nobody directly in front of us."

"There's a stairwell here," said Mara.

She paused, put her hand to her ear.

"What's going on?" Josh asked.

"Kerfer's got somebody behind him."

"We gotta bail him out," said Josh.

Mara didn't say anything.

"I'll go," said Stevens. "You guys get across the road with Ma."

"No," said Mara, frowning. She took off the glasses and handed them to Josh. "I'm going to have to go through the lobby. If someone sees me, I can tell them I'm an employee. You won't be able to understand what they're saying."

"How are you going to hide the gun?" asked Stevens.

"Josh is going to give me his shirt. I'll make it look like a bag."

Josh pulled off his shirt and handed it to her. Mara folded down the stock on the submachine gun, then rigged the shirt around it. It wasn't the most fashionable bag, but it wasn't obviously a gun, either.

"Get across the river and wait there," Mara said. "Worst case, meet the helicopter."

"All right," said Stevens, still reluctant.

"I think we should back her up," said Josh as soon as she left.

"I don't know. We got the little girl to worry about."

"We can go back the way we came, get up the elevator shaft the way Kerfer did. We'll be right behind whoever's behind him."

"It'll be too confusing. And I got to keep you two safe. You're more important than anyone else. Come on—let's see about getting across the road."

Mara caught her breath at the closed door separating the restaurant from the balcony overlooking the atrium. She pulled the radio up and asked Kerfer if he was okay.

"Get out of the hotel," he said, his voice a hoarse whisper.

"I'm up here near the restaurant. The people who are shooting at you—where are they?"

"Get the hell out of the hotel."

"*Ric*. I didn't goddamn come back for you to blow me off. Come on."

"They're two floors below me. On the sixth. The Chinese are on the fifth and seventh, in the stairwell. At least two top and bottom. They have police uniforms, but they must be Chinese."

"Anybody above you?"

"Negative at the moment. There's hotel security somewhere, but I haven't seen them."

"Whose side are the Vietnamese on?"

"No one's. One of them got shot on floor five when the Chinks opened up on my guys."

"You sure they're Chinese? Not Vietnamese police?"

"I didn't ask for passports. That was what they were speaking."

Mara took the submachine gun out of the shirt-bag and slipped it to her side. Then she took a deep breath, brushed her hair back from her forehead with her left hand, and stepped out through the doors.

Candles had been placed in several spots below, and at each end of the hall, providing just enough light to see. She walked swiftly to the right, heading past the elevators to the staircase, which was located around a corner. She turned it quickly and found herself behind two policemen, who had their pistols drawn. The door to the stairs was propped open beyond them.

"What are you doing?" she snapped in Vietnamese.

Startled, the men turned around.

"Who are you?"

"Security for the prince," she said, keeping the gun down against her leg. "What's going on?"

"There are thieves in the hotel," said one of the policemen. "There was a gunfight. We have them trapped in the staircase."

"Are they thieves or assassins?" she demanded.

"Thieves in black broke into the hotel," said one of the men. "Some police have come in. Reinforcements are on the way."

"They're after the prince," said Mara. "We have to get him out."

The security man closest to her started to say that help was only a few minutes away, but Mara cut him off. She couldn't afford a conversation, and knew that if she gave them time to think—or even ask which prince she was talking about—she would be in trouble.

"Come," she said, starting up. She took two steps, then stopped. "Are you coming?" she demanded.

Sheepishly, the men started up behind her. The staircase came up to a level of convention rooms on the third floor. Mara was now two floors below the SEALs and one floor below the closest group of Chinese.

"This way," she said, pointing to the door.

Neither man moved.

"Squeaky, can you hear me?" said Mara over the radio.

"Yeah."

"I'm two floors below you. I'm coming up a flight. Get the attention of whoever is below you. I'll take them out."

Gunfire rattled in the stairs. Mara put her shoulder to the door and pushed open. There were two shadows on the landing above.

She fired until she had no more bullets. The stairway

filled with smoke and the acrid fumes of spent ammo. The policemen huddled below, unsure what to do.

"Clear!" she told Squeaky. "Kerfer?"

"Guys? On three . . ."

The stairway exploded with gunfire as Kerfer began firing from above. With the Chinese sandwiched between them, the SEALs below him used the distraction to run up the steps. Within seconds, the two Chinese agents were sprawled in the staircase, dead.

"Kerfer?" said Mara.

"Coming, Mother."

Mara trotted down the stairs, leaned out the door, and spotted the two policemen. "The prince is leaving," she told them sternly. "Make sure the lobby is secure."

Ho Chi Minh City

Jing Yo recognized the van, or more specifically its round window at the side. It was a Ford, relatively rare in Vietnam, a twin of the van he had seen at Ms. Hù's.

Or the same one.

"There are soldiers there, on the corner," Jing Yo told Hyuen Bo, pointing to the truck whose gray sides grew black as the red fires behind them flickered in the night. "I'm going to move up the street, away from their view, then cross. I'll get into the building from the back. You wait for me here."

"They'll ask why you're at the hotel," she said. "I should go with you—we'll say we are looking for a place to stay. We can say our house burned down."

It was a good idea. And it would keep her with him. Safer.

"All right. Come on," said Jing Yo.

They walked back up the side street before crossing. Jing Yo took Hyuen Bo's hand, tugging her gently as he started across the street.

His leg muscles stiffened as he reached the other side. He shrugged off the fatigue and started down the street, toward the van. As they approached, Jing Yo realized someone was sitting in the passenger seat.

Mr. Tong.

He *must* confront him. Fate had placed them together here. To ignore it was too dangerous.

"Stay here," Jing Yo told Hyuen Bo, letting go of her hand.

Mr. Tong didn't see him until he was only a few feet from the truck. Surprise flickered across his face, then resignation. He lowered the window as Jing Yo approached.

"Why are you here?" Jing Yo asked.

"You're the one I should ask," said Mr. Tong. "Why have you not apprehended your man?"

Jing Yo caught a glimpse of the pistol rising from Mr. Tong's lap. He shot his arm forward, fist smashing into Mr. Tong's jaw. The blow cracked his windpipe.

A second punch broke Mr. Tong's nose. He started to fall forward in the seat.

A chop to the back of his neck killed him.

Jing Yo reached into the truck and took the gun.

So it was clear now. There was no room for questions or doubt.

There was a commotion around the corner, at the front of the hotel. Jing Yo unlocked the door and climbed into the van, pushing Mr. Tong's limp body into the back. He slid into the driver's seat. The keys were in the ignition.

A sawed-off shotgun sat in a holster next to the central console. Directly behind the passenger seat was a case with two rocket-propelled grenades, and a pair of submachine guns, along with a backpack filled with ammunition. There was a handgun and grenades as well.

Enough for a small army. Or one commando.

Hyuen Bo ran to the van and climbed into the passenger seat as Jing Yo started the engine. He drove up the block and back around, just in time to see half a dozen men running across the street to the park. The soldiers in the distance made no effort to stop them.

The men were taller than average Vietnamese were. One of them, Jing Yo knew, must be the scientist.

He continued down the block, driving slowly but steadily past the soldiers. He nodded at them, trusting—hoping, really—that the militia bandanna he was still wearing would spare any questions. Apparently it did; the soldiers didn't say anything.

He was just turning up the street, back toward the heart of the city, when Hyuen Bo grabbed his hand.

"We can't go back to the apartment," she said.

"I know," said Jing Yo.

"We should leave Saigon. There must be many ways out of the country."

"I can't just leave. I have a mission."

"We should leave," she said.

For the first time since he had returned, Jing Yo heard pleading in her voice. And pain. Great pain.

"Aren't they trying to kill you?" she asked. "Wasn't this the van of the people you went to see?"

Mr. Tong had tried to kill him. Jing Yo had to assume that Ms. Hu wanted him dead.

But that didn't relieve him of his duty. He had let the scientist escape. He had to fulfill his obligations.

Beijing might know nothing of the plots here. And in any event, they were irrelevant.

"I'm sorry," he told Hyuen Bo. "I must do my duty. Whatever the cost."

They were silent for a moment.

"And then I will be free," he added, though the words sounded false, even to him.

Ho Chi Minh City

Josh and Stevens waited with Mạ in a low clump of brush just south of the ferry station as the others ran across the road. The soldiers at the end of the block made no move to stop them.

"We're all here," said Kerfer, trotting over. They'd sustained a few cuts and bruises among them, but no serious injuries. "All right, next problem: Stevens, how we getting across?"

"The ferry will have lifeboats," said Josh. "We can take them."

"Smart," said Kerfer, starting toward the building. "Must be why you're a scientist."

Josh picked up Mạ and followed as the team ran to the ferry house. Two of the vessels were tied up inside. The building and ships were deserted. There were two rafts tied to the side of the vessel above the main deck.

"Why don't we just grab the whole ferry?" said Kerfer as Stevens and Little Joe climbed up to release the rafts. "We can sail it downriver."

"Do you think we can get past the gunboat?" asked Mara.

"Why not? They're not going to stop us if we look like we know what we're doing."

"There's probably an order against using the river," said Mara.

"You just convinced two policemen you were protecting a prince," said Kerfer. "You don't think you can talk your way around a bunch of sailors?"

"Can you get the engines started?" Mara asked.

"Piece of cake."

As Kerfer had predicted, the gunboat didn't bother with them, apparently assuming that a craft as large and official as a ferry would not be moving without orders. Josh made a makeshift bed for Mạ in the passenger cabin. Mara joined Kerfer and Little Joe on the bridge as they guided the ferry into the river channel and moved southward. Kerfer took the wheel himself, smiling broadly as he steered downriver. There was enough light to make out the shoreline and the larger vessels along the way, but Kerfer posted his men as lookouts at the bow to watch for small boats or obstructions.

The ferry wasn't particularly fast—eight knots looked like their top speed, even with the engines at full—but it was stable and big. If they had to get off it quickly, they could sail toward shore and swim for it.

Hopefully it wouldn't come to that. Mara turned on the radio, listening for transmissions. There was a cacophony of military traffic, but none of it seemed to be coming from the river, and it didn't appear that any was directed at them.

The sat phone rang—DeBiase, looking for an update.

The transmissions—that must be how the Chinese were tracking them.

Mara turned the radio off without answering.

A mile beyond the patrol boat they passed another naval ship that had been hit by a missile and was burning. A dozen smaller boats moved around it, some taking survivors to shore, others trying to put out the fire. An array of barges sat farther on, tied up in front of warehouses and wharfs filled with goods. Mara guessed that they would be the targets of the next wave of Chinese missiles.

A pair of junks and several small craft were tied together at the edge of the channel. Some had small lamps hung beneath the tentlike canvas sheltering the families and goods aboard. Others were completely dark. But there were people on all of them, watching silently as the ferry chugged along, one of the few craft moving on the river.

The river bent northward, then twisted back south toward Phu My Bridge.

"Missile boat, port side," yelled Little Joe as they sailed toward the mouth to the Nha Be River.

The Vietnamese naval craft was protecting an oil refinery and storage area on the Nha Be. They stayed clear, heading southward, just barely clearing some rocks at the sharp corner of the peninsula.

The ferry's radio came to life with a challenge.

Mara picked up the microphone.

"This is Sai Gon Ferry Two," she said. "We have been ordered to report to Dong Hoa to take soldiers to reinforce the city."

"We will speak to the captain," said the voice on the radio.

"I am the captain," said Mara.

"What is your name?"

"Speak to the general who sent me if you have questions," said Mara. "Call central command."

"What command?"

"Division command. I am not one to question orders," she added. "If you think you can override a general, then do as you please."

She snapped off the microphone and looked at Kerfer.

"Sounded bitchy to me." Kerfer nodded. "They following us?"

She went across and stepped out onto the narrow deck that ran along the port side.

"They're not moving," she told him.

"Good."

The Vietnamese ship didn't have to follow to blow them up; a salvo of missiles would send them to the bottom in seconds. Mara climbed up the ladder that ran up topside to benches used by passengers on clear days. The river smelled like rotting fish, and she was sure that if she looked closely at the water, she would see plenty of beady eyes like those she'd seen in the storehouse—the Saigon River was legendary for its swimming rats.

The missile boat was lost in shadows behind them, its ominous tubes and the gun at the bow blurring into the mass of blackness.

"How long before we get to Vung Tau?" asked Josh, coming up from below.

"A couple of hours," said Mara.

"What happens there?"

"We find the airport, helicopter comes to rescue us. You anxious to get home?"

"I wouldn't mind it."

"Your parents are probably worried."

"My parents . . ." Josh's voice trailed off. "My parents died when I was little. They, uh . . . It was a bizarre thing. Like a serial killer. Like *In Cold Blood*."

"Oh."

She wasn't sure what to say. Finally, Josh filled the awkward silence.

"I was raised by my uncle and his family. They're farmers."

"Oh yeah?"

"Yeah. They seem to be doing pretty well with the climate change. That's the irony of it. Some places make out. Of course, who knows—a couple of years, their farm may be a desert."

"Really?"

"Yeah, really. It's funny: change the amount of rainfall just a few inches, one way or another—the effect can be tremendous. There are so many things in play. Look at Vietnam. This country is suddenly the most arable land in Asia. Those fields we're passing—they were swamps two or three years ago. Now they're industrial rice farms."

"I'm not sure I'd eat the rice," said Mara, thinking of the sewage smell in the river.

"You probably already have."

"Looks like something's following us," said Little Joe, who was standing a few feet away, looking toward the stern. "One of those little mama-san boats."

Mara walked aft. Little Joe gave her his night goggles, but Mara couldn't quite make out what he was talking about. She increased the magnification to max but still couldn't see anything that approximated a boat.

"How fast can those little boats go?"

"Mama-san boats? Eh, if they got a motor, couple of knots. Twelve tops."

"What's a mama-san boat?" asked Josh.

"Little craft they use to get around with. Sometimes people live in them and stuff," said Little Joe. "Smaller than a junk. Narrow. Longer than a skiff. Mostly they push 'em around with these long poles. But a lot of 'em have engines."

Mara went back to the bridge. Kerfer had already heard from Little Joe over the radio.

"Probably nothing," he said.

"You don't really think that, do you?" asked Mara.

Kerfer smiled, and turned his attention back to the river.

19

Nha Be River, south of Ho Chi Minh City

The ferry's size made it easy to see, even in the dim light of the river, but the small motor on the side of the boat Jing Yo had stolen couldn't drive them fast. They fell behind steadily, little by little, until at last Jing Yo couldn't see them at all.

Where would they go?

Perhaps a safe house somewhere farther south. Or perhaps out to a boat waiting in the mouth of the river, at Soi Rap.

He had to think like his enemy if he was going to succeed. Jing Yo lowered his head, concentrating.

They were smart, and there were several of them. Half dozen at least.

Clever people. Worthy enemies, not the vulnerable prey he had assumed earlier.

His mistake. One he kept repeating.

The ferry would have been a spur-of-the-moment decision. Planning to take it would have been too difficult—too many contingencies. It had been an opportunity that presented itself.

And what did that tell him?

That they had a destination somewhere south. That it was far enough away to risk taking a large boat.

"We are coming close to shore!"

Jing Yo slid his hand on the tiller, taking them back toward the middle of the channel.

"I'm sorry," he told Hyuen Bo.

She leaned back over the bow, keeping lookout.

Most likely, the scientist had come to Ho Chi Minh City to meet an airplane. When the airport had been bombed, he had changed his plans.

The most logical thing to do would be to find another airport.

"Is there an airport south of here?" he asked Hyuen Bo.

"Vung Tau?" she suggested tentatively. "It's small."

Vung Tau was on a small peninsula that jutted out from Ganh Rai Bay. Some years before, it had been a tourist area, but the discovery of oil offshore had altered its complexion. Large platforms lined the shallow waters near the shore, extending well into the ocean. The airstrip at Bai Sau was not a large one—it didn't appear on many maps—but it would be big enough to accommodate a propeller-driven aircraft or a helicopter.

It was a destination at least. He would follow down the river, and if he didn't see the ferry, he would head in that direction.

20

Aboard USS *McCampbell*

"Cruiser is increasing speed, skipper. New speed is fifteen knots."

Commander Silas glanced around the ship's combat information center. Not one head was turned toward him; every sailor in the compartment was working his or her gear.

Absolutely as it should be.

"Their distance?" Silas asked.

"Fifty-two miles," said his executive officer. "On that heading, they should be within sight in two hours. If they keep their speed up."

"I'll be on the bridge," said Silas, making his voice firm and sharp, if not a little curt.

He could feel the adrenaline starting to build. They were in the open water, and there was no reason for the two Chinese ships—besides the cruiser, there was a smaller frigate about a quarter mile to the northeast—to challenge them, much less fire on them. But Silas sensed they would. He knew it the way he knew how to walk.

So maybe the old ways weren't completely dead.

His orders from fleet were to avoid conflict and to remain in international waters. Those were his only orders—the request to pick up the CIA officer had not been passed on through official channels.

Which could be interpreted in many different ways, unless you were an old Navy hand, in which case there was only one way to see it: the admirals didn't want to get caught with the splatter if things went wrong.

21

Quach Van Dhut took a long drag on his cigarette, then blew the smoke out in a cloud that engulfed his head. "Eight Zodiac boats is the entire inventory," he told Zeus. "You are lucky that they are all here."

"Eight?" Zeus couldn't believe it. "The Vietnamese navy has only eight rigid-hulled boats?"

"They are marine boats," said Quach. "The navy has none."

"You're sure?"

Quach turned to the colonel whose unit had been assigned to supply the manpower for the mission and said something to him in Vietnamese. Quach, a short, thin man in his early fifties, was a member of the intelligence service, and unlike the others, was dressed in civilian clothes. He hadn't given his title, but he clearly had status—Zeus had noticed how even the senior officers straightened when he walked by.

But status wasn't what they needed at the moment. Zeus, tired—he'd been working on this all night, and it was now nearly dawn—rubbed his forehead and looked back at the map. It was roughly 120 miles across the Gulf of Bac Bo to Hainan; while the water was generally calm, that was a long way to go in the small open boats. They weren't the largest models, either—barely seventeen feet long, the tiny craft were designed for seven men and were intended as utility boats, the sort of little runabouts that might be used off cabin cruisers or maybe to host a diving party. The debris that Zeus needed to bring—the entire reason for the mission—would add considerable weight; even divided up among the eight boats, there'd only be room for two or at most three people aboard each.

"The colonel assures me there are no other boats," Quach told Zeus. "I'm sorry."

"Me, too."

Zeus glanced around the conference table. The colonel had brought three aides to the meeting; besides them, there was an officer from the general staff and another member of the intelligence service. The room stank of tea and cigarette smoke. Ordinarily, Zeus didn't like tobacco of any kind, especially the stale remains of cigarettes. But right now he was glad for the stimulant.

"They have done exercises like this before," said Quach. "And I have been put ashore from one of the craft. I believe they will work."

"I guess they'll have to."

The inflatables weren't the only limitation. The marines didn't have night glasses, short-range radios, or GPS systems. Zeus had a satcom he could use to get intelligence from the data that was being sent to Vietnam's army headquarters, but he'd have to use it sparingly, on the assumption that the Chinese would be able to detect, though not decrypt, the signal. Just knowing someone was in the middle of the gulf might increase the alert status on Hainan; everything depended on things remaining calm there.

Still, it was doable. The marines had Chinese police uniforms, which might come in handy. And the unit had received considerable training in infiltration and sabotage.

They worked for a bit longer, sketching out contingencies.

"We're going to need a contact here," Zeus said. "A contact at headquarters I can talk to directly if the shit hits the fan."

"Shit?"

"If there's a problem," Zeus told Quach. "Someone who can stay on the phone with me. And get things done."

"The colonel," suggested Quach.

"He's gotta speak English."

Quach and the colonel spoke again in Vietnamese. Finally, the colonel turned to one of his aides. The aide seemed to be arguing, but then finally put his head down.

"Tien will be happy to help," said Quach. "His English is very good."

"Why is he frowning?" Zeus asked.

Quach said something in Vietnamese to the captain. Tien shrugged. Quach said something else. Tien looked toward the floor.

"What's wrong?" Zeus asked Tien, deciding that if he spoke English, there was no need for a translator.

Tien rose, bowing his head slightly in what impressed Zeus as an overly subservient display. "Working as your translator here means I cannot go on the mission," said Tien.

"Oh. I'm sorry."

"No one else on the staff speaks English," said Tien. "It is unfortunate."

"Well, maybe Mr. Quach can act as the coordinator here," said Zeus.

"That will not be possible," said Quach. "I am going with you."

Zeus looked at Quach. He was perhaps five four, and weighed no more than 110. And that was counting the packs of cigarettes he had in his shirt pocket.

"I don't know," said Zeus.

"I speak Chinese, and have been to the island many times. We will have one other of my agents with us," added Quach. "This is a difficult plan as it is, Major. You would not do well without people who know the island and can speak the language."

"Don't take this the wrong way," said Zeus. "But you're—"

"Old?"

"Well—"

Quach smiled. "That is not considered a handicap in Vietnam."

"It may be, out on the water. We have to swim to the ships to set the charges."

"I believe you will find that when the time comes, I will perform adequately," said Quach. He pulled on his cigarette, right down to the filter. "And if we find ourselves too much in the water before we reach the harbor, there will be other problems to worry about greater than my age."

They broke up the meeting a half hour later. Zeus waited to speak to Tien.

"I know what it feels like," he told the captain. "I'd rather be with my men."

"We all have a role," said Tien stoically.

"Your English is good."

"Thank you. I have studied since I was eight." Tien took out a cigarette and offered the pack to Zeus.

"No thanks."

"You Americans invented cigarettes," said Tien. "Now you give it up."

"Funny, huh?"

"We are very grateful for your assistance," Tien said. "Your strike at the dam was legendary."

"I didn't hit it myself," said Zeus. "I just came up with the idea."

"Vietnam is grateful. You saved us."

The praise made Zeus a little uncomfortable. The strike had stopped the Chinese advance, but surely that wouldn't last.

As for this operation . . . the odds of success were stacked very much against it.

Still, there was no sense dashing the captain's hopes or enthusiasm. They spoke for a few minutes about what Zeus might need. Tien gave him some pointers about working with the marines. He also suggested that he look at the boats himself.

"Just because they say they are there does not always mean it is so," said Tien. "I would go myself and make sure."

"All the way to Hai Phong?"

"Yes."

"All right."

"One of my sergeants would be able to drive you," offered Tien.

"I'd have to leave soon," said Zeus. "Right away if I could. I have a lot of other things to do."

"The sergeant will be at your disposal."

"Great." Zeus stuck out his hand, deciding he would leave right away. Then he remembered Mara Duncan's cell phone. "Damn."

"Major?"

"I need—one of my friends may need some help. Probably not at this point."

Zeus explained that he had a cell phone. He was as vague as possible, saying only that his friend was trying to get out of the country, and he had promised to give her information on the Chinese advance if necessary. But he couldn't do that if he wasn't in Hanoi.

Tien offered to help.

"Nothing classified," Zeus said. "But if she needs to find an open airport or highway or something."

"I would certainly help a friend of yours," said Tien, taking the phone.

Soi Rap, near Dong Hoa, southeastern Vietnam

The Ne River was a calm, meandering stream, gradually widening as it made its way to the ocean. It took them nearly six hours to get down to near Soi Rap and the delta. Mara spent much of the time walking back and forth across the top deck, watching for other ships. As they approached the coast, Kerfer called her down to the bridge to listen to the radio. A Vietnamese navy patrol boat was challenging vessels near the mouth of the river. Which gave Mara an idea.

The SEALs rigged the ferry so that it would continue to sail on its own at about six knots. Then they took the lifeboats and, after veering temporarily toward the eastern side of the river's mouth, snuck off the boat, taking advantage of the lingering dawn's early shadows. They paddled away as silently as possible, hoping to escape notice, at least until the patrol boat approached the ferry.

Kerfer was the last one off, waiting until the others were away and then steering the ferry back to the middle of the channel. He made sure it was headed directly for the patrol boat before going off the side. The current pushed him toward the life rafts, which had stopped near the dark part of the shore to wait for the Vietnamese ship to take the bait.

Kerfer had to swim a considerable distance, and for a while Mara fretted that he wouldn't make it. A jittery anxiety took over. She felt her hands shaking as she dipped her paddle into the water, holding the small raft steady.

It was ironic, she thought—he'd been almost a total jerk toward her since they'd met, yet here she was, actually worried that he was dead.

Of course, she thought; he was part of the team, and she would be concerned about all of the members of the team.

But it was more than that. And as much as she wanted to distance herself from any sort of sexual attraction—the idea was revolting—she still felt exhilarated when she spotted his head bobbing in the waves thirty yards from their boat.

"This way!" she called.

He gave a wave and continued swimming, not toward her boat but to the other, which was a little closer to shore and farther from him.

She felt disappointed.

"All right," she told the others in the boat. "Let's move south along the shoreline. Hold off the motor until we're beyond the patrol boat."

"How long before we get to the airport, you think?" asked Josh, who was sitting across from her with Mạ.

"If we can get across the bay before daylight, we'll be less than a mile," Mara told him. "If we have to put into shore before then, it may take longer. We're going to make it, Josh. You don't have to worry about that."

"I'm not worried."

"How's your stomach?"

"Good."

She could tell he was lying. "Are you okay to paddle?"

"I'm fine," he insisted. He put his paddle into the water, making a show of pushing off.

"You're not sneezing," Mara said.

"Yeah, I'm not allergic to seawater, I guess. I've never had problems with that."

She put her hand against his forehead. "Your fever's gone," she told him.

"Fear," he said. "Miracle cure."

J osh felt the coolness of Mara's fingers on his forehead long after she had taken her hand away. He tried to focus on the water in front of them, avoiding her gaze. He was definitely attracted to her, but of course the circumstances made that completely inappropriate—impossible, really.

His body still ached, though not as badly. Soon they'd be the hell out of here, he thought.

Then what?

Then he'd be talking to the president of the United States, telling him what the Chinese had done.

And would he tell him about the Vietnamese soldiers they'd killed? Or the men in the hotel?

The men in the hotel had been Chinese agents. He was pretty sure of that. They definitely had meant to kill him. So killing them in turn had clearly been justified.

But the soldiers, the Vietnamese . . .

What would he tell God, if he died now?

It didn't work that way, not like the old-fashioned

books claimed, where you stood in front of Saint Peter
or God himself and answered for each sin.

Mạ shifted against him. The poor little girl was so
tired she was sleeping again.

He'd have to find her a home. Maybe his uncle would
adopt her.

So what would he tell God about the soldiers? If it
did work that way, if he did have to account, meta-
phorically or literally, what would he say?

I didn't kill them.

That was true. But not exactly the entire story.

Those men deserved to die so that I could live?

So that Mạ could live.

Don't blame it on her.

What of the soldiers he had killed? The Chinese captain whose head he'd bashed in?

Were the extra blows justifiable? Were they relevant
at all?

"Zoning out on us?" asked Squeaky.

"No, I'm here," said Josh, realizing that he hadn't
paddled for several minutes. He pushed his oar back
into the water.

"You do a J-stroke, right?" said Squeaky.

"I guess."

"You know what I'm talking about?"

"Kinda. If we were in a canoe, we'd be steering it."

"Exactly."

"I was a Boy Scout," said Josh. "For a little while."

"There you go."

"Mind if I ask you a question?" said Josh.

"What's that?"

"When you shot those people—does it bother you?"

"Which ones?"

"The guys in the train."

"Better us than them," answered Little Joe, who was in front of Mara.

"Yeah," said Josh.

"It's true," said Squeaky.

"I had to—I killed a couple of the Chinese soldiers behind the lines, before you guys got to me," said Josh. "I think it was the right thing to do."

"It absolutely was," said Mara.

"Yeah."

"You don't have to second-guess yourself, Josh," she said, putting her hand on his arm. "We're in survival mode here. You're getting back and telling the world what's really going on. It's going to make a big difference. Believe me."

"Mạ, too."

"And her. But you're an adult. And a scientist. A reliable witness. People will believe what you say."

"I hope so," said Josh.

She smiled at him, then let go of his arm. He wished he could lean across and kiss her.

"They're taking the bait," said Squeaky, pointing to the Vietnamese navy ship. It had changed course and was heading for the ferry, which had started to angle itself slightly toward the western end of the channel.

Two sharp blasts of the patrol ship's horn rent the air. A moment later, its forward gun cracked.

"Let's start up the motor and get out of here," said Mara.

They steered close to land as they rounded the peninsula near Dong Hoa, tucking into Ganh Rai Bay near Cao Gio. Aside from a pair of ancient fishing boats, the bay seemed deserted. The sun peeked over the land to the east, edging upward like a child stealing into his parents' room on Christmas morning. Smoke rose in a pair of funnel clouds to the south, an ominous reminder that they were not yet free of China's reach.

Mara needed to talk to DeBiase to arrange a time for the helicopter to pick them up, but she didn't trust the sat phone anymore. She still had the cell phones.

She turned one of them on, and was surprised to get a signal.

Should she use it to call DeBiase? Assuming the call went through, it wouldn't be encrypted. And the cell phone could be traced as easily as the sat phone.

But they wouldn't know to look for it. Even if all communications were being routinely monitored, it might take hours for the information to reach someone who could act on it.

Mara dialed one of the access numbers for Bangkok.

"This is an open line," she said as soon as an operator picked up, even though it would be obvious. "I need the Million Dollar Man."

DeBiase came on a few seconds later. "Is this my favorite niece?"

"I need a time."

"We're still working on it."

"That's not good enough."

"It's the best I can do."

"Call me a half hour before it happens," said Mara. "Use my old number."

She hung up, then tossed the phone into the water.

23

Soi Rap

Jing Yo's boat had two spare cans of gasoline, but even so, he had to stop twice for fuel, quickly stealing gas from wharfside pumps. The second time he stopped, he spotted a small fiberglass speedboat tied to the dock near the pump. He was able to start the engine without too much trouble. He and Hyuen Bo transferred their gas cans and things to the new boat and took it south, moving much faster than before.

They drew in sight of the ferry just in time to see the Vietnamese navy ship send a round from its deck gun into the wheelhouse. The ferry, its wheel and steering mechanism damaged, veered sharply toward shore.

The next shot landed in the large passenger compartment. At first, it seemed to have passed straight through without causing much damage. Then a thin finger of black smoke rose from the side where the shell had entered. Within moments, flames were leaping from the hole.

"Prepare to be boarded!" declared a loudspeaker. A rigid-hulled inflatable with four or five men left the side of the patrol boat and headed toward the ferry.

Jing Yo idled the engine and waited in the shadows of the shoreline, watching the boarders clamber onto the battered ferry. Two of the Vietnamese sailors climbed to the top deck of the ferry. They waved their arms at the patrol boat and fired into the air.

All clear.

So the scientist had gotten away.

Jing Yo glanced down at Hyuen Bo, curled against

the side of the boat, sleeping. He felt a pang of both love and shame, for putting her into so much jeopardy.

Jing Yo eased his engines up, starting across the channel to the far shore. He was almost past the warship when he heard a challenge over the radio, a broadcast on the emergency band that told him to stop.

That was the last thing he was going to do. He pushed the throttle to max. The boat jerked its bow upward and began speeding downriver.

The patrol boat replied with a long blast from its horn. Jing Yo lowered his head, as if he could urge the speedboat faster. A second later, a geyser erupted to his right.

The ship had fired one of its guns.

The speedboat rocked violently through the roiling waves, pitching its nose down and its stern east simultaneously. Jing Yo fought to hold the wheel steady, plowing sideways in the water. He put his hand on the throttle, hoping to force it faster. A direct hit would kill them.

Hyuen Bo rose from the deck, hooking her arms around his waist.

"Hold tight," he said, regaining control of the craft.

This time he heard the crack of the gun, and the shriek as the shell flew overhead. It hit the water two hundred yards ahead. Jing Yo jerked farther out into the channel, a feint to trick the patrol boat while lessening the impact of the swell as it rocked them sideways. Then he spun the wheel back hard to take the boat closer to shore. A third shell landed in the middle of the channel, this time behind them.

The ocean lay before them. Jing Yo turned hard to port, heading eastward beyond Dong Hoa. The patrol boat fired several more shells, but these landed far behind them, the angry flailing of a neighbor yelling at children who had fled his yard after making mischief.

"Was that a Chinese ship?" asked Hyuen Bo when they were clear.

"It was Vietnamese."

"Why are they trying to sink us?"

"The world's gone crazy," he said.

With the scientist having abandoned the ferry, Jing Yo could only guess where he had gone.

The airfield near Vung Tau seemed the most likely possibility, but it would be just as easy for him to find another boat or ship and sail out to sea, where a ship might be waiting to pick him up.

What would Jing Yo do then? Follow him to America? Easier to run. He could take a boat himself.

But the monks had taught him that there was no way to escape one's fate. The Way could not be avoided, any more than air could not be breathed.

The sat phone's sharp peal startled him. Jing Yo took it from his pack. He had not expected it to ring. Indeed, he thought he'd turned it off.

Hyuen Bo looked at him but said nothing.

He picked up the phone and answered it. "This is Jing Yo."

"What is your status, Lieutenant?"

It was Colonel Sun.

"The Chinese network in Ho Chi Minh City attempted to assassinate me," Jing Yo told him.

"You're sure of this?" said Sun.

"An operative named Mr. Tong sent me into an area of the city where he hoped to have me apprehended. When that didn't work, he pulled a gun on me and tried to assassinate me. He was not successful."

"I trust that he paid for that mistake with his life," said Sun.

Jing Yo didn't answer. Was Sun acting surprised? This might be a trick.

Surely it was a trick.

"Where is the scientist?" the colonel asked.

"He took a ferry to the Soi Rap mouth," said Jing Yo. "A Vietnamese patrol boat tried to stop him, but he escaped into the water. Where exactly he is at the moment, I am not sure."

"We have his satellite phone frequency under surveillance," said the colonel. "When he transmits again, I will give you the exact location. Have nothing more to do with any spies of any force."

"Yes, Colonel."

"Tell me—did Ms. Hu know of this?"

Jing Yo was surprised that Sun mentioned the spymistress.

"I am not sure."

"I do not believe that she did," said Sun. "But I will find out."

The colonel killed the line.

"Who was that?" Hyuen Bo asked.

"A friend," said Jing Yo. "Or an enemy. I am not sure which."

24

Aboard USS McCampbell

"They're asking our intentions, skipper."

"My intention is to sail the open sea," replied Commander Silas.

"Sir?"

"Lieutenant Commander Li, have a message sent to the Chinese captain," said Silas, his tone formal and strong. He was speaking for the record.

For posterity, if necessary.

"Inform the Chinese commander that I intend to sail the open sea," said Silas.

"Aye, aye, Captain."

The sun was just creeping over the horizon behind them, throwing steel gray shadows across the ocean. The cruiser was a quarter mile off the starboard bow. Silas could see men on her forward deck, near the gun. His own people were at general quarters—their *battle* stations.

"How's the Seahawk?"

"Aircraft is prepped, crew aboard. Engine start on your order."

They needed to get a few more miles before the chopper could take off. Silas had spoken personally to the helo pilots, making sure they understood the mission, and getting his own sense of how close they had to be to have adequate reserves. He would continue east after they launched, making it easier for them on the return trip. Still, the helicopters were gas-guzzlers at high speed, and this mission called for as much speed as they could muster. The launch point had been calculated down to the meter to make sure they had enough fuel.

The Chinese cruiser's bow turned toward the *Mc-Campbell*. But it was the frigate that drew the Americans' attention—it set a course directly for them.

The commanding officer aboard the cruiser was sending the smaller frigate to do its dirty work, Silas realized. The cruiser would stay just close enough to fire if necessary.

They'd love that, Silas thought. Undoubtedly they'd have video cameras rolling. Very possibly there was a live, direct link back to Beijing. As soon as the first missle or shell flew, it would be posted for the world to see.

"They want to ram us!" yelled one of the extra lookouts the captain had posted.

"Steady as she goes," said Silas.

This was the way it was done—in a calm voice, a prepared voice.

Outside. Inside, a voice was screaming: *Try it, motherfucker!*

"Sir, the Chinese ship is on a collision course," said the helmsman. "We will hit them if—"

"Steady!" commanded Silas.

Silas knew he was playing more than a simple game of chicken. His primary concern was to accomplish his mission. At the same time, he had to do so without starting a war. Sinking the frigate and the cruiser would be personally satisfying—would it ever—but would have an immense impact on geopolitics.

Even firing a warning shot would be considered an act of war under the circumstances. Indeed, it could easily backfire, as the cruiser's dual water-cooled 130s on the forecastle might actually give it an edge in a quick gun battle. Silas had to be prepared to fight, but under the circumstances couldn't take the first shot himself.

On the other hand, Silas couldn't appear to back down. And he certainly wasn't about to let his ship get rammed.

Chicken indeed.

"Crew, we're going right by the Chinese," said the captain over the ship's 1MC system. "They're trying to bluff us. Be very prepared to fire back. If they give us just cause, we will sink them. Until that point, we must not, and we shall not, blink."

The frigate was churning through the water. Silas drew a breath, mentally calculating the angle.

No doubt at this point. They were going to hit.

The video cameras aboard ship were rolling. They could show that the Chinese had caused this. But would he be able to get close enough to launch the helicopter, then recover it?

"Helm, stand by," said Silas.

"He's heaving to!" yelled the watchman.

"Give me everything, engine room," said Silas, though in fact the engines were already at 110 percent. "Helm, avoid collision. Maintain us as close to course as possible."

The Chinese frigate turned off, but its momentum was such that Silas could have reached out and spit on the crewmen.

He was tempted.

"**C**aptain, we are within range for helicopter launch," said the exec ten minutes later.

"Get 'em off the ship," said Silas.

By then, the Chinese frigate had moved off to a more comfortable distance. The cruiser was now almost alongside her. Silas pulled up his binoculars, watching the missile launcher on the cruiser carefully. The Seahawk was an easy target at this range, even staying low and using the *McCampbell* as a screen.

One missile launch and he'd sink the cruiser. And the frigate.

If their crews were any good, they'd get a few shots in on their own. At this range, on the open sea, anything could happen.

Anything.

He was ready.

"Seahawk is away, sir!"

"Steady," said Silas. "Steady."

A moment later, he knew the Chinese weren't going to interfere. He'd won. This battle, at least.

"Helicopter is out of range of their antiair weapons," said Lieutenant Commander Li a minute later. Her voice was noticeably calmer—not casual, but no longer tense. "Pilot reports they are on course and on schedule."

"Steady as she goes, Commander. Remind the crew that we have more to do."

"Aye, aye, Captain."

25

Bai Sau, southern Vietnam

Mara's boat was in the lead as they started across the bay. A breeze kicked up, sending sprays of water across the bow. She angled her face to dull some of the effects of the wind.

The inner bay area was still a major tourist spot, a favorite of many residents from the Ho Chi Minh area who drove down on weekends to enjoy the sand and sun. But the oil boom was steadily encroaching on paradise, and for a few years now the eastern end of the large cove had been dominated by an oil-storage area and a small refinery. Three ships sat at harbor, taking on fuel for export. To the south, barges were stacked two deep in a line extending along a half-mile pier, waiting to disgorge raw petroleum collected from offshore platforms. Workboats were parked in another line against the wharf, some idling, others seemingly abandoned.

It was nearly 8 a.m., and in theory the workday should be well under way. But the war had disrupted regular routines, and Mara saw few people on the wharf.

Once they were across the bay, they took the boats back to the west, cruising past a swampy delta area toward an inlet populated by fishermen and their families. Only about half the fleet had gone out, leaving the channel glutted but passable. The two boats moved slowly, crossing the occasional swell from a nearby motorboat.

On the shoreline, buildings stood shoulder to shoulder, leaning against each other. A few were large, solid-looking structures, metal-sided warehouses and small fish-processing factories. But most were shacks, small houses built fifty or sixty years earlier, witness to several generations' worth of hardships and war.

A handful of children watched them come in, staring in curiosity.

Mạ stared at them as if they were animals she had never seen before.

"Wave," said Josh.

He prodded her to raise her hand. When she didn't, he waved his own. The children ran away.

What kind of life is she going to have? thought Mara. *What kind of life are any of those kids going to have?*

They found a place to tie up at the southeast, forty or fifty feet from the road.

"The airport's a mile that way," said Mara, pointing to the east. "Let's start walking."

The first quarter mile took them around the outskirts

of the residential area. The swamp to their left had only recently been filled for new construction; two buildings had been started but not yet completed.

They took a turn to the right and entered a dense pack of houses, crisscrossed by narrow roads and even tighter alleys. Unlike the houses they had passed before landing, these were vacation homes. On the whole their owners were much better off than the fishermen farther to the west. Four- and five-story buildings dotted the area.

The SEALs had tucked their weapons back into their rucksacks, but people stared at them as they passed. It was clear that they were out of place.

"What do you figure someone's going to call the cops on us?" Kerfer asked, catching up to Mara.

"We look like oil workers," said Mara. "There are plenty of Russians around."

"With a kid?"

"What do you want to do, stuff her into one of the rucks?"

"I thought of that."

"If the police come, I'll do the talking," said Mara.

He frowned at her.

"What do you want me to tell you?" said Mara, exasperated. "We won't be bothered?"

"Don't get bitchy on me."

"You're the one that's being bitchy," she told him. "Just relax. If we can find a motel, we can check in."

"What are we using for money? Your good looks?"

"Get us further than yours," said Josh behind them.

The SEALs laughed. Mara felt her face flush slightly.

There were no police or soldiers in front of the airport, and while Mara initially took that as a good sign, it turned out to be the opposite. The doors to the terminal were locked; a handwritten message taped to one of them declared that it had been closed, and that only military flights would be using the strip for the near future. Sure enough, there were a small number of soldiers in the back, working on helicopters and guarding a pair of MiG fighters near the hangars. Mara decided they'd be better off finding a different place to wait.

There was a hotel across the highway from the airport. From the outside, at least, it looked on par with a Motel 6 back in the States. The architecture was similar, and the rooms were spread out among three buildings.

Mara left the others outside and went in with Little Joe, whose clothes seemed the neatest. The clerk eyed them dubiously.

"Some of my friends and I need rooms for the night," she said in Vietnamese.

The clerk held up his hands and said they had none.

"You have no rooms?" said Mara.

"Many reservations."

"There are no rooms for anyone?"

"Very sorry."

The reception area was small, with a pair of Western-style couches and some fake flowers. There was no one inside, but of course that didn't mean the hotel was empty. Still, Mara had a hard time believing that there were no rooms available.

"I know hotels sometimes keep places for special guests," she said. "Perhaps if we paid extra."

"No. I'm very sorry," said the man. "All rooms are reserved."

"Is there a place where we could shower?" she asked.

"I'm sorry."

Mara thought of using Mạ, whom she'd left outside, to plead her case. But she worried that Kerfer was right about the girl making people more suspicious.

"Could you recommend another hotel?" Mara asked.

"We are all booked," said the man. "Because of the war."

"There's nothing else?"

"No. I am sorry."

Mara gradually wheedled more information out of him. The oil companies had booked the hotel rooms for their employees, whom they were trying to evacuate. A cruise ship was supposed to be on its way to take them away.

The only problem was that the cruise ship was two days overdue.

Mara decided it wasn't worth going to each hotel to hear the same message. Instead, she took Josh, Mạ, and the SEALs up the road to an athletic club, where she spent the last of her Vietnamese money buying them a day pass to the tennis court in the back. She didn't care about tennis; she wanted the showers.

The shower helped Josh as much as the pills had, though pulling on his sweaty clothes took some of the edge off his improved mood.

Little Joe had liberated some snacks from a vending machine and shared them with the others. Josh didn't realize how hungry he was until he ripped into a bag of soy-soaked strips of puffed rice and gobbled them down. But the food only stoked his hunger.

Mara met them outside near the entrance. She'd changed into a flowery shirt that fell to her thighs.

"I found it," she told Josh. "What do you think?"

"Nice."

"It's a dress. It's a little tight, but it works."

"Stealing clothes," said Kerfer.

"It was a barter. I left mine."

Ma, meanwhile, had found a tennis ball. The SEALs took turns playing with her, improvising a game of little kid soccer as they walked back toward the airport. She smiled and even laughed as they played with her.

"Maybe there's hope for her," said Mara.

Josh glanced at the CIA officer gazing intently at the little girl he'd rescued. He knew exactly what she meant, but was surprised she was thinking that. Mara had seemed . . . not uncaring, but focused on her job.

It made him like her even more.

They walked down along the western side of the airport, along the far end of the runway. Only a field separated them from the concrete strip, and they had a clear view of the back of the complex.

The airport's main runway was a thousand meters, long enough for a turboprop or perhaps a small jet. But most of the aircraft that used it were helicopters. Three large Russian choppers—civilian Mil Mi-58s— sat in front of hangars.

"Maybe we oughta take our own chopper," said Kerfer.

"Can you fly it?" asked Josh.

"Don't get funny with me, kid."

"I'm serious."

"Flying lessons are next month," said Kerfer.

There was no fence at the far end of the field; they could have walked straight onto the runway if they'd wanted. Instead, they walked down the long shrub-lined boulevard that marked the southern edge of the complex, passing a row of new but seemingly deserted warehouses. Josh wondered if they had been abandoned because of the war, or if they were just unused; there was no way to tell. Near the end of the block they saw another hotel complex. Mara went over to see if there were rooms, but soon came out saying there weren't.

"What is it with Vietnam and tennis courts?" asked Squeaky as they began walking again. "Tennis courts all over the place here."

"It was a big sport when the French were here," said Josh. "And it was associated with being rich. So when people in the country started having money, they started paying a lot of attention to it."

"You're a big tennis fan?" asked Kerfer.

"One of our translators gave me the whole story," said Josh, thinking of Li Huy, who'd told him how good his son was at the sport.

His ten-year-old son. Now fatherless. As Huy said he had been after what he called the American war.

Josh glanced down at Mạ.

"Police car, six o'clock," said Squeaky.

Mara acted as if the police officers were godsends, speaking as quickly as she could manage, saying they had been told to come here by their company only to find that there were no rooms. The men were oil workers, expecting to get off by ship, but unsure when it was arriving. She and her daughter—they were careful to keep Mạ back by Josh and Kerfer—had come to visit her father and grandfather and were now hoping to get out with the rest of the workers.

Mara leaned into the car as she spoke, practically pressing her boobs into the nearest officer's face.

"Is there a hotel where we could stay?" Mara asked. "Our company will pay the best prices."

The policemen began talking among themselves.

Mara pressed closer until the cop started to roll up the window.

She stepped back.

"Throw yourself at him, why don't you?" said Kerfer.

"Don't speak English," said Mara in a stage whisper.

The police car began backing away slowly. Mara put a disappointed look on her face, pretending to be sad that they couldn't help.

"What happened?" asked Josh.

"I think they were afraid that we were going to ask for a favor that they couldn't grant," said Mara. "Or maybe they have an emergency somewhere else. Whatever—they're gone. For now. We ought to find a better place to hang out."

"When the fuck is that helo coming?" asked Kerfer. "They said daybreak."

"They said after daybreak. Maybe not until noon."

"It's after daybreak. As far as I'm concerned, it's going on noon."

"It's a Navy helicopter," said Mara. "Your guess is as good as mine."

"Call them."

"Every time I call, the Chinese show up," said Mara.

She spotted a grove of trees near the highway that ran along the eastern end of the runway, and began walking toward it. Mạ, who was walking with Josh and Little Joe, began sobbing and holding her stomach.

"What's with the kid?" Kerfer asked.

Mara bent and spoke to her. Mạ said she was hungry.

"We oughta get her some food," said Kerfer. "How much money you guys got?"

They dug through their pockets, but the only one with cash was Josh, who found two twenty-thousand-dong notes—about two dollars.

"The problem is finding someplace to get food," said Mara. "We haven't passed anything."

"I'm kinda hungry myself," said Squeaky.

"You got money you ain't tellin' us about?" asked Stevens.

"I'm just saying."

"Maybe we can trade something for food," said Josh.

"Yeah, like we won't shoot you if you give us food," said Little Joe.

The others laughed.

"Not a good idea," said Mara.

"Relax," said Kerfer.

Mara's sat phone rang before she could say anything else.

"This better be good news," she told DeBiase.

"Helicopter is inbound. It'll land in forty-five minutes."

"Tell him there's a concrete turning area at the eastern end of runway thirty," said Mara, looking directly at it. "It's kind of between the ends of the two runways."

"Okay."

"We'll meet him there. The terminal is closed and there are soldiers by the hangars."

"I can stay on the line," offered DeBiase. "In case—"

Mara snapped the phone off.

"Forty-five minutes to pickup," she told the others.

"Good," said Kerfer. He looked down at Mạ and patted her head. "When we get back to the ship, kid, you and me are having the biggest damn bowl of ice cream we can find. I promise you that."

26

Bai Sau

"He's near the airport," Colonel Sun told Jing Yo. "There is an American ship offshore that has just defied the blockade. Most likely he is to meet them. Either they will go to the port, or send a helicopter."

"I will do my duty," said Jing Yo.

"Ms. Hu had nothing to do with it," Sun added.

"Colonel?"

"I believe her. But don't trust her, nonetheless."

The colonel cut the connection.

Jing Yo steered his boat to the southeastern end of the peninsula, where the beach backed into a golf course. The airport was roughly a mile from the water to his north, on the other side of a highway. There were few houses nearby, and fewer people to ask questions.

"Stay on the beach, near the boat," Jing Yo told Hyuen Bo after he pulled the boat up onto the sand. "I will be back very soon."

"Yo." She took hold of his arm as he slung the bag containing the grenades and extra ammunition he had taken from Tong's van over his shoulder.

"You have to stay," Jing Yo told her. "Hold on to the shotgun—hide it in the sand in case you need it."

"We must escape together."

"We will," said Jing Yo.

The rocket grenade launchers were in metal boxes. They were cumbersome, since he had to carry the case by the handle as if it were a long suitcase, but it wouldn't attract as much attention if anyone saw it. He kept one launcher and loaded two of the spare grenades into its box.

Hyuen Bo wrapped her arms around him and pressed her face into his neck.

"I love you," she said.

"I must do this," he told her, steeling himself. "I will be back. And we will be together. I promise."

Gently, he pushed her away, then quickly started up the beach. It wasn't until he reached the golf course that he realized his shirt was wet with her tears.

Bai Sau Airport

The SEALs spread out in the fields surrounding the edge of the airport property, establishing a perimeter to keep the area under surveillance. With only forty-five minutes before pickup, they didn't want to let their guard down. Mara, Kerfer, and Josh stayed out of sight with Ma, waiting near the tree.

Mara adjusted the volume on her earset, glanced at her watch, then looked toward the southern horizon.

Forty-five minutes. Now forty-four.

She knew from experience they were going to be among the longest of her life. She wished she could just fast-forward through them. Or better, take them and save them for some other time she wanted to move slowly. Undoubtedly, on her deathbed she was going to want them back.

Assuming, of course, that she died in bed. Not likely, given her profession.

"Company," said Little Joe over the radio.

"What?" Mara asked.

"Army guys in one of those Chinese Hummer trucks. Comin' at you."

"How many?" asked Kerfer.

"Two. Officer and a driver. Cops must've sent them."

"We're better off trying not to be seen," said Mara. "If they send reinforcements, the helo may have a tough time landing."

"Truck behind them. Looks like it's full," said Little Joe.

"Stay down," said Mara. "I think I have a solution."

"What?" asked Josh.

"Stay down," said Kerfer. "Keep Mạ quiet. All right?"

Josh put his fingers to his lips, then ducked down. Mạ did the same.

Meanwhile, Mara took out one of the cell phones she'd bought in Hanoi and pressed the speed dial for Zeus. But instead of Zeus, another voice came on the line.

"Hello?"

"I need Zeus."

"He is not here."

"You have his phone."

"Major Murphy told me to do whatever you asked," said the man. "What do you need?"

Mara hesitated. Would Zeus really have given over the phone?

"Troops are getting out," said Little Joe. "A dozen at least."

"Where is Major Murphy?" Mara asked.

"He's on an important assignment. I am his liaison. I can help."

Mara could see the truck. It wouldn't take long for the soldiers to get too close for comfort.

"There's a unit at Bai Sau Airport that must be pulled back, into the city, away from the airport. Right now. Immediately."

"This moment."

"Absolutely now."

"It will be done," said the man.

Mara hung up.

"Twenty yards," said Squeaky.

"Hold your fire," said Mara.

"You got a plan here, lady?" asked Kerfer. He had taken his gun out and squatted next to her, ready.

"A friend is going to pull them back."

"He is, huh?"

The soldiers walked through the field slowly. Stevens dropped back behind a warehouse to avoid detection. Meanwhile, a second troop truck arrived, parking up by the buildings across from the airport. Those soldiers began searching there.

The commander of the unit, a Vietnamese lieutenant, walked on a beeline toward the tree. A communications man walked with him, while a pair of soldiers lagged behind, rifles in hand.

"If we can grab the louey, maybe we can set up a hostage situation," said Kerfer.

"Just hold on," said Mara.

"I don't know that that's going to work, spook." Kerfer put down his gun and took out his knife. He turned to Josh. "You know how to use that, right?"

"Yeah."

"Just hold on," said Mara.

The soldiers were ten yards away when the communications man suddenly stopped and reached for the controls of his field radio. The private listened for a moment, then handed the radiophone to the lieutenant. He was so close Mara could see his face, even smell his sweat. If the wind shifted suddenly, he'd smell theirs.

"Tôi hiêu!" he said loudly. I understand!

He reached for his pistol. Mara felt her stomach knot.

The lieutenant fired into the air. Mara felt Kerfer's body coiling, ready to attack.

"Back to the truck!" the lieutenant shouted in Vietnamese. He turned abruptly. "We are needed at the port! Back to the truck!"

S tepping onto the golf course was like stepping onto a mattress. Jing Yo's feet sprang up with each step, his energy increasing.

He worked to control it. Too much excitement would cloud his mind.

Jing Yo took his submachine gun out of his backpack, trying to balance caution against readiness. Then he ran into the woods lining the northern edge of the course. He spotted a building to his left, a large mansion or clubhouse. He changed course to avoid it, trotting through an open field, then past a narrow band of trees to the highway.

The road was empty. The airport sat a half mile beyond, at the top of the hill above a patchwork of fields and houses.

Jing Yo readjusted the strap holding his submachine gun, making it easier to tuck down near his leg behind the RPG box, then dashed across the road.

W hy didn't you use that magic cell phone before?" Kerfer asked.

"We didn't need it until now," Mara told him. "I might have used it on the train, if you'd given me a chance."

He scowled at her, then began checking in with his men, making sure the soldiers had gone.

Thirty-two more minutes, thought Mara, checking her watch. A few lifetimes.

"You feeling good now?" she asked Josh.

"I'm ready."

Mara leaned over to Mạ and asked her in Vietnamese if she was all right.

"*Vâng,*" said Mạ. Yes.

"The helicopter I told you about—it's coming. Are you ready?"

"Yes."

"We will fly to a new home. Okay?"

"Josh," said Mạ, grabbing him. "He will come with us?"

"Yes," said Mara. "Okay?"

"Yes. I am ready."

"We won't let the bad men hurt you," said Mara.

Mạ's chin began to quiver. Mara glanced at Josh, who tucked Mạ close to him.

"We got somebody moving up through the fields," said Stevens over the radio.

"A soldier?" asked Kerfer.

"I don't know. Maybe a militia guy—has a lighter shirt. Khaki. Carrying something. Could have a weapon. I don't have an angle. Ducking into one of the lanes. Shit, I lost him."

"Hold your position," said Kerfer.

"Where is he?" Mara asked.

Kerfer pointed toward the house that sat on the edge of the hill to their right. "Gotta be looking for us," he said.

"I agree."

"Probably avoiding the rice paddy," he said. "If he keeps going straight, he comes out right over there, across from the houses. Stevens is back this way." He pointed to the left, meaning beyond the rice paddy.

Mara glanced at her watch. If they took him out now, would the helicopter arrive before the police? Or before whoever had just helped them changed his mind?

"He may just be a scout," said Kerfer. "If he's not armed and alone. We should still take him out, though."

"Shooting him will complicate things," said Mara. "Is he close enough to grab?"

Kerfer touched his radio control to transmit. "Hey, Stevens, can you grab this guy without too much fuss?"

"Negative. He's out of sight. Good fifty yards away anyway."

"Can you sneak up behind him?"

"If he's armed, what do you want me to do?"

Kerfer turned to Mara.

"Watch him until the helicopter gets closer," she said. "Or until he's a threat. There's too much time for the soldiers to come back."

"Yeah, okay, I agree," said Kerfer. He hit the radio. "Stevens, can you parallel him?"

"Yeah, I'm on it."

"All right. Keep him in sight."

"See, you can cooperate," Mara told Kerfer.

"Don't get too comfortable with it."

J ing Yo heard the dog yapping in the backyard as he turned out of the alley. He had been planning to go over the fence there but decided to try the next yard instead.

His heart was pounding. He needed to calm down. He needed to work out a plan.

He'd get onto the airport grounds, find a place to hide the grenades and stow the guns. Then he would go to the terminal. He'd go inside, posing as a maintenance worker.

First, he needed a uniform.

He'd find a worker outside. He'd kill him quickly, with his hands. He'd take his shirt, and pants if necessary.

They'd be in the terminal. He could take them there, or he could take them on the helicopter when it arrived.

Either way.

A grenade into the motor of the chopper as it took off would be very efficient.

Two grenades into the terminal would be almost as easy.

And then?

Should he go to Hyuen Bo? They might be able to escape in the boat.

Difficult.

It would be easier for her if he disappeared. She would be killed if the Vietnamese caught him.

Getting out of the terminal might be hard. Hitting the helicopter as it took off presented its own difficulties, however. He'd have to be pretty close to ensure that he hit it.

Jing Yo saw a lane to his right. He started down it, saw a pair of children playing in the nearby yard. There was another lane, a dirt driveway, to his left. He turned, avoiding the kids, then saw a clear path to the road.

As he started to trot across the road, he spotted a man crouched near some bushes about a hundred meters ahead, up the hill.

A member of the scientist's security team.

He threw himself down.

"**T**otally fucking lost him," cursed Stevens.

Mara turned to Kerfer. The SEAL commander frowned but said nothing.

"He probably lives in one of the houses," said Mara. She checked her watch. "We have twenty-five minutes. Let's start pulling back and get up closer to the runway."

"Twenty-five minutes is a long time."

"It's a quarter mile from the perimeter access road to the landing pad, and we have to get past two warehouses," said Mara. "That's ten minutes, crawling."

"Sixty seconds, running."

"You really want to wait until the last minute? Besides, everybody's getting restless. You can hear it in their voices."

Kerfer touched his radio. "Start pulling back very slowly. You got ten minutes to get back to the tree."

Jing Yo watched the American begin to back up the hill slowly. Had he been spotted?

He craned his head, but he couldn't see very far in either direction without getting up, and he dared not do that.

The American stopped. Jing Yo held his breath, waiting. Finally the man began to move again. Jing Yo slid his body to the left, edging backward at the same time. He dragged the case with him, pushing through the rough grass and dirt.

If the American hadn't seen him, where would he be going?

He was obviously posted as a perimeter guard. He'd be pulling back to the terminal building.

Why?

Because it was time to leave, and he was being evaced as well.

Except the American didn't seem to be moving toward the terminal. Rather, he was moving toward high ground near the end of the runway.

For a better view? Simply a guard rotation?

Jing Yo edged upward, crawling on his belly, then stopping as the American rose and jogged about twenty meters before diving back to the ground, out of sight.

There was another guard on Jing Yo's left, a hundred meters away, stalking through the field.

Jing Yo breathed slowly, relaxing, readying himself. They'd seen him; they were coming for him.

The man had a submachine gun.

Jing Yo heard him say something. His ear was unaccustomed to English, so he had trouble deciphering the words.

Clear. That's what he thought the man said. *Clear.*

Maybe it was wishful thinking. It meant he wasn't spotted. It also meant the guards would relax now, easing their watch.

Time to advance.

Jing Yo took another breath. Patience was critical. And yet if he waited too long, he would lose his chance.

Now, he told himself, and started moving up the hill again. He spotted a group of boulders on his left. He rose on his hands and knees, then scrambled toward them.

A culvert extended across the access road below, up the slope, and over to the end of the runway. If he could get into the ditch, he could move in the direction the

Americans were going without being seen. He'd also have a path to the runway.

Of course, there might be someone in it already.

The only way to find out was to run there.

Jing Yo emptied his lungs, pressing the stale air out.

He got up and ran to the ditch, diving in, not sure if he had just run into the enemy's sights, ready, gun in hand. Ready.

The ditch was empty.

Stevens was the last of the team to arrive. Just as he dove in next to Kerfer, Josh heard the sound of helicopter rotors in the distance.

"You think that's them?" asked Josh.

"I hope," said Mara. She glanced at her watch. "They're early."

"How far off, you figure?"

"Couple of minutes," said Kerfer. "Navy Seahawk. You'll know when it's real close. Ground starts to shake. We wait until then. It shakes, we go. You got the girl?"

Josh put his arm around Ma. He felt a surge of relief. He'd been through so much. It was almost over.

"All right, let's wait, and make sure this is it," said Mara. She looked at Josh. "When we see it, we run straight across the road, across the end of the runway, to the cement pad. Got it?"

"Memorized," said Josh.

"Make sure you're locked and loaded," said Kerfer. "You, too, Junior, Mara. If we need them, we're going to want them right away."

"You have maybe six rounds left," Mara told Josh.

"Yeah, I know."

None of them had much ammunition. But they didn't need it now. The helicopter's rotors were getting louder and louder.

"Seahawk," said Stevens, pointing.

Kerfer held his hand up, watching for a few seconds. "Go," he said.

J ing Yo could feel the beat of the helicopter as it approached the airport.

This was it.

He snapped open the grenade launcher. The 40 mm shell had an effective range of roughly three hundred meters. The end of the runway was easily within that. But what if it landed farther down, away from him?

He'd run to get closer. He wanted to get it just after it took off, just after the scientist was aboard.

He'd have only one chance. He'd have to run as closely as he could. He'd run with both legs, as the monks said.

Jing Yo picked up the launcher. He wished he'd taken the other. Reloading for a second shot would take time; having the second launcher would have been easier.

Just make sure you don't miss, he told himself.

He checked the strap on the submachine gun, ready to fire. The rucksack was on his back. He'd need it later, for the extra bullets, for the escape.

There'd be no escape. That was not his fate.

The helicopter flew over the beach on his right, heading for the runway. Jing Yo took another long breath.

They were running!

The scientist was right there, running, not fifty yards away.

The woman he'd seen in Hanoi. And . . . a girl.

A girl?

Mara ran next to Josh and Mạ, the center of the circle as the SEALs hustled toward the landing spot. This was the sort of thing the shooters practiced time and again, and the team ran as one, swarming across the scrub and leaping over the ditch like a well-trained dance company moving across the stage.

As they reached the asphalt apron around the runway, they dropped their pace. The three SEALs at the back of the group turned to make sure no one was sneaking behind them.

Squeaky suddenly shouted. "Man, man—I got a man!"

Then he started to fire.

Jing Yo saw the muzzle flash. Instinctively, he raised his weapon and fired.

The grenade hit the man shooting at him square in the chest and exploded.

Josh felt himself launched into the air. He didn't know what had happened. He couldn't hear—it was as if someone had clapped his hands on Josh's ears.

He landed in the dirt.

A sneeze welled up from deep in his chest.

Someone grabbed him, pulling him.

Mara.

"What?"

If she said anything, he couldn't hear what it was.

Mạ?

The girl had been behind him. He twisted around, thinking she was under him.

She wasn't.

Oh God, after this, after all she had been through—was she going to die? It couldn't work that way.

But of course it could.

He saw Mạ lying in the field, a few feet away.

God! God! Why!

He ran to her, tears welling in his eyes.

"Josh?" she muttered, starting to rise.

He grabbed her. The helicopter was turning toward them, turning toward the cement pad. He began to run for it.

J ing Yo dropped his grenade launcher and grabbed his submachine gun. But even as he pressed the trigger, the ditch erupted with a hail of bullets. He threw himself down, waiting for a break in the storm.

M ara pushed Josh and Mạ toward the chopper, then turned back to see where the others were. Stevens, Eric, and Silvestri were firing from their knees, covering the ditch. Little Joe, Kerfer, and Squeaky were down.

Squeaky was more than down. The grenade had ripped through his chest and severed his head, which lay on the ground a few yards away.

Mara jerked her head back toward the ditch.

"Get that motherfucker!" yelled Stevens.

Something moved. Mara fired. Her bullets sped through the gun; within seconds she had no more.

The others must be almost out as well.

"Get to the helicopter!" she shouted at them.

She ran to Kerfer, who was lying faceup. There was blood all over his chest.

"Hey," he said.

"Come on." Mara reached down and tried to pull him up, but Kerfer didn't budge.

"Go. Get the hell out of here."

Mara grabbed his submachine gun.

"Come on," she told Kerfer. "On my back."

"Ain't worth it, spook lady. Go!"

Mara reached down and scooped him up as one of the SEALs started firing again. She ran a few yards toward Little Joe, intending to help him up as well, but as she got close, she realized he wasn't getting up—the exploding grenade had blown his leg off, leaving his body in a pool of blood. His eyes were closed, as if in sleep, but it was clear he was already dead.

"To the helicopter!" she yelled. *"Go! Go!"*

J ing Yo raised his head, then quickly ducked back as the Americans began firing again.

There were more grenades in the case. He needed them.

The gunfire stopped. He grabbed the box, opened it, then reached for his launcher. But when he tried putting the grenade in, he saw that the barrel had been hit by bullets. It wouldn't accept the grenade.

He'd have to take them with the submachine gun.

He punched out the old magazine, even though it was half full. Slamming a new box in, he grabbed two more, then jumped up and began running toward the helicopter.

J osh turned a few feet from the chopper, looking back for the others. He saw Mara, dragging Kerfer on her back. Eric ran to her and helped.

Where was Squeaky? Where was he?

One of the chopper crewmen jumped to the ground.

"Take the girl," Josh yelled, pushing Mạ toward him. "Go!"

Josh let go of Mạ, then spun and started to run for the others.

E ric took hold of Kerfer as Mara stumbled toward him. Silvestri took the other side. Mara twisted out from under them and spun back.

The bastard who'd been following them was jumping out of the ditch.

She squeezed the trigger on Kerfer's gun.

He was out of bullets, too.

J osh saw the man in the ditch lowering his gun to fire. He pressed the trigger, but without good aim, his bullets went low, striking the dirt in front of the man.

But it was enough. He went down.

"Into the helicopter!" Josh screamed, turning back for the helo. "Into the helicopter!"

J ing Yo collapsed as the ground erupted in front of him. He couldn't lose now.

He raised his weapon to fire. But there was someone behind the scientist, a sailor from the helicopter, shooting with an M-4. The fire was so intense he had to stay down. He dug his chin into the dirt, waiting for the fusillade to lift.

———

Just as he reached the nose of the helicopter, Josh saw something from the corner of his eye. He stopped and turned. There was a small figure with a gun, two guns—a grenade launcher, he thought.

He raised his weapon. This time his aim was true, striking the figure in the midsection.

"Into the chopper!" screamed Mara, grabbing his back. "Go! Go! Go!"

They dove headfirst into the body of the Seahawk. Before Josh could get to his feet, they were off the ground.

28

Bai Sau Airport

Jing Yo rose as the helicopter rose, emptying his gun at the fuselage. But the helicopter was charging away, up the runway and back toward the sea. He started to run, screaming at it in frustration.

And then, with the Seahawk banking hard to the southeast, he saw the body of his lover, prone in the field, hunched over the grenade launcher.

If he had been truly a man of duty, he would have scooped up the launcher at that moment and tried somehow to down the helicopter, even though it was out of range.

But he would have had to be a man of stone to do that.

Jing sank to his knees, bent over Hyuen Bo's dead body, and wept.

Fury

愤怒

Greene Urges Patience on Economy

WASHINGTON (AP–Fox News)—Sounding a theme he has used since taking office, President Greene told a press conference today that he is confident the economy will rebound soon.

"Sooner, not later," said Greene. "But we must be patient."

Greene made the remarks during a press conference called specifically to discuss the situation in Southeast Asia, where Vietnam has attacked China in a dispute over borders. However, not one reporter asked a question about the conflict; the economy took center stage. . . .

Solar Panel Blouses Turn Up Heat

PARIS (NBC–Agence France-Presse)—With wearable solar panels all the rage, three French designers today unveiled a new line of shoulder-board blouses they say will power MP3s and cell phones for up to 12 hours.

They'll turn up the heat as well, with plunging necklines and see-through fabric that leave little to the imagination. . . .

1

Washington, D.C.

"Frost needs you right away," said Dickson Theodore, sticking his head through the door of the Oval Office. "Line three."

President Greene smiled at Cindy Metfort, the MS-NBC reporter who'd been interviewing him. "I really do have to take this call."

"I don't mind."

Greene kept smiling. He didn't care much for MS-NBC, but Cindy was . . . an impeachment waiting to happen, probably.

"I know it's really late, but I'm afraid I'd like to take this one alone," he said. "Maybe we can wrap this up tomorrow or sometime next week."

He winked at his assistant press secretary, Debra Scacciaferro. Scacciaferro was already at the reporter's side, ready to physically remove her if necessary.

That wasn't necessary, probably to Scacciaferro's chagrin. She wasn't a big booster of the cable networks.

"Of course, Mr. President," said Cindy, rising. "Tomorrow or next week will be fine. I hadn't realized how late it was myself."

Greene watched her leave. Ah, to be twenty years younger . . . then he'd only be old enough to be her father.

The president picked up the phone. "This is the president."

"We have them," said the head of the CIA. "They're en route to the Philippines."

"All of them? The little girl, too?"

"Yes, sir."

"Great."

"There's one thing you should know, George," said Frost. "Peter Lucas had his people set up something with the captain of USS *McCampbell*. The destroyer sailed past a pair of Chinese ships and sent a helo through the blockade. There was almost a collision, but no shots were fired. I stand behind Peter one hundred percent," added Frost. "He did what I would have done."

"Then congratulate him," said Greene. "And get me the name of that destroyer captain. I want him promoted."

Over the South China Sea

Josh felt as if a blanket had been thrown over him. His whole body vibrated, and not just from the rotating rotors above the Seahawk. He slipped back on the bench at the side of the helicopter, still stunned and unable to process everything that had happened.

A Navy corpsman was working over Kerfer on the floor. He had an IV bottle and was poking at his chest. He reached into a box and took out a syringe, then plunged it into the SEAL commander's rump.

Mara stood over the corpsman, watching. Eric was next to her, his face white.

"What happened to Squeaky?" Josh asked.

No one answered.

"Squeaky," he said. He looked at Mara.

"No, Josh," she said. "He and Little Joe are dead."

Josh exhaled slowly.

"We didn't get them out of there," said Stevens loudly. "We should have gotten them out of there."

"We needed to get ourselves out," said Mara.

"We should have gotten them the hell out of there." Stevens whirled and put his fist into the frame of the helicopter. He punched it hard, then punched again. Tears streamed down the sides of his face.

Josh stomped his feet, sharing Stevens's anger and frustration. He'd liked both of the SEALs, Squeaky especially—a big bear of a guy with a stupid little girl's voice.

"Damn," he said, pounding the floor.

Mạ grabbed his side in fright. The medic looked up at him. One of the Navy crewmen put his hand on his shoulder.

"Sir," said the sailor. "Please. Calm down. You saved the chopper. You did your best."

"I didn't save the chopper. My friends—they died. They died for me."

"You killed the gook with the grenade launcher," said Eric. "You couldn't've done any more."

Stevens came over and wrapped his arm around him. Neither of them spoke.

The medic continued to work on Kerfer. He had gauze and bandages and tape.

Did he have magic? Josh wondered. Because that's what they really needed—magic to get them the hell out of here, to take them back, far back.

He'd killed the gook with the grenade launcher. Or he'd killed a gook.

A gook?

Or a human being?

Someone who was trying to kill him. That's whom he'd killed. Someone who wanted him dead.

"It was a girl," said one of the crewmen.

Josh looked up at him.

"We got it on the chopper video. It was a woman."

"I killed a girl?" Josh asked. He sat on the bench. Mạ sat close beside him.

"You saved our lives, Josh," said Mara. She came over and kissed him on the cheek. "Thank you."

Bai Sau Airport

There is but one purpose. *There is but one Way. To forget this truth is to forget yourself. To forget yourself is to surrender to the chaos.*

The words of his mentors came to Jing Yo in the fading beat of the helicopter's rotors. They were fact and recrimination, accusation and inspiration, a call to return from the path where he had strayed.

Hyuen Bo was dead, killed by the man he had pursued. Her death was Jing Yo's fault, as surely as if he had put the bullet through her skull himself.

Her long dark hair, the white skin of her wrist—the image burned into his brain. But already the stench of death had claimed her, the smell of rot and return.

He despaired.

There is but one purpose. There is but one Way. To forget this truth is to forget yourself. To forget yourself is to surrender to the chaos.

"I must move myself," he said aloud.

In the next instant, Jing Yo jumped to his feet and began to run. He fled across the field, across the road and through a yard, down the soft green fairways, over the rocks and to the boat. He moved so fast that his conscious thoughts trailed far behind, outpaced.

By the time his brain caught up to his body he was an hour upstream, nearly out of gas. He found a small marina and would have stolen fuel had a man not appeared on the dock and offered to sell it.

"You look battered," said the man. "Were you in the shelling?"

Jing Yo blinked at him, handing over his spare gas cans.

"There are rumors that the Chinese attacked the shore," said the man. "Missiles and artillery from ships. Did that happen?"

"There was an attack," said Jing Yo.

"Where are you going? Saigon?"

"I don't know."

"There have been attacks there as well. You're better off in the highlands. They are forming bands of resistance. A young man like you would be of some worth."

"That's where I'm going," said Jing Yo, not sure what else to say. "To the hills. To fight."

"I thought so," said the man grimly.

He gave him the fuel for free, then pressed him to take some food and a few thousand dong.

"We are counting on you," said the man, tears in his eyes. "Go with our prayers."

A half dozen plumes of black spiraled from the center of Ho Chi Minh City. Above them, thick piles of black cotton seemed pasted on the sky.

A Vietnamese gunboat sat in the middle of the river channel, its gun raised and slightly off center. There were half as many small boats on the river as normal, and their movements seemed slow and tentative, their owners skittish.

A policeman stood on the first dock Jing Yo passed. There was one on the second as well. Jing Yo continued up the waterway until he found a jetty where no one was waiting to ask questions.

He had the submachine gun and a half dozen rounds of ammunition in a rucksack. If questioned he planned to say he had been given them by a friend in the militia, for protection; he had no idea if this would be an adequate explanation.

Soldiers and police guarded the intersections and patrolled in front of storefronts, even in Chinatown. Knots of militia clustered around trucks or kept the curious from smoldering ruins. Last night's marauders had returned to become the day's order keepers. Some were cleaning up the mess they or their comrades had made—Jing Yo passed two work crews of militiamen sweeping glass from the streets and replacing broken windows with large sheets of wood.

They were acting under orders, he was sure. Which would last longer—their hatred for the Chinese, or their respect for authority?

Getting into the area where Ms. Hu lived was not easy. Jing Yo had to circle around the center of the city on foot. There were several places where he might have slipped across the barriers to take a shortcut, but he decided the risk wasn't worth it. The police were not bothering people who went about their business, so long as they didn't go where they weren't supposed to. And Jing Yo knew that the less he had to explain to anyone, the less chance he had of being apprehended.

The bicycles and motorbikes were still relatively plentiful on the streets. Their riders seemed more anxious than even on the day before, less willing to yield to pedestrians or change their course as another vehicle approached. Private cars, always a minority in the city, were almost nonexistent, as were commercial trucks.

Jing Yo walked through the precincts of the city, absorbing not just the sights and sounds, but the jittery emotions of the people. They moved mostly with purpose, not meandering—he guessed they were getting things in order, buying food and water for a siege, making sure they had batteries and other emergency supplies. He saw no one smiling.

The missiles and bombs had brought a powdery, metallic smell to the air, something close to fire and yet not completely burned. The sun was bright, and the damp air hot.

Three men in Western jeans and soccer shirts leaned against an old pickup truck on the dirt road near the fuel tanks around the corner from Ms. Hu's compound. Jing Yo walked toward them, his gaze fixed in the distance. One of the men stepped toward him, hand on the back of his hip. A bulge on the opposite side of his belt betrayed his revolver.

"I have business with Ms. Hu," he told the man.

"Ms. Hu? I don't believe we know of a Ms. Hu."

"Oh," said Jing Yo, easily guessing this was a lie.

He took a step forward. The man stepped in front of him.

"Listen, friend," said the man. "This is not a good place for you."

"Nonetheless, I have business," Jing Yo told the man.

If the man had gone for his pistol, Jing Yo would have killed him on the spot. He would have made short work of the others as well.

In truth, he thirsted for provocation. He wanted to unleash some of the anger he felt. But instead of fighting, the man took out a small radio.

"Your name?" asked the man.

"Jing Yo."

Whatever the person on the other side said surprised the man.

"Go on," he told Jing Yo, holding both hands up as if in surrender.

M s. Hu was in her garden. It was as if nothing had happened.

"Sit, please," she told Jing Yo.

"I have no need to sit. Your man tried to kill me. He has met with a regrettable end."

"So I understand."

"I require transportation to complete my mission."

"Where to?"

"To America, I assume."

While Sun had told him otherwise, Jing Yo suspected that Ms. Hu had either ordered the killing herself, or at a minimum had passed the order on from his commander or Beijing. He knew that he could not trust her, just as he could not trust anyone now, not on his own side or the enemy's. Indeed, the enemy was more reliable than his friends, for the enemy's motives were clear and unchanging. By contrast, those belonging to Colonel Sun and Ms. Hu were much more difficult to fathom.

"You think that I can arrange passage to America," said Ms. Hu. She had the tone of someone making a statement, not asking a question.

"Whether you personally can do it, I could not say." Jing Yo stared at her face as he spoke, fighting the urge to turn his eyes downward. "But I know it can be done.

And I know that my mission has been ordered from the highest authority."

Ms. Hu took the tiniest sip of tea from her cup.

"You are very stoic," she told him after returning the cup to the table. "And brave to trust me."

"I don't trust you," said Jing Yo.

"If I tried to kill you once, why would I not try again?"

"If it is my time to die, so be it. You are not the keeper of my fate."

"You have surrendered to your religion, Jing Yo," said Ms. Hu. "Is that wise for a commando? To trust to superstition? Obviously the monks didn't—if they did, they wouldn't have trained in kung fu. They would have remained in their monastery, praying, those many centuries ago."

"There are many forms of prayer," replied Jing Yo.

"It is useless to debate you." Ms. Hu smiled for the first time. "The monks have taught you all the answers."

"No answers. Only questions."

"Trusting me is a way of testing your faith," said Ms. Hu pointedly. "If I do not kill you, you will assume that your beliefs are correct. You will think that you are a warrior, following the Way, and that the Way calls you to this mission."

Jing Yo remained silent.

"So you believe I betrayed you," said Ms. Hu, "and ordered you killed?"

"It is the most logical conclusion."

"Have you considered that Mr. Tong betrayed us both?" asked Ms. Hu. "He saw killing the American as a way to advance beyond me. You were in the way."

"What happened does not matter to me," said Jing Yo. "Only the present is of interest. I seek only the means to complete my duty."

"You have done a favor for me, eliminating the viper," said Ms Hu. "Whether you knew it or not. I will see what I can arrange. Go back to the house where I sent you last night. Be ready to leave at a moment's notice."

Washington, D.C.

The encounter between the *McCampbell* and the Chinese ships was now being seen around the world, thanks to the Chinese news service, which wasted no time presenting high-definition video to every news organization it could think of, as well as posting a variety of snippets on YouTube. In the Chinese version of things, the American had been aggressive and then turned away; and indeed, from the way the video was edited, it did appear that way.

The American version—much longer and unedited—gave a completely different perspective. Not only did it show the destroyer staying straight and true until after the frigate veered off, but it also caught three Chinese sailors basically running for their lives in the moment before the ships came close.

Greene especially liked that. He considered offering to pay for dry cleaning at a press conference to answer the charges, but decided that would seem a little too cheeky, even for him.

Unfortunately, many of the rest of the world's leaders had a different response to the exchange than Greene did. The French and Italians wondered why the U.S.

was provoking China. India was considering recalling its Washington ambassador for "consultations"—a step not even the Chinese had undertaken. The British prime minister was calling for "considered reflection"—clearly the prime minister was taking the Dalai Lama's recent visit to London a bit too seriously.

The response that most unsettled Greene, however, came from the U.S. Congress. He expected the opposition to raise holy hell, and they did. Greene was being pilloried as a warmonger. His critics accused him of trying to pick a fight with China, possibly to get out of paying back American debts to the country. He wasn't exactly sure how that was supposed to work, but in any event he wasn't surprised. Given that during the campaign his opponents had likened him to Mussolini— "not smart enough to be Hitler," snarked several—he considered the present criticism from that quarter mild.

The screams from his own party were a different matter. The House majority leader was questioning whether the destroyer had been ordered to initiate the conflict. In the Senate, a dozen of Greene's former allies were lining up behind Senator Grasso of New York, who had already scheduled hearings into the matter.

Those hearings could be a forum for the White House to make its case, if the president could bring Grasso around. But short of adding the senator's face to Mount Rushmore, that wasn't likely to happen.

Greene decided he had to at least soften him up a little. So he put in a call. And then a second one.

Grasso called back after the third.

"The Gulf of Tonkin," said Grasso when Greene picked up the phone.

Greene rolled his eyes, but reminded himself that he would not be baited. "Senator. How are you?"

"George, you're as transparent as a cheap hooker's robe," said Grasso.

"I hope you're not basing that on personal experience," said Greene.

"Johnson did the same thing in Vietnam—created an incident so Congress would give him carte blanche over the war. The Gulf of Tonkin. That is not happening here," said Grasso. "Negative."

"I assure you, Senator, the destroyer was severely provoked and acted with model restraint. A ridiculous amount of restraint. And it was quite a distance from the Gulf of Tonkin."

"Cut the Senator crap, George. You and I have been around the block. I know a power play when I see it. Crude as it is. The tail wagging the dog."

"What will it take for you to see that China is the villain?" said Greene.

"I don't care if China is the villain. Frankly, I don't give a crap about them. Or Vietnam. Especially Vietnam."

"Neither do I," said Greene.

"I'm glad to hear you say that," said Grasso. "Because a lot of people think this is psychological—some sort of payback for the people who protected you in prison."

"Nobody protected me when I was a prisoner, Phil. They tortured me. There were no secret deals to keep me alive. It's all been reported. But ask the men I was with if you don't believe me."

Grasso was silent for a moment, an unusual state for him. Greene hated to play the POW card, but he wouldn't avoid it, either, especially when someone was spewing bullshit.

Part of him wouldn't mind seeing the Vietnamese

government—not the people—crushed as payback for what they'd done to him, and more important, to his friends. But as president, his personal feelings were beside the point. And they were, no matter *what* armchair politico-psychologists said in their blogs.

"You know, I think I can put the entire conflict in the proper perspective when I speak at the UN Friday," said Greene.

"You're still pushing for sanctions?"

"I think they're inadequate, but we have to start somewhere."

"You don't have a single vote in the Senate in favor of them."

Actually, Greene figured he had about three. But why quibble?

"Why don't you come to the UN with me and listen for yourself?" said Greene. "Have lunch with me. Prime Minister Gray will be there. He's always good for a few laughs."

The invitation was supposed to flatter Grasso, who would be able to hobnob with world leaders as if he were one of them. But it seemed to fall flat.

"I have a very busy schedule," said the senator. "I don't think I can make it."

"I think you'll like what you hear."

"I doubt it."

"You have to be in New York anyway," said Greene. "You're going to the Governor Smith Dinner, right?"

"Yes."

"So am I."

Grasso didn't respond. Greene guessed that his invitation to New York's biggest political bash of the year—a charity dinner where all the top politicians and top wannabes attended—was a surprise and a challenge to Grasso.

He certainly hoped it was. It had taken quite a bit of arm-twisting to get it.

"Come with me to the UN," Greene urged again. "It will be worth your while, I guarantee."

"Do I get a copy of your speech beforehand?"

"You don't have to endorse it."

"I'd like to read it."

"It's not written yet, or I'd have a copy sent right over."

"You'd better get your staff working. You only have a few days."

"I'm writing it myself. So—can I count on you?"

"I'll see if I can fit it on my schedule."

Grasso hung up.

Greene dropped the phone on the hook, wondering if it would not be a good idea to spray it with Lysol.

En route to Vandenberg Air Force Base, California

The Air Force crewman was almost comically respectful, hovering over Josh and Mara like a doting uncle caring for a pair of visiting newborns. When Josh got up to go to the restroom, the sergeant nearly leapt from his seat near the rear of the plane. "Is the baby okay?" he asked.

"She's fine. She's sleeping," said Josh.

Mạ had been checked out by a corpsman on the destroyer and by a doctor in Thailand, where they'd landed to meet the Air Force transport. Everyone said she was in great health.

Physically. Given her age and what she had been through, her mental state remained unknown.

"So, can I get you something?" asked the sergeant.

"Just gotta use the head," said Josh.

"Sir, by all means. Anything you need."

When Josh came out, the crewman asked if he wanted some more coffee.

"Coffee's going through me, thanks."

"We have beers, sir."

"That's all right. Beer would put me to sleep."

"The book okay?"

"I'm good."

"Say the word. Anything you want."

The sergeant had scrounged up some reading material from the base in the Philippines where the plane had refueled. The choices were an odd mix but included a classic by Patricia Highsmith, *Strangers on a Train*. It was an odd and twisted book: two men, thrown together, end up committing a murder for each other—one willingly, almost gleefully; the other as an act of strange desperation.

Thrown together by chance, to discover what they were made of? Or to discover the darkness every man is capable of?

Which was the author's point?

Josh went back to his seat. Mara was sitting behind him. The small jet, a military version of a Learjet 85, with an extended range, was less opulent than a civilian corporate jet but still had such amenities as plush, fully reclining seats and video screens that rose from the cabin sides. The sergeant had snagged a half dozen movies, but they were all thrillers, and Josh was in no mood to see anything that might remind him of the real thrills he had just escaped.

"We'll be down in a couple of hours," said Mara. "You'll be able to stretch your legs."

"Then what?"

"Direct flight to Washington. Meet the president." Josh nodded.

"You up for it?" she asked.

"I guess. You think Ma is?"

"She's a tough kid," said Mara. "She'll make it."

He peered over the seat to where the girl was curled up, sleeping. She was a tough kid. No doubt about that.

"Kerfer's going to be okay," Mara said. "I got a text from Bangkok. They heard from the fleet."

"Good."

"We couldn't do anything about Squeaky and Little Joe."

"I know."

"The Vietnamese recovered their bodies. They'll get home."

"Do you do this stuff all the time?" he asked.

"Which stuff? Rescue scientists and eyewitnesses to massacres? No."

"Don't make fun of it."

She reached her hand out and touched his leg. "I've seen death, if that's what you mean."

Josh nodded.

"The people who died, the people you shot—they were trying to kill you, Josh," Mara said. "And her. Her whole family was wiped out. Her village. Everything."

"I know."

"That's why war sucks. That's why you have to tell the world what happened."

Josh slumped in his seat. What about the soldiers in the train, he thought. What about them? Should we have killed them?

But he was too tired to ask the question. Way too tired.

He leaned his head back and closed his eyes.

Suddenly he felt Mara next to him, over him, her face next to his.

His heart leapt.

She reached to his side as he opened his eyes. He thought she was going to kiss him. He longed for it.

"You have to buckle your seat belt," she said gently, slipping it together. "Before the sergeant does it for you."

Washington, D.C.

Peter Frost caught President Greene's sleeve as he stepped toward the tee. "You're sure you want to do this?"

"I'm a lousy golfer, Peter," admitted Greene. "You think I should be using a five-iron?"

"I mean Vietnam. The Zeus plan."

"Oh, and here I thought you were talking about something *important*." Greene laughed and walked toward the ball. The laugh was a bit too sharp, he realized, but there was no way of taking it back, and he wouldn't if he could.

"I'm serious, George," said Frost.

Greene squatted down, as if inspecting the grass around the ball. He didn't like golf, but had discovered that the game had various uses, the most important of which was allowing him to get out in the fresh air away from the constant pressure of the White House. It also gave him a way of talking with his aides and confidants— the press called them cronies—in a more relaxed atmosphere.

Golf was one of the benefits of climate change, at least from Greene's perspective. A few years ago, February golf even in the Washington, D.C., area would have been a chilly affair. Global warming wasn't all bad.

"Shouldn't be too hard to hit," said Greene, rising.

"What you're doing is borderline legal," said Frost.

"I don't think there's anything borderline about it," said Greene. "As long as I hit the ball squarely. It goes down the middle of the fairway. No one will complain."

"After the beating you've been taking all day, I'm surprised you're willing to take the risk."

"Not much of a beating, all things considered," said Greene.

"Gulf of Tonkin? A thousand blogs have used the analogy."

"Senator Grasso said that on the phone. Do you think he got it from them, or the other way around?"

"George—"

"I like the Zeus plan," said Greene, lining up the head of his club.

The CIA had obtained the missiles from Dubai and sold them, through a third-party government, to a South African company. The South African company was owned by a man who had once worked for the CIA but was now a private entrepreneur—a term favored over the less generous but better-known "mercenary." The entrepreneur had hired an ex–Malaysian air force general to ship the weapons to Malaysia via his air freight company. The missiles were at this moment being loaded onto a pair of MiG-21s owned by a private company and leased to the Malaysian air force. There was paperwork indicating that the missiles were being tested as part of a feasibility program to see if the country should buy them, though it was hoped that such paperwork would never have to be reviewed.

The Malaysian general *was* Malaysian, but he was also on the CIA payroll, and had been for several years, pretty much since the beginning of the covert war there. Most of the technicians working on the plane were Americans under contract to the private company that owned the planes—a private company formed by an ex–CIA employee immediately on his "retirement" from the clandestine service. The two "test" pilots who would fly the planes were Australians, though neither could return to Australia without facing a variety of criminal charges.

According to the spec sheets, the MiGs themselves did not have the range to reach the target area, a slam-dunk argument against anyone who came up with a wild theory alleging that they had somehow been involved. What the spec sheets did not indicate was that both MiGs had been fitted with more efficient engines and conformal tanks that increased their fuel capacity.

The conformal tanks were modeled after those in the Stealth Eagle program, helping decrease the MiGs' radar signature to the point that, with care, they would not be detected by even the American ships in the area, let alone the Chinese. Indeed, the MiGs looked very little like standard MiGs, with angled fins taking the place of the normal tail configuration, and nose extensions that would have made a plastic surgeon drool.

Greene, the former aviator, knew and loved all these details. Frost had passed them along, knowing he'd love them. It was also a way for Frost to cover his behind if the mission blew up in their face. Greene had no doubt that the CIA director would take the sword for him before a congressional committee, but when it came to writing his memoirs in a few years, a lot of blood would be on the floor.

Greene's blood.

So be it. The way he figured it, he'd be senile by then anyway.

Greene whacked the ball. It flew straight down the fairway—for fifty yards. Then it began shanking hard to the right.

In the direction of the doglegged pin, as luck would have it. It cleared a rough, bounced over a trap—just— and plopped at the edge of the green.

"Better lucky than good," said the president. He turned to the Secret Service detail and aides behind them. "We'll walk."

"Now I know you're crazy," said Frost. "Walking?"

"Come on, Peter. Do you good."

The aides shot ahead. The Secret Service detail stayed a respectful, but watchful, distance behind.

"I got all the exercise I need forty years ago," groused Frost. In actual fact, he was in as good a shape as the president—probably better, since he wasn't feeding at the trough of so many state dinners.

"We have the finding indicating that American lives are at risk and have to be protected," said Greene, addressing the legality of the action—such as it was. "I'll hang my hat on that."

"That's a thin nail," said Frost. "And more than your hat is resting on it."

"This is nothing more than any president has done. Look at Reagan in South America. He fought a war there for years. Never had congressional support. Never went to them. What does posterity think about that?"

"That was against drug dealers, George. Nobody cares about drug dealers. Besides, it was Reagan. People loved Reagan. They don't love you."

"Ah. I have a depression to deal with," said Greene. "I don't expect them to be patting me on the back."

"Stabbing you in the back isn't a good alternative."

Greene stopped. "Why so negative today?"

The president searched his old friend's face. Ironically enough, they'd met back in Vietnam, both of them idealists in the process of being sharply disillusioned.

Greene's naïveté had ended a few weeks later, somewhere around fifteen thousand feet, as he descended from his airplane and realized he was so far over Injun territory that he was going to end up either dead or a POW. He wasn't exactly sure where Frost's had run out.

"We always said that if we were running things, we would do what was right," Greene told him. "No matter how we had to get it done. You know this is right—if we don't stop China now, there'll be a world war inside of five years."

"There may be a world war anyway, no matter what we do."

"I realize that," said Greene. "I wish I could get the rest of the country to realize that. At the moment, I'll settle for UN sanctions. And a congressional vote in favor of them. It's a start. Where's your damn ball, anyway?"

7

Edwards Air Force Base, Maryland

The jet's engines suddenly grew very loud. Josh raised his head, then felt gravity slam it back against the seat. For a moment he felt weightless, and panicky. He'd been sleeping, and all he could think of was that they'd been shot down.

But no one was firing at them. They were in the States, safe, at least for now. The war was literally half a world away.

"Have a good dream?" asked Mara.

"Was I dreaming?"

"I guess." She laughed. "You were mumbling something, and laughing."

"Laughing?"

"Yeah."

"Wow." Josh couldn't imagine what he'd been dreaming. All of his thoughts were dark, very, very dark.

"Where's Mạ?" said Josh, seeing her seat empty.

"Behind you, coloring," said Mara. "The sergeant had some markers."

Josh leaned around the seat. Mạ was making pictures on a yellow pad. They looked like black, violent scribbles. She was very intent on what she was doing.

"We're landing?" Josh asked Mara.

"Landing."

The jet taxied to the far end of the base. It was night, and a foglike humidity clung to the runway, the lights' yellow and white beams struggling against the moisture. Out the window, Josh saw a pair of F-22 fighters sitting at the edge of the parking area, their canopies open, security officers standing at attention.

The jet pulled to a stop just beyond a pair of black MH-6 helicopters. The sergeant who'd shepherded them opened the door, unfolding the ladder to the ground.

"Sir, it's been an honor having you," he told Josh.

Josh mumbled his thanks.

"Please watch your step, okay? Careful with that little one. Ma'am, a real pleasure. Thank you for your service."

Mara caught Josh's elbow from behind as he stepped away from the plane.

"That's our car," she told him.

A Lincoln Town Car stood at the edge of the cement apron. The rear door opened. A short, middle-aged man got out. He looked a bit like an accountant, in a dark suit and rumpled white shirt. "Josh?"

"You're Peter."

"I told you I'd get you home," said Lucas. He was beaming, a proud father greeting the prodigal son.

His handshake was a little limp, Josh thought.

"And you must be Mạ," said Peter, stooping down. "*Xin chào.* How are you?"

He reeled off some Vietnamese. Mạ pressed closer to Josh.

"We're going to be great friends," Lucas said, rising. "I have some nurses and a doctor who will take really good care of you."

"Child psychologist?" asked Josh.

"The best." Lucas turned to Mara. "You! How the hell are you?"

They hugged. Mara pecked him on the cheek. It was almost like a family reunion.

"You did good, Mara. Damn good." Lucas shooed

them into the car. "Come on, we have an appointment
to keep and we're a little late."

"Where are we going?" Mara asked.

"White House. President wants to talk to you right
away. As in, now."

When Josh McArthur was in seventh grade, his
school had arranged a visit to Washington,
D.C. The highlight of the trip—if one didn't count the
scandalous game of strip spin the bottle after hours at
the hotel—was a visit to the White House. Josh wasn't
one of the six or seven kids who'd gotten to shake the
president's hand when they visited the Oval Office, but
the memory of standing around the room was still
vivid.

And here he was now, an adult, an important person, waiting in the back of the limo as it whipped up
the driveway toward the West Wing.

"Ready?" Lucas asked as the car came to a stop in
the circle below the portico entrance to the building.
Two limos, with only their drivers inside, were blocking the drive in front of the doorway.

"I could use a cup of coffee," said Mara.

A uniformed Marine Corps guard opened the door.
Josh stepped out, then reached back and helped Ma.
The night was warm, nearly as hot as Vietnam and al-
most as sticky. A swarm of small flies buzzed nearby.

"Damn gnats," said Lucas. "Damn things are everywhere."

Mycetophilidae. One of the indicators of extreme climate change—an increase in fungi in the environment,
generally caused by increased dampness, meant there
was more food for them. The bugs' diversity—there were

more than three thousand described species—meant that they could rapidly adapt to pesticides.

Josh had been involved in a study examining the genus as an undergrad.

And there was a great deal of mold in the air—he struggled to hold back a sneeze.

Mạ had no idea what was going on. She held Josh's hand tightly as they walked. Then she said something to Mara in Vietnamese.

"She's hungry," Mara told Lucas.

"We'll get some food in a minute."

"Mr. Lucas, good to see you, sir," said a young man in a black suit. He had a clipboard in his hand. "You're Mr. MacArthur?"

"Yeah," said Josh, trying to keep from sneezing.

"Really, really good to meet you, sir. After all you've been through."

"Uh-huh." Josh turned and sneezed.

"Ms. Duncan?"

"That's me."

"Thank you for your service, ma'am. And this is . . . ?"

"Mạ," said Mara. "We don't know what her other name is."

"Follow me, please."

Josh sneezed a few more times. The aide raised his clipboard and waved them toward the doors. Josh had imagined there would be a crowd of reporters, even though it was night, but the only people he saw were the Marines and uniformed Secret Service agents prowling nearby. He, Mara, Lucas, and Mạ went through a metal detector at the door, then followed the aide up the stairs to a small room used as a waiting area.

"Can I get anyone anything?" asked the aide.

"Can you get something for the kid?" asked Lucas.

"Sure. What would she eat?"

"Peanut butter and jelly?" said Josh.

"I don't think she knows what that is," said Mara.

"I don't know what I can find in the cafeteria this late," said the aide. "But I'll look for something. What else?"

"Coffee," said Mara. "With a little milk. No sugar."

"Me, too," said Lucas.

Josh passed.

"Sneezing done?" asked Lucas.

"Probably have another round, adjusting to the AC," said Josh. "Allergies."

"Vietnam didn't help, huh?"

"No."

Josh felt some of the excitement draining from him. He was tired, jet-lagged; he wished he could go to sleep.

The door opened. A bald man with a round face leaned inside. "Peter, you ready?" he asked.

"Absolutely," said Lucas, jumping to his feet.

"You're MacArthur, right?" said the bald man. He stuck out his hand. He was wearing a blue blazer over khaki pants, a blue-striped shirt, and a rep tie. "Glad to meetcha."

Josh shook his hand. It was a solid, though moist, grip.

"Turner Cole. I'm the assistant to the deputy national security adviser on Asia."

"Nice to meet you."

"My pleasure."

"Mara Duncan," said Mara.

"Mara, thanks for coming. This is the little girl, right? Josh? You saved her?"

"She found me. Her people were killed."

Cole pressed his lips together tightly. The gesture seemed a little too pat to Josh.

"This way, all right?" said Cole.

Cole led them down a short hallway to a rounded hallway. Two Secret Servicemen were standing outside.

This is it, thought Josh. Finally.

As soon as Greene heard the knock at the door, he raised his hand to quiet Frost. The CIA director stopped speaking midsentence.

"Come," said Greene. He leaned back in his chair, watching as Turner Cole led in Lucas, Mara, Josh, and Mạ. In an instant, Greene sized them up, analyzing how they would come across on television.

Regular people. Kids.

God, they were kids—Josh looked like he was still in high school. But then everybody seemed to look that way to him these days.

The little girl was adorable. She reminded him of his grandkids.

"Mr. President, this is CIA officer Mara Duncan, and scientist Josh MacArthur," said Cole. "And Ms. Mạ."

"Mara Duncan, Josh MacArthur," said Greene, rising and stepping out from behind the desk. "Damn, I'm glad to meet you."

He grabbed Josh's hand and pumped it, then stepped over and gave Mara a hug and kiss on the cheek. She was a big girl—nearly as tall he was.

"And who are you?" Greene asked, sliding down on his haunches to look at the little girl.

She turned and buried her face in Josh's leg. The scientist put his hand on her protectively.

"She doesn't understand English, Mr. President," said Mara.

"Have you sent someone to talk to her? A psychologist?"

"We haven't had the chance."

"I want someone." Greene stood. "Turner. A psychologist and a translator. Actually, see if you can find a child psychologist who can speak Vietnamese."

"We did find one, Mr. President. She'll be here in the morning."

"Excellent. Excellent. Well, sit," he added, turning to Lucas. "Good work, Peter. Again. Good work."

Greene sat on the edge of his desk. "Josh, I've seen the footage," he said. "Terrible stuff. Tell me in your own words what happened."

"Well, um, I'd gone to Vietnam to, uh, study the effects of climate change, as I guess you know. I was with a UN team and we were studying the flora and fauna—"

"You might just want to skip to the essential parts," said Frost.

Greene gave Frost a wink. Josh recounted the night when he had woken and left camp to relieve himself, just escaping the massacre. Then he spoke of the village where he'd gone, the hand he'd found in the dirt. His voice grew stronger as he continued.

Greene liked that. They could use that.

"Do you have the location of that site?" Frost asked.

"I'm not really sure," said Josh. "I ended up a lot closer to the border than I thought I was."

"All right," said the president. "Now how did you find our little princess here?"

J osh felt his nose starting to act up, tickling as if a sneeze was about to follow. He tried to ward it off, but it was difficult while he was talking.

Something about the way that the president's people were treating Mạ bothered him. They were too—was "unctuous" the right word?

They wanted her as proof of the massacre. But something about it, something about the way they treated her—she was important only for their political agenda.

Not that he didn't agree with the agenda. China must be stopped. But still: he felt as if he had to protect Mạ, and bringing her here, contrary to his expectations, seemed to be doing the opposite.

The CIA director turned a notebook computer around and showed him a map of northern Vietnam, trying to pin down where exactly the massacre had taken place. Josh located the camp where they had been when the Chinese first attacked, but the map showed the stream where he had been chased on the wrong side—or at least what he thought was the wrong side.

"Should be up here," he said. And as he pointed, he sneezed, barely covering his nose and mouth with his forearm.

"God bless," said the president. "Peter, I think you can work on the exact location and narrow it down later. In fact—"

The president paused, a thought forming in his mind. Josh and the others looked at him expectantly. Then Josh sneezed again.

"Hope that's not catching," said the president. He smiled at Josh, letting him know it was a joke.

Or at least Josh thought it was.

"I, uh—no. Allergies," said Josh, sneezing again. "Excuse me, sir." He got up and moved toward the door, trying to discreetly blow his nose.

"It may be more useful to us to be vague," said the president. "For now. To make it seem as if we don't know exactly where it is."

Frost and the president began discussing the political implications. Josh, though consumed by his sudden sneezing fit, was shocked, not only that they were planning how best to use the information, but that they would consider holding back some of it. Facts were facts—data points, whether convenient or not, had to be shared and dealt with. That was the only way one reached truth.

Scientific truth, at least.

The president turned to him abruptly. "Josh, here's what I'd like you to do. I'm going to address a special session of the United Nations on Friday." Greene pushed off from the desk and walked past Josh toward a large globe that stood near the fireplace. He put his hand on it, moving it gently, gazing at it distractedly. "I'd like you to be my guest. And to repeat what you've told me."

"Everything?" said Josh.

"Well, shorten it a bit," said the president.

"The interesting parts," said Frost drily. "And we can do without the sneezing."

The president laughed. So did Frost, after a moment.

"It's all right, Josh. The director has a very droll sense of humor."

"Yes, sir."

"And you, little girl"—Greene leaned toward Mạ; his voice was soft and gentle—"would you tell your story to the world?"

"I don't think that's a good idea," blurted Josh.

Everyone looked at him.

"Why not?" asked Frost.

"Because—she's just . . . a little kid."

"Well, I agree with you there, Josh." The president straightened. "But—well, let's take the matter under advisement." He turned to Cole. "The psychologist will be here in the morning?"

"Yes, sir."

"We'll get his input."

"Hers."

"Hers."

Greene frowned. Josh could tell he didn't like being corrected.

"But, Josh, you'll definitely be there, yes?" said Greene enthusiastically.

"Well, yes, sir."

"Ms. Duncan, I'd like you there as well," said the president. "The media will be interested in your impressions. And how you got our friend out."

"The SEALs played a part," said Mara. "Two of them died."

Greene looked at Frost. "The Chinese killed them, right?"

"That's what we believe."

"Then there's not a problem with that," the president told Frost.

"I don't want to be giving away craft," said Frost. "I think we should just produce Josh and leave it at that."

"She adds authenticity," said Greene. He looked over at her. "And she's an attractive young woman. Ms. Duncan, hope you don't mind my compliment. I'm afraid that's how things are with the media. People will look at your pretty face and focus on that rather than your intelligence and resourcefulness, which I'm sure were the real reasons for your success."

Mara had flushed. "Thank you, Mr. President."

"Not at all. You're the one who deserves thanks. And you, too, Mr. Lucas. I know you and your staff have been working hard on this."

"Thank you."

"Get someone from my staff to help Josh whittle down his speech," Greene told Cole. "One of the political boys. Billy would be best. Jablonski. You know what? I'll call him myself."

The president walked to his desk, picked up the phone, and told the White House operator to get him William Jablonski.

Josh glanced at his watch. It was nearly 1 a.m. Was Jablonski still in his office?

"You'll like Billy," said Greene, looking over at them from the phone as he waited for the call to go through. "He's a bit of a pill, but he knows his stuff. He got me through New York. And that took some doing. Don't offer to buy him lunch though."

"Josh," said Ma, tugging on him.

Josh turned to her. "What's up, honey?"

"Josh," said Ma.

Mara leaned over to her and whispered something in her ear. They exchanged a few words in Vietnamese.

"She's tired," said Mara. "She should get some sleep."

"We have a nurse who can take her," said Cole. "There's a bed all ready for her."

"In a hotel?" asked Josh.

"My house." Cole beamed. "My wife and I have two kids, eight and five. She'll fit right in."

"She only speaks Vietnamese," said Josh.

"I have a translator coming," said Frost.

Meanwhile, the president's line connected.

"Billy," said the president, his voice rising several decibels. "Listen, I have an incredibly important assignment for you. . . . The hell with that. I'll square that for you. . . . No, that's crap. . . . Listen, I have a real hero here—a pair of heroes. Josh MacArthur and Mara Duncan. Josh witnessed the Chinese massacre of a village in Vietnam. Ms. Duncan rescued him from behind the lines."

"There were SEALs involved, Mr. President," said Lucas.

"SEALs, too," said the president. "It sounds like a movie plot, but it's real. I want Josh to talk with me Friday in New York. He needs a little polish. Not too much—it shouldn't be Hollywood. Find him some clothes, too. Get Sara on it. . . . Well, whoever you think can do a decent job. He should look like a scientist, though, not some wiseass rap star. . . . You won't have to do anything with her."

The president gave Mara a wink, then told Jablonski that he would be hearing from Josh and Mara later in the day.

"No, you know what? Get up to New York. You can meet with them there," the president told Jablonski. "And, Billy, this is quiet until the session. No advance notice, you understand. That columnist at the *Times* you have in your pocket—if he finds out about this before I step to the podium, you are going to be flailed and I'll be using your skin as a bear rug at Camp David. *Capisce?*"

Mara watched the president, considering how to explain tactfully that she didn't want to go public, since doing so would effectively end her career in operations.

It bothered her that neither Frost nor Lucas had pointed this out. Lucas especially.

The risk wasn't just to her. Anyone who had dealt with her would presumably be in danger: guilty by association. She hadn't been a spy recruiter, but a good portion of her work in South Asia had called for the use of aliases and other covers, and there would be a decent trail of potential exposures.

So why the hell hadn't Lucas pointed this out? Frost, maybe—*maybe*—wasn't completely aware of her résumé, but Peter Lucas certainly was.

The president hung up the phone. Before Mara could say anything, there was a loud knock on the door. Turner Cole, the aide who had taken them there, stepped into the office and told the president that the NSC adviser and staff, along with the secretaries of state and defense, were waiting in the Cabinet Room.

"Good, very good." Greene practically sprang from his seat. "I think we're going to keep you two under wraps," he said, pointing to Mara and Josh. "I just need the director and Mr. Lucas. Get up to New York, both of you."

"Mr. President," said Mara. "Sir—"

"Mr. President, Ma is very tired," said Josh quickly.

"Ma? Oh, right—well, of course. It's past her bedtime," said Greene. "Turner—are all the arrangements made?"

"Yes, sir. We just—we were getting a translator."

"Well, where is she?" said Greene. He got up and started walking toward the door. "Come on now. I want this girl taken care of. Marty!"

The president disappeared through the door, calling for one of his aides. Cole and Frost followed him.

"Peter, I have to stay covert," Mara said to Lucas as he got up. "If I go public, my career is over."

"I'll take care of it," said Lucas. "Don't worry."

J osh stood, waiting with Ma for the president to return. She pushed against his side, sucking her thumb, her eyes narrow slits.

"She's got to get some sleep," he told Mara.

"Mr. Cole is going to take care of her."

"You think that's okay?"

"Well—what else do you want to do?"

"I don't know. She can—she could stay with us."

"Us?"

"Me."

"You ever take care of kids?"

The answer of course was no. And Josh couldn't speak Vietnamese. Still, he didn't want to leave her.

"Look who I found," said Turner Cole, returning to the Oval Office. A young Vietnamese-American, his eyes drooping, and a woman with a small backpack followed. The translator and nurse, Tommy Lam and Georgette Splain, respectively.

The translator dropped to the floor, legs curled, and began talking to Mạ. She looked at him for a few moments, not saying anything. Then suddenly she started talking, words racing from her mouth.

"She wants more ice cream," explained Mara. "Mr. Lam says he knows where they can get some."

"All night Friendly's," said Lam, beaming. You'd never know he had a sweet tooth to look at him; he couldn't weigh more than a hundred pounds.

"Mạ really should be getting to bed," said the nurse.

Josh felt pangs of jealousy as the translator, the nurse, and Cole talked with Mạ. It was silly. He couldn't take care of her.

Actually, he had taken care of her. In the jungle. But here there were professionals and people with kids. He wasn't exactly Mạ's dad.

Mạ looked up at Josh as Lam explained that she was going to go with them to Mr. Cole's. He would stay the night on a couch to help translate.

"I'm—I—I'm going to stay in a hotel, Mạ," said Josh. "All right?"

Mara bent down and started talking to Mạ in Vietnamese. When she was done, Mạ turned to Josh and hugged him. He reached down and grabbed her.

Tears welled in his eyes.

"I'll see you soon," he said.

He looked away as she left.

"I told her that we'll see her," said Mara. "And that there are other kids."

Josh nodded.

"We want to find the site, but keep it quiet," Greene whispered to Frost as they walked toward the Cabinet Room. "Put it under surveillance. When word leaks out, dollars to doughnuts the Chinese will try and dig up the bodies. We'll have it on video."

"Dollars to doughnuts?" said Frost.

"That's my stomach talking." Greene laughed. "Let's get Josh and Mara up to New York, get them ready for Friday. Have them leave tonight."

"What about the girl?"

"She can come up with me."

"You think she should testify?"

"Of course. Why not?"

"We have to vet her first."

"What do you mean vet? The scientist found her in the jungle, right?"

"We have to hear what her story is. We just heard what Mara said."

"That's good enough for me."

"George . . ."

"Have your man Lambert talk to her and hear her story. He has until Friday."

"You really think it's a good idea? We have the scientist."

"Christ, Peter. All these years and you still don't know crap about what sells in the media, do you?"

Hanoi

As a military strategist, Major Win Christian was plodding and predictable, exactly the sort of opponent Zeus would love to meet on the battlefield. In fact, the only time Zeus ran into trouble when facing him in the Red Dragon war games was when he failed to account properly for Christian's stupidity. Faced with what looked like an idiotic development, Zeus had trouble believing his opponent wasn't setting him up for some brilliantly clever and devious counterplay. But that was never the case.

As an engineer, however, Christian had real talent. Charged with helping the Vietnamese navy and air force—such as they were—come up with fake submarines and aircraft, he was creative and efficient. His hastily arranged collections of sheet metal, wood, and bamboo at Hai Phong not only gave Vietnam a dozen submarines overnight, but showed stockpiles of what looked like long-range torpedoes, along with the external modifications that allowed the weapons to be strapped to launchers on the hull. He also added the capacity to carry an unspecified but suitably nasty-looking antiship missile to a pair of otherwise inoperable Hormone helicopters.

"I call it the Zeus Murphy weapon," said Christian proudly. "A lethal dose of bullshit in every breath."

"Har-har," said Zeus, stooping over the coffee table in General Perry's hotel suite to examine the photo.

The weapon and the subs looked so real that even trained satellite analysts couldn't tell that they were fake—as the intelligence alert posted by the U.S. National Reconnaissance Office an hour earlier attested.

"Vietnam Moving Antiship Weapons onto Helicopters" was the title of the brief but credulous report.

"I wonder if the CIA would be able to leak this intelligence to the Chinese," said General Perry.

"The Chinese are already seeing this on their satellites," said Christian. "There's no need to leak it."

"If they think that we think this is happening, it adds more credibility," Perry added.

"I may be able to try something," said Zeus. He remembered that Mara had warned him not to deal with the CIA station at the embassy; while she hadn't been explicit, it was obvious from her hints that there was some sort of mole there, working for either the Chinese or the Vietnamese. In any event, it would be an easy matter to leave this for them in hopes of its getting back to Beijing.

"Do you have time?" asked Perry.

"I don't leave for a couple of hours," said Zeus. "Now that I know where Hai Phong is, it shouldn't be a problem."

The driver assigned to him earlier in the day had gotten lost. Vietnam was a small country, but it turned out that many of its residents, even soldiers, had never visited anywhere very far from the place they had grown up.

Perry turned to Christian. "Major, would you excuse us for a moment?"

Christian nodded.

"Drink?" Perry asked, going to the credenza at the side of the suite room.

"Sure." Zeus jumped to his feet.

Perry was short and very thin; Zeus guessed he was no taller than five six, and if he weighed 130 it was only with his winter uniform on. But Perry had *two* Silver Stars and *three* Bronze Stars with the V device—V as in Valor, an award given only if its recipient had been under fire. He'd more than proven his mettle.

Until this assignment, Zeus had had only brief contacts with the general during war games, and thought he was very standoffish and cold. His opinion had changed considerably in the past few days, however; the general had proven not only warmer, but much more clever and unorthodox than Zeus had suspected.

"I would offer you your choice," said Perry, picking up a bottle, "but it will all come down to the same thing—Johnnie Walker Black Label, or Johnnie Walker Black Label?"

"I'll take the Black Label."

"Neat?"

Since there was no ice, neat would have to do. Perry poured two fingers' worth into the clear glass and handed it over. Then he poured three fingers' worth for himself.

Rank had its privileges.

"After the war, an import-export business focusing on liquor," said Perry, holding up his glass.

"I'm not really sure international trade is my thing," said Zeus.

"I meant for me."

Perry smiled and took a slug of the Scotch. Zeus took a small sip.

"You," said Perry, "I expect will stay in the Army, go

on to become a general, and eventually chief of staff. Assuming you don't get killed on this mission."

"I'm not planning to, General."

"None of us do." Perry took another sip of Scotch. This time he savored the whiskey.

"The submarine base near Sanya on Hainan," said Perry. "We're reasonably sure the submarines aren't there?"

"They've used the bay as an overflow area for landing craft. I don't think they would if the subs were there."

"Hmmm."

"The subs would add to their alarm," said Zeus. "Just make them more nervous."

"Maybe."

Zeus fidgeted. He hadn't been able to get the Navy to give him information on the precise whereabouts of the submarines—it was too closely guarded—but earlier alerts had indicated that the two boomers generally stationed there had put out to sea. Chinese doctrine called for them to be deepwater, within range of their American targets, during times of attack.

On the other hand, the harbor facilities were generally considered capable of hiding up to twenty submarines. There could easily be more there.

"You don't have to go," said Perry abruptly.

"I know that."

"I'm serious. You're pretty damn valuable—I should have vetoed it. I should have told the president no. It's not too late," added Perry. "I'll take the heat. None of it will come back on you."

"I think I can do it, General."

Zeus almost said that he *wanted* to do it—that he was dying to do it. His small tastes of action in the aircraft bombing the dam and then later driving the truck behind the lines to help get the SEALs and Josh Mac-

Arthur had fired him up. Accepting his promotion to major had meant leaving the Special Forces unit. He hadn't realized how much he missed it until the first few shots had whizzed over his head.

That part he didn't miss. Escaping them, the exhilaration of beating an enemy—that was the good part. That was the part to live for.

Not that he could say that out loud. Saying it out loud would make him seem like a mindless bozo. It was one thing to be dedicated, and another to be dedicated to the point of recklessness. Perry saw the mission as reckless. Zeus didn't: he saw it as difficult, not reckless. But recklessness was in the eye of the general.

"Hmmph." Perry walked to the window. Despite the bombings, the hotel windows had not been broken. In fact, none of the large foreign hotels in the area had been hit. The Chinese seemed to be making at least a token effort to avoid hitting areas where tourists and businesspeople were concentrated.

"What do you think about taking Win with you?" asked Perry, gazing toward the river. The top of a Vietnamese gunboat, struck a few hours before by Chinese warplanes in broad daylight, was just visible. About three-quarters of the ship was underwater, the hull resting in the shallows where the captain had beached the craft to make recovery operations easier.

"You want me to take Win?" said Zeus.

"Actually I don't." The window reflected Perry's grin. "But the major asked me to ask you. And whether I think it's a good idea or not, I feel obliged to follow through on the request. Just as I would for you."

"Yes, sir."

"It's not an order, Zeus." Perry went over to the couch and sat back down. "I know you and he don't exactly get along."

"We don't have to be friends to do our jobs, sir."

"It can help, though. Win does have some talents," added Perry. "He does speak some Chinese."

Just enough to read off a menu, thought Zeus.

"I expect he was quite a pill at the Point," said Perry.

"Top in the class," said Zeus. It was a double entendre—Christian had been both the valedictorian *and* the biggest jackass.

"He is handicapped," said Perry gravely. "That ego must make it hard to get in and out of doors."

Zeus guffawed, utterly surprised by Perry's remark. Generals never spoke of their underlings so candidly. Or at least this one never had.

"But as you say, you don't have to like someone to work with him," continued Perry, going back over to the Scotch. "Sometimes you can influence people the way gravity influences them. Push them in certain directions by exposing them to different things. Sometimes that breaks people. But sometimes, if you have the right person, it can help them overcome their flaws."

Perry had just given Zeus the reason he had put Christian on his staff. He recognized that the major was headed for the very high ranks, and wanted to help him become a better officer. Maybe it would work—maybe Christian was becoming more human, less of a jerk.

But was he becoming more of a soldier? Soldiers couldn't go around with sticks up their butt, or complain when a foreign army officer didn't give a by-the-book salute. Or bitch because the seat in the helicopter had no padding.

"He did good work with the decoys," said Perry. "That may be useful on the island. And he claims to know a bit about explosives."

Not nearly as much as I do, thought Zeus.

"Your call," said Perry.

"He does know some Chinese," said Zeus. "So maybe he would be useful. If he can swim."

Christian did know how to swim, though he couldn't figure out why Zeus was asking.

"Because if we run out of fuel, we're going to swim to shore," Zeus told him.

"Running out of fuel is not an option," said Christian.

"It's not a planned option, no shit," said Zeus. "Which is why I'm asking you again, can you swim?"

"Shit yeah."

"Then you're in."

"Okay."

"Don't jump up and down."

"I'm not."

Be nice to the handicapped, Zeus told himself, even if the handicap is only an irony deficiency.

He laid out the basic game plan, which called for eight Zodiacs to rush across the Gulf of Bac Bo as soon as night fell. They'd have only sixteen Vietnamese soldiers, along with two spies; the rest of the space in the boats would be taken up by the engineered debris. At the same time, a pair of gunboats and the two real submarines that Vietnam had would leave port, trying to attract the attention of the Chinese ships offshore. The diversion would both help the Zodiacs cross and plant the idea that the submarines were responsible for part of the attack.

Once across the gulf, they'd land on Hainan near a fish-farming operation about twenty-five miles southwest of Ledong Lizu. There they would steal a pair of boats and take them around the southern end of the island, arriving at the target area by first light. They'd scout the harbor, find the easiest targets to plant their charges on, then go to work again at nightfall, setting charges and debris to make it look as if the ships had been hit by torpedoes from the minisubs. Charges would be planted in the boats they stole to make them look as if they'd been hit by torpedoes as well. They'd aim to coordinate with a 3 a.m. attack from the missiles on the tenders.

"Then what happens?" asked Christian.

"Then we go home."

"How?"

"We steal a truck and drive back to the Zodiacs."

"And if the Zodiacs have been discovered?"

"Then we steal a boat," said Zeus. "But I'd rather take the Zodiacs. They're faster, and the Chinese won't be patrolling that far north. But we can take another boat from the fish farm area if we have to."

"I think we ought to land farther north to begin with," said Christian. "Steal something from up there. Then hit the fisheries on the way back. Once we take something from one place, they'll be on guard there. If we switch it around a bit, there'll be less chance of being caught."

It wasn't a bad idea, even if it was Christian's.

"Okay," said Zeus. "That's what we'll do."

The president ordered a military jet to fly Josh and
Mara to New York. To keep Josh's existence secret, the
aircraft flew to Stewart International Airport, about an
hour north of the city. They were met by a pair of U.S.
marshals who packed them into a black Jimmy SUV,
hopped onto the thruway, and raced toward the city at
speeds approaching those the jet had used. Josh fell
asleep, but between the bumpy pavement and the speed,
Mara was more than wide awake. She shifted nervously
in the front passenger seat, trying to tamp down her
anxiety, or at least hide it.

When she saw a sign for a rest stop ahead, she told a
marshal to stop for some coffee.

"Orders are to go straight, ma'am," said the driver.

"We're either stopping or I'm going to pee right here
on your seat," she told him.

The driver took his foot off the gas.

The rest stop was basically a slightly oversized Mc-
Donald's, manned by sleepy-eyed retirees. It was a
little past five in the morning, but more than a dozen
people were already in line for coffee and breakfast
sandwiches, the first wave of the far-suburb rush hour.

Mara had been away from the States for over a year,
and while she was not generally a fast-food junkie, the
smells stoked her appetite as soon as she walked in the
door. She ended up ordering two Sausage McMuffins
with Egg, hash browns, and a large coffee.

Then she realized she didn't have any money.

"Don't worry, hon," said the woman behind the counter. "Your husband can pay. Can't he?"

The marshal standing behind her looked like he wanted to melt through the floor. He ordered a coffee, then paid—reluctantly.

"I better get reimbursed," he said on the way out.

"Bill the agency," Mara said.

"Oh yeah, I bet that works."

Josh was still sleeping in the car. The other agent, slumped behind the wheel, asked why they hadn't brought him back something.

"Your partner's a cheapskate," said Mara. "You can have one of my McMuffins if you want."

"Got sausage?"

"Of course."

"Nah, I don't want take your food. Besides, I'm supposed to stay away from that stuff." He started to back out of the parking space, then pulled back in. "Maybe I'll just go grab something."

Mara tried to make conversation with the other marshal while they were waiting, but he remained in a bad mood. He was middle-aged, the sort of man who by now was more interested in the job's pension plan than in its possibilities for travel. He answered her questions with as few words as possible. Most of his assignments involved protecting witnesses in federal cases, though he'd never protected anyone more interesting than a low-level mobster. He hadn't been involved in any interesting busts, either, at least to hear him tell it.

Mara let him drink his coffee in peace. She was still worried about having to go public. Lucas said he was going to take care of it—but would he really? How strongly could he argue against something the president wanted?

Josh didn't need Mara. She could blend into the

background easily enough, even pretend to be part of his bodyguard contingent.

Here was the funny thing: she was prepared to give up her life for her country, but not her career. Going public meant she'd work a desk for the rest of her life.

Maybe not. Technically, it was possible to work in covert operations once you were known. It was highly unlikely, but possible.

No way would that happen. They'd give her some sort of gig as a trainer, pretending it was a reward.

To them, maybe.

Then she'd get some BS assignment that would be, at its heart, an analyst's job. Visit, drink, report. Not necessarily in that order. Repeat as necessary.

Mara glanced at her watch. Was it too early to call Peter and see if he had fixed things? Would he have gone home after the briefing and gone to bed? Possibly he was still in the session; Greene and his cabinet were known for marathons.

She decided she would try anyway, and reached for her phone—only to realize she didn't have one. She's surrendered her gear as soon as the helo landed in Thailand.

"Son of a bitch," said Mara.

"Problem?" asked the driver.

"Coffee's hot," she told him, reaching over to turn on the radio.

J osh leaned against the door of the car somewhere less than fully awake but not quite sleeping, either. He kept seeing the village where the people had been buried. And Mạ, hiding from him in the jungle the next day, at yet another massacre site.

It had taken so much to win her trust.

And now he was just going to let her go?

But he couldn't take care of her. There were experts. She'd need psychologists and tutors for English.

He felt as if he were letting her down somehow. That he was abandoning her.

She'd be at the UN with him. But how was she going to deal with that? It'd be crazy. She'd think the Vietnamese were after her again.

"She should just be left alone."

"Problem, Mr. MacArthur?" asked the marshal next to him.

Josh opened his eyes. He hadn't realized he'd been speaking out loud.

Mara turned around in the seat in front of him. "You okay, Josh?"

"Just a bad dream," he told her.

10

John F. Kennedy Airport, New York City

"Let's see the passport."

Jing Yo hesitated a moment, as if he didn't understand the words. Then he raised his hand and gave over the small book. The customs officer took it and held it under a light at his station before comparing it to something on his computer screen.

The U.S. and China were not at war, but Jing Yo had been given a Thai passport and an assumed name to travel under nonetheless. He had a false background story and an entire biography memorized; he was a student returning to America to work on his medical degree. He could give any number of details relating to this, from his three previous (but false) addresses to the difficulties he had (supposedly) had finding suitable cadavers to work on.

What he could not do was speak much Thai beyond a few simple phrases. The agent who had given him the passport, some other travel documents, and a supply of cash and credit cards, had told him it wouldn't be necessary to speak the language; no customs official would waste his or her time with him.

This one certainly seemed interested, however. He moved the passport back to the little light, fanning it gently, as if maybe he thought the ink would flow off.

Jing Yo told himself to be patient.

"What's the purpose of your visit?" asked the officer. "Mr. Sursal."

"Srisai," said Jing Yo, correcting the pronunciation in case this was a trick. "I am studying to be a doctor."

"You're a doctor?"

"A student. I learn to be a doctor."

"You're going to stay in this country?"

"Only for school," said Jing Yo.

"I'll bet."

The man shoved the passport back at him. Jing Yo took that as a sign that he was cleared to go. He took his bags and moved on, passing through the dimly lit hall with its grimy walls and well-scuffed floor. A set of double doors swung open ahead, activated by a motion detector. He walked through and found himself going up a ramp into a large hall cluttered with voices and echoing sounds. People were standing at the edge of a velvet rope, looking anxiously for relatives. Drivers held up cardboard signs with names: SMITH, FENTON, BOZZONE.

SRISAI.

The crowd swelled at the end of the rope. Jing Yo walked through it, circling around to see if he had been followed. It was hard to tell in the terminal—there were so many people, and many places to hide or appear otherwise engaged. He pulled his bag with him, circling around a set of chairs, then edged back into the crowd.

"I am Srisai," he said to the man holding the small cardboard sign.

The man jerked around, surprised. "Oh, I'm sorry," he said. "I missed you."

His accent was difficult to understand, but he took Jing Yo's bag and led him out through the main doors.

It would be easy for him to kill me when we reach the car, thought Jing Yo as they walked through the parking garage. He let himself fall a step behind, glancing left and right to make sure he wasn't being watched.

The trunk on a black Cadillac opened as they approached. Jing Yo's stomach knotted in an instant.

There is no way but the Way, he told himself. You must surrender to your fate.

The driver touched another button on his key fob, and the car started.

No way but the Way.

"So, your hotel?" said the man, slapping the trunk down.

"The Janus Ambassador," said Jing Yo.

"Nice place," said the driver.

Jing Yo opened the back door to the car and slipped inside. The driver seemed to remember belatedly that he was supposed to have done that, and rushed over to close it.

"Long flight?" asked the driver as he pulled out of the parking spot. He was Hispanic, and spoke with an accent that was difficult for Jing Yo to understand.

"Yes."

"Visit here on pleasure or business?"

"I am a student," said Jing Yo.

"Ah. What do you study?"

"Medicine."

"You are a doctor?"

"A student."

"A good thing, to be a doctor."

The man began talking about a cousin or a nephew— Jing Yo had trouble understanding—who wanted to be a doctor but was having difficulties with his undergraduate classes. The man seemed content to talk without any encouragement, and Jing Yo let him talk. He looked out the window at the early-morning traffic, taking in New York.

It was his first visit, not just to the city, but to any part of the Americas.

His first glimpses were less impressive than he had imagined. The airport was ancient, not even close to Beijing's. The buildings along the highway were mostly small and dirty—again, he compared them to Beijing and found them wanting.

There was one place where New York had an advantage. The thick brown fog that hung over the Chinese capital wasn't present here. The sky this morning was about three-quarters filled with clouds, but they were bright white, inviting instead of threatening. And behind them was an azure blue that reminded him of a dress Hyuen Bo had worn the first time he saw her.

Jing Yo held his breath, trying to push the memory away. He felt the pressure in his lungs, urging it to replace the sorrow. He pushed his chin to his chest, the pressure growing.

Think only of the breath, welling up.

Think only of the Way.

Or revenge. Revenge was an easier thought.

"We'll take the tunnel," said the driver.

Jing Yo let go of the breath. His head tingled, blood resuming its normal flow.

"The tunnel is okay?" asked the driver, a little concerned.

"The way you think is the best."

"Your hotel is on the East Side, so we will do better getting out there," said the driver. "We could go different ways. At this hour sometimes there isn't much difference. The traffic can back up unexpectedly. Would you like some coffee?"

The question caught Jing Yo by surprise. He was not sure, at first, what the words meant. Or rather, he knew the words, but wondered if there was another meaning.

"Coffee?" said Jing Yo finally.

"Breakfast. Would you like to stop for breakfast?"

Was this a spur-of-the-moment question? Jing Yo wondered. Or was it part of a plan? The man was almost surely a hired driver, with no knowledge of anything. But . . .

"Do you have a place?" Jing Yo asked, leaning forward against the front seat.

The man waved his hand. "There are many places."

"I do not drink coffee," said Jing Yo, not sure whether the man was actually trying to get him to a meeting place or was just being hospitable.

"Tea, then?"

"Can I get tea at the hotel?" asked Jing Yo.

"Oh, I'm sure you can. We'll just go there," said the driver.

They drove through an electronic toll both at the entrance to the tunnel, a large sign proclaiming the toll in red lights: $50. Jing Yo stared at the words beneath the sign, trying to decipher them:

TOLL DOUBLED AT HIGH TRAFFIC TIMES.

"The toll is higher because of traffic?" Jing Yo said to the driver.

The man laughed. "In a way. It's always fifty except from one to three. They pass the law to double it, but then they change the hours. A racket. To raise money by Billionaire Mayor. Always rackets. Bogus."

The tunnel was narrow, with yellow lights and large, old-fashioned tiles that reminded Jing Yo of the shower room at his army training camp. The pavement was uneven, with jagged cracks running from side to side. Suddenly, the driver braked and blared his horn. A man had darted into the road. He ran in front of the car, something black under his arm.

Jing Yo turned toward the door, ready, sure he was being ambushed. "Go!" he hissed in Chinese. "Don't stop! Get us out of here."

The driver gave another blast of the horn, then hit the gas. "I don't blame you for cursing," he said when they were well past. "That jackass."

Jing Yo said nothing, still unsure of what had happened.

"Risking his life for a muffler," continued the driver. "And what will he get for it? Five hundred dollars, if that. If it was his muffler, it would be different. Weld it back on the car. But you can tell it wasn't his muffler. Do you know what it cost my boss to replace the muffler on this? Two thousand dollars. That was just the muffler. Two years ago, ten times less . . ."

The driver moved on to other complaints. Jing Yo sat silently, trying to recover. His heart was pounding.

It would take him time to find his balance here, he thought. He might never find it.

The driver took him to a small business-class hotel in midtown. The door was flanked by four bulky men in dark suits, hands held together at their belts. They eyed Jing Yo as he got out of the car, then went back to staring blankly into the distance. A doorman appeared and ushered him in.

Jing Yo presented his passport to the desk clerk, who took it with a quizzical look, then entered the name into the computer for the reservation. Jing Yo was surprised when he handed it right back. In most Asian countries, the passport would have been held on to at least until the hotel had copied it, if not for the entire stay.

"What I need is a credit card for additional charges," said the clerk.

Jing Yo gave him an American Express card.

"This is your first stay with us," said the clerk.

"Yes."

This seemed to please the clerk, who began running down a list of the hotel's amenities, including its gym and free Internet. Jing Yo had no use for either, but he listened politely, nodding occasionally. Finally, the clerk gave him his key card. Jing Yo picked up his bag.

"I'll have that sent right up," said the clerk. "You don't have to carry it."

"Carry?"

"Your bag, sir. We'll take care of that."

Jing Yo hesitated. There was nothing in the bag that would give him away—it had to be "clean" to get through customs, in case it was inspected—but as a matter of general principle, he didn't want to lose control of his things, even temporarily.

On the other hand, he didn't want to seem suspicious.

"I think I will carry it," he said finally. "For a shower."

"Suit yourself," said the clerk.

Jing Yo had no idea what that meant, though the man's smile indicated he was releasing him. He went to the elevator, got in, and pressed his floor number, 6.

The room was at the end of a twisting hall, across from a door to the back stairwell. It was a good size, with two king-sized beds and a small couch. Light flooded in from the windows.

Jing Yo put his suitcase down on the bed closest to the door and began looking around. The Americans were clever, he knew; they could have mounted a bug anywhere and he would be unlikely to find it. But examining the furnishings helped him assimilate. He needed to know his environment.

There were no bombs hidden here, at least. No messages from the intelligence service or its spies, either.

Jing Yo flipped on the television and began trolling through the channels. He stopped on Fox News.

There was a map of Vietnam on the screen. It showed what it claimed were the approximate lines of the war. Jing Yo looked at them and decided they must be wrong—they were no farther south than when he had left the battlefield in pursuit of the scientist several days before.

A pair of experts were discussing the war. One was a historian, the other a general. The general declared that Vietnam would be forced to surrender within a few days.

The historian disagreed. The government would last

at least another month, and then a guerrilla war would follow.

"I could see that," said the general. "But unlike their war with us, they won't have outside support from Russia. The insurgency will wither on the vine."

Jing Yo wasn't sure what that meant, though both men seemed to agree that the war would end soon in China's favor.

"The Vietnamese should never have attacked China," said the general. "It was a classic blunder of hubris. Their egos got the better of them."

Jing Yo flipped the television off.

The West was populated by fools. While this benefited China, it nevertheless disgusted him.

11

Off the Vietnamese coast

The spy Quach Van Dhut brought along for the Hainan mission was even smaller than he was. She was also a woman, and a very pretty one.

Her name was Solt Thi Jan; her given name (the last) was short for Janice. The name as well as her exotic features revealed a mixed family background that included an American grandfather. Despite her ancestry, she seemed to speak little or no English, relying on Quach to translate when Zeus spoke to her. But Quach assured Zeus that she was a skilled operative who also had been on Hainan before. He had no trouble, he said, putting himself in her hands.

As small as she was, Jan shouldered all of her own

gear, which included a rubber pouch for her AK-47, which had a paratrooper-style folding stock. Zeus had no reason to object.

They set out an hour before the sun went down, giving themselves a few extra minutes to avoid the approaching Chinese surveillance satellite, which crossed just before dusk. They paired up, each group leaving sixty seconds after the other. Poorly equipped, the Vietnamese marines had no radio communication among the boats; they used small flashlights to signal each other. It was, Zeus mused, an effective means of radio silence.

Zeus and Christian borrowed wet suits to wear, along with small Mae West–style life vests, tac vests, and special bags for their gear. They also had civilian clothes for Hainan. The wet suits were the largest the Vietnamese had, but they were still tight, especially around the crotch; too much of this, Zeus thought, and he wouldn't have to worry about birth control for a while.

He had the helm in the lead craft, where he could use his GPS and act as a pathfinder for the others. Besides two marines, Solt was in the boat as well; her Chinese would be handy when they came to shore. Christian was in the third boat. Quach took the last craft, on the theory that he would have the easiest time if separated from the others.

Unlike the infiltration boats American units used, these Zodiacs and their engines were not purpose built. Starting life as normal pleasure or work craft, they had undergone a few modest modifications—they were now black instead of the original gray, their motors had detachable mufflers, and they carried extra fuel. But otherwise the little craft were so sturdy that there was no need for extensive changes. The marines had a lot of practice with them, and even with the heavy load of debris each carried, they made good time across the open water.

An hour after setting out, Zeus checked their location on his GPS unit and found they were almost ten miles farther than planned. Under ordinary circumstances, this would have been an excellent start, but they were running ahead of the diversion. At least three Chinese ships were in the area east of them; if they kept going they were sure to sail right into them.

Zeus gave the order to stop, then signaled for the other boats to draw close. The waters were choppy, with the wind kicking up, but the marines brought the boats together expertly.

"We need to wait," Zeus told the others, explaining what had happened. "We need to give the Chinese destroyers to the east time to grab the bait."

"I think waiting is a fool's mission," said Christian. "We're as likely to be seen here as anywhere."

"The major is right," said Quach. "To wait now tempts fate as much as going ahead."

Zeus checked his watch. The Vietnamese patrol boats were leaving with the satellite. By now they would be broadcasting their position with a series of "sloppy" radio messages sure to be intercepted. So the Chinese should already be on their way south.

Or not. There was no guarantee that they would take the bait at all.

"All right," said Zeus. "Everybody have their knives?"

The marines held them up. It was a not-too-subtle reminder that, to protect the mission, the Zodiacs and the weighted debris were to be scuttled to avoid capture.

"Let's move ahead."

Twenty minutes later, Zeus lifted binoculars to his eyes and strained to see into the distance. The night had darkened and the ocean smelled of rain. That was probably good, he reasoned; a storm would preoccupy the Chinese ships, making them much less likely to be on guard.

"There!" said the marine across from Zeus. Zeus turned to the north. There was a low black shadow on the horizon. It was heading in their direction.

A destroyer.

They'd make it past, he calculated; so could the boat following them. But he couldn't be sure about the others.

He swung back to find the other boats.

They sat on the ocean for a half hour, waiting for the Chinese vessel to pass south. The ship's outline was barely visible, and only when the waves took the Zodiac to their highest crest.

Quach sat in his boat next to Zeus, smoking the entire time. They'd killed the engines, and his smoke-laden breaths were louder than the slap of the waves against the rubber hulls.

Zeus was tired. Even though his heart was pumping with adrenaline, he felt his eyes sliding closed. He had to lean over the side and throw water on his face.

"Do you want a cigarette?" asked Quach. "It will help you keep awake."

"I'm okay."

They started out again a few minutes later. The monotonous drone of the engine and the slacking waves reinforced Zeus's desire for sleep. He found himself wishing he'd taken up Quach's offer of a cigarette—or better, had taken along a stash of the "go" pills doctors often prescribed for USSOCOM members on critical night missions.

Within minutes they were passing through a small rain squall. The water struck the boat so hard that it shook. Within five minutes they were beyond it, the ocean considerably calmer, but the night just as black.

The boats drew tighter together. An hour passed, boredom giving way to excitement as they neared land. Every apprehension Zeus had had about the mission began asserting itself; every possible argument against it echoed in his head.

He stretched; he moved around in the boat as much as its small size and the weighted bags of cargo and gear allowed. He knew he'd be fine once he got to shore. Once he was actually doing something, all the doubts dropped away. It was like playing quarterback—get on the field and the butterflies stopped flapping their damn wings.

"*Major!*" said the marine at the bow, pointing right.

Zeus looked into the shadows.

It was land.

He pulled his GPS out, surprised that they were so close already.

Then he realized it wasn't land; it was a small ship, cutting north with no running lights.

"Gas!" yelled Zeus. "Give it the gas!"

The marine nailed the throttle. The ship just missed them. Its wake nearly threw the small Zodiac under the water.

Their second boat wasn't as lucky. As the ship cleared, Zeus heard a scream behind them.

"Turn us around, turn us around!" he yelled, anxiously scanning the waves.

12

Washington, D.C.

Once a week, President Greene and his wife spent an hour having coffee together in the morning. It was a ritual they had begun decades earlier, when their schedules were easier to manage, but the practice was sacrosanct as far as the first lady was concerned; she insisted that her husband make the time.

If matters had been left completely to him, of course, he might never have made it. But the first lady knew a thing or two about politics—Greene's appointments secretary and the chief of staff not only knew how important the time was to her, but also realized there would be hell to pay if the president missed the coffee.

Greene did, however, occasionally bring work to the sessions, which were held in the residence. He also pretended to be surprised by interruptions that he had arranged, knowing that his wife would not object if they at least *seemed* spontaneous.

"I really think we should invite Brin and the children to spend the holiday at the White House," said his wife after they sat down in the dining room. "It would be so nice to have the little ones around."

"That's not a bad idea," said Greene, glancing toward the door. As if on cue—and actually it was—Turner Cole appeared. "Oh look, Martha, here's Turner. Come on in, Turner. Grab some coffee."

His wife rolled her eyes at the interruption, then proceeded to welcome Cole graciously, as Greene knew she would. Ms. Greene's real name was Sally; Martha, a reference to the very first first lady, was a joke between them.

"Coffee, Turner?" asked the president.

"I'm a little caffeined out, Mr. President."

"Already? It's barely nine o'clock."

"Don't give the poor man the jitters, George," said Ms. Greene. "You should try the mini cannolis, Turner. They're very good."

"Turner, I'm glad you came. It's a good coincidence," said the president. It wasn't a coincidence at all, of course—Greene had made it clear that Cole was to be sent over as soon as he arrived. "Here's something you should hear, Sal. We have this little girl, an orphan girl from Vietnam. The cutest thing. Her name is Mạ. Right, Turner?"

"There's a down tone on the vowel, Mr. President. Maa."

"Yes," said Greene. Actually, it was Turner who had the accent a little off, but the president didn't feel like giving the aide a language lesson. "Now the horrible thing is, Sal, her family was assassinated by the Chinese."

"My God."

"How is she, Turner?"

"She's very good, Mr. President. She, uh, she misses Mr. MacArthur."

"Well she'll see him soon enough. She's going with me to New York Friday, Sal."

"She's not going to that dreadful dinner, is she?"

"No, she's testifying before the UN. She'll make a great case."

"Testifying?"

"Just saying what happened to her family."

Ms. Greene frowned.

"What's wrong, Sal?"

"How old is this little girl?"

"Teri's age—six or seven."

"We believe six, sir," said Cole.

"You're going to have her speak before the UN?" said Ms. Greene.

"Why not?"

The first lady shook her head.

"She has held up remarkably well, Ms. Greene," said Cole.

"I'm sure she has. On the surface," said the first lady.

"We're having a psychologist look her over," said Greene.

"They're with her now," said Cole.

"You'd better be gentle with her, George," said Ms. Greene.

"She's not going to break."

"She's still a child. Would you want Teri to speak before the UN?"

"She'd have them eating out of the palm of her hand. God, she'd be fantastic."

"A week after her parents were killed?"

Greene frowned. His wife was smart, but sometimes she didn't bring the proper perspective to things.

"These are good," said Cole, reaching for another cannoli.

"She's going to get the best care possible," said Greene. "Believe me."

"I'm sure," said his wife. She looked over at Cole. "Try some milk with that," she told him. "You look a little tired, Turner. I hope my husband isn't working you too hard."

13

Off the Vietnamese coast

The ship that had struck the Zodiac continued speeding northward, most likely unaware that it had hit anything. Zeus stood in the rubber-sided raft, trying desperately to see if there were any remains of the boat. Meanwhile, Christian's two boats came up from the west and started searching as well. They moved in small, concentric circles, the marines grimly looking for their comrades.

"What happened?" asked Quach as his boat drew near the others.

"There was a ship without its lights running north. It struck the other Zodiac."

"A smuggler," said Quach. "Avoiding the port taxes. Or something else."

"I heard someone call out," said Zeus.

"We can't wait to look."

"We'll take another look around, then catch up to you," said Zeus.

"We don't have the GPS," said Quach. "You have to lead."

Quach was right. Zeus was sure the marines and the girl were still here somewhere, but the timetable was tight, and waiting jeopardized the mission.

"Where are you?" he yelled. "Where are you?"

"We have to go, Major," said Quach.

"Hey, Zeus, he's right," yelled Christian from his boat.

"Cut the engines for sixty seconds," Zeus commanded. "Quiet everything down. And then we'll go."

One by one, the engines shut off.

"Where are you?" yelled Zeus. "Where are you?"

"Đây," said a weak voice in the distance. Here.

"Where?"

If there was an answer, he couldn't hear it.

They restarted the engine and turned the boat toward the north. Even though it was on its lowest setting, the motor drowned everything out. He took the binoculars and scanned the water, but it was next to impossible to see anything. Finally he went to the bow and leaned out across the water with the flashlight, shining it across.

He saw a head, two heads, in the distance.

"There!" he yelled. *"There!"*

The Zodiac slipped toward them slowly. The heads rose on a wave, cresting above them, then disappeared.

Zeus cursed. He grabbed the marine on his right and put the flashlight in his hand. Then he went over the side, looking for the men he'd just seen.

It was darker and far colder in the water than he'd realized. He came up quickly, empty-handed. He swam forward, then to his right, then back. The salt water stung his eyes, making it even harder to see.

If it weren't for the flashlight, he wouldn't have known where the boat was. He realized he had to give up, and swam back to the Zodiac, clinging against the side.

Quach pulled nearby. "Major, your dedication is admirable. But we must go."

Wordlessly, Zeus pushed himself into the boat. Clearing the salt water from his eyes, he opened his bag and took out the GPS, regaining his bearings.

"This way," he told the marines.

They started back to the east. The air felt as if it had turned cold, close to freezing.

"Commander! There!" shouted the marine with the flashlight.

Zeus struggled to focus his eyes. All he could see was a black blur, with a dim yellowish white light moving back and forth across it.

The marine leaned over the side. Zeus crawled over the bag of debris in the middle of the raft and reached his hands out, blindly helping as the Vietnamese soldier pulled something into the boat. It was long and dark, and for a moment Zeus thought it was a giant fish.

It was the female intelligence agent, Solt Thi Jan. They laid her out across the large body bags containing the debris. Zeus thought she was dead, but when his fingers touched her face, it felt warm. His training kicked in, and he began following first-aid procedures buried somewhere deep in his consciousness. He bent and started giving her mouth-to-mouth resuscitation. Within three breaths he felt resistance; she started to vomit. He managed to get her up and over the side of the raft for most of it.

"Back on course," he told the marines. He pointed east, then realized he wasn't sure that it was east and had to hunt around for the GPS to make sure his instincts had been correct.

14

New York City

Josh woke in the middle of the bed, the covers off, his body naked. He had no idea where he was or how he'd got there.

He was cold. Very cold.

And he had to sneeze.

He pushed himself out of the bed. The curtains were drawn, but light was peeking through the sides.

He was in a New York hotel. Mara was in the next room.

The bathroom was near the door, to the right.

Up, up, up!

Just as he reached the bathroom, he sneezed. The sound echoed against the marble floor and walls.

He couldn't find the light. Finally he got the switch that turned on the overhead heat lamp. There was just enough dim light for him to see the box of tissues.

The sneezes ripped through his nose.

"Goddamn," he cursed. "I'm not in the jungle anymore. Stop, already."

But his sinuses wouldn't give in. Sneezing like a maniac, he reached into the shower, turned on the hot water, and let the room steam up, soothing his nasal passages. He buried his face in a towel.

A soft beep began to sound, quickly growing louder. Josh looked around for the source before realizing it was coming from the shower faucet. The water flow slowed, gradually falling to a trickle.

There was a cardboard placard on the sink counter.

Dear guest:
Please conserve energy. Be sparing with the hot water. Due to NYC and state regulations, we have placed limiters on our hot water. Showers will cut off after three minutes' use. The device prevents the water from being turned back on for twenty minutes.

Josh turned the faucets off, then went and got dressed. His stomach and bladder felt better, but he'd lost track now of when he'd taken his last pill. Better to take an extra one, he decided, and so he took one, then checked the time. It was just after one.

He decided he'd go get some lunch. He opened the door and was surprised to see a man sitting across the way on a chair, a newspaper on his lap.

"Hey," said the man.

"You talking to me?" Josh asked.

"Saying hello," said the man. He wore a plaid flannel shirt under a zip-up sweatshirt, along with a pair of black corduroys and Nikes.

"Who are you?"

"Michael Broome." He reached into his pocket and took out an ID. He flipped it open and closed quickly. "I'm with the marshals."

"Oh. Okay."

"You've been sleeping late," Broome said. "Right out when I got here. It's after one. You know that?"

"Why are you here?"

"I'm just hanging to make sure everything is copacetic. Okay? Figured I'd let you have your privacy."

"I guess." Josh closed the door behind him.

"Where you going?" asked the marshal.

"Get some food."

"Great," said Broome.

Josh looked down the hall, trying to get his bearings. The elevator was to his left. He started for it. Broome followed.

"You coming with me?" Josh asked.

"That's the general idea."

Josh shifted back and forth, waiting for the elevator. Broome stood only a few inches away, too close for Josh to feel comfortable. The marshal smelled of whatever he'd had for lunch—some sort of Mexican food, Josh guessed.

An elevator chime announced that the car was arriving. The gondola was empty. Josh stepped in, Broome right at his side.

"Give me a foot, okay," Josh said as the door closed, stepping away.

"Claustrophobic?"

"Something like that."

"My cousin's got that bad. You lock him in a closet, he'll sign over all his bank accounts just to get out."

Josh figured Mara would still be sleeping, but he was surprised to see her sitting in the lobby, arms folded, watching a plasma television mounted in the wall beside the main desk.

"Hey, sleeping beauty," she said, rising as he walked over. "Where are you going?"

"Get something to eat. Wanna come?"

"I'd rather you stayed in the hotel."

She looked at Broome. He shrugged.

"I don't think it's a big deal," said the marshal.

"Come with us," said Josh.

"I have to meet this guy Jablonski." She made a face. "We'll catch up. What restaurant are you going to?"

"Haven't a clue."

"There's a Mexican place around the corner," said Broome. "Decent takeout."

"I want something light," said Josh.

"You can get a quesadilla."

"Not Mexican light."

"Call me and tell me where you are," she said. "Broome has the number. Right?"

"Memorized."

What amazed Mara was the distance between the reality she had seen in Vietnam and what the commentators on television claimed.

It wasn't just that they didn't know all the facts, or that they misinterpreted them. That was to be expected. It was that they were so *sure* they were right, so passionate about their misinformation.

Vietnam had been the aggressor in a pointless border dispute and was now getting its rightful comeuppance. China's actions so far had been modest and restrained.

It was almost as if the people talking had been paid by China to give its side of the conflict. Or drugged and reprogrammed.

And these were people who should know better: a retired Army general who'd served in Southeast Asia, a retired ambassador to the Philippines, a former CIA analyst.

As she thought about it, Mara realized that the titles didn't confer any real authority or knowledge about the subject area, let alone the present conditions, though the television show implied they did. Still, given their experience, the speakers should have known to be more circumspect in their views.

Why was China getting such a free pass in the media? Since when had it come to be viewed as a benign, or at least semibenign, foreign power?

Maybe because it was America's largest debt holder. Maybe because nearly everything Americans bought had been made or assembled there.

Mara thought it had to be more than that. CNN switched to an audience-participation program, with a congressman taking questions. He was there to talk not about the world situation, but about a proposal to cut taxes to bring the country out of the recession. One after another, the people talked about the terrible economy. They seemed depressed, beaten down, and more than anything else, scared.

One woman rose and said that her husband had been out of work for eighteen months. She was working full-time at a department store in the local mall, but because of inflation they didn't have enough money to pay all their bills. Their house was in foreclosure.

"When will he get a job?" asked the woman.

The crowd applauded. The congressman, of course, had no answer.

"But the problem is, we needed the solution five years ago," said a voice behind Mara. "Now it is almost too late. We need to restructure the economy. Make things. That is not a thing to turn around in a few months. Not with a war threatening. Or already begun."

Mara stood up. The man who'd made the comments was standing right next to the couch. Fortyish, vaguely professorial, he wore a rumpled green plaid sports coat, mismatched to his blue pants. His hair was thin and hopelessly tangled. He wore thick framed glasses in a hipsterlike style, though this brush at fashion was clearly an accident.

"You're Jablonski?" said Mara.

"Yes." He blinked at her from behind the glasses. "Mara?"

"Yes."

"I just called up to your room. You didn't answer."

"Because I'm sitting here."

William looked around. "Where's the scientist?"

"He's getting something to eat. Why don't you and I talk first?"

"Good, very good."

Jablonski suggested the bar. Mara, having sat in the hotel lobby for a while, wanted to stretch her legs. She suggested they find a bar somewhere else. This wasn't hard; there were six or seven to choose from within sight of the lobby.

Jablonski seemed to know them all.

"O'Ryan's has Guinness. The Tap House is mostly German on tap," he told her, pointing from the edge of the red carpet as the electronic eye opened and closed the door behind them. "Choose your poison."

"I'm not drinking."

"Then we'll go German. I haven't had a *Weissbier* in a while."

The bar also served lunch, and was fairly crowded. Jablonski found a quiet spot at the far end of the bar. He didn't seem to know the people who worked there, but he had a certain ease that implied that they should know him.

"I understand you have an incredible story," he told her as they waited for their drinks—she'd ordered seltzer.

"Yes, but I don't want to tell it."

He blinked behind his glasses. She couldn't tell if it was a habit or astigmatism.

"The president sees this as an important thing," said Jablonski. "You're made for TV. You, our scientist, and the little girl."

"They're made for TV. I'm not that pretty."

"You're not bad-looking."

"Thanks." She wasn't sure whether it was a compliment or not.

"You're real. That's what's important. And you're not the Wicked Witch of the West. You don't have a model's body—"

"Thanks." That one definitely wasn't a compliment.

"You don't have a model's body, but you're young, athletic. You're good-looking," said Jablonski quickly.

"You're trying to flatter me."

"I will if I have to." The speechwriter had kind of a Donald Duck lisp when he talked too fast. He breathed and swallowed his words. "Why don't you want to talk?"

"I'll blow my cover."

"That's not already blown?"

"No. Not the way it would be blown if I went on television. My career will be over."

"Nonsense. The president will take care of you."

"How long will he be in office?"

The question was more pointed than Mara realized. Jablonski frowned, then looked up to get his beer. It had a lemon slice wedged into the top of the glass. He dropped the slice into the drink and took a sip, the froth sticking to his lips.

"It's a real uphill battle to convince people how critical the situation is," he told her. "A story like yours would be dramatic and help a great deal. You'll be on all the talk shows."

"You can tell the story with Josh and Mạ. He'd be happy to go on the talk shows." Probably he wouldn't, she thought, but that was Jablonski's problem. "Or the SEALs who were with us."

"The SEALs?"

"They should get the lion's share of the credit. Ric Kerfer got shot in Ho Chi Minh City, getting us out. They lost two guys there. He's a hero."

"So are you."

"Yes, but wouldn't SEALs be a better story? People love talking to SEALs."

"Hmmm."

Jablonski took another sip of his beer, then pressed his lips together, thinking about it. "Everybody expects the SEALs to be heroes. This is better," he told her.

"Not if it kills my career."

"I'd have to talk to George," he said.

"You mean the president?"

"I've known him awhile. Before he ran for Congress, actually."

"I want to talk to him, too."

Jablonski frowned, then sighed, then frowned again. Finally he took another sip of his beer. "This isn't bad," he told her.

"That wasn't the way it happened," Josh told Jablonski. "It was dark. I didn't see the other scientists being killed. If I'd been that close, I would have been killed."

Jablonski grimaced. "Josh—you mind if I call you Josh?" he asked.

"Go ahead."

"I'm not asking you to lie," Jablonski said. "Some of the blanks will need to be filled in, that's all."

"I need a break," said Josh.

He got up from the couch and walked to the door. After meeting them at the restaurant, Jablonski had taken them to a building two blocks away. The twenty-third and twenty-fifth floors of the office building were leased by a law firm friendly to the president, and he'd arranged to use this conference room. It seemed an unusually quiet law firm, Josh thought; aside from the receptionist at the door, he hadn't seen anyone on the entire floor.

Broome was standing outside the door, slumped against the wall, eyes glazed into a spaced-out stare.

"Just going to the john," said Josh, walking down the hall.

"You're gonna need a key," said the marshal.

They reversed course and walked down to the reception area, where a woman in a short black skirt presided over a glass-topped desk that was twice as long as most kitchen counters. The only things on the desk were a telephone and a small platinum-cased Macintosh laptop. She swung around in her chair and reached down to the bottom drawer of the credenza behind her, flashing a good amount of leg and cleavage in the process. She fished out the key, which was attached to a large, oddly shaped piece of Plexiglas. It wasn't until they were down the hall that Josh realized the Plexiglas was shaped in the letters of the law firm's partners, J&H.

"What a set of knockers, huh?" said Broome.

"I didn't notice."

"I'll bet."

Josh pushed into the restroom. Broome followed.

"You don't have to watch me this close, do you?" Josh asked.

"Gotta hit the can myself."

Josh went into one of the stalls. He wanted privacy above anything else.

He wasn't going to get any, was he? Once he went public, he was going to get more attention than he'd ever dreamed possible.

And they wanted him to lie. Or not "lie." Present the truth in a dramatic fashion.

Bullshit.

He was a scientist. He didn't lie. Or shade the results.

But he did have to help those people. He had to.

And Mạ. He had to help her. Her whole family had been wiped out.

Was that why he had shot the soldiers in the train? To help them?

Josh shook his head. He *hadn't* shot the soldiers.

He'd shot the person trying to kill them getting on

the chopper. It was different. The Chinese soldiers earlier—all different.

Why did he even think he'd shot anyone in the train?

He didn't think it. But it seemed almost like a memory, an intrusion.

Guilt, maybe.

The person he'd shot at the helicopter had been a woman, a Chinese agent. She'd had to be killed.

For perhaps the hundredth time that day, Josh wondered how Mạ was doing. Did she have nightmares? Were they doing this to her?

She shouldn't testify, he thought suddenly. It would be too much for a kid.

Maybe not. Maybe being a kid made it easier—she probably didn't go over and over it in her head.

He wasn't going to lie. That was for damn sure. The real story was dramatic enough. And important enough.

At least he was feeling better. It didn't hurt to piss anymore.

Josh flushed the toilet, went out, and washed his hands. Broome had gone outside to wait.

All Josh really wanted to do was rest. Sleep for ten years.

And maybe lie down next to Mara.

Jablonski was more subdued when Josh returned.

"I gave you the wrong impression," he said. "I want you to be completely and totally honest. This works only if you're honest. So let's go through it again."

Josh glanced at Mara. She sat with her arms folded, silent like a sphinx. He wanted to thank her, but he couldn't even catch her eye.

He started to talk, to remember what had happened.

"I think that's enough for now," Jablonski said when

Josh finished the part about finding the buried people in the village. "Let's take a break."

"I think we're done for the day," said Mara.

"I didn't get to Mạ," said Josh.

"The girl?" asked Jablonski. "Why don't you tell me that one. That's a good one."

"I really think we need a break now," said Mara. "For the rest of the day."

Josh looked at her. She was tired, more tired than he had realized.

"I agree," he said.

"All right," said Jablonski. "I have some calls. And I'd like you to get some new clothes. So maybe I can meet you for dinner?"

"New clothes?" said Josh.

"The president wants you to be presentable."

"Uh—"

"We'll pay for it, don't worry." Jablonski reached into his jacket pocket and pulled out a thick wad of business cards. He sorted through them, then found one for a store called Schwartz's Menswear. "Talk to this guy. Give him this card," said Jablonski, writing on the back.

"I don't know," said Josh.

"You can pay me back if you want," said Jablonski. "Don't worry about it now. You have a lot to worry about."

Josh took the card and flipped it over. The scrawl was hard to make out, but he deciphered it as one word: *Billy*.

"So, we're set on dinner?" said Jablonski, rising.

"I'm not sure," said Josh. He glanced at Mara.

"Call me and we'll see," she said.

15

New York City

Jing Yo took a shower. The water pressure was strong, the first thing about America that truly impressed him. He examined his clothes carefully as he dressed, trying to make sure no electronic devices had been sewn into them. But this was always a possibility—the CIA was as clever as it was devious—and the first item on his agenda was to deal with it. He checked his phone to make sure there were no messages, then left the hotel.

It was late winter. The temperature was just over sixty, cool to Jing Yo, though warm to most of the people he saw on the streets, who were going around in their shirtsleeves.

Jing Yo walked a few blocks south and west, choosing his turns randomly. He stopped and looked in windows, trying to see if he was being followed. The environment was so foreign that he couldn't tell. There was no one *obviously* following him, but if the Americans were onto him they would have their best operatives, and they would have a decided advantage.

He wasn't about to concede. He wasn't even prepared to assess the odds of his success.

After twenty minutes of wandering, he set his mind on finding new clothes. This took him farther downtown, where a panoply of small shops and even street vendors offered items for only a few dollars.

Ironically, nearly all were made in China.

Shirts and sweatshirts were easy to find, and so were shoes—though he had to settle for athletic shoes rather than something sturdier. It took longer to find a place that sold pants, but finally he was finished, outfitted from head to toe in completely different clothes.

Jing Yo dumped his old clothes in a garbage can, then walked toward the East River. At First Avenue he turned uptown. As he crossed East Thirty-fifth Street, he heard crowd noises—loudspeakers blaring, and the vague buzz of people gathering somewhere nearby. Cars were backed up on the avenue, a few beeping, most simply looking for a way to get out of the gridlock.

He noticed people moving down the street toward him, younger people mostly. One or two had signs, but he couldn't make out what they said, and didn't want to stare, let alone ask.

At Thirty-sixth Street, people were sprinkled along Saint Gabriel's Park and the green islands that flanked the entrance to the Midtown Tunnel. A few were eating sandwiches. By now it was the middle of the afternoon, and Jing Yo was confused—they seemed to be having a picnic in the middle of a workday.

There were police sawhorses at Thirty-ninth Street; behind them stood a crowd of people, their backs to him as he approached. A policeman was trying to wave the traffic from First Avenue onto Thirty-ninth, but it was like trying to fit the contents of the ocean into a milk jug. Every time a vehicle inched onto the side street, three more tried to nose into its slot. They were packed so densely together that Jing Yo had trouble finding a way across.

Safely on the sidewalk, he walked through the gaps in the crowd, weaving between the clusters of people. These signs he could read:

NO NEW VIETNAM!
LEAVE CHINA ALONE!
WE DON'T NEED THE UN.

Unknowingly, Jing Yo had stumbled onto a protest against the war. It was aimed at the UN a few blocks away.

The prudent thing would have been to take one of the side streets and walk away. Jing Yo guessed that the police would have agents in the crowd taking pictures, and if the authorities decided to move in, they wouldn't care if he said he was just out for a stroll. But he was too curious to simply turn around. He was surprised, even fascinated by the fact that these people seemed to be supporting China, or at least not criticizing it. None of them seemed to be Chinese.

A man was speaking from the back of a pickup truck that had been driven onto the island divider at East Forty-first Street. The loudspeaker blared. "Vietnam started this war. Let the Chinese finish it. Keep the UN out."

There were several dozen policemen nearby, lining the street behind him. Police cars, lights flashing, blocked the road.

Jing Yo turned and surveyed the crowd. As he looked at the signs, he realized many had nothing to do with the war.

BRING DOWN GAS PRICES!
BIG $$ BLEEDING US DRY!
HAVE YOU SHOT A BANKER TODAY?

There had been demonstrations like this in China. Many had turned violent, generally with provocation. The police would pick their moment and wade in to make arrests. Knowing this, the people would pick up rocks and other things to throw. Bricks. They would be waiting, something in each hand, for the inevitable charge. A few would have guns.

People began jostling Jing Yo, trying to get closer to the speaker. Deciding he'd indulged his curiosity long enough, he started moving back through the knots of people. A few shouted at him, making points that he couldn't understand through their accents.

Finally he managed to reach the side street. He walked back west through midtown, then cut around once more in the direction of his hotel.

Jet lag was setting in by the time he reached it. The four men who'd been outside earlier were still there, still staring blankly across the street as he entered. He glanced at the clerk at the front desk. The clerk smiled but said nothing.

The elevator seemed to take forever to arrive. Jing Yo stood perfectly erect, as he had been trained from his first day at the monastery.

Revenge was his purpose, not politics. He had wasted his time at the UN.

He corrected himself. His mission was repentance, not revenge. He had to atone for causing Hyuen Bo's death.

The elevator door opened. A short black man with a chubby face got out. He was wearing a tracksuit and listening to music on an iPod.

Jing Yo pressed the button for his floor, then stepped to the back of the car. The elevator began to rise.

It stopped at the next floor. A mother and small child started to get in. Then the woman stopped. "Is this elevator going down?" she asked.

"No."

The doors started to close. Jing Yo threw his hand forward, halting them.

"Oh, I'm sorry," said the woman. She bent, then straightened. "You dropped this."

She handed Jing Yo a business card, then stepped back as the doors closed.

The card was from a diner on Second Avenue, in the shadow of the Queensboro Bridge. Not knowing how close it was, Jing Yo took a taxi, handing the card to the man.

The cabbie's English was far worse than Jing Yo's, but he found the place easily and left Jing Yo off in front. Not knowing what to expect, Jing Yo went in and was offered a table toward the back. He asked for a cup of tea.

He was halfway through the tea when the same black man he'd seen in the hotel elevator came into the diner. Seemingly lost in his music, the man didn't acknowledge Jing Yo as he passed, walking to a booth at the very end of the room.

"There is my young friend," said a cheerful voice across the room.

It belonged to an elderly Chinese man walking toward Jing Yo from the front of the restaurant. He had a cane, though he didn't seem to need it for walking; he wielded it like a wand or poker, punching the air before him. He was dressed in a perfectly tailored gray pin-striped suit, with a crisp white shirt and a red patterned tie. A few wisps of hair clung to his temples, but otherwise he was bald. He wore thick bifocal glasses.

Jing Yo rose as he approached.

"Sit, sit," said the old man, raising his cane and waving it at him. "Have a seat. I am sorry for being late."

He asked the waitress for tea and a banana muffin. Then he eased himself into the seat, maneuvering slowly, as if he had something in his pockets that he didn't want to break. "My hips," he said cheerfully in English. "Both steel."

"I don't understand," said Jing Yo.

"Replacements. They taught me to sit a special way."

The old man smiled, adjusted his jacket, then looked up at the waitress, who was approaching with his order.

"Would you like more tea, sir?" she asked Jing Yo.

"No," said Jing Yo.

"You can call me Wong," said the old man when she left. It was the equivalent in English of asking to be called Jones. "I am in your service."

He spoke in Chinese, but not the Mandarin dialect—he used Jing Yo's own native Jin, with an accent heavily tilted toward Shanxi.

"Thank you," replied Jing Yo.

"English," said Wong, though he too was using Chinese. "For now. It will raise less suspicion."

Then he switched seamlessly to English.

"What brings you to America, Mr. Srisai?" asked Wong.

"I am a student," said Jing Yo. "I have come on an assignment."

"Mmmmm." Wong nodded. "A very difficult assignment. I was surprised when I heard of it."

"I need to get to Washington, I believe. I'm not yet sure. I only just arrived."

Wong reached his hand across to Jing Yo's. It was brown, marked with liver spots, and wrinkled. But the grip was strong. "You will have more help here than you suspect. Your progress was marked at the very highest levels of the school. The faculty has taken quite an interest in you."

"Thank you."

Wong took a sip of his tea. He savored it, then took another. "This tea has gotten better. Or my taste buds have declined. The exact reason doesn't matter, if the result is the same." He picked up his muffin and broke it in half. "What do you think of America?"

"I've only just arrived."

"Mmmmm." Wong put a small piece of the muffin in his mouth. "You might order one. They're very good."

"Thank you." Jing Yo bowed his head slightly. "But I am fine."

"I heard you studied to be a monk," said Wong, shifting to Chinese. "Do you have any dietary requirements?"

"No."

"We believe the Americans plan to use the scientist for propaganda," said Wong softly. "We have not yet located him. There are several places a person like this could be. We're watching his family very closely."

Wong paused and took another bite of the muffin. He chewed it slowly, as if each movement of his teeth were a dialogue with the food.

"We have other friends. We have ways of finding things out," said Wong. "It would be ideal to discover him before he is used. After that, there are questions about what course to take. But . . ."

He let the word hang in the air, the silence suggesting many possibilities—and none.

"I have a theory," said Wong, returning to his tea. "The president is coming to the United Nations on Friday. When the president makes a speech, perhaps we will see him then."

Jing Yo said nothing. Finding the man would be difficult enough, but killing him inside the UN, where security would surely be high, would be nearly impossible.

Only because of the time limit. If he had infinite time, he could easily find a way. He would prepare carefully, and infiltrate. But with only a day and a half to get ready, it would be impossible.

"You look daunted," said Wong.

"Jet lag."

"You have more help than you can imagine. Even now, hundreds are at work."

Wong took the last morsel of muffin and ate it, a bit more quickly than he had the others. Then he took his cane and started to rise. Jing Yo rose as well, out of respect.

"Your clothes, even for a student, do not suit you. The clothes make the man." Wong chuckled. "I have a cousin who is a tailor. He will make you something very suitable, and quickly." He handed Jing Yo a card.

Jing Yo took it, and watched as Wong walked to the front and paid the bill. Someone jostled him from behind. He turned quickly. It was the black man with the chubby face.

"Yo, bro, you dropped this," said the man, handing him a BlackBerry cell phone. "Better be careful. Brick's worth a lot of dough."

This time, the cabdriver spoke very good English but had a great deal of trouble finding the address. He ended up dropping him off at the corner of Clinton and Houston. Jing Yo walked for a few blocks before finally deciding he had to ask someone for help. It took three passersby before he located the address, a small walk-up shop on the third floor of an old building just up from Rivington Street. There was no number outside; the only confirmation that he was in the right place was a small business card taped below the mailbox. There was no business name, no phone number or address, but the logo, a needle and thread, was the same.

The number 3 was written on the wall next to the card.

Jing Yo went up the stairs and knocked on the door. A young woman, maybe sixteen or seventeen, answered.

He froze as soon as he saw her. She could have been Hyuen Bo's cousin. Slim, long black hair, breasts that seemed to pull him toward her.

"Yes?" she asked.

He told her in Chinese that he had been sent by Mr. Wong for a new set of clothes.

"I don't speak very good Chinese," she told him in English. "You want my father?"

"Mr. Wong sent me," he said.

"Come in."

Where Hyuen Bo would have been warm and accommodating, this girl was cold and distant. But that was a blessing. He couldn't afford to think about his dead lover. He needed to stay far from the memories, away from the longing.

The front room was as small as any of the shops Jing Yo remembered from Hanoi. Old newspapers were stacked chest high against one wall. Fabric samples were scattered in loosely organized piles everywhere. Two wooden chairs, their white paint chipped away, sat on either side of the window. An orange curtain made of velvet hung over a door to the rest of the apartment.

A large oscillating fan stood in the corner. The girl bent to plug it in before leaving.

The shape of her body as she bent was so like Hyuen Bo's that Jing Yo closed his eyes.

When he opened them, the tailor had shuffled into the room. He wore gray cashmere pants and a blue denim work shirt whose tails hung below his waist.

"Up," he said in English.

Jing Yo rose. A measuring tape appeared in the man's fingers. The man was as old as Wong had been, and much more frail, but he worked quickly, silently taking Jing Yo's dimensions. His hands opened and closed, spreading the tape and reeling it in like a magician manipulating cards. He wrote nothing down, and said nothing until he'd finished.

"Three hour. You come back."

"Three hours?" said Jing Yo.

"Three hour. Done."

J ing Yo used the time to get dinner. He had a hamburger in a small combination bar-restaurant two blocks from the tailor. Jing Yo had had hamburgers before, but this was unlike any of those. The meat had a different taste—bloodier, it seemed to him. And definitely fresher. It tasted as if the cow had been slaughtered in the back. It was also much cheaper than it would have been in Asia.

The Americans did have this advantage. They wouldn't have it for long. And perhaps it explained their arrogance—if you were able to eat like this, you must think you were better than everyone else.

A television was on in the bar, set to a news program. When Jing Yo finished his burger, he watched the report, trying to see what news there was on the war.

To his great surprise, there was nothing. The news was about sports, movie stars, and crime. There were three different stories about robberies in Manhattan. "Home invasions," the reporter called them.

"Serves those rich bastards right," said a man sitting on a stool. "They got all our goddamn money. I'd shoot 'em all. The Wall Street bastards."

When Jing Yo returned to the tailor's shop, he found the door ajar. He pushed in slowly, suspicious and unsure.

A pair of suits, one blue, one pin-striped gray, were sitting on a black suitcase.

"Hello?" said Jing Yo. He put his hand on the curtain and pulled it back a few inches. "Hello?"

There was no answer.

He took the blue suit jacket and pulled it on. It fit perfectly, as did the other.

There were more clothes in the suitcase: underwear, socks, shoes. There was also a map of the city, and a tourist guide. A small traveler's wallet contained several MetroCards, along with two debit cards and several hundred dollars in different bills.

Jing Yo's phone rang as he was sorting through the wallet.

"Mr. Srisai, I am calling for Mr. Wong. A taxi will meet you downstairs. It will take you to a new hotel. There'll be an envelope in the backseat of the taxi. In it will be a key for the room. The room number is 1203. You are not to go back to the old hotel. You will receive further instructions shortly."

"Thank you," said Jing Yo, but the caller had already hung up.

16

"Damn it!"

Greene slammed the phone down, releasing a small portion of the anger he'd kept in check during the conversation.

A very small portion. The only way to release it all would be to throttle Senator Phillip Grasso.

Then cut him into little pieces with an ax.

And he was a member of his own party!

Greene got up and began pacing around the office. What he really should do was go down to the gym and work out a bit. Or even go upstairs and hit his bike. But he had too much to do. He was supposed to be on the phone right now, sweet-talking Congressman Belkin into voting for his health-care appropriation.

Belkin would ask for a few more dollars in one of the highway allocations. Greene would bargain a bit, but in the end he would have to relent.

Everything was a deal. Everything required some sort of quid pro quo.

And Grasso—

His phone buzzed.

"Yes, Jeannine?" he snapped.

"I'm sorry, Mr. President. Um, you have, uh, Mr. Jablonski is on three-four."

"I'm sorry I yelled," Greene told the operator. "My bark is worse than my bite."

"Yes, sir."

He picked up the line. "Billy, what the hell is going on?"

"All good," said Jablonski. "The scientist is a little, uh, well, scientific. Stiff. But he'll be okay."

"That's in our favor, right? Shows he's authentic."

"I guess."

"Did you get him clothes?"

"I sent him to a friend of ours. Same guy I had cut you the suit."

"You don't think Anna or someone like that would have been better?"

"You said you didn't want him to look like a movie star."

"All right. It's in your hands. How's Ms. Duncan?"

"That's why I'm calling. She doesn't want to go on."

"What?"

"If she goes public, she loses her cover."

"This is more important than her goddamn cover," said Greene. "The hell with her cover. Who the hell cares about her cover—what does she think she's going to do, sneak back into Vietnam after the Chinese take it over?"

Jablonski didn't say anything. But that was reproach enough.

"Why the hell didn't Frost mention that it would be a problem?"

"I wasn't involved in the conversation, George."

"Yeah, yeah, Billy. I know." The president rolled his head around his neck, stretching his muscles. They always seized up when he got angry. "What do you think?"

"I don't see any need to use her, to be honest. She's a good story, but if she's not into it, she won't add much. The little girl, on the other hand."

"Don't worry about her," said Greene. "She's got a hell of a story."

"And our scientist rescued her."

"Damn straight."

"That is pretty compelling. She doesn't speak English?"

"Christ, Billy. The child is six. She probably doesn't even speak Vietnamese very well."

"When do I meet her?"

"She's coming up with me."

"All right. We'll figure something out. Now—the SEALs."

"What SEALs?"

"Mara told me there were SEALs involved in this."

"Yes, they came in and helped her get out. She deserves most of the credit though."

"Two of them died on the mission. That—"

"I'd rather not emphasize that point," said Greene. "I don't want *any* mention of soldiers in Vietnam."

"Uh—"

"No."

"Of course. I'm sorry. Let's drop that whole angle. We mention that some CIA people were involved, but we don't get specific. That's better anyway. People expect the CIA to be involved."

"Just say assets."

"I'll figure something out."

"Listen, I'll tell you what else I want you to figure out. That jackass senior senator from New York is a pain in my behind."

"Phil is a pain in a lot of behinds."

"You get along with him."

"Not really, George."

"Sure you do," said Greene. "I need his damn vote on the committee. What can we do to get it? Short of sexual favors."

"I'm not sure those would work with him."

Neither man spoke for a few seconds. The president remembered Jablonski on primary night in New York, pacing up and down the corridor, rethinking every move they had made in the state. Jablonski was sure they were going to lose—Greene could read it on his face.

Oddly, that was what convinced Greene they would win, and win big.

He did, by nearly 8 percent—huge at the time.

"You have to butter him up," said Jablonski finally.

"I thought you said sex wouldn't work."

Jablonski's laugh sounded like a bull snorting. "What might work," he said, "is to have our scientist meet him, tell him the story personally. Give him the Lincoln Room treatment. Take him up to New York on your plane, make a big thing out of him getting the information beforehand, the whole deal."

"That's only going to encourage him. He already thinks he's more important than he is."

"He controls Armed Services. You need him."

"Hmmmph."

"He's probably heard something about this by now anyway."

He'd better not have, thought Greene. He had the biggest mouth in the Senate. It had gotten him kicked off the Intelligence Committee two years before. And not a second too soon.

"He's in Syracuse or wherever the hell it is he claims to live," said Greene. "If he goes to the UN, it'll only be to oppose me. He's already threatened to do that."

"So make the move. Turn on the charm. Hold your friends close. Hold your enemies closer."

"Don't quote Machiavelli to me."

"That was Jablonski 101, not Machiavelli."

"Oh all right. I'll try. Set it up, Billy. Make it work." Greene dropped the phone onto the receiver.

17

New York City

Broome was replaced when they got back to the hotel by John Malaki, half African-American, half Asian-American. There was no polite way to get him to disappear when Mara invited him to eat with them.

Which bugged Josh. He wanted to be alone with her.

A driver working for the Marshals Service took them to a small French place uptown, where they were seated alone in a back room. Josh spotted steak and fries on the menu and quickly made his choice. Mara and Malaki bonded over the menu, talking about terrines and pâtés and sauces that Josh had never heard of. He ordered a bottle of wine—Malaki recommended a Rhône—but ended up drinking alone, as Mara didn't want any and Malaki wouldn't drink while working.

Jablonski was waiting for them in the hotel lobby when they got back.

"We're looking a little refreshed," he told them. "Josh, did you get the suit?"

"It'll be delivered in the morning."

"Did you get a shirt and a tie? Couple of shirts?"

"Just one."

"You may need a few. I'll take care of it."

"I don't need any charity."

"It's not charity. Relax." Jablonski pointed to the elevator. "Why don't we go upstairs and talk?"

They went to Mara's room. Malaki stayed outside, which was fine with Josh. He would have preferred that Jablonski stay there as well.

Mara propped herself up at the head of the bed. Josh and Jablonski took the chairs.

"The president needs you to do a favor for him, Josh," said Jablonski. "The senator who heads the Armed Services Committee needs to know what's going on. The president would like you to brief him."

"Uh, okay. How?"

"The speech is Friday afternoon. The senator is flying into New York City tomorrow. I spoke to his staff and we're getting something arranged for either tomorrow or maybe Friday morning."

"Kind of nebulous," said Josh.

"That's how these things go," said Jablonski. "Especially with this senator."

"Did you talk to the president about me?" asked Mara.

"Yes. All taken care of."

"You're sure?"

He held up his hand. "It's all good."

"I don't have to talk to the senator?" she asked.

"No, but you might be—it would be useful to have you along as an aide," said Jablonski. "We can be vague about your background."

"You're not going to testify at the UN?" asked Josh.

"If I go public, I lose my job."

Josh suddenly worried about the career implications for himself. Was he going to come off here as a political hack, working for the government?

"Something wrong, Josh?" asked Jablonski.

He had to do it. It was his duty. The dead people needed someone to talk for them.

"Nothing."

"There'll be some video," said Jablonski. "Some of the material you brought back. You can explain—the fewer words really the better. The hardest thing will be the questions, because they're impossible to predict. I'd like to go over some of them tomorrow, okay? There'll be media questions, and then later, speaking with some of the dignitaries. All right?"

"Yeah, sure."

"What about Mạ?" asked Mara.

"The little girl?" asked Jablonski. "She's going to come up with the president. There'll be a translator. She won't be on too long."

"You think it's a good idea?" asked Josh.

"Which?"

"For her to talk?"

"Her story is pretty overwhelming, from what you've said."

Josh looked at Mara, but she didn't say anything. She was clearly relieved about not having to go before the UN.

Jablonski repeated some things that he had said earlier about how to make his presentation. Josh didn't pay much attention. He mostly watched Mara.

"I know you guys are still tired, so I'll see you all tomorrow," said Jablonski, finally getting up. "For breakfast?"

"What time?" asked Mara.

"I get up at five."

"That's too early," said Josh.

"Eight?"

"What are we going to do that we need that much time?" asked Josh.

"We want to go over this so you're prepared for the questions," said Jablonski. "It's pretty important, Josh."

"I already know what I'm going to say." Josh looked at Mara. "I'm just going to tell the truth."

"That's all we ask," said Jablonski. "Believe me, it's better that you're sick of me than unprepared."

"Eight's good," said Mara.

Josh stayed in his seat as Jablonski got up and Mara showed him to the door.

"What's up?" she asked, coming back inside the room.

"Do you think we're lying?" he said.

"I don't think you should lie at all." She seemed surprised. "He's just trying to make sure you get all the details."

"He keeps suggesting how I phrase things."

"Well, don't lie."

"I'm not going to." He folded his arms. "What about the soldiers we killed?"

"Where?"

"The ones in the train car."

Her brow knitted. "What about them?"

"I shouldn't mention them, right?"

"That wouldn't be useful."

"Why not?"

"Because it confuses things."

"Leaving them out is not a lie?"

"Josh, right now, the world is on the brink of war. People don't understand what's going on. You can help. More people will be massacred," Mara added.

"They'll get killed no matter what I do or say."

Mara didn't answer. Josh looked at her, wanting to say something else—wanting not to talk, but to go over and take her into his arms.

Why didn't he?

"You're worried about Mạ?" Mara said.

"Yeah, that too."

"I think she'll be fine. They'll get really good people for her."

"Yeah."

"Listen, I'm a little beat right now. We can talk better in the morning."

I should go over there right now, right next to her, and kiss her, thought Josh.

But he didn't. Even as he got up, even as he left the room, he asked himself why not.

He kept asking the question, over and over, when he got back to his room. He stared at the ceiling while a Knicks-Lakers game played on the television.

What was the worst thing that could have happened?

After everything he'd been through, he was afraid of her telling him no.

Why?

Just am.

I shouldn't be.

But I am. Just am.

New York City

Jing Yo's new hotel wasn't nearly as nice as the first. There weren't any doormen, let alone armed guards; the clerk had to be summoned from the back office by ringing a tarnished bell on the battered desk at the side of the entry vestibule. The bedsheets, though clean, shaded toward gray rather than white.

Jing Yo wasn't here for the amenities. Once more, he acted as if he were under surveillance, though now it was more likely that he was being watched by Mr. Wong than by the CIA.

It was all the same in a way. He slept well, certainly better than he had at any time since parachuting into Hanoi, and with the exception of the time with Hyuen Bo, probably the best he had slept over the past six months.

Rest restored his equilibrium. Equilibrium made him confident that he would succeed. And confidence filled him with energy.

Jing Yo rose at four, did his exercises, and meditated. Then he went out for breakfast.

There were bums on the street, homeless people sleeping against the buildings. Many of them—he stopped counting at a dozen. America was a far richer country than China, but in China, these people would be with their families, or at least kept from sight.

They were an inferior, mongrel race.

Jing Yo ordered tea and an egg at a small coffee-shop two blocks from the hotel. The waitress asked if he'd seen the paper. He said no, not realizing that it was an invitation to read one—she handed him the *Post-News*.

The first few pages were given over to accounts of crimes—murders and robberies. Then there were four pages of stories on movie stars and actresses. The lead was a two-page spread on a singer who'd been hospitalized for drug abuse. The picture showed her nearly naked.

Jing Yo scanned the other headlines inside. It was slow going. He could speak English better than he could read it, and he had to sound most of the words out first in his head, then translate them, as if someone were speaking inside his skull.

But he recognized the word "China" easily enough.

Senator Phillip Grasso has become a key player in the administration's campaign to drum up support against China.

Grasso is rumored to be coming to New York today or tomorrow to meet with advisers for the President. He is said to be unconvinced.

The story was on the opinion page. Unconvinced about what? Jing Yo wondered.

But he was meeting with advisers. Jing Yo guessed that the scientist would be one of them.

"I wish to buy this newspaper," Jing Yo told the waitress, stopping her as she passed.

"The *Post*? That rag's been free since it combined with the *Daily News* two years ago," she said. "Help yourself, hon. More tea?"

The man who answered the preprogrammed number on the cell phone greeted him in Mandarin Chinese.

"I need to speak to Mr. Wong," Jing Yo told him.

"You will speak to me, and I will relay the message."

"There is a news item on page O-2 in the newspaper."

"Which newspaper?"

"The *Post-News*," said Jing Yo, flipping the paper to the front. "I believe it is important. I think it will tell us where to find our man."

"We will be in touch."

Hainan Island, China

The boats rocked gently against the wharf, sheltered from the tide by a long sandbar and an elbow of trees that jutted from the land. The storm was well past by now, and light from the stars shimmered in the space between the waves and hulls. There were seven boats; they needed only two. "Which ones, do you think?" Zeus asked Quach.

"The largest."

They all seemed the same size, not much more than thirty feet long, the sort of craft used to take small amounts of merchandise to local markets. More critical than their size were the engines, but simply starting them would not be much of a test.

"We'll take three," said Zeus. "This way, if one fails, we can get rid of it."

"As you wish."

Zeus pointed to the first three vessels, and the marines moved in to take them.

The three he'd singled out had enclosed wheelhouses, small structures barely big enough for two people to stand in. Two had forward cabins as well. The engines on all three craft started right up, and within a few minutes Zeus's small flotilla rendezvoused with the Zodiacs just beyond the sandbar. They transferred the flotsam bags and other gear, tied the extra Zodiacs to the boats, and continued south.

So far, so good—if you didn't count the loss of the Zodiac and two men.

Solt Thi Jan had a large bruise on her forehead.

Zeus suspected that she had hurt her arm and maybe some ribs as well, but she wouldn't let him or any of the marines look at her. She wouldn't even cough for him. He asked Quach to tell her to try, but Quach just shook his head.

"A big girl," the Vietnamese spy told Zeus. "She takes care herself."

"Maybe her lungs are hurt," said Zeus.

"And how would you change that? You have a hospital?"

Zeus let it go.

Quach guided them to a small cove south of the fisheries so expertly that it was clear he had used it before. When Zeus suggested that Solt and two marines stay with them, Quach refused to even discuss it with her.

"Why would she stay?"

"She's hurt," said Zeus.

"She is fine."

"I don't know."

"She is fine."

The spy said this without any animosity, just a gentle insistence that for some reason Zeus found more difficult to deal with than hostility. The girl watched him talk, saying nothing. Finally he decided it was useless to argue, and had her brought on the boat with him. Christian and Quach took the second. They left two men on the third fishing boat, dividing the rest of the marines between them. The men pulled clothes from the sacks, changing so that they looked like Chinese fishermen. Solt put on jeans and an oversized sweatshirt, and pulled a cap over her head. She looked like a teenage boy, small for his age.

The boats they'd taken were solid, but their motors were considerably slower than the outboards the Zodiacs had used, and by 4 a.m. they had not yet reached the southern tip of Hainan. Zeus therefore modified the plan—rather than going ashore near their target area, they'd stay at sea, pretending to be fishing.

An hour later, they saw the outline of a Chinese destroyer in the distance, its silhouette framed against the gray twilight of the false dawn. Zeus recognized it from the silhouettes he'd studied as a Type 051 Luda-class destroyer: a long, lean vessel with two widely spread smokestacks and a pair of old-style missile launchers mounted amidships. Fairly old—the existing boats dated to the 1970s—the ship was still potent against other surface vessels and would be able to sink Zeus's small fleet with a few shells from its 130mm guns.

The few Luda-class ships remaining in the Chinese inventory were used for home defense. If Zeus remembered correctly from the war games, they would normally have been deployed much farther north, generally working in low-threat areas. The ships had limited surface-to-air capability, and their antisubmarine systems were antiquated. But their 130s made them good for naval gunfire support during an amphibious assault.

Which was great. The Chinese would not be surprised that the minisubs had gotten past the defenses, or that the helicopters supposedly carrying the antiship missiles were able to get close enough to fire their weapons.

The destroyer stayed on the horizon as they passed. Zeus stood on the bow in front of the forward cabin, watching the water ahead. The first fishing boats were just starting out from shore, heading toward their favorite trolling grounds. They passed quickly, leaving the three strangers to themselves. They steered their boats a little farther from shore, keeping the island's gray-brown mass to the left.

A jet took off from the airport to the northeast. It was a commercial airliner.

Business as usual, despite the war.

"Navy," said one of the marines.

Zeus turned around. A Chinese patrol boat was approaching from behind. Unlike the destroyer he'd just seen, there seemed no doubt that it had spotted them. It was moving at a good clip, and a searchlight blinked on its deck.

"They're going to board us and look at our papers," Zeus told the marine captain. "Can you deal with the Chinese?"

"I will talk with them," said Solt.

It was the first complete sentence in English Zeus had heard from her mouth.

"Are you sure?"

"It is why I am here, Major."

"Get the bags in the nets and put them overboard," Zeus told the captain. "Make sure the nets don't break."

Zeus had two choices. One was to try to hide below. The other was to go over the side. The side seemed a better bet.

He stripped off his shirt and pants, leaving just the wet suit, then lowered himself into the water, hanging on to the rubber tire that served as a bumper.

Zeus's teeth immediately started chattering. A head appeared over him, motioning. At first he wasn't sure what the marine was trying to tell him. Then he heard the loud rumble of the patrol boat's engines, and realized that the ship was cutting in front of them and he'd be exposed to view.

He worked his way to the stern, moving under the platform at the fantail. Grabbing a line that hung off the boat, he wedged his feet against the hull, hoping to ease the strain on his arms.

Not more than a minute later, he saw the Chinese navy ship passing them, turning to port as it circled before them.

His boat's engine suddenly started. Zeus pushed to the left, still holding the line but worried that he was going to be thrown into the propeller.

"What are you doing?" he yelled.

There was no answer from above, but the engine quickly dropped to idle. The short burst had sent the boat toward shore, angling it so that unless the Chinese patrol boat turned around again, it could only come up along its starboard side.

"Here!" yelled one of the marines, warning Zeus that the patrol boat was nearly there.

The marines could take the ship. There'd be thirty men aboard at the most. Catch them off guard, they'd be easy pickings.

Too late for that now. Why hadn't he thought of it earlier?

The vessel put down a small utility boat. A minute later, Chinese sailors climbed aboard the stolen boat, yelling instructions to the marines. Zeus could hear Solt's voice above the din of the patrol boat's engines, yelling back at them in Chinese.

He pushed closer to the hull. The bow of the patrol boat was just visible beyond the stern.

The yelling got louder. Zeus took that as his cue to duck beneath the waves. He closed his eyes and held his breath for as long as possible. Finally, his lungs about to burst, he surfaced, took a gulp of air, a second one, then ducked back down.

The second time he came up, he saw a hand over the side, waving.

He ducked back down quickly, and stayed until the pain in his lungs had spread to his mouth and nose, and his chest felt as if it would implode. He put his head up and took another breath.

The boat jerked forward. Zeus reached for the line, but couldn't find it. He started to swim for the tire on the side, but after two strokes he realized it was too late; the boat was moving too fast.

Just as the patrol boat's bow came into view, two marines ran to the stern of Zeus's boat and jumped into the water near him, splashing and hooting. Solt stood above, yelling in Chinese for them to act their age.

The Chinese sailors on the patrol boat waved and shouted at them.

One of the marines grabbed hold of Zeus. "Okay," said the marine. "It okay."

"Okay," replied Zeus. "Okay."

Back aboard the fishing boat a few minutes later, Zeus thanked the marine captain for sending the marines in.

"Not my idea," he said. "Ms. Solt's."

"Thanks," Zeus told her.

"The Chinese were surprised there were so many men aboard," she told him. "I told them they were relatives, and had to earn their keep. But they were not fishermen, and most of the time they were lazing around, or swimming. Then I sent them into the water when I realized the boat would see you."

"I thought you didn't speak much English," said Zeus. "It sounds pretty good to me."

Solt shrugged.

"You know, you got a hell of a bruise on your forehead," said Zeus. "Are you okay?"

"I said before, I'm fine."

"Are your ribs okay?"

"Eh?"

"Your side."

"You want me to take my shirt off?" She shook her head. "No. Not so easy."

"I'm not trying to see your tits," said Zeus. "Come on. Let's see your ribs."

Solt hesitated. Slowly, she put her hand on her shirt and rolled up the side.

"God, that looks like hell," said Zeus. He put his finger on the large purple blotch. Solt winced.

"It's got to be broken," he told her. "How far up does it hurt?"

She shook her head. He eased his finger up. Two of the bones seemed to have snapped; she must be in terrific pain.

"Do they have morphine or something like that in their med kits?" he asked her.

"If I take that, my head will be cloudy," she told him. "I am fine."

"It's got to be killing you."

"I am grateful for your saving my life," she said.

"Yeah, but that's not what we're talking about now. Can you cough?"

"Cough?"

"Yeah. What happens with those is your lungs get screwed up. Cough for me."

Solt coughed. Even puzzled, she looked beautiful.

"All right. Can you breathe okay? Big breaths."

She was breathing fine. So it was just a question of managing pain.

"If you won't take morphine, at least take some aspirin," he told her. "Your head will be clear."

"I took some earlier. I am not a fool for pain."

He smiled at the expression; it seemed pretty poetic.

"Why haven't you been speaking English?" Zeus asked.

"I had nothing to say."

"Mr. Quach says you don't speak it at all."

"He said I do not speak it well."

"Sounds pretty good to me."

"Thank you."

"You afraid of him? Your boss?"

Solt frowned, but said nothing.

Zeus went and changed in the forward cabin. When he emerged, he found Solt and the marine captain standing at the stern, arms folded, worried looks on their faces.

"What's going on?" Zeus asked.

Solt pointed to the patrol boat, which was about a half mile away.

"They boarded Quach's boat," she said. "They've been there a long time."

"How many sailors were on the patrol boat?" Zeus asked.

"Eighteen," said the marine captain.

"They are working with small crews," said Solt. "They have trouble feeding their sailors. The ones who came aboard were skinny. And they asked about food. We gave them some rice we had."

"How many went aboard the fishing boat?"

Neither the captain nor Solt had seen. Six had come aboard theirs.

"We can take it," said Zeus. "If we go now."

The two keys to the operation were speed and taking out the Chinese patrol boat's radio.

That task was assigned to the marine crouched just aft of the cabin, holding his RPG launcher below the gunwale. He had to strike the radio mast dead-on, preferably without taking apart the bridge below.

The Chinese were either so focused on Christian's

fishing boat or so shorthanded that they didn't bother posting lookouts on the stern or port side of their ship. It wasn't until Zeus and the marines were ten yards away that someone emerged from the superstructure aft of the bridge and turned in their direction, spotting them.

The timing was nearly perfect.

"Fire!" yelled Zeus. "Board them!"

The grenade hit the antenna mount and exploded. A second grenade struck the forward gun mount, shattering the side armor, killing the gunner stationed there and destroying the gun mechanism as well.

The boat crashed into the side of the Chinese patrol craft. Zeus stumbled to his knees as he leapt across, his balance upset by the rocking waves. He got up, fixed his grip on his AK-47, then glanced to his right to make sure the rear gunner's station was still unmanned. With that clear, he left it for Solt to take the gun as planned and started forward.

The machine gun on the starboard side had already been secured by one of the Vietnamese marines, who was using it to pepper the Chinese boarding party. Zeus ran past to the ladder, thinking he was trailing the main boarding party. But instead he ran into three Chinese sailors. Two bursts from his AK-47 took them down. Then something pushed him to the deck, hard—the air shock from an explosion.

He rolled up in time to see the Chinese captain and his helmsman running past him, trying to escape. Zeus cut both of them down, his bullets hitting them in the legs and dropping them like the teeth of a chainsaw gnawing saplings in the woods.

Inside the bridge, he went to the control board and made sure the ship's engines were still on idle. Then he went back out to the deck, passing the marine who'd been assigned to secure the bridge.

"Keep us close," said Zeus.

Down on deck, the marines were pulling out bodies from the cabins directly below the bridge. Zeus looked over at Christian's fishing boat. The marines there had taken out their weapons. Two Chinese sailors were on the deck near the wheelhouse, their hands high.

"Christian? Win? You all right?" yelled Zeus.

Christian and Quach came out of the wheelhouse. Zeus went over to help them aboard.

"You all right?" Zeus asked.

"I'm good, I'm good," said Christian, who looked more than a little shaken up.

"Very risky thing," said Quach. "But thank you."

"It looked like things were getting out of control over here," Zeus told him. "What happened?"

"They found one of the bags," said Christian. "Quach told them we'd fished it from the water. I don't think they were buying it."

"Did they radio that in?"

"I don't know."

Quach went up to the bridge to check on the radio. Solt was already there. With the radio out, they couldn't be certain that the Chinese hadn't broadcast for help; they hadn't heard anything on their radios, but there was always a chance they had missed it.

Only one marine had been injured in the takeover; he'd fallen and broken his arm. Zeus took charge of immobilizing it with a splint and fashioning a sling. When he finished, he came out on deck just in time to see Quach take a pistol and hold it to the head of the one of the two Chinese prisoners. Before Zeus could say anything, both men were dead.

"Why the hell did you do that?" yelled Christian, clambering up from the fishing boat where he'd gone for his gear. "Those men were prisoners."

"They were liabilities," said Quach calmly. "We can't keep them. And we can't take them back to Vietnam. They'd do the same to us."

"Damn," said Christian.

He looked at Zeus. The truth was, Quach was right, as unpleasant as that was to face.

"Let's get everything together," said Zeus. "We have a long way to go."

New York City

Josh stood at the edge of the airstrip, the helicopter poised in midair behind him. His AK-47 was out of bullets. Kerfer and the other SEALs were in the grass somewhere, down.

He was all alone, surrounded by Chinese soldiers. He kept firing at them, but they didn't die. They were like zombies, standing in the field, on the runway. The wash of the helicopter's blades swirled dust around him. He turned, just in time to see the chopper taking off.

Then he woke.

It was five past five.

Josh jumped out of bed and took a shower, finishing just as the water began to turn off. There was a small coffeemaker with a package of premeasured grounds on the bathroom counter. He poured in a cup of water and turned it on.

The coffee surged through the machine while he got dressed. The first sip was terrible; the second, worse. He left the room, determined to find something better.

Broome was out in the hall, sitting on a chair and leaning against the wall.

"You're back," Josh told him.

"Like a bad penny," said the marshal. "So whatcha doin'?"

"I need some real coffee."

"Me, too. Hey—mind if I use the john? I gotta pee *bad*."

Josh let him in. At least he didn't smell like Mexican food this morning.

They found a coffee place down the block. Broome groused about the high prices—eight dollars for a medium cup of coffee. Five years before, it had been two, and even that was considered outrageous.

"No wonder there's so many people in the streets," he said as they walked back to the hotel. "Coffee bankrupted them. Look at this—they're two deep over there. And you need guards all over the place. And New York ain't even that bad," continued the marshal. "You should see Atlanta. L.A. L.A. is a pit. It was never that good to begin with."

"You think there's going to be a war?" Josh asked.

"How's that?"

"With China going into Vietnam?"

"Nah. They're just kicking their butts around for a bit. That's not a real war."

"You don't think we'll be involved?"

"Nah. Besides," added Broome, "who the hell cares about China and Vietnam? Let them do what they want. It don't affect us."

"Yeah," said Josh.

J osh found breakfast with Jablonski nearly unbearable. The food itself, served in the back room of a fancy restaurant about a block from the hotel, was excellent. But the work was tedious. The speechwriter had him go over the same points several times, each time telling him to say less and less. Josh resisted, but only to a point. He was so tired of hearing himself that he wanted to cut it short as well.

"So what's the president going to do with this?" Josh asked finally.

"He wants a resolution condemning China."

"And then what? Do we intervene?"

"Maybe," said Jablonski cautiously. He glanced at Mara, who'd been sitting silently through the entire session. "What do you think about that, Josh?"

"I don't know."

"The Chinese want to take over Asia, Josh," said Mara. She leaned across the table. "You've seen how ruthless they are."

"I don't know if they want to take over all Asia."

She shook her head. "They do."

"Kerfer thinks it's just for the oil."

"Kerfer's wrong. You said so yourself."

"Maybe I was wrong."

"I think we probably all need a little bit of a break," said Jablonski. "I have more phone calls. I'm still trying to nail down the senator."

"Why don't we do some sightseeing?" suggested Mara. "How about the Statue of Liberty?"

"What about Central Park?" said Josh. "I just want to walk."

"We can do that."

The last time Mara had been to New York, there was no charge to go into Central Park. Now it was five dollars. The sign said that it was a "requested donation," but everything about the entrance suggested it was mandatory, with elaborate pay booths and policemen watching the large chain-link gate topped with barbed wire.

Another sign explained that the charge was due to the city's "ongoing fiscal crisis." The mayor hoped to rescind it soon.

It was midmorning, but it was already sixty-two degrees. Mara took off her light sweater and tied it around her hips. The trees had started to bud. It seemed closer to April or May than February. Josh started talking about the trees, identifying different species and talking about how they were doing.

The main effect of the rapid climate change had been to increase the amount of rainfall. The wetter growing season had encouraged more disease, Josh said, and he pointed out different kinds of blight as they walked down a path from the entrance. In theory, the longer growing season would also strain the nutrients in the soil, though this wouldn't be obvious for some time. Meanwhile, bushes and the grass were doing better than ever, thanks to the wet weather.

"And weeds. All sorts of weeds," said Josh. "It's a great time to be a dandelion."

"Damn things are all over my lawn," said Broome.

"What do you do with them?" asked Josh.

"Pull them the hell out."

"You ought to think about eating them. They're supposed to make a great salad."

"Yeah, right."

"The climate change isn't all bad," said Josh. "It has a lot of different effects. We just have to adapt to them."

"Yeah, like buy a lot of umbrellas," said Broome. "I can deal with the warmer weather. That's good."

"I wouldn't get too used to it," said Josh. "This hot right now might just be a temporary aberration. Using the averages—it's very misleading. The actual programs that model climate change have a vast amount of variables, but even then they're really just sophisticated guesses. Hell, if you put the right formulas in, you see that the world will cool down."

"So what's the point, doc?" said Broome. "We just tough it out?"

"Maybe. We can slow it down—"

"It's that old saying, Everybody talks about the weather, but nobody does anything about it."

They stopped at a hot dog vendor for lunch, then walked in the direction of the Metropolitan Museum, passing behind the large white building and continuing toward the lake at the center of the park. At the north side, Mara saw a large area of what looked like old ruins, with boards and metal scattered in heaps, and small mounds of dirt and debris in low piles like pimples dotting the barren ground. She thought it was a temporary dumping area, a place appropriated by a city tight on space. But that wasn't the case.

"Squatter's field," explained Broome. "People lived here last winter. A lot of people, when the prices started shooting up. They didn't want that happening again. That was the real reason behind the fee. So they could kick people out."

"Where'd they go?" asked Josh.

"There's plenty of shelters and stuff. It was just temporary for most of them anyway," said Broome. "We should start heading back. This isn't the best area anyway. Even in daytime."

They turned around and headed across the park in the direction of Columbus Circle. The skyline loomed in the distance. Sleek high-rises peered over the older buildings close to the park's edge. The clouds had thickened, and the tops of the towers were festooned with gray and black wreaths.

They were nearly at the southeastern corner of the park when the first drops of rain started to fall. The rain felt different here than in Asia, Mara thought. A little sparser, more welcome in a way. It didn't have the acidic smell or taste it had in Malaysia.

"We should get out of this, because it's going to be a downpour," said Josh.

"How can you tell?" asked Broome.

"Look at those clouds." He pointed to a series of dark black clouds on the horizon.

"The subway's over there," said Mara, pointing.

Broome wasn't sure about the subway, but as the rain began to pound heavier, he relented, ushering them toward the entrance. A flood of people had the same idea, and there was a long line for the fare cards. Only one machine was working.

"Twenty dollars for a single fare?" said Mara, reading the sign.

Someone nearby snickered. "Frickin' mayor," he said. "Like all the rich bastards, stick it to the little guy."

Broome just shrugged. He bought two cards because rules prevented more than two swipes at a station.

"It's kind of a rip-off," said Broome. "And they expire pretty quick, too. But the city needs money."

Broome suggested they go down to Little Italy and Chinatown. Mara thought of vetoing Chinatown, expecting trouble, but when they emerged there were no protests or any other outward signs of the trouble in Asia, just tourists walking along Canal and the side streets, gaping at the stylized storefronts. The stores had about as much connection with China as with the King of England, and a good portion of the employees looked to have come from Central and South America, not Asia.

They had an early dinner, finding an Italian restaurant—Mara insisted on Italian—in the small stretch on Mott Street that remained of Little Italy. By now, Josh had become extremely quiet, and Mara wondered if he was brooding over what he was supposed to say tomorrow at the UN, or worried about Mạ.

Jablonski had called twice to say that he was still working on finding a good time to hook up with the senator, but Mara was starting to doubt that the meeting was going to come off. Just as well, she thought. What Josh really needed was a long break, a vacation somewhere safe—somewhere cold, maybe, far away from anything that would remind him of Vietnam. What he'd been through must surely be taking a toll. He needed to decompress.

She wouldn't mind a break herself. Though there was undoubtedly a lot more to do back in Asia.

Broome's evening replacement, John Malaki, met them at the restaurant just in time to order. It was amusing watching the two marshals talk—they were nearly polar opposites, though clearly they liked each other.

"Great spaghetti, huh?" asked Broome as they ate. "Best place down here. If you really want Italian, though, ya gotta go up to Arthur Avenue in da Bronx. Or over in Brooklyn. There's a million places there. Or Staten Island. Nobody knows about Staten Island. But there's good Italian there. And Jersey."

The two marshals began debating the likelihood that the Mets would make the playoffs thanks to the addition of Albert Pujols, and whether the adoption of the designated-hitter rule would improve or harm the National League.

Mara tried to get Josh talking about his scientific work, but he gave mostly one-word answers to her questions, and after a while she, too, fell silent.

He came to life, briefly, when they were leaving. A pair of men in suits came inside the dining room, looking around carefully before holding their sleeves to their mouths and whispering into microphones hidden there. A few seconds later, a pair of men in suits walked in swiftly, trailed by a waiter and two more members of a security team, wearing suits identical to the advance men.

"Look at that," said Josh. "Gotta be mobsters, huh?"

"Nah," said Broome as they walked out to the waiting marshal car. "Just Wall Street guys. Worried about kidnapping. The usual stuff."

"Oh," said Josh, clearly disappointed.

New York City

Jing Yo spent the day mostly in wait.

He got hardly any sleep. He could feel his enemy nearby, but the sensation was one of frustration and failure, of worthlessness. He knew the scientist must be close to him, almost in the next room. Yet he was very far away.

A story in the morning newspaper, this time the *Wall Street Journal*, confirmed his hunches. The story declared that there were rumors of atrocities in the China-Vietnam border conflict, and these rumors were likely to be brought up at the UN when the president spoke on Friday. The paper speculated that the president would offer proof that they were real.

Or the paper said that the president had to offer proof to be taken seriously. Jing Yo wasn't sure which. But the scientist would be plenty of proof.

Where was he? Jing Yo walked uptown and then east to the UN. The crowds were gone, or hadn't gathered yet, but there were fresh barriers, this time several blocks away. The police turned back everyone a block away unless they could prove they either lived in the neighborhood or worked at the UN. Jing Yo tried three different approaches, mentally recording everything that happened. Coming from the north would be the easiest, he decided, but it would be better to have a worker's ID than a resident's. Workers were questioned less.

There were plenty of work trucks on the surrounding blocks. He could grab a driver, take his license. Though it would be better to have his own license.

Jing Yo continued his survey of the area, growing more and more restless. He began to doubt his instinct, and the inexplicable feeling that his foe was nearby. Logic dictated that the scientist would be in Washington, at the CIA, being debriefed by government officials. He might already have made a video statement. It might be too late to prevent him from doing harm.

Of course it was too late for that. And to Jing Yo, it was irrelevant. He cared only about killing the scientist. That was his mission. Everything else was irrelevant.

Wrath was all he was after. Revenge.

And yet, that was the greatest temptation, the sin of ego, a turning away from the path. He was motivated by anger, not by his allegiance to the one true Way. And what good came of that?

Jing Yo had heard nothing from Mr. Wong by noon. He moved westward on the island, deciding to seek out a place where he might obtain a false ID, and perhaps a weapon, in case he had to act on his own. He had two important handicaps: his difficulty with the language, and his lack of knowledge about the city.

It would be foolish to go up to a person on the street and ask where he could get a phony license. And even worse would come from asking where to buy a gun in a city where owning one was against the law.

He thought of making himself a target for a thief and then taking his weapon from him. But perhaps he looked too little like a victim: for all the stories and rumors of crime run rampant in the city, no one approached Jing Yo or even menaced him with a stare. He found a store to stay in while it rained, leaving as the shower began to diminish a half hour later. By 2:45, even the mist had cleared, though the sky remained overcast.

At 3 p.m., with still no word from Mr. Wong, Jing Yo went to Central Park. He found a large rock outcropping with no one nearby and sat to make a phone call.

Someone picked up before the second ring.

"What has happened?" asked Jing Yo in Chinese.

"What?" said a voice. It answered in Chinese, but was different from the one that had answered the phone the night before.

"Have you found him?" asked Jing Yo.

"We are working. You will wait for your instructions."

"Perhaps he is in Washington. Let me go there."

"When we have an assignment, we will tell you."

"It may already be too late," said Jing Yo.

"Time is not your concern. You will do as you are told. No longer call this number unless it is a true emergency."

The line clicked dead. Jing Yo put the phone in his pocket, slid down the rock, and began walking once more. He found himself at the entrance to the zoo. He paid the separate admission—surprised to receive change—then wandered through the exhibits.

The rain forest made him long for Vietnam, and for Hyuen Bo.

Jing Yo left the park and walked in the direction of his hotel. He was a block away when a black Hyundai Genesis L pulled up to the curb next to where he was walking. The rear window rolled down.

"You will join me please," said Mr. Wong from the backseat.

The backseat of the stretch sedan had three flat-screen displays embedded in the false seat back below the glass separating the driver and passengers. Each one was tuned to a different television news station, Fox, CNN, and MSNBC, from right to left. The volume was off, but a Chinese translation of each show's sound track ran across the bottom of the screen.

"Would you like some tea?" Mr. Wong asked as the car pulled from the curb.

"No, thank you."

"How have you spent your day?"

"I have walked around the city."

"Thinking about your assignment?"

"My mind was not quiet," answered Jing Yo. It was an answer the monks would give.

"Then it was productive," said Mr. Wong. "Problems must be attacked from many directions."

That answer was also one a monk might give.

Jing Yo looked at the screen on the left. An analyst was talking about the price of oil, which had risen fifteen dollars a barrel during the day. The change was considered minor.

"Your theory about the UN is an interesting one, and has perhaps borne fruit," said Mr. Wong. "We have obtained the senator's schedule from a friend. It has several stops in the area, tonight and tomorrow, before he goes to the UN."

"I understand."

"If you follow him, your scientist will perhaps meet him. But it is possible he will not."

"If he meets him, I will be there."

The edge of Mr. Wong's mouth turned up slightly.

"You are said to be a most capable man, Jing Yo. Worthy of great trust. But there were problems in Vietnam."

"There were difficulties."

"You were on the wrong side of the people there?"

"I did nothing to offend them, except my job."

"Their attitude toward you was a mystery?"

"Yes," said Jing Yo.

"And your commander: he may feel you a great warrior, but he is not your friend."

"I need only orders from him, not friendship."

"What would you do if you were ordered home?"

Jing Yo considered the question. It was an obvious test, but what did Mr. Wong really want? A lie, so that he could satisfy himself that Jing Yo would do what he was told—or more likely, so he could report back that Jing Yo was still a faithful soldier? Or the truth, so that he could properly judge his character?

Jing Yo decided that he could not tell, and because of that, he admitted that he would disobey the order.

"Why is the matter personal?" Mr. Wong asked.

"The scientist murdered a companion."

"You speak of murder in war?"

Jing Yo did not explain the circumstances. Finally, Mr. Wong continued.

"In this matter, your interests and your country's interests lie in parallel," he said. "But you must be careful. Putting yourself ahead of your country is not desirable. You know that from your apprenticeship."

Jing Yo finally realized that Mr. Wong had himself trained in Shaolin. It should have been obvious, he realized now—but the most obvious things were always the last to be learned.

"I am a prisoner of my ego," Jing Yo admitted, lowering his head in shame as he would have at the temple.

"We are all, in one way or another," said Mr. Wong softly.

Mr. Wong had the car drive him to Queens. They turned onto local roads immediately after the bridge, threading their way onto a residential block midway between Astoria and Long Island City.

"This opens both doors," said Mr. Wong, handing Jing Yo a small silver-colored key. "You will find everything you need inside. One last thing—your phone. You no longer require it."

Jing Yo handed over the phone, then got out of the car. Mr. Wong lowered the window.

"Thank you," Jing Yo told Mr. Wong.

"Remember your training," said Wong. "And be true."

The building was a small two-family row house. The key was to the apartment downstairs; there appeared to be no one living upstairs. It was sparsely furnished with generic furniture; it would have been difficult to guess the ethnic background of the person who lived here.

A satellite phone sat on the kitchen table. Jing Yo turned it on, then put it in his pocket.

At first, Jing Yo thought that the place was simply "clean"—an empty shell where he would wait for orders. But as he began to examine it more closely, he realized that it was in fact outfitted specifically for him. The closet in the rear bedroom had a variety of clothes in his size, from casual to formal suits. The ones that had been made for him by the tailor had been transferred here, and supplemented with others. Underwear and socks in his size were in the dresser drawers. Two pairs of shoes, one dress, the other casual, sat in the closet. There was a wallet in the small box in front of the bureau. Inside the wallet was a set of identification cards, business cards for several professions, credit cards, and a thousand dollars in bills ranging from fives to a hundred. Beneath the wallet were magnetic card IDs, including one that showed he was a temporary translator at the UN, specializing in different varieties of Mandarin Chinese, and another that indicated he was an aide to the Malaysian ambassador.

A nice irony there.

He found a door to the basement in the hall and went downstairs. A door at the far end led to a small backyard, fenced off from the alley behind by a tall, solid fence. The yard was only a few feet deep, and covered with old cement.

The basement was mostly empty, with a small metal kitchen table near the outside door. A set of old flower pots sat in the middle of the table. Closer to the stairs were a washing machine, a dryer, and the boiler. Next to the boiler was an old room used to store coal when the building was new. The door had a padlock, with a key still inserted in it.

Metal shelves lined the walls. On the shelves to his right were four pistols, in varying sizes, from a two-shot derringer to a Magnum. There were sub-machine guns—an FN-P90 bullpup-style gun, a mini-Uzi, and an MP-5N. And there was a Remington bolt rifle, outfitted with sniper scope and small bipod, in a black case that looked as if it were for an electric guitar.

Strongboxes filled with ammunition were stacked on the opposite shelves. At the base was a kit for an RPG-29V rocket-propelled-grenade launcher, with four thermobaric antipersonnel rounds and four rounds designed to pierce a main battle tank's armor.

Jing Yo took only the Glock 9 mm pistol and the small derringer, locking the door and taking the key with him back upstairs.

The second bedroom had been converted to a study. The desk was an old secretary, packed with books and dictionaries, the sort of thing a scholar might have had in his house before the Internet.

A briefcase sat next to the desk. Jing Yo opened it, and found a custom-built laptop inside. When he booted it up, it asked for a password.

His name in pinyin unlocked it.

There were several programs installed, including a Web browser that connected via a satellite modem card. Jing Yo clicked on an icon for Google Earth. The program zoomed on the house he was sitting in.

The detail was extremely fine—much better than he would have seen with Google. As he moved the cursor, he saw a time stamp at the bottom right-hand corner of the screen. The image had been taken earlier in the day.

He opened the Web browser and examined the bookmarks. One led to Senator Grasso's calendar, apparently posted on an internal Web site used by the senator's staff. Others led to pages with information about the places where the senator was due to appear the following day: a Catholic school on Long Island, a science museum in Queens, and the UN.

As he examined the links, Jing Yo's stomach began to growl. He'd skipped lunch and forgotten dinner.

He got up and went to the refrigerator. It was stocked with a variety of food. He took out a frozen pizza and began to preheat the oven. As he waited for it to reach temperature, he noticed a coffee cup with two sets of keys on the counter beneath the cabinet. One set said Ford on it; the other was blank, but looked to him as if it went to a motorbike.

He placed the pizza in the oven, then went out to the front stoop and looked up and down the block. There was a Ford Taurus parked across the street. He walked over slowly and, after making sure no one was around, placed the key in the lock.

It didn't fit.

He spotted a pickup truck near the corner, but decided not to try it when he saw some people approaching.

Jing Yo turned the corner and continued walking. He'd have to wait until it was much darker to check the truck. He spotted an alley up on his left and, realizing it must be the one behind the house, turned down it.

Cars were parked along the backs of the property, with just enough room to back out without scraping one another or the tall fences on the other side.

There was a van parked at the back edge of the house where he was staying. The key opened it.

The scooter was in the back. The registration documents were in the van's glove compartment, as was the key for the storage case between the front seats. Jing Yo opened the case and discovered a pair of boxes. One had a hand-held GPS unit. The other looked similar, but when activated flashed only a single-word message:

Searching . . .

It was a locator unit, used to track shipments. In this case, Jing Yo suspected, it would help lead him to the senator.

"If I fail at this," Jing Yo thought as he returned to rescue his burnt pizza from the oven, "the fault will be only mine."

Hainan Island

Now that they had the Chinese patrol boat, it was easy to scout the harbor area, though Zeus was careful to keep the ship well away from other military vessels. They moved east slowly, Zeus and Christian both scanning carefully with their binoculars.

There were so many landing craft jumbled together that it was impossible to get a precise count. The preparations seemed far more ad hoc than an American or

NATO operation would have been. They were using much smaller boats, more like what would have been seen during World War II than those favored by current NATO planners. The support craft that the U.S. would have used—most notably the large amphibious-warfare ships that were essentially helicopter carriers—were nonexistent. Then again, the Chinese already had a substantial fleet out in the water to the south, where presumably they were going to invade. They would be able to use the airports on Hainan and the mainland for support.

The airport at Sanya remained open to civilian flights, with a steady stream of airliners coming in and going out. But it was also being used for military sorties—Zeus saw two flights of J-8 fighters land in the hour or so it took for them to sail leisurely across the outer harbor.

Leisurely being a relative term.

Their pass complete, they moved the ship farther offshore, reasoning that the farther away it was, the less likely it was to attract attention. They moored the fishing boats nearby. The marines took turns sleeping, trying to get some rest for the operation later that night.

Wiping out the radio had been necessary to avoid being detected, but now it was needed to monitor broadcasts and figure out if the Chinese authorities were concerned about the missing ship. Christian went to work rigging up a substitute antenna. It worked well enough to pick up transmissions on the standard Chinese navy frequencies, as well as some other chatter on the general maritime bands.

The main com handset had also been damaged in the battle. Christian also rigged a substitute that seemed workable, though Zeus put off testing it until absolutely necessary—no sense taking the risk of drawing more attention to themselves than they had to.

If he weren't so obnoxious—or maybe obnoxious in a different way—Christian might be a decent officer, Zeus thought. But he seemed always to be doing something to rub Zeus the wrong way.

After covering the damage done to the superstructure with a tarp, one of the marines found some gray paint to make it less noticeable from a distance. Christian complained about the smell as if it were the most putrid scent he'd ever taken a whiff of.

Worse, as Zeus finished sketching out the basic layout of the Chinese ships, trying to figure what their easiest target would be, Christian began beefing that technically, he, rather than Zeus, should be in command of the mission. Zeus gave him a dirty look, then went on with his work.

"Seriously, Zeus. You think you're better than me. I graduated at the top of the class. Not you."

Fortunately, they were alone. Zeus continued to ignore him.

The most vulnerable parts of the force were located at the two extremes of the secondary harbor, away from a pair of gunboats that sat at its mouth. Striking some of the landing craft there would not be terribly difficult, and if they blew up the gunboat at roughly the same time, the effect would be dramatic.

"So why does Perry like you better?" insisted Christian.

"Maybe because I don't whine about the smell of paint," said Zeus. "Or brag about the grades I got in kindergarten."

"You're calling the Point kindergarten?"

"Want some coffee?" Zeus asked, putting his pencil down on the chart table where he'd been working.

"You're not going to answer?" Christian said. "It's a serious question."

"I'm sure it is. Coffee or not?"

Christian frowned. He was serious. He didn't get it at all.

"Stop acting like a jerk," said Zeus.

"I don't think I am."

"You are."

"I just don't get it."

Well maybe that was the first step toward recovery, Zeus thought: the admission of ignorance.

"We'll discuss it another time," said Zeus. "Coffee or not?"

If there was coffee in the galley, Zeus couldn't find it. There was plenty of tea, though, and he settled for that. Solt came down while he was waiting for the water to boil.

"Mr. Quach wants you," she told him. "Ship nearby."

Zeus turned off the kettle and went up to the bridge. A Chinese destroyer, possibly the one they had seen earlier, had appeared on the horizon to the west.

"They're hailing us?" Zeus asked Quach.

"We haven't heard. But we don't know whether to trust the radio."

"Let's pretend we're busy. Take us over to the fishing boats," Zeus told the helmsman.

The destroyer kept coming. The marines, dressed in sailor uniforms, made a show of boarding the fishing boat. Meanwhile, Christian and the marine captain manned the forward and rear gun turrets, ready to rake the larger ship if necessary.

It would be a desperation move. Even though old, the destroyer was much larger than the patrol craft, and while they could shoot up the bridge easily enough, disabling all of the destroyer's guns would be virtually impossible. Meanwhile, even if the destroyer's complement had been reduced proportionally as the gunboat's had, they would still be outnumbered four or five to one.

Quach played with the radio, scanning the frequencies and trying to conquer the squelch, desperately trying to hear if they were being hailed. Finally, with the destroyer closing to fifty yards, he heard it hailing them.

"This is patrol vessel 2328," he said in Chinese. "We are conducting our patrol."

"Do you require assistance, 2328?" asked the radioman aboard the destroyer.

"Negative. The fishermen are stupid and ignorant, but present no problems."

"Why didn't you answer earlier?" asked a different voice, deeper and more scolding. Zeus gathered that it belonged to the destroyer's first mate or captain.

"The captain has ordered the mate to re-inspect the radio," said Quach.

"Your mast has been damaged?"

"We have been due for repair for three weeks," said Quach. "Since our accident. Our captain has low priority with the fleet."

"Be more alert next time," scolded the radioman.

The destroyer passed so close to one of the fishing boats that from Zeus's angle it looked as if it were going to collide.

"Did they buy it?" Zeus asked Quach as it cleared.

"For now. It's not rare for maintenance to go a long time, especially if the vessel's captain is held in low esteem."

Zeus watched the destroyer turn off, making a wide wake as it headed back to the southwest. It was funny—in the computer simulations, he tended to think of the destroyers as relatively small assets, of little use. Here it loomed huge.

"You are a good gambler," Quach told Zeus after the destroyer disappeared behind them. "You would make an excellent spy."

"Gambling's easy when you're desperate," said Zeus. "Problem is, sooner or later the odds nail you right between the eyes."

Around three in the afternoon, Zeus began planning where to set demolition charges on the patrol boat to make it look as if it had been hit by a torpedo. The marine captain, realizing what he was doing, began arguing that they shouldn't blow it up at all.

The patrol boat represented a large prize—if it was brought back to Vietnam, it would be a substantial addition to the fleet. He also thought it would make getting back much easier—the Chinese wouldn't stop one of their own ships. By they time they realized it was missing, the raiding party would be in Hai Phong.

"Our job isn't to steal their ships," Zeus told him. "We have to make them believe they're vulnerable to attack. If they think the patrol boat was blown up by submarines, they'll believe every one of those landing craft over there, and the troopships around them, are vulnerable. Even better, they'll worry about their aircraft carriers. They'll hesitate. They may even call off the invasion. That's our goal. That's why we're here."

The captain began pressing his case with Quach in Vietnamese. The spy listened a little more intently than Zeus would have liked.

"The fishing vessels are a better way to escape," Zeus told them. "They'll be looking for military ships.

Even the Zodiacs. They'll have every asset out. You don't think they'll notice a patrol boat that's not where it belongs?"

"They have not stopped us so far," said the captain.

"That's because they see us patrolling. We just came pretty damn close. Eventually, we'll miss something and they'll come over to see what the hell is going on. We may have missed it already. We're pressing our luck, believe me. Mr. Quach, tell him."

"The ship would be a big prize," said Quach.

"What good will it be against a Chinese aircraft carrier?"

That logic seemed to settle it, though the marine captain clearly wasn't happy.

"They're getting greedy," said Christian a little while later, as they stood on the fantail eying a pleasure boat passing about a half mile away. "That can be fatal."

"Yeah."

Zeus knelt down and opened the box with the timers. They were primitive, though undoubtedly reliable. Their fuses could only be set an hour in advance. That made getting off the ship a little tight, but it wasn't an insurmountable problem.

"What do you think of this boat?" asked Christian.

Zeus rose. Still holding one of the timers in his left hand, he took the binoculars in his right. There were two men in the boat. The men seemed a little too intent to be just taking a pleasure cruise, but they weren't headed in their direction.

"I thought the Asian mind always followed orders," said Christian. "Does it apply across the board, or is it because we're white?"

Zeus focused on the men. They seemed to be looking in his direction, but that might just be curiosity.

"You listening?" Christian asked.

"Vaguely." He handed the binoculars back and turned around just in time to see the marine captain and three of his men emerge from the cabin with rifles. "Shit."

"You will not plant the explosives on the ship," said the captain. "You cannot do it."

"You're being foolish," said Zeus.

"If you were to die, it would be easily explained," answered the captain.

"Hey, relax," said Christian. "This isn't that big a deal."

"What do you mean, big deal?" asked the marine captain.

"I mean it's not a problem."

Christian reached over to the timer Zeus had in his hand. "Put it down, dude. Come on."

Zeus let Christian take it.

"It ain't worth your life," said Christian. "Or mine."

"We will take the timers and the explosives," said the captain. "I am sorry, Major. But this ship is too important to lose. I hope you understand."

"I don't understand," said Zeus.

"I am very sorry."

New York City

Josh slept for nearly ten hours, without dreams that he remembered this time. It was a deep sleep, but it didn't leave him relaxed or at ease. Instead, his body ached when he woke up, his muscles cramped and twisted.

He just wanted to get the whole damn thing over with. He just wanted to go home.

Where was that, though?

The Midwest, where he'd grown up. Where his parents had been murdered.

God, how dark his life had been.

He thought about Mạ. He was really looking forward to seeing her, though he still had a lot of doubts about whether she should talk or not.

God, she'd had just as horrible a childhood as he had. But he'd overcome it. Or at least dealt with it.

She would, too.

Josh took a quick shower—the only kind possible—then got dressed. Broome was outside once again, reading his newspaper. He had a cup of Starbucks coffee waiting for Josh.

"Figured you'd like a shot of joe," said the marshal, handing it to him. "Sleep okay?"

"Like a baby, thanks."

"Babies sleep like crap," said Broome. "At least mine did. Mara's downstairs, with that guy Jablonski. Just went down. They were going to wait for a while before waking you up."

"Aren't they nice?" said Josh sarcastically.

"There's the prince," said Jablonski when Josh and Broome entered the lobby. "Ready for breakfast?"

"Yeah."

"I think you ought to get dressed for the presentation," said Mara. "The schedule's going to be tight."

"What schedule?" said Josh.

"We're going to meet the senator at eleven ten at the New York Hall of Science in Queens," said Jablonski. "Then we're going to come back to Manhattan and meet the president before his speech. He wants to go over a few things with you."

Josh looked at Mara. She was wearing a dark black skirt that fell to her knees, with a matching jacket.

"You look nice," he told her.

"Thank you. Mr. Jablonski picked it out."

Josh felt a slight twinge of jealousy.

"No, actually my wife," said Jablonski. "Very professional looking."

"I'm with the State Department," she told Josh, winking. "Public relations."

"Uh-huh."

"Well, let's get you ready," said Jablonski, taking Josh's elbow and steering him toward the elevator. "Let's run through your speech, and there're a couple of things I want to tell you about the senator. First of all, he has an ego the size of Mount Rushmore. Never interrupt him. And never answer your cell phone or text a message while he's talking."

"I don't have a phone."

"That's a start," said Jablonski.

"So basically, this guy thinks he's God," said Mara.

"No, he thinks he's a senator," said Jablonski. "That's a whole rung higher than God."

24

Long Island, New York

Jing Yo turned off the Long Island Expressway, following the GPS's directions toward the high school in Jericho where Senator Grasso was to appear at 9 a.m. He had more than two hours to get into position, and he drove slowly, looking around, trying to memorize everything he saw, comparing it to what he'd seen the night before.

It'd be easiest to take the scientist here. There was a parking lot right across the street where Jing Yo could park and watch. Once he identified his car, the rest would be easy. He could take him then or, more likely, get him when he returned from the building. If he was with the senator, so much the better.

The problem was, Jing Yo didn't know if the scientist was going to be here. The senator's schedule noted that a meeting was supposed to be arranged to talk to an expert "prior to UN."

"TBA" was the annotation.

TBA. Jing Yo had had to look the abbreviation up on the Web. "To be announced," it said. Or "to be arranged." So the appointment was still tentative.

If he had to kill him at the UN, he would have to use his bare hands. The bookmarked references made it clear that security would be very tight, even for employees. Jing Yo's passes would take him pretty much anywhere he wanted to go, but even a diplomat could not bring a gun into the building.

The school, on the other hand, would be easy. It was not yet in session, but there were already teachers and other staff members inside. A pair of policemen stood at the front, looking bored.

Jing Yo swung through the parking lot and went back onto the street, continuing to a second minimall a few hundred yards away. He pulled in and took out his laptop.

The senator's schedule had been updated. The meeting with the scientist was now on it, an addendum beneath the entry to the senator's second appointment of the morning, an 11 a.m. presentation at the New York

Hall of Science, where the senator was being thanked for obtaining a federal grant.

CHINA/VIET BRF—J. MACARTHUR—11:10

Jing Yo put the laptop into sleep mode, then backed out of the parking space.

"New York Hall of Science," he told the GPS, even though he thought he could remember the way.

25

Washington, D.C.

One of the perks of being president was never having to wait at an airline gate for the flight to leave. Air Force One was always ready when you were ready.

On the other hand, getting to the airport could be a major hassle, especially when you couldn't just hop aboard Marine One. Even stripped to its essentials, the presidential motorcade made the process a bit cumbersome—though at least it didn't have to stop for traffic lights.

But this morning's trip through the Washington suburbs was President Greene's fault, a direct result not just of his decision to take the little girl to New York with him, but of his opinion that Mạ should be allowed to sleep as late as she wanted. So rather than having Turner Cole take her to the air base and meet them there, Greene decided he would stop off at Cole's house and take her himself.

Cole's house was, in fact, very close to the airport, which calmed the Secret Service objections about the arrangements, at least to the point where the agents didn't protest for too long when Greene told them in the morning that they were making an unscheduled stop. In his short time in office, Greene had made a habit of overruling his bodyguards. To hear them tell it, he had already vetoed their arrangements and advice more than any three of his predecessors.

It might very well be true. Having survived a shooting war, not to mention Washington itself, he knew a thing or two about risk taking.

Picking up Mạ himself, Greene decided, would give him the chance of talking to her alone for a while in the car. He needed to build a rapport. It wouldn't be tough; he was a great grandfather. All his grandkids said so.

The limos stopped in front of the brick colonial. Secret Service agents were already spread out on the lawn. The front door was open; Turner Cole stood centered in it.

Greene got out. He was going to do this right—this child was going to see exactly how grandfatherly he could be.

Hell, maybe they'd take in an amusement park over the weekend. It had been ages since he'd been on a roller coaster. He loved those damn things.

"Mr. President, very good to see you this morning," said Cole as Greene strode up the walk.

"Turner. So, where's my little girl?"

"She's upstairs, sir. Uh . . ."

Greene didn't like the sound of that "uh." "Out with it, Cole," he snapped.

"Sir—"

"You might want to get in the residence," suggested one of the nearby Secret Service agents.

Greene stepped inside.

"Mạ is upstairs," said Cole, still mispronouncing the name. "She, uh, she's a little resistant."

The translator and the psychologist, along with a CIA officer, two federal marshals, and some of the Secret Service detail, were standing in the living room. Cole's wife had taken the children to school. A nurse was upstairs with Mạ.

"All right, the president wants the entire story," said Greene, addressing the small crowd. "And he wants it unvarnished. This is a no-bullshit zone. Out with it."

"Well, the psychologist seems to feel that reliving the—going back over what happened to her family would be traumatic at this point," said Cole when no one else would speak. His tone was reluctant in the extreme.

"It's no more traumatic than what happened to her in the first place," said Greene.

He looked at the psychologist, a kind of dorky-looking type with unkempt hair and blue jeans.

"You're the psychiatrist, right?" said Greene.

"Child psychologist, sir."

"Whatever. What's the problem?"

"Reliving the trauma, at this point—"

"She's not reliving it. She's telling the world about it. She's saving her people."

"I . . ."

"Damn it," cursed Greene, "sometimes individuals have to make sacrifices for the better good."

"She's already made a hell of a sacrifice," said the psychologist. "With respect."

"Maybe we could tape her talking," said Cole. "Not bringing her in front of all those people."

"Where is she?" demanded Greene. "Upstairs?" He started for the steps. "I want to talk to her. Myself. Now."

The retinue paraded up the stairs. Cole had given Mạ her own room, sandwiched between the master bedroom and his oldest daughter's.

"Everybody but the translator stay out," said Greene. "You, too, Frankenstein," he joked to the Secret Service agent next to him. "No offense, but you'll scare the kid."

"Sir, I—"

"If I can't handle a seven-year-old, this country is in serious trouble," said Greene.

The nurse, who'd been sitting in a rocker, jumped to her feet as Greene came in. Mạ remained sitting on the floor, in front of a scattering of wooden blocks, Legos, and a toy kitchen set. She had an airplane in her hands. She looked up at Greene with a puzzled expression when he came in.

"Josh?" she said.

"Josh had to go do some important work," said Greene, sitting down next to her. As he listened to the translator explain, Greene realized she wasn't going to understand, no matter what words he used.

"Nice airplane," he told her, pointing.

She handed it to him. It happened to be an F-4 Phantom.

"Thank you. I used to fly one of these. The stories I could tell." He circled it around the air, ducking and diving, making airplane noises.

Mạ tucked her elbows against her ribs, apprehensive.

"You saw these from the other direction, huh?" said Greene, suddenly realizing that she was scared of the plane. He stopped flying it and handed it back to her. She took it, then threw it angrily against the wall.

"Bad plane, huh?" said Greene.

The Vietnamese words came back to him as the translator spoke.

"Demon plane," they meant specifically.

He remembered those words very well.

And then more came back. Everything.

"*Tên tôi lá* George," he told the girl in Vietnamese. "My name is George. And you are Mạ."

"Yes," she told him.

"Terrible things happened to you," he continued in Vietnamese, stumbling a little, as he was at the limit of his vocabulary. But the translator didn't interrupt. "I am very sorry."

She stared at him.

"*Tôi không biet tiêng Việt*," he said. "I don't speak Vietnamese very well. I was in your country long ago. During a war. Another war."

He glanced at the translator, who nodded. He'd gotten the words right.

"War is terrible," continued Greene. "We have to stop it. You can help."

"Josh?"

"He's helping," said Greene, resorting to English. "Will you help us?"

Mạ looked at him, her eyes wide. She looked like a child on a poster they used as public service announcements against child abuse. The posters had adorable kids, with two-word captions.

Protect me.

It was impossible to protect everyone in the world. As president, he had to protect the most people he could. If he thought too much about individuals, he'd never be able to do his job.

And yet, he did have to protect individuals. Little girls and boys, if he could.

They used to plan the bombing missions over the north meticulously to avoid civilian deaths. It always pained him that critics of the war didn't realize that.

They didn't appreciate the dangers the pilots subjected themselves to, just to lessen the chances that the inaccurate bombs of the day wouldn't hurt people like Mạ.

Bad things did happen. That was the nature of war. That was why you did what he was doing, trying to head bigger conflicts off.

Mạ began speaking in Vietnamese. She had tears in her eyes.

"She will help," said the translator.

Greene rose. "We'll do it without you, honey," he said. "Your friend Josh should be able to pull it off. We won't hurt you again."

Greene looked at the translator. "You don't have to translate that. Tell her she's a brave little girl, and she'll see her friend Josh very soon."

New York City

"They came in the middle of the night. I found out later they were Chinese commandos. They snuck into the camp while I'd gone off into the woods to relieve myself. The next thing I knew, there was gunfire. The entire scientific expedition—the UN's expedition—was slaughtered. All in their sleep. The bodies were buried, and the site was wiped out.

"A day later, as I wandered . . . as I moved around the jungle, trying to find my way back to the highway leading to Hanoi, I saw . . . I came to a village. It was deserted. Well, I thought it was deserted. There was a field above the village. It looked freshly plowed. Then . . . but when I put my foot into the ground I realized it was, that it had been dug up. I saw something on the surface. I pushed the dirt away with my hands.

"It was a body. Buried. It belonged to a woman. Young, maybe a teenager. She'd been shot in the head. And there were more bodies beneath her. I couldn't take it. I got sick.

"Later, I think it was that day or maybe the next, I found a little girl. Her whole village . . ."

Josh stopped speaking. He felt light-headed; his tongue felt as if it were stuck to the roof of his mouth.

"That's good," said Jablonski. "That's perfect. You can just stop there and let it go. The video will be playing. It's perfect."

The bastard thought it was a performance. People dead, butchered in their sleep, and he looked at it like a goddamn performance. Points for his political bullshit.

"It's okay, Josh," said Mara, touching his elbow. "It's all right."

They were sitting in an empty section of the hotel restaurant, reserved by Jablonski so they could talk without being bothered. The hotel had provided a buffet breakfast, but Josh hadn't bothered with any of it, except for the coffee.

He got up, anxious, angry, feeling as if he was part of something he really didn't want to be part of. He walked to the serving table, took a new cup from the tray, and pushed it under the spigot of the silver pot. The ornate handle squeaked as he pushed it forward. The coffee sputtered, then streamed out, steam escaping with the liquid.

"I know this is hard for you," said Mara behind him. "You did everything you could. You're doing everything you can now."

"That's not the point," said Josh.

Jablonski was still at the table, concentrating on his food and pretending not to hear. Josh tilted his head, then walked over near the door, wanting Mara to follow. He pushed out into the hall, frowning at Broome before walking down to a pair of upholstered chairs sitting by themselves in a small alcove. He sat down. Mara remained standing.

"What's up, Josh?"

"I just—the whole thing. It's kinda, it's like a production."

"Of course it's a production. This is a huge event. Millions of people's lives are involved."

"It's not an event. It's not a show. It's a war."

"I used the wrong word," she said quickly. "We have to save people. China is going to run over Vietnam if something isn't done."

"I know that. I don't want Mạ involved in this."

"Why not?"

"I just don't."

Josh looked up at her. The suit looked good on her, but he wondered what she would look like in a dress. She didn't have a classic female figure. She was too tall for that, with broad shoulders, a little more muscle than the typical woman. But she'd look pretty, he was sure.

"It's just so . . . political," said Josh, flailing for the right words.

"Of course it is. But we have to do this."

"You're not . . ."

She stared at him. Their eyes locked.

"I'll blow my cover if you want," she said. "I'll stand with you."

He could have kissed her at that moment, jumped to

his feet and hugged her, told her he loved her. He could have married her and had an entire future in that instant; he could have died and been content. But instead, he just nodded.

"It's all right," said Josh, his voice catching. "I can do it. I just wish the whole damn thing wasn't so political. But we have to keep Mạ out of it."

"I'll talk to my boss. And Jablonski."

Josh looked down at his hand. He was surprised he still had the coffee cup, and took a sip.

Hainan Island

After the mutiny, Zeus went up to the bridge, thinking he might try to talk some sense into Quach. But the spy had been placed under guard as well. He shrugged when Zeus came in, and stayed at his post near the radio, listening to the transmissions from shore and other Chinese vessels.

Zeus took his binoculars and went above, watching the water and considering what to do.

At this point, the marines might very well decide to scuttle the whole mission, since it would jeopardize their escaping with the ship. If they went that far, then it would eventually occur to them that killing Zeus and Christian was the next logical step.

If it hadn't already.

They'd probably kill the spies as well. Except that they wouldn't do that while they still needed to speak

Chinese. Which might be the real reason they hadn't killed the Americans—no sense getting rid of them while they were still useful.

Zeus and Christian would have to escape on their own. They could make their way back to the area where they'd left the Zodiacs, steal their own boat.

The marines might look for them. But the Chinese would be looking for the marines. The boat was a pretty big target. They'd never get away with it.

Assuming the Chinese realized what was going on. They might not. They hadn't so far.

Maybe he didn't have to escape. Maybe the marines knew they'd have no problems once they were back— they'd be considered heroes. The Americans' objections would be insignificant.

It would be a risk for them. Better to escape.

Zeus and Christian had their U.S. passports taped in small plastic bags to their chests. China and the U.S. weren't at war, and once on shore the Americans should have no trouble—in theory. But they didn't have any of the necessary paperwork, and just washing up on shore in the middle of a battle in wet suits— that wasn't going to look good.

Better than turning up MIA. They'd never even be acknowledged.

"How grim is it, you think?" asked Christian, coming up the ladder after visiting the galley. One of the marines was right behind him. Zeus had no idea how much English, if any, the man spoke, but he couldn't take chances.

"Grim." Zeus pointed in the distance. "There's a highway there."

Christian pulled up his glasses and looked. Did he understand what Zeus was trying to tell him?

There was no way of knowing. Zeus scanned the shore again, mentally calculating the distance. It had to be nearly three miles.

Could he swim that far if he had to?

What did it matter? As soon as the marines saw he was gone, they'd chase him down anyway.

Around 5 p.m., they got a communication from a command unit. The unit was wondering why they had not checked in. The marine captain told Quach not to answer at first, then sent Solt up to ask Zeus for advice.

Zeus went down to the bridge.

"Tell them we're continuing to inspect some suspicious boats," said Zeus. "Be as vague but as positive as you can."

Quach spoke to them for a few minutes in Chinese, apparently satisfying them.

"It'll be dark enough to set out soon," Zeus told the marine captain, deciding to try and push up the timetable. "We should get ready."

"Go over the plan."

Zeus mapped out the attack he had envisioned earlier, with minor revisions. It called for the two fishing boats to go into the harbor. A team of two men aboard each would swim over and plant charges on the landing boats closest to the open water. The debris would be released nearby and the fishing boats would then retreat. Rather than blowing up the patrol boat—still his preference, he said—he suggested putting charges on the third fishing vessel and leaving some debris nearby. The patrol boat would start westward as soon as the teams arrived back.

"It is a good plan," said the marine captain.

"Christian and I will take this landing boat," said

Zeus, pointing to the craft farthest west. "Mr. Quach should come with us in the fishing boat, in case we're stopped by the Chinese."

"Mr. Quach has to stay with the ship," said the captain. "Solt will go."

He assigned one of his men as well. Zeus let him pick the other crew.

"Once you see the explosions, make a transmission that you've spotted a periscope," said Zeus. "Lay down the depth charges from the fantail."

"We should be back aboard by then," said Christian.

"I mean if we don't make it," said Zeus, staring at the marine captain.

The captain held his glare for a moment, then turned his eyes toward the deck.

S ince the timers they had for the charges were only good for an hour and they wanted the explosions to coincide roughly with the missile attack, leaving before 10 p.m. didn't make much sense. But Zeus wanted to be on the island before the attack, which meant leaving as soon as possible. And with the marines itching to get out of the area, they set a new H-hour for the explosions: 10 p.m.

They climbed aboard the fishing boats at 1807—seven minutes after 6 p.m. They would have a little over three hours to get close to the landing ships and set the charges, then return.

Or not.

"I'm surprised they let us go," whispered Christian as Zeus steered the boat away.

"Maybe."

Zeus took a wide turn, heading westward. The plan

called for him to sail to the west of the city, then tack back, following a pattern they'd observed some of the fishing boats take earlier. But after a few minutes he changed course and headed directly for the landing craft.

"What are you doing?" Christian asked.

"Going to Plan B."

"B?"

"It's more like W or X," admitted Zeus. "Hang on."

He pushed the engines to full throttle. The marine watching them stayed at the aft end of the cabin, not saying anything. Nor did he object twenty minutes later when Zeus cut the motor and let the boat drift.

"You're coming with us," Zeus told Solt.

She looked up at him, her eyes studying his face. She was a beautiful woman, he realized. Very beautiful.

"Will you be able to swim?" Zeus asked.

"Yes," she said.

They took the bags with the debris with them over the side, pushing off one by one. The night was cloudy and fairly dark, but the boxy shadow of the landing craft stood out against the light from shore. Zeus was the last to leave the boat, watching after Solt as she swam. But within a few strokes she started to pull away, and he ended up being the last one to the landing craft by quite a margin.

"Hey, slowpoke," said Christian when he got there.

"Set the charges," said Zeus.

"Ya think? Already done. All we have to do is push the button and the timer starts."

"Do it." Zeus swam to the stern of the landing boat and climbed up the ladder with the body bags. He threw the pieces of metal and plastic inside the empty craft, then went back to the water and let the weighted bags sink to the bottom. He pulled a waterproof ruck from the last bag—clothes.

"We're good?" Zeus asked Christian.

"You bet. I say we get to shore."

So at least he can add two plus two, Zeus thought. He turned to Solt.

"We're not going back to the fishing boat," he told her. "I'm afraid the marines will kill us before we get back to port."

"I know," she said.

"I'm sorry about Mr. Quach."

"Don't be," she said. "He's with them."

The landing craft were anchored about ten meters apart, in long rows. They hopscotched toward shore, resting every few minutes and making sure that there were no patrols nearby. They were nearly to the wharf when Zeus spotted an army truck trolling along the far side.

"We'll have to look for another place to land," he told the others. "I think farther east."

"We should go this way," said Solt. "We can take one of the small boats and go to the beach."

"Back by the city?" asked Christian.

"We can change our clothes," she said.

"You brought some?"

"Under the wet suit. In case."

"I don't have any clothes," said Christian.

"I have yours," said Zeus. He held up the ruck.

"Well then lead the way," said Christian.

Solt waited until the truck had turned around before pushing off from the side of the landing craft. The dock she was talking about was nearly a half mile off. Zeus felt tired before he'd taken more than a dozen strokes. He put his head down, willing himself forward.

He'd almost reached the boat when he heard an explosion in the distance. He stopped and turned, looking back in the direction of the landing craft they'd put the charges on. He couldn't see it because of the other landing craft in the way.

A fireball shot up from the ocean. Then there was a loud crack, and a red glow in the distance where the patrol boat would have been.

"I set the charges on the patrol boat," said Christian. "I didn't figure you'd object."

"When?"

"I did it right after we took it over. You think I'm going to leave something like that for the last minute? All I had to do was press the button."

"Good work," said Zeus.

"We better get moving. The landing craft should explode any second. My bet is the fishing boat will, too."

28

**New York Hall of Science,
New York City**

It took Jing Yo three turns around the parking lot to get a feel for the place, matching the photos and brochures he'd seen online with the building's exterior. Besides the main entrance, there were four different service doors and a loading dock. Each had a card reader; gaining access would require obtaining an employee ID.

Jing Yo parked the van in a cluster of cars near one of the doors, backing into a spot that allowed him to observe the loading dock and another service entrance on the side. He got out, planning to look in the nearby cars for spare IDs—a violation of security protocols so common that it was generally unpunished, especially at a place like the museum, where security was usually not a high priority.

The first car was locked. Not seeing anything that would make it worth breaking into, Jing Yo moved on to the second car. He was just opening the passenger door when a worker opened the service door at the side of the building and walked out.

The man stuck his hand into the pocket of his blue mechanics overalls and pulled out a cigarette. Cupping his hands against the light breeze, he lit up, took a puff, then began walking toward the two heating company trucks parked a short distance away.

Jing Yo watched. He expected that the man would get into the cab of the truck and drive off. Instead, the man went to the back of the truck and opened it, climbing in for some part or tool he needed inside.

Jing Yo left the car and circled back, angling toward the rear of the truck just out of view from the interior.

He would take him with his hands. Shooting would be too loud.

Jing Yo was almost at the back of the truck when the employee jumped out, the vehicle rocking on its shocks. The man looked at him in surprise. Jing Yo was surprised as well—the man was a Chinese-American, which for some reason Jing Yo hadn't expected.

"I wonder if you have a cig," said Jing Yo.

"Cig?" The man looked bewildered, and slightly annoyed.

"Cigarette?"

"Yeah, I guess I got one," said the worker, digging into his pocket. "Damn things cost a fortune," he added, taking the pack and shaking a cigarette out. "Here."

It seemed odd to be complaining about your own sense of charity. Jing Yo took the cigarette, then watched the man pull out another for himself. The worker put his parts down—there were small pieces of electronics gear—and lit up. Then he handed Jing Yo the lighter.

"You work here?" asked the man.

"Yes."

"Nice place, huh? Pay okay?"

Jing Yo shrugged. The other man laughed.

"Don't worry. I'm not looking to take your job."

"What are you fixing?" Jing Yo asked.

"The safety cutoff on boiler two is your big problem," said the man. "You guys are lucky I found the parts in the truck. Boss wanted me to drive back to the warehouse. Forget that, man."

"Don't you need an access badge?" asked Jing Yo.

"You mean a card to get in? Nah—I stuck a doorstop in there. You'll open it for me, right? If I need it."

"Sure."

"Have we met?" the man asked. "You look familiar. You live in Kew Gardens?"

Jing Yo shook his head. "I come from China," he said in Chinese.

"Huh?"

If the man had answered him, or even shown some recognition of the language, Jing Yo might have spared his life. But the man's ignorance of his ancestral language broke the small spell his Asian roots had cast.

Jing Yo stepped forward quickly and swung his left leg up in a hard kick that caught the worker in the chest, doubling him over. A chop on his neck sent him to the pavement.

Two kicks to the side of his head finished him.

Jing Yo picked him up and put him in his truck. The man was a little shorter than he, and the coveralls didn't quite fall to his shoe tops. But they were roomy enough for him to move his arms easily, and gave him a good place to hide his pistol.

A toolbox hid the P90 submachine gun.

A woman called to him a few feet into the building. "Where are you going?"

Jing Yo turned abruptly, angry that he was being stopped. "Your heating system has difficulties," he said.

The woman frowned at him. "I know it has *difficulties*," she said. "When is it going to be fixed?"

"It may take a few hours."

"A few hours? It was supposed to be fixed by nine. It's a quarter past."

Jing Yo stared at her.

"We have some important guests coming," she continued. "You have to fix it quickly."

"We need parts."

"Get them. And get it fixed."

The woman turned on her heel and stomped away in the direction she'd come. Jing Yo shifted the mental map he had constructed of the interior: she must be walking toward the staff offices, which he had thought were on the other side.

He went to the stairway door and opened it, as if going down to the basement. But he went up instead of down, coming out on the second floor.

He found himself in the middle of a display of rocket ships. A black man about his age wearing a tan turtleneck and faded blue jeans looked at him expectantly.

"I need to find thermostat," said Jing Yo, his English failing as he tried to come up with an excuse for being there.

"All the thermostats are in armored cases," said the man.

"Are there any on this floor?" asked Jing Yo.

"Out near the restroom, over there. Better hurry. There's a hundred kids on their way into the building. And the first place they go is always the john."

The left side of the hallway opened on the side of an atrium that rose to the top of the building. Standing by the rails, Jing Yo could see the front entrance. Two school buses were parked in front of the doors. Children were being lined up on the sidewalk.

The door opened. The kids were not nearly as disciplined as Chinese schoolchildren would have been. They spoke loudly and rudely. Their line was barely distinguishable from a mad jumble. The teachers seemed not to notice, talking to one another rather than herding their charges back in line.

Americans really were a doomed race.

The children were directed toward an auditorium at the left side of the atrium, just out of Jing Yo's view. One peeled off and headed for the stairs. A second and third followed. Soon there were a dozen, running and laughing, heading for the restroom, as the man inside had said.

Shooting someone from here was simple. The P90 would make quick work of him.

Jing Yo wasn't concerned with getting out. If he got out the way he came without any trouble, then he would. If not—what did it matter? Very possibly Mr. Wong or the government would arrange for his death even if he did escape.

It would be better to die sooner rather than later, rather than waiting to be tortured and questioned, forced to betray his country. If possible, he would die in a firefight. If wounded, he would end his suffering honorably.

"What are you doing up here?"

Jing Yo turned slowly. The woman who had accosted him downstairs was standing in the hall near the rocket exhibit.

"Thermostats," he told her.

"What?"

"I have to check them."

"Get moving. Senator Grasso is going to be here in half an hour. Do you even know who he is?"

"He's a U.S. senator."

She shook her head, disgusted, and stomped past him. Jing Yo resisted the urge to throw her over the railing. He went to the thermostat, pretending to look at it.

"She's a bitch on heels, huh?" said the man he'd seen earlier in the rocket display.

Jing Yo didn't understand the idiom, but realized he should agree. He tapped the thermostat as if he had just finished what he was doing, then began walking toward the stairway at the far end of the open space.

A uniformed guard was standing near the top of the landing as he came up. The guard, in his late sixties with a gray buzz cut and a trim belly, nodded at him. Jing Yo nodded back. The man didn't have a gun.

He did have a radio, which might be useful.

Jing Yo went over to the thermostat, which was on the wall right next to the opening down to the atrium area. He opened his case and took out a screwdriver, then quickly closed it so that the submachine gun couldn't be seen.

The screws on the thermostat were star-heads rather than conventional screw or Phillips heads. With the guard watching, he couldn't fake working on the device without taking it apart. He dropped down to his knee to see if he had the right driver.

"Whatcha workin' on?" asked the guard as he zipped his bag open.

Jing Yo turned to him. He was still over near the steps.

Stay there, old man, he thought.

"Heating system," said Jing Yo.

"Thermostats are bad?"

"Just need checking."

The guard took that as an invitation to come over. Jing Yo pulled a large screwdriver from the bag and zipped it closed quickly.

"These commercial systems a lot different than residential?" asked the guard.

"Different."

"I used to do some work with a plumber," said the guard. "Before I joined NYPD."

"Mmmmm," said Jing Yo.

He still didn't have the right screwdriver in his hand. He looked at the thermostat.

"This one's okay," he said, pointing.

"How can you tell? Jump them and look for a spark?"

"Yes," said Jing Yo, hoping that was the right answer.

"Nothing changes, huh? You don't use a meter?"

Jing Yo had no idea what the proper answer would be, and certainly could not have identified the meter the guard was talking about.

He could grab him by the throat, clamp his hand over his mouth, and drag him somewhere.

Where?

The restroom must be nearby.

The guard gave him a quizzical look.

"Restroom?" asked Jing Yo.

"Just over there." He took a few steps back and pointed.

Jing Yo took his tool bag and walked over to the men's room. Inside, he waited near the door, hoping the guard would follow. But he didn't. When Jing Yo came out, he was gone.

The nearby exhibition halls were empty as well. One was dedicated to exhibits on the human body; the other demonstrated how evolution worked. The displays were in glossy colors. The place looked more like a toy room than a science lab.

He went back out to the walkway over the atrium. The children had been sequestered inside the auditorium, joined there by a second group whose buses had just arrived.

As Jing Yo watched, a limo pulled up to the door, angling in front of the buses. Two men in suits came out from the area directly below Jing Yo, followed by the woman who had scolded him twice earlier. They waited at the door as a young man in his early twenties got out of the limo, holding the door open for another man.

Senator Grasso. Short, balding, with a round belly, Grasso swaggered as he walked the short distance from the car to the door.

Jing Yo unzipped his tool bag. The gun was right on the top, easy to grab.

"Senator, so pleased to see you," said the woman, her voice easily carrying across the open space. Her tone was 180 degrees from the one she had used to address Jing Yo.

"Maria—so nice to see you again. How is my favorite museum administrator doing?"

The senator pulled her toward him and kissed her on the cheek. She didn't resist.

"You know the chairman of our board, Dr. Giddes. And my assistant, Ralph Kinel."

"Doc, Ralph—how are yas?"

The senator didn't introduce his aide, who stood in the background.

"We have a lot of children here today," said the museum director. "We thought you'd like to accept your award in front of them."

"Oh-ho," said the senator. "Wouldn't that be nice?"

"The senator does have a busy schedule today," said the aide. "He also needs to meet with some aides to the president after the presentation. If there is a room available."

"Will my office do?" asked the director. "Let's take a look."

The director began leading them to the hall beneath the open walkway. The aide looked up and saw Jing Yo. He didn't say anything, simply stared until Jing Yo stepped back from the rail, out of view.

If the senator had used the main entrance, so would the scientist. All he would have to do was wait.

29

Queens, New York City

The Grand Central Parkway looked more like a parking lot than a highway. Traffic on the RFK-Triborough Bridge was at a standstill, with two accidents eastbound, one just before the tollbooths and the other on the Queens side near the exit to the local roads.

"Are we going to make it?" Jablonski asked the driver, leaning forward.

"It'll be close."

"I'd better call. The only thing worse than being late is not telling Grasso we're going to be late."

Josh leaned against the door as Jablonski fished in his pocket for his phone. The aide had unfortunately decided to sit between him and Mara.

"Kevin, this is Will. How are you? Listen, we're stuck on the damn Grand Central, in the middle of the Triborough. Where are you? . . . Oh, you're at the museum already. How'd you get through the traffic? . . . Too late for us. Look, our driver isn't sure we're going to make it, so I thought I'd better give you a heads-up. . . . Uh-huh. It's very important to the president that the senator speak to Josh. He wants the senator to hear about this firsthand, from the source. The horse's mouth, so to speak. . . . That would fine. Fine. We'll see you in the parking lot. Excellent."

Jablonski killed the phone.

"We're going to ride with the senator," said Jablonski. "We'll meet them at the parking lot. You and I will go with them to the UN."

"What about Mara?" asked Josh.

"She'll follow. The marshals will stick with us, right, guys?"

"I'd kind of like her there."

"I'll be with you at the UN, Josh. You don't need me to talk to the senator."

"All right," Josh said, pushing closer to the door of the car.

Jing Yo glanced at his watch. It was exactly 11:08. Where was the scientist?

The view to the front door was perfect. Jing Yo went down on his knee, next to the canvas tool bag. He put his right hand on the P90, slipping his finger around the trigger.

He was ready. His mind was at peace. Every muscle was relaxed, his breathing slow and full. There was only one true Way, one true existence.

Laughter filled the atrium below. The children were coming out of the auditorium.

One true Way.

A car drove up outside. Jing Yo saw its tires in the glass. If he'd taken the grenade launcher from the truck, it would be over now.

No bother. It was only a matter of moments.

No one got out of the car. It was the senator's limo.

A second car pulled up behind it.

Security? Had he been seen?

Adult voices filled the hall below. Jing Yo looked down. The senator was walking out, threading his way through the children.

Jing Yo would shoot the scientist and then the senator. He would try not to kill the children, but if they were there, there was nothing he could do.

One Way.

The senator veered to his left, toward the front of the building. He wasn't going to the office. Something was wrong.

Jing Yo looked toward the door. A person got out of the car behind the senator's.

The scientist—no, someone else.

"This way, Senator," said the aide, ushering him out of the door.

It was a trick, thought Jing Yo, jumping to his feet. I've missed my chance.

Josh got into the back on the driver's side; Jablonski slid in from the other end. After seeing so many movies and television shows featuring big politicos and businesspeople being ferried around in outrageously equipped limousines, the senator's car was a real disappointment. There was no television in the backseat, let alone a computer or a bar; it was little different than the backseat of the marshal car, a plain vanilla Chevy Caprice. Papers and files were piled on the shelf behind the seat, so high that Josh doubted the driver could see out the back window.

"The Triborough's a mess," Jablonski told the driver.

"So I hear. We'll go over the Fifty-ninth Street Bridge. The Queensboro. It's closer to where we're going anyway."

Josh felt his heart pounding. He looked at his hands. Sweat was pouring from the pores.

"Nervous?" asked Jablonski.

"I guess."

"You'll do fine. Just tell what happened. Your own words. Like at breakfast."

The door on the other side of Jablonski opened. Senator Grasso climbed in, the car rocking with his weight. His aide got in the front seat.

"Billy, how goes the speechwriting?" said the senator as the car pulled from the curb.

"Just fine, Senator."

"Do you actually write any speeches?"

"I've written a few."

"Was Peaceful Vigilance yours?" Grasso was referring to a speech the president had made two weeks before, suggesting that America's troops would stay at a high state of alert.

"I contributed a few lines."

"Now I know you wrote it. Any time you're being modest like that." Grasso leaned over. "And you must be Dr. MacArthur, right?"

"I'm Josh MacArthur."

MacArthur extended his hand. Grasso grabbed it and shook it vigorously.

"Any relation to the famous MacArthur?"

"A great-great-great-uncle."

"That's a lot of greats." Grasso winked at Jablonski. "Good to meet you, son. Are you from New York?"

"Iowa, actually."

"Looking for votes?" Jablonski asked.

"Always, Billy. Without you working for me, I have to get all the votes I can find. Why don't you come over to us anyway? Working for that old fart can't be that much fun."

"He is the president."

"All that means is you get to ride in a better airplane. Kevin?" Grasso turned to the front seat, where his aide was working his BlackBerry. "How are we fixed for time?"

"We have to go right to the UN," said the aide. "There

are demonstrations outside. A lot of them. Police should meet us on the other side of the bridge."

"See?" Grasso turned to Jablonski. "Your guy wants us to vote for a war. You know how unpopular we'd be? We'll be crucified."

"The president isn't asking for a war vote," said Jablonski.

"Not yet. But this is the first step. Sanctions. Of course, the vote would fail if it were in the Senate, you know."

"It's not in the Senate."

"So what do you want to talk to me about, young man?" asked Grasso.

"I just wanted to, uh, tell you, uh—"

"Josh was in Vietnam when the war broke out," said Jablonski. He was behind the lines for a while."

"Wait—you're with the CIA?" asked Grasso.

"Uh, no, sir. I uh—I'm a scientist."

"Scientist?" Grasso was acting confused. Josh realized it was an act—he was trying to draw him out, trying to be clever by playing dumb.

It made Josh angry. And that relaxed him. Slightly, at least.

"I was with a UN team. I was on a grant," Josh told the senator. "We were in Vietnam. The Chinese came over the border one night. They were in black. Commandos or something like that. They killed the rest of the team. While they were sleeping."

"No shit?"

Josh finally had the senator's attention.

"Tell him about the village, Josh," said Jablonski.

J ing Yo flew down the stairs, the submachine gun in his hand. There was no sense hiding it now. It didn't matter if anyone saw him now; if they tried to stop him, they were dead.

He reached the first floor and threw himself against the door, expecting to be met by a hail of bullets. But there was no one there.

It hadn't been a trick. It was a change in plans.

He told himself to remain calm. To be the man he had trained to be.

He could still take the scientist. It would still be easy.

Jing Yo ran to the van behind the building. He started the truck and pulled forward, wheels squealing as he drove to the front lot.

Which way would the senator have gone?

Jing Yo stopped. He reached over to the glove compartment and took out the GPS tracking monitor.

There was a yellow dot on a map, along with a green square showing where he was.

The senator was to his left, going east, away from the UN.

Away from the UN? Was Josh with him? If so, it didn't make sense.

But it was all he had to go on. Jing Yo looked at the map, then headed for the exit.

"**S**tay close," Mara told the marshal who was driving.

"I'm only three cars back, for cryin' out loud. I can't help it if that jackass cut me off."

"There's a merge up there, and traffic will pick up."

"He's only going to Manhattan. I'm sure I'll find him."

"Don't be a backseat driver," said Broome, leaning forward behind her.

"I'm in the front seat," she said.

"Yeah, whatever. Watch it or Fred will give you the wheel."

Mara folded her arms, staring at the traffic on the bridge ahead. She felt bad that she hadn't gone with Josh, as if she'd chickened out.

That was stupid. The senator wasn't exactly dangerous. She'd been with Josh in Vietnam, behind the lines—she'd been with him when things were truly bad.

Still, she felt as if she belonged with him now.

N either the senator nor Jablonski spoke when Josh finished telling them about the vehicles he had seen coming down from Vietnam.

"They were definitely coming out of China," repeated Josh. "It was a setup."

"Tell me about that village again," said Senator Grasso. "That little girl."

"Ma," said Josh.

"Yes."

"The president is bringing her," said Josh.

"Really. She's someone I'd like to meet. Now, you're sure that village was in Vietnam?"

"Yes, sir."

"Could you find it on a map?"

"I'm not positive. I've tried, from satellite photos. It's not easy to get your bearings in the middle of the jungle."

"I see."

"I can show you where the camp was, and where I went."

"Okay." Grasso leaned forward. "Kevin, we have a map of Vietnam somewhere, right?"

The traffic frustrated him. Jing Yo knew from the sensor that the senator's car was somewhere ahead, but he couldn't see it.

He had to merge with a line of traffic to his left. Meanwhile, another stream of cars was moving in from the right a short distance ahead. The traffic was as bad as anything around Beijing. The sound was worse: the heavy thump of bass lines from several nearby cars shook the van, and every so often their disjointed symphony was interrupted by the blaring of horns.

The steel web of the bridge's cantilever shell rose in the distance. Jing Yo urged the van forward through the traffic, wedging it into the flow as best he could. Manhattan lay ahead, high-rises and office buildings spread along the horizon.

Jing Yo needed to get the scientist before he got over to the other side. If he got too much of a lead once he was in Manhattan, he'd get to the UN before Jing Yo could.

He'd take him there if necessary.

The car in front of Jing Yo eased ahead, then hit its brakes. Brake lights were lit as far ahead as he could see.

The van was useless here.

He opened the window and craned his neck out the side. If the senator's car was nearby, he'd just jump out and blow it up with the grenade launcher—climb on top of the van and let loose.

He couldn't see it.

The scooter was in the back. He could use that.

Jing Yo threw the van into park and pulled on the emergency brake. Then he got up and squeezed into the back of the van, hitting the overhead light so he could see.

The senator's car was undoubtedly armored. He

opened the box to the grenade launcher, mounted an armor-piercing shell, then slung the gun over his shoulder. He put the P90 over his other shoulder. He still had the plumber's coveralls on; the big Glock was in a holster and the derringer was in his pocket beneath them.

A horn sounded behind him. Jing Yo pushed open the door to the van. It slammed into something about midway—the hood of the car that had been following him.

The horn sounded again. Jing Yo pushed the other door open, but it too stopped halfway.

A cab was behind him. The driver was pounding on his horn, screaming out the window at him to move, asking what the hell he was doing.

Jing Yo kicked at the doors, then crouched in the open space between them. He swung the RPG launcher into his arm.

"Move back!" he yelled in English. *"Back!"*

The cabdriver was too shocked to do anything. Stunned, his hand stayed on the horn.

"Out of my way!" Jing Yo yelled to the taxi driver in Chinese, menacing him again with the grenade launcher.

Firing would have done him no good—at this range, the shaped charge on the grenade's nose would have sent it right through the unarmored windshield, and very possibly through three or four more before exploding.

He put his foot on the door at his left and pushed, wedging it across the bumper and front end of the other car. Then he grabbed the scooter and pushed it toward the door. The taxi driver, meanwhile, had regained enough of his senses to throw the car into reverse. He tried getting around the van to the left. But he hit the bumper, pushing the front of the van sideways into another car before managing to get into a small wedge of open space. The space closed quickly—he hit a pickup truck trying to veer away, bounced off and smacked into the side of an SUV, which in turn hit the car in front of it. Within seconds, the entire bridge was one big pileup.

Jing Yo tumbled to the floor of the van, the scooter tumbling on top of him. Rage took over, flooding past the last bits of discipline that had been holding it back. He grabbed the scooter and pushed it over, falling with it to the pavement. Then he scrambled to his feet, pointed the bike at the left side of the crowded traffic lanes, and got on. He gunned it to life, looking for an opening, desperate to fulfill his destiny.

M ara couldn't see what was going on up ahead, but clearly there was some sort of crazy commotion—car horns were going off, and suddenly an alarm began to bleat.

She unbuckled her seat belt, opened the door, and propped herself up on the floor ledge, trying to see over the cars and trucks. Someone on a scooter cut sideways across the lane of traffic.

He had a gun strapped across his back. Two guns.

One was a grenade launcher.

Mara ducked back into the car.

"Give me your pistol," she told the marshal driving.

"What?"

"There's someone on a bike up there with a gun. Your pistol!"

"What's going on?" demanded Broome in the back.

"Come with me!" Mara grabbed the pistol from the driver's holster, then jumped out of the Chevy. Running toward the scooter, she reached for her cell phone to call Jablonski and warn him.

30

Hainan Island

By the time the landing craft and fishing boat exploded, Zeus, Christian, and Solt were in a small runabout, racing past the main harbor at Sanya.

"Beach the boat there," said Solt, pointing to a ledge of rocks at the end of the sand. "We want to get ashore as quickly as we can, before they begin to organize."

Christian began pulling off his wet suit. So did Solt—she unfurled a thin pair of pants from under the suit, and stepped onto the beach barefoot.

"We should get some better clothes," said Christian. Zeus had inadvertently taken the wrong set of sailor's pants, forcing Christian to wear a pair at least two sizes too small.

"Let's grab a car and get out of here first," Zeus told him.

"We can get clothes at the hotel," said Solt, pointing to the high-rise building almost directly ahead. "There is a gym and a locker room. Westerners are there," she added. "Your size."

"I hope so," replied Christian.

The patio was filled with people craning their necks to see the fires out in the ocean. A pair of fighter jets rocketed overhead, and a helicopter approached from the north. Zeus and Christian followed Solt into the building. She walked quickly through the hall, ducking right. She'd obviously been here before.

"That way," she said. "Meet in the lobby in five minutes."

"They all have locks," hissed Christian, spotting combination locks on the row of metal boxes. "What the hell?"

Zeus started opening the lockers that didn't have locks, but gave up after finding a few empty. He looked at one of the combination locks. It was a simple device, the sort common in high schools and junior high schools across America. He knew they were fairly easy to pick, but he had no idea how to do it.

"Clothes!" yelled Christian near the back of the room. He sounded like a kid who'd found an unexpected cache of toys under the Christmas tree. What he had found was nearly as good: a box of items that had been left behind over the past few months. He began sorting through them, pulling out a pair of jeans. They were loose and not exactly fashionable, but they fit.

"Come on, let's get out of here," said Zeus, deciding his clothes, though damp, would do.

"Wait—you trust her?"

"Solt? Why not?"

"I got a bad feeling," said Christian. "She brought us in here. All the lockers are locked—"

"If she was going to kill us, she could have done it in the water."

"Maybe we're her prize," said Christian. "The way the ship was to the marines. If she's working for the Chinese."

"I don't think so."

Christian frowned, but followed Zeus out to the lobby. It was a large, marble-walled space, with soaring ceilings and four pairs of golden chandeliers. Solt wasn't there. Zeus walked as nonchalantly as he could to the couch farthest from the registration desk.

"Where is she?" whispered Christian.

"Don't know. You got your passport?"

"Shit yeah."

"Emergency money?"

"A hundred bucks ain't gonna get us off the island."

It wouldn't get them a night at the hotel, either. But they could call the embassy, maybe, have some emergency money wired in.

There'd be lots of questions, and not just from the Chinese. But what was the alternative?

Solt appeared across the hall. She was wearing an ankle-length silk dress that seemed to be made for her. It was supported off her shoulders by two thin straps and hugged her breasts and sides.

She'd covered the purple welt on the side of her head with makeup. Zeus guessed she must still be hurting, but you couldn't tell from the way she walked.

"She's damn hot, I'll give her that," said Christian. "Matala Hardy or whatever that woman's name was."

"Mata Hari," said Zeus, referring to the famous spy.

To Zeus's surprise, she came over and kissed him. It happened so quickly he could barely enjoy it.

"We should leave quickly," she whispered.

"Yes, let's go."

"How come you get the kiss?" muttered Christian as they walked out the front door.

Solt glanced around the horseshoe-shaped drive, then started down the sidewalk to the right. Zeus and Christian followed.

A taxi came up the driveway.

"Let's take the cab," said Zeus, stepping into the road. "Get us away from the harbor."

Solt went to the driver's window. He had been dispatched for another guest, but one of Zeus's fifty-dollar bills easily changed his mind. Within a few minutes they were on the highway, Solt in the front, Christian and Zeus in the back.

Solt told the driver to pull off at the second exit.

Zeus didn't understand the directions until they went off the highway.

"What are we doing?" he asked.

"I need to make a stop."

Christian shot him a glance. It turned into a glare as they found themselves in the center of town, heading toward a building with a troop truck and several police cars parked in front.

Zeus held his breath as they passed. The cab stopped in front of a bank.

"Keep him here," whispered Solt. She hopped out. It looked as if she was going to the ATM, but she hurried past and disappeared around the corner.

"Now what?" asked Christian.

"Relax, would you?"

"I'm relaxed. Just relaxed enough to get arrested. If we're lucky."

The cabdriver started talking to them. At first it sounded as if he were speaking Chinese. Only after he stopped did Zeus realize the man had asked him something in English. His accent was so thick it was impossible to tell what he'd said.

"I'm sorry," said Zeus. "I don't understand what you're saying."

"You do business Hainan?" repeated the man.

"Not really," said Christian.

"We hope to," said Zeus quickly. "We have plans for importing Scotch. We wanted to, um, set up a trade for fish. For the fish imports. So we're going to look at, uh, fish farms."

"All fish stay in China," said the man. There was an edge to his voice. "Important to feed Chinese."

"That's what they told us," said Zeus. "I respect that."

"Respect?"

"Chinese fish for Chinese people," said Christian.

"That is right," said the driver.

"But the trade would be valuable for the Chinese as well," said Zeus.

Christian interrupted. "You don't like Americans?"

"American business—big," said the driver. "Does not care. Too big. Steal from Chinese."

They sat in silence for a few minutes. Zeus wanted to strangle Christian, or at least gag him. Two police cars pulled out behind them and raced past, sirens blaring.

"Where miss?" asked the driver. "We must go. Cannot stay here."

"She's coming," said Zeus.

"Must go."

"Please stay."

"Must go."

The driver started to put the car into gear.

"Hey, this will get you to stay, right?" asked Christian, holding out one of his fifties.

The driver grabbed the bill, then put the car back into park.

"Good idea," whispered Zeus.

"Yeah."

The door opened. Solt slid in. She told the driver something in Chinese and they started out. But they found the nearby entrance to the highway blocked. So was the next one. The driver began talking very quickly, arguing with Solt.

"We're not going to be able to get on the highway," Solt told Zeus finally. "I'm going to have him take us to the airport. We can get there on local roads."

"What the hell are we going to do at the airport?" Christian asked.

Zeus shook his head. The driver might not speak English very well, but clearly he understood it.

A few blocks later, it was clear they weren't going to

get to the airport, either. The roads were jammed, either closed or choked with chaotic traffic. Solt told the driver to let them out.

"Do you have passports?" she asked after the taxi had managed a three-point turn and started away.

"We do," said Zeus.

"We can get a plane to Hong Kong, and from there to Japan," she said. "If they're still flying."

"We don't have the money. Or baggage."

"That won't be a problem. As long as you still have some dollars to bribe the security people with."

"I have fifty."

"Me, too," said Christian.

"Then we should start. If we get separated before the gate," Solt added, reaching into her purse, "call the number on this business card. Tell them than Mr. Jenni sent you. Do what he tells you. You can trust him."

"Can we trust you, though?" asked Christian.

Solt looked at Zeus, as if to say, *Why do you hang out with him?* Then she started walking in the direction of the airport.

31

Queens, New York City

"I'm willing to believe the Chinese did arrange this," Senator Grasso told Josh. "I can believe they'd do something like that. They can be very—clever is the word here. Very clever. But let's say for the sake of argument that they did. Which I'm not disagreeing with," Grasso added quickly, cutting off Josh's objection before he could voice it. "I agree. They started this. Not only that, but as the president says, they're out to take over Southeast Asia. No doubt about it now that I think about it."

Grasso paused. The blaring of the traffic behind them was so loud he had to raise his voice as he continued.

"But why should the U.S. intervene? Why should we get involved in another costly war? What's in it for the American people?"

Josh started to answer, but the senator wasn't done.

"And let's say there's sanctions against China. How do they help us? China holds trillions of dollars of our debt. Don't you think there'll be repercussions?"

"I think the repercussions will be more serious if we do nothing," said Jablonski.

Jablonski's phone rang. He ignored it.

"That's what the president says." Grasso swung his hands up, making his point. "But I think he overstates it. I think he wants confrontation. It's all he knows. What do you think, Josh? Are the repercussions so serious that we should risk everything? What are we risking it for, anyway? Who cares if Vietnam becomes a colony of the Chinese? Do we really care?"

We should care, thought Josh. There was something fundamental—something so unjust and unfair that it had to be countered. But Josh couldn't find the words to express it.

"I know what you're going to say," continued the senator, who really didn't want an answer from anyone except himself. "We should be idealists. But where has idealism gotten us? Look at Vietnam. You're too young to know what that was like, but the president isn't. He of all people should know the limits of idealism."

Josh turned away from the senator, looking out across

the traffic toward the Manhattan skyline—ideals, he thought, made tangible.

Something streaked through the line of cars at the far end of the left lane. A man on a motorbike.

With guns on his back.

Josh stared at the man, sure he was having a psychotic episode.

The man was Asian.

It was a hallucination, his mind flashing back to Vietnam. He was seeing the man who had pursued them, the man who had attacked the helicopter just before they escaped.

He was losing his mind.

It's real!

"Out of the car!" yelled Josh. He turned and pushed Jablonski and Grasso toward the opposite door. "Senator! Get out of the car! *Now!*"

J ing Yo saw the limousine to his right as he drove up the narrow space between the row of cars and the barrier dividing traffic on the bridge. He was just past the first tower on the bridge. The cars were bumper to bumper, with no space to get between them.

It didn't matter now. He had him.

Jing Yo continued on for several car lengths until finally a large panel truck blocked his path. He hopped off the scooter just behind it, pausing for a moment to get his bearings and plan his route to the limo.

The driver of the car next to him was talking on a cell phone. He looked up suddenly, just as Jing Yo's eyes turned in his direction. The man's expression was one of profound fear.

The look of a hen before the hawk struck.

Jing Yo felt a wave of disdain. He leapt onto the hood of the man's car, pulled up his grenade launcher, sighting for the limo. He saw it, and pressed the trigger.

Mara saw the flash and smoke, then the streak toward the limo. The missile crashed into the front of the car. In the same moment, there was a loud crack and an explosion. Flames appeared, giving way to a white cloud that turned brown in the next second.

"Josh!" yelled Mara, raising her gun and firing in the direction the grenade had come from.

Josh felt the rush of a tornado as the grenade blew up the limo. The bridge vibrated madly.

The cone of white-hot gas and metal that had been the warhead set the inside of the vehicle on fire, filling it with flames and hot gas. Glass shattered, body crinkled, the limo started to disintegrate into bits of molten metal and evaporating plastic.

"The gas tank!" yelled Josh. He saw Grasso and Jablonski on the other side, stunned, lying next to a damaged car.

"Get off the bridge!" Josh yelled. "Go that way." Josh pointed back toward the Queens side. "Go! Get away from the car!"

He glanced at the vehicle, knowing there were two more men inside. But they were beyond hope now. He started to follow Jablonski and Grasso on his hands and knees, then saw Mara running up through the cars, gun drawn, coming for him.

Jing Yo felt the bullet hit him in the right thigh, the sting of a bee on an early summer day, a diversion, an attempt to shake his focus. He concentrated on the limousine, working the stream of bullets into the front of the car, firing until a second shot grazed his left side and pushed him off the car, sent him tumbling to the pavement.

Jing Yo scrambled to his feet, a little wobbly but still able to move. He dropped the box from the P90 and fished another from the pocket of the coveralls. It took him a moment to fit it into the unfamiliar gun.

Someone began firing from the right, near the divider. Jing Yo slammed the magazine home and returned fire.

Mara saw Broome go down as the Chinese assassin fired in his direction. She fired two more shots even though she couldn't see the gunner, hoping to distract him. Realizing it was futile and that she wouldn't be able to reload, she stopped.

Josh and the others were up ahead somewhere. She started crawling for them. People were jumping from their cars, rushing to get off the bridge. The smoke and dust were so thick she started to cough.

Bullets crashed into nearby cars, punching through the metal and plastic. She flattened herself on the pavement and glanced around, trying to locate where they were coming from.

The gas tank in the limo exploded, the flames from the interior igniting the gas fumes. The force of the explosion pushed the car into the air; it slammed down on the hood of the car behind it, setting it on fire. Fortunately, the driver had already fled.

A plume of smoke enveloped the bridge, a thick cloud of soot, dust, and debris. Josh started to sneeze.

Panic gripped him. He started to get up. Something hit him, pushed him back against the car—a woman, running from the chaos.

Josh fell to the ground, smacking his head on the bumper of the car. He was back in the past—not Vietnam, but the distant past, a child again, running from the men who had killed his parents.

It was the same paralyzing fear, an emptiness at the center of his body, a certainty that he was going to be killed. He was a little boy again, desperate for life, desperate to live out the dreams he'd started to imagine for himself, half-formed wishes to be a hero, to accomplish something, to be a great man.

Rather than a coward. Rather than a dead boy cowering.

He was not a coward.

Josh pushed himself to his feet, scrambling across the back of another car. He ran through a knot of dust, angled westward along another car, then turned behind a pickup truck.

The cement barrier was a few feet away. He sneezed, put his arm over his mouth to block out the smoke and took a deep breath, then jumped over it. As he went over, he saw a body lying on the ground, next to the barrier, on the eastbound side of the road.

The image didn't register until he was over the cement, on the other side.

Broome, lying on the ground. Wounded or dead.

Jing Yo realized it was just a matter of time now. No one was firing at him anymore. All he had to do was walk down the line of cars and find the scientist.

Assuming he was one of the people who'd gotten out. Jing Yo wasn't sure. The limo was on fire now.

Jing Yo steadied himself against the vehicle stalled next to him. Most likely the scientist was already dead, but he had to make sure.

And then?

It was his duty to try to escape. He was not seriously wounded. He would run until he was cornered, and then he would have an honorable death, a fulfillment of his fate.

The next life would take care of itself.

His leg dragged as he walked, his injured thigh holding him back.

Someone was moving forward from the line of cars. He raised his gun and fired, but he didn't have a good enough angle. He climbed up on the hood of the car next to him, then got up on the roof. He still couldn't see. The car had crashed into the rail, trying to get away. Jing Yo sidestepped toward it, still trying for a good angle. His balance shaky, he reached up toward the bridge support. But it was too far away.

The height of the side of the bridge would give him the right angle.

If he hadn't been wounded, he could have easily jumped up. He leaned now instead, clambering up.

There was a woman with a gun. He twisted himself in her direction and fired.

Mara realized a half second before he fired that she would be in the gunman's sights. She ducked down, then raised the pistol, firing blind.

A burst of submachine gun bullets told her she'd missed.

She stayed down, crawling to the side of the car and looking up toward the limo. Where the hell was Josh?

As soon as Josh heard the gunfire, he rolled back over the divider, landing on his side. He pushed forward, moving almost like he was swimming, crawling toward Broome.

Broome was breathing.

"You all right?" Josh asked.

"Brother, I'm good. Stay down."

"Give me your gun," said Josh.

"What?"

"Your gun."

"Stay down!"

Josh saw the gun a few feet away, under a Lexus GS350. He started crawling for it.

"Hey!" yelled Broome.

"Stay down," said Josh, grabbing the pistol.

The top of the bridge railing was wet, and the grit from the explosion made it muddy and slippery. Jing Yo moved along the side, having trouble keeping his balance.

The woman with the gun was three cars away. If the scientist wasn't in the car, he would be with her.

Just as Hyuen Bo had been with him.

He would kill the woman. Kill her first, so the scientist saw what it was like, felt a shadow of the pain he had felt.

He edged forward, sliding. Walking on the bridge was like walking on the beam—it was an exercise he had done when small, an exercise that tested not so much his balance but his faith in the Way, his trust of what the monks told him.

"Close your eyes and walk," said his mentor. "Walk simply, with your head erect. Trust that you will not fall."

He did trust.

She was there, on his right. Jing Yo let go of the bridge post, lowering the P90 to fire.

"It's me you want!" yelled a man's voice.

Jing Yo turned toward the voice. As he did, his balance shifted, and he felt himself starting to fall.

J osh fired at the commando on the bridge. The nose of the pistol jumped up slightly, his hand a little shaky. He grabbed with both hands and fired again, twice.

The man twisted back, falling away from the third shot.

The assassin disappeared from the bridge.

Josh began to run. He didn't have a conscious plan, wasn't sure whether he was still in danger or not. He saw Mara on his right, yelled at her.

"Over the side!" he shouted.

He reached the rail and looked over, looked down.

The shooter was gone, somewhere in the water.

Mara grabbed his shoulder. "Don't!"

Josh twisted around. "Don't what?"

"Just let him go."

His face was two inches from hers.

"I wasn't going to chase him," he said, staring into her face.

"Good," she managed, before he kissed her.

32

UN Headquarters, New York City

The head of the Secret Service detail literally had tears in his eyes as he repeated his advice to the president.

"The most prudent thing is to get of here now," said the agent. "We have a path north—we close down the FDR, have Marine One meet us at Yankee Stadium."

"See, now, if it were spring and we stood a chance of catching a ball game, that might be a winning strategy," said President Greene. They were sitting together in the presidential limo in the garage under UN headquarters. Green reached across and put his hand on the agent's shoulder. "It's all right, Ted. I know you're only doing your job. Excuse my black humor."

"Sir, we don't know how many of them there are. We don't know what else they may have planned."

"You checked the building for bombs, right?"

"Three times. But—"

"And nobody could come in or out in the last two hours?"

"Yes, sir—well except for your people. But—"

"You think I'm going to let the Chinese win this without even taking a shot? They weren't shooting at me, were they?" Greene glanced at his national security adviser. "Walt, you think they were shooting at me?"

"I can't say at this time, Mr. President," said Jackson.

"But I can. We go on as planned. What did you do with Josh?"

"He's with the police on his way," said the agent. "Mr. President—"

"I'll fire you if you say anything else," said Greene.

"Then I'll have no protection. That's not going to be a better situation, is it?"

"No, sir."

"Well then, let's move, gentlemen."

Greene got out of the car. As best as he could determine, the situation was under control. The Chinese had tried to assassinate Josh MacArthur on the Fifty-ninth Street Bridge. Josh and Mara Duncan had turned the tables on them. The NYPD had arrived and ushered not only Josh and Mara, but Senator Grasso across the bridge, then taken them through the line of protesters in an armored car.

The confusion had dulled the crowd a bit as well. People were shocked at the violence, not entirely understanding it. Even the Secret Service detail had reported the crowd had "diminished," as close as the bodyguard ever got to saying things weren't quite as dire as they had first appeared.

"There's Senator Grasso now," Greene said, seeing the senator across the garage. He was standing with two emergency medical technicians. "Senator! Phil! Are you okay?"

"George. George"—Grasso grabbed the president's arm—"the Chinese are *crazy*! They tried to kill me!"

"You're all right?"

"Yes. They're out to kill everyone."

"I've been trying to tell you that."

"We have to stop them. They got Smith. My aide. They killed him. And my driver. My God!"

"It's terrible," said Greene. "It could have been you."

"MacArthur shot him. He got the Chinese bastard. I saw the whole thing. I would have taken a few shots myself, if I'd had a gun."

Greene had gotten a full description of what had happened from Jablonski; according to his blow-by-blow, the senator had cowered beneath an SUV for most of the encounter, and had to be pried out by the paramedics who responded. But Greene wasn't about to contradict a senator, as long as his vote could be counted on.

"Where is Josh?" asked Greene. "Is he okay?"

"Mr. President, Dr. MacArthur is by the truck with Ms. Duncan," said Jess Jordan, one of the NSC staffers traveling with him.

"Thank you. Senator, excuse me a second."

Greene strode across the garage. He was a little apprehensive. He didn't want to push Josh too far, and was genuinely concerned about his safety, and Mara's. But his testimony was critical. Especially now—the delgates would know what had happened, or would hear of it before the end of the day. It would add an exclamation point to his testimony.

Josh and Mara were standing near the back of the armored car. A nurse was cleaning the cuts on her forehead.

"Josh! Mara! You're all right?" said Greene, walking to them. He hugged Mara, then hugged Josh as well. "You're all right? Are you all right?"

"I'm okay," said Josh. "Where's Mạ?"

"You're sure you're all right?"

"Yes, sir. Where's Mạ?"

Greene looked at Mara. She seemed as calm and collected as ever. He turned back to Josh.

"You know what, Josh? I thought about it. She's pretty young. For her to go over this. I don't know." He shook his head. "Are you really okay?"

"Yes, sir. We—it's been like this ever since that night."

"I can imagine."

He could do more than imagine. He could remember. For just a moment, Greene felt as if he were back in the cell in the Hanoi Hilton. Every day was intense.

Every day there was more and more pressure. It went on like that, becoming the norm.

"Josh, if you can't go on, I understand," said Greene. "I know it's—it may be difficult."

"I can do it," said the scientist. He glanced at Mara, then turned back to Greene. "I have to do it."

"Then let's go tell the world what's really going on out there," said Greene, taking hold of his arm and turning toward the elevator.

Turn the page for a preview of

LARRY BOND'S
Red Dragon Rising

SHOCK OF WAR

LARRY BOND AND
JIM DeFELICE

Now available from
Tom Doherty Associates

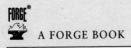

A FORGE BOOK

Hainan Island, China

Major Zeus Murphy tried not to look too conspicuous as he walked down the concourse toward his flight. In theory, he had nothing to fear: the United States and China were not at war, and while his U.S. passport had caused a few seconds of hesitation at the security gate, the check of his baggage had been perfunctory at best. But theory and reality did not always mesh, especially in this case: the war between China and Vietnam had greatly strained relations between the two countries, and even in the best times Chinese customs officials and local police were not exactly known for being evenhanded when dealing with citizens from other countries.

And in this case, Zeus had a little extra to fear: he had just led a guerilla operation against the Chinese naval fleet gathered in the harbor, hopefully preventing it from launching an attack against the Vietnamese.

He could see the red glow of distant flames reflecting in the dark glass of the passageway as he walked toward the gate. Too much time had passed for the fire to be on one of the boats they had blown up; Zeus suspected instead it was due to friendly fire, panic set off by the supposed attack of Vietnamese submarines on the landing ships that were gathered in the port.

All for the better.

A television screen hung on the wall near the gate ahead. Zeus slowed down to get a look. In the U.S., it would be set to a local or all-news station; by now it would be carrying live feeds from the attack, breathless correspondents warning of the coming apocalypse. Here it showed some sort of Chinese soap opera, or maybe a reality show; he couldn't quite tell and didn't want to make himself too conspicuous by stopping.

He passed two more screens as he walked. Both were set to Chinese financial news stations. Though it was night here, it was still daytime in the U.S., and tickers showed stock prices across the bottom.

A lot of red letters and down arrows, Zeus noticed. War wasn't good for anyone's economy.

"I thought you'd never get here," said Win Christian, who rose from a seat across from the television.

Christian was also a major, was also in the U.S. Army, and had also just helped blow up part of the invasion fleet. The two men had snuck ashore with the help of a Vietnamese agent, assumed identities as businessmen, and headed for the easiest way out—a Chinese flight to Hong Kong, and from there to Japan.

Zeus nodded. They'd gotten into different lines at the security checkpoint, splitting up in case they were stopped.

"Where's the girl?" Christian asked, referring to the Vietnamese agent, Solt Jan.

"I thought she was with you," answered Zeus.

Christian seemed even more nervous than he had earlier. Fidgeting, his eyes shifted continually, glancing in every direction. "I hope she didn't bail."

"We got our tickets. Relax."

Christian glanced around. There were about forty people at the gate, waiting for the 11 p.m. flight to Hong Kong. The destination was written in English as well as Chinese on a whiteboard that sat on an easel next to the podium in front of the door to the plane tunnel. The door was closed, and the podium itself was roped off by a velvet-covered chain. There were no attendants nearby.

Zeus glanced at his watch.

"Half hour before boarding," he told Christian. "Let's get something to eat."

"You think that's wise?"

Zeus started toward a kiosk about ten meters away in the center of the gate area. Maybe some food would calm Christian down.

"Guess it can't be any worse than Vietnamese food," said Christian, catching up.

Zeus closed his eyes at the word *Vietnamese*. He glanced at Christian, who'd turned beet red.

"I know," muttered Christian almost inaudibly. "Sorry."

Zeus didn't reply. At least Christian realized he'd been an idiot; they were making progress.

The vendor was a few years younger than Zeus, twenty-one or twenty-two at most. Zeus pointed at a bag of American-style potato chips.

"Ten yuan," said the young man in English.

Zeus dug into his pocket. Solt had given him some Chinese money on the way over. He had some American money in his wallet as well—fifty dollars, barely enough to bribe the passport control people in Hong Kong, which would be necessary to get to Tokyo since his passport lacked the proper visa stamps.

"Here are your crisps," said the man, using the British term for the snack as he handed them over.

"I'll have a bag, too," said Christian.

The man kept his eyes locked on Zeus's. It was a menacing stare, a dare.

Why?

"My change," said Zeus.

The man's mouth twisted into a smile. Zeus held out

his hand. The man looked down at it, and for a moment Zeus thought he was going to spit. Instead, he reached into the cash register. He took a bill and some coins, then dropped them into Zeus's outstretched palm.

Zeus locked his eyes on the man, not even bothering to count the change.

"All of it," he said.

The clerk's smile broadened. He reached into the register and fished out the right change, placing it into Zeus's hand.

"What the hell was that about?" Christian asked as they walked back to the gate.

"Got me," said Zeus.

"He spoke English pretty well."

"Yeah," said Zeus. "Good enough."

An airline employee had appeared at the podium and was fiddling with a microphone. She began to speak as Zeus and Christian approached. A few passengers got up from their seats; the rest looked anxiously toward her as she continued.

"What's she saying?" Christian asked.

"I didn't learn to speak Chinese in the last twenty minutes," snapped Zeus. "Did you?"

He reached into his pocket for his ticket, expecting she was trying to organize the boarding—probably asking for people with small children first. But no one moved forward.

A short, balding man near the gate began speaking to the woman, haranguing her in slightly angry Chinese. Zeus turned around, looking for Solt. She should have met them by now.

Admittedly, she hadn't told him that she'd been on the flight; he'd just assumed that when she pressed the ticket into his hand in the lobby before disappearing in the crowd.

"They're not moving," said Christian. "What's going on?"

"Flight cancel," said a grim-faced man nearby. He added something in Chinese.

"Excuse me," said Zeus. "The flight's canceled? Why?"

The man shook his head.

Zeus tried repeating the question, phrasing it more simply and speaking slower. "Why is the flight canceled?"

"Flight cancel," said the man. "Problem at airport. All flight."

"Shit," said Christian.

"Is it temporary?" asked Zeus.

Again, the man shook his head, not understanding. The passengers at the podium moved closer to the woman, apparently asking questions.

"Do you know . . . the next flight? When?" asked Zeus, trying to simplify what he wanted to know. "Is there another flight?"

The man said something in Chinese. Zeus didn't understand the words, but the meaning itself was clear: He had no idea.

Most of the people at the gate remained in their seats. Zeus guessed that the airline was making other arrangements, and they had been told to wait.

Or maybe not. Maybe the entire airport was closed. Maybe they thought they were under attack.

He told himself to calm down, to relax and think it through. He was a businessman, not a saboteur—be aggravated, annoyed, not alarmed.

"What are we going to do?" Christian asked.

"I'll ask what the story is," said Zeus. "Maybe some of the airline people speak English. Come on."

"Right behind you," hissed Christian.

They joined the small knot of people near the

attendant. Zeus stood patiently, hoping to hear someone speaking English. He didn't.

The people around him were mostly men, speaking quickly and not very politely. The woman fended them off with short bursts, giving as good as she got. It struck him that she was speaking the universal language of airline gate attendants: *Sorry, you're shit out of luck.*

"Excuse me," said Zeus as the cacophony around him hit a lull. "Do you speak English?"

"Flight cancel," said the woman.

"Why?"

She turned to another passenger, who was saying something else. By the time she turned back in Zeus's direction, it was obvious she had forgotten what he had said.

"Is there another flight?" asked Zeus. "Will there *be* another flight? To Hong Kong."

"Oh, yes."

"When is the flight?"

Again she started to turn away to answer a different passenger. Zeus reached forward and touched her arm. The woman jerked back.

"I'm sorry," said Zeus. "When is the flight?"

"No flight," said the woman. She added something in Chinese, then began answering a man to Zeus's right.

Deciding he wasn't going to get any more information from her, Zeus took a few steps back.

The first order of business was to look for Solt Jan. Zeus turned to his left and faced the large aisle at the center of the gate area. He began scanning the faces of the crowd, examining each one in turn. The Vietnamese agent was a small woman, thin and petite. *Pretty* and petite. Dark hair, exotic looks: Asian and something else as well, probably Western, French maybe, or even Scandinavian.

Zeus turned almost completely around without spotting her.

"What do you think?" Christian's voice trembled.

"She must have gone back into the city," said Zeus. "It's just as well; they might suspect her. Let's just play this through. We find an airline person who speaks English. We're businessmen, stranded because of our flight. Just play it through."

"What if we can't get to Hong Kong?"

Zeus shook his head. There were plenty of alternatives.

"I don't like this," said Christian.

"Here. Have some crisps."

Zeus held the top of the bag in his two hands and began pulling the sides apart slowly, trying to keep the bag intact as he ripped it. It required a certain amount of finesse, strength, and restraint at the same time.

The bag top separated cleanly. He held the chips out to Christian. "Here," he said. "Have one."

Someone tapped Zeus from behind. He spun around, surprised.

"You are Mr. Murphy," said a short man in a Chinese army uniform. It didn't sound like a question.

"Excuse me?"

"You are Murphy?"

Zeus hesitated. If he said no and the man asked for his passport, then what would he do? Run?

Zeus looked at his uniform. It was light tan. He was an officer, a captain.

What did the insignia mean? Air force?

Would the airline have sent him?

We're not at war. Relax.

The officer started to put out his hand; Zeus guessed that he was about to ask for his ID.

"I'm Murphy," he admitted.

The Chinese officer said nothing, turning instead to Christian.

"You are Christian," he said.

Christian had nearly crossed his eyes. He looked at Zeus, undoubtedly wondering why the hell he had agreed.

Play it through, Zeus thought. We're businessmen.

"Mr. Christian?" repeated the officer.

"Yes?" said Christian finally.

"You are to come with me."

The officer turned sharply. Two other men, these in blue uniforms, stood a short distance away, watching. Zeus noticed that they had unsnapped the protective strap at the top of their holsters, allowing free access to their sidearms.

"What's going on?" asked Christian.

The officer stopped abruptly. He wore a deep frown.

"You will follow me," he said again, in a voice that brooked no argument.

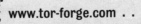

An explosive new military thriller from
New York Times bestselling author

LARRY BOND

EXIT PLAN

Embark with aviator turned submariner Jerry Mitchell.

Jerry Mitchell is on exercises off the coast of Pakistan when his submarine is ordered to a rendezvous off the Iranian coast. Once there, disembarked SEALs, experts in seaborne commando operations, are to extract two Iranian nationals who have sensitive information on Iran's nuclear weapons program.

But while en route, the minisub suffers a battery fire, forcing the survivors to scuttle their disabled craft and swim for shore. There they find the two Iranians waiting for them, and their attempts at returning to the sub are thwarted by heavy Iranian patrol boat activity. And when they find themselves surrounded by Iranian Revolutionary Guard Corps troops, they create a bold plan to escape by sea. It's a desperate gamble, but it's the only way to get the proof of the Iranian plot to the United States…and prevent a devastating new war.